MIDNIGHT RIDER

BY
JOANNA WAYNE

MILLS
BOON

Published in Great Britain 2015
by Mills & Boon, an imprint of Harlequin (UK) Limited,
Eton House, 18-24 Paradise Road, Richmond, Surrey, TW9 1SR

© 2015 Jo Ann Vest

ISBN: 978-0-263-25294-1

46-0115

Harlequin (UK) Limited's policy is to use papers that are natural, renewable and recyclable products and made from wood grown in sustainable forests. The logging and manufacturing processes conform to the legal environmental regulations of the country of origin.

Printed and bound in Spain
by CPI, Barcelona

Brittany knew she should back away, but her body ignored her brain.

His lips were soft at first, then more demanding. The thrill of their mingling breaths roared through her like fire. The inhibitions that had become part of her being melted away and she kissed him back, letting the heat of him wash though her.

The unexpected hunger for him was primal, untamed. Her arms slid around his neck, pulling him closer as her body arched toward his.

When he had the good sense to pull away, her body went weak.

"Don't think the doctor would approve of this." His voice was a husky whisper.

"Probably not," she agreed, though it wasn't her physical health she was worried about but her inability to control her emotions where Cannon was concerned. It wasn't the time or the place. Likely not even the right man, no matter how right it felt right now.

"Good night, Detective."

"Good night, cowboy."

Joanna Wayne began her professional writing career in 1994. Now, more than fifty published books later, Joanna has gained a worldwide following with her cutting-edge romantic suspense and Texas family series such as Sons of Troy Ledger and the Big "D" Dads series. Joanna currently resides in a small community north of Houston, Texas, USA, with her husband. You may write Joanna at PO Box 852, Montgomery, Texas 77356, USA, or connect with her at www.joannawayne.com.

To my twin sisters, Linda and Brenda,
and to all my readers from big families who know
what it's like to love, chat, laugh, eat and
sometimes cry with a houseful of siblings.

Chapter One

Brit Garner woke to the irritating rattle of her cell phone vibrating against her bedside table. She pulled the pillow over her head and tried to ignore it. It finally stopped only to start again a few seconds later. If this was her partner, she was going to kill him.

She checked the caller ID and then took the call. "This had better be of life-threatening importance, Rick Drummond."

"Not life threatening, but I think you better get down to the morgue."

"What part of 'I'm on vacation with plans to sleep until noon every day' do you not understand?"

"I get it. You've worked your gorgeous butt off the past few months. But I think you'll want to see this."

"I've seen dead bodies before." Too many of them, which was why she needed a few well-deserved days off. A walk in a park or along the beach would do wonders for her state of mind. Time to read a book or visit friends would be heaven.

Her dad had warned her it would be like this.

"Just come down. No work involved. I really think you should see this."

"Why is it so urgent I see this particular body?"

"Just get down here, Brit. I'll buy you coffee and breakfast after."

"A real breakfast. No coffee and doughnut on the fly."

"Anything you want—under ten bucks, of course."

"Splurging and secrecy. You're starting to freak me out. I'll be there as soon as I can throw on some clothes. Not work clothes. I'm on vacation, remember?"

"Hard to forget when you keep bringing it up every ten seconds. Come on up to Autopsy when you get here."

Brit kicked off the top sheet and stretched her legs over the side of the bed. She went to the bathroom, splashed her face with cold water and brushed her teeth. After that she shed her nightshirt and wiggled into a pair of faded jeans and a long-sleeved green T-shirt. A quick brush of her long hair and she was ready.

She'd go to the morgue but, no matter how interesting the case, she wouldn't let Rick sway her to jump in. She really needed the time off. And not only to rejuvenate, but also to try to figure out where she'd gone wrong on a very important case.

The colder a case got the harder it was to solve. She'd been working on her father's murder for three years without a decent lead. She had to be overlooking a key element. No murder was perfect.

Less than a half hour later, she was walking into the autopsy section of the morgue. The facilities were state-of-the-art and as familiar as her neighborhood grocery store, though the odors were far more unpleasant.

Her partner, Rick, was standing next to the gray examining table. Her favorite pathologist, Elise Laughton, was at the other side of the table and slipping out of her gloves.

"Looks like she put up a hell of a fight," Elise said. "Evidently she was just no match for the strength of her attacker."

"Cause of death?" Brit asked by way of greeting, determined to stick to the basics.

"You made good time," Elise said, looking up.

"Traffic was light. And as you can see, I didn't bother with makeup since I'm not sticking around long."

Elise shared a concerned look with Rick and then looked back to her. "To answer your original question, the evidence includes new bruising on the hands and arms and having her throat slashed."

Another morning in Houston. Not that all murders weren't bad, but any detective in the department could handle this, including Rick. There had to be something more going on for him to call her in this morning.

"So start talking, Rick, and this had better be good."

Rick frowned. "Take a look."

Brit stepped closer for an unobstructed view of the body. An icy chill seeped deep inside her as she studied the victim.

She could have been staring into a mirror. The lifeless victim spread out on the cold metal slab looked exactly like her.

Chapter Two

One Week Later

"How about passing that potato salad before Leif goes back for seconds and doesn't leave any for the rest of us?" Travis joked.

"Look who's talking," Leif said as he handed down the serving bowl. "You've been hogging the platter of fried chicken like a starving man."

"That's 'cause I had him out baling hay all afternoon," Adam said. "Nothing like a little ranch work to build up an appetite."

"Save room for the apple pie à la mode," Hadley said. "I made it myself and I'll be insulted if there's a bite left on a dish."

"Ice cream!" four-year-old Lacy added. She pushed her plate back. "I want mine now."

"Me, too," R.J. said, "but I better clean my plate first. You better eat a few more bites of dinner, too."

R.J. smiled and leaned back in his chair. There was a time not so many months ago that he'd have been sitting at this table all alone. Or passed out somewhere skunk drunk. Now he was alcohol-free, thankful to be surrounded by family. Best medicine in the world for a dying man.

He didn't have much of an appetite these days, even though his daughters-in-law Hadley and Faith had become dadgum good cooks. His third daughter-in-law, Joni, was too busy being the best dang vet in the state of Texas to spend much time in the kitchen.

Besides, he suspected she might be pregnant. She'd turned green and rushed away from the breakfast table a couple of days ago and she'd developed a little swell in the belly. He wouldn't ask. She'd tell them all when she was ready.

It had been over a year now since the neurosurgeon had given R.J. the death sentence. A malignant, inoperable brain tumor that would eventually take his life. For some miraculous reason, the tumor had decided to slow down a bit and give R.J. time to enjoy his family— the family he'd never bothered to get to know when he was drinking and carousing like the SOB he'd been for most of his life.

He'd given little thought to contacting his estranged kids until the grim reaper had looked him square in the eye and chuckled. But getting to know Adam, Leif and Travis and their families had given his life more meaning than he'd thought possible. Why, already there had been three weddings on the Dry Gulch Ranch. Fortunately, none of them his. Four weddings were enough for any one man.

Still, with each passing day, the longing grew stronger to connect with his other three children. So far, no luck there. His youngest son, Cannon, was either too resentful or too busy with his bull riding to give R.J. the time of day.

His daughter, Jade, was the baby of the family, though she was in her early twenties now. The only times he'd seen her was when she came to the ranch for the reading of the will. She hadn't cared much for his requirement that a beneficiary would have to spend a year living on and helping work the Dry Gulch Ranch to get a share in his estate. Hadn't seemed too pleased that he'd had the reading of the will while he was still breathing, either.

Had let him know it, too, in no uncertain terms. As feisty a hellcat as her mother had been. The ranch had never offered enough excitement for Kiki. Apparently it didn't for their daughter, Jade, either.

And that left his oldest son, Jake, rich Texas rancher and oilman. The wealth inherited from his mother's side of the family. Jake had everything a man could want. Fancy cars. Private jets. Gorgeous women half his age draped across him in every picture of him that appeared on the society pages of the *Dallas Morning News*.

Jake had moved on so far he couldn't even see R.J. in his mind's rearview mirror. No doubt his mother had done the same. Stupidest mistake R.J. had ever made was letting her walk away. He wondered what she was like now. He still pictured her as young and beautiful as she'd been at eighteen when they'd married. Best-looking girl in the small country high school they'd attended. Hell, she was probably the best-looking girl in all of Texas back then.

The doorbell rang.

"Are you expecting company tonight?" Faith asked.

"Nope," R.J. said. "Probably a neighbor stopping by."

"I'll get it," Adam offered, already scooting back from the table.

"You just keep eatin'," R.J. said. "I need a little exercise. Old bones get stiff if I sit too long."

He held on to the edge of the table for extra support as he stood. Never knew when one of those dizzy spells would hit. He ambled to the door, taking his time about it. The doorbell rang again.

"Hold your horses. I'm coming."

He swung open the door and stared into the bluest eyes he'd ever seen. He took in the rest of the stranger, enjoying the tour. He might be near dead. But just because he couldn't sample the wares didn't mean he couldn't window-shop.

"You must be lost," he said, sure he'd never seen the tall, willowy strawberry blonde before.

"Is this the Dry Gulch Ranch?"

"Was the last time I looked at the sign over the gate."

"Are you R. J. Dalton?"

"Yep. You're batting a thousand so far."

"Then I'm not lost."

A baby whimpered.

R.J. followed the sound to a baby carrier resting on the porch, next to the stranger's right foot. The young woman reached down and grabbed the handle, lifting the carrier so that he could see the adorable infant peeking from beneath a yellow blanket. The baby kicked and made a few boxing moves with its tiny fists.

"And who might this be?" R.J. asked.

"This is your three-month-old granddaughter, Kimmie."

"My granddaughter. Well, don't that just beat all?"

"Yes, it does." She pushed the carrier toward him. When he didn't take it, she set it on the floor inside the door.

"Come on in," R.J. urged, opening the door even wider.

"No, thank you. I'm just here to drop off Kimmie."

"What do you mean drop her off?"

"Just that. I'm leaving her in your care."

"You can't do that. I'm a sick man. I can't take care of a baby." Had never done that when he was young and healthy.

"Then I suggest you hire someone to take care of her or call your son Cannon and tell him to stop by and pick up his daughter."

So Cannon was playing around with more than bulls. A chip off the old block. But the old block had made a lifetime of mistakes.

"Why don't you go tell Cannon that yourself?"

"I don't have time at the moment to go chasing down some irresponsible bull rider."

Apparently not time to raise her child, either.

She pulled a business card and an envelope from her pocket. "If Cannon has questions, he can reach me at this number. Inside the envelope, you'll find everything you need to know about caring for Kimmie."

"I'm gonna need a lot more than some notes."

"Yes, you'll need this to get you started." The woman slid a large canvas tote from her shoulder and handed it to him, as well. "There's formula, bottles, diapers and a few changes of clothing inside."

"You got a momma for her in there, too?"

The woman didn't answer, but he could swear those striking blue eyes of hers were moist when she turned and walked away.

She stopped just before she reached her car. "I play classical music for Kimmie when she gets fussy. It calms her down."

There was a definite quiver in her voice but no hesitation as she got into her car and drove away.

Once her taillights disappeared, R.J. took a look at the card she'd pressed into his left hand.

Brittany Garner, Homicide Detective, Houston Police Department.

Cannon sure knew how to pick them. Gorgeous, sexy and she could handle a weapon. *All good traits in a woman—unless she turned the gun on you.*

R.J. was still staring at the newest addition to the family when his daughter-in-law Hadley joined him at the door. She stopped and stared at the baby. "Oh, my gosh. Look how adorable."

Hadley reached down, unbuckled the baby from her chair and picked her up, all the while gushing baby talk.

"Hello, little sweetie. Did you just drop from heaven and land at our door?"

"Something like that," R.J. said.

Hadley's eyebrows arched. She dropped the baby talk. "What are you talking about? Who is this?"

"Name's Kimmie, or so her mother said."

"Who's her mother?"

"Apparently a lady cop."

"What do you mean apparently? You must know whose baby this is?" Hadley walked to the door and looked out. "Where is her mom?"

"Gone back to Houston, I s'pect."

"Without her baby? What's going on here?"

"Supposedly this is my granddaughter."

"Who's the father?"

"Allegedly, it's Cannon, but I bet he's gonna be as surprised about this as we are."

R.J. smiled in spite of the situation. Not the ideal bargaining tool, but it was one way to get Cannon back to the Dry Gulch Ranch. His neighbor Caroline Lambert was right. God sure worked in mysterious ways.

Chapter Three

Macabre kicked his way out of the creaky gate with a vengeance that sent adrenaline exploding through Cannon's veins.

One. Two.

The bull bucked wildly. The rope dug into Cannon's gloved hand. His lucky Stetson went flying. Bad omen.

Three. Four.

The crowd's cheers mingled with the thunderous stamping of the bull's hooves and the frantic beating of Cannon's heart.

Five.

Cannon's body shifted and began to slide. Instinct took over. He struggled to hang on, leaning hard, fighting to shift his weight.

Macabre's fierce back hooves propelled the animal's powerful muscles, twisting and spinning the two-ton mass of fury. The rope slipped. White-hot pain ripped through Cannon's shoulder.

He was on the ground. The rank breath of the snorting bull burned in his own nostrils. Flying dirt blinded him. He blinked, covered his head with his hands and rolled away.

Shouts from the rodeo clown echoed though the

arena, but the bull didn't back off. It swerved and came back at Cannon.

Cannon rolled in the opposite direction. The crowd gasped in unison as one hoof came so close to his head that Cannon could feel the vibrations rattle inside his skull.

Then the bull turned and went after the clown. Cannon owed Billy Cox big-time.

He picked himself up, grabbed his hat and waved it to the crowd as he scrambled back to safety. Cox was safe, as well. Only then did Cannon check the results.

Seven seconds.

Disappointment burned inside him. One more second and he would have scored big. He'd drawn Macabre, the most vicious of the bulls on tonight's docket. The animal that could have put Cannon in pay dirt.

Already December, one of the last of the rodeos in what had been a great year for Cannon. Still, he could have used that prize money. Like most rodeo addicts who loved bull riding, the day would come when he'd have to retire. He'd need *mucho* cash to do that right.

What was a cowboy without a ranch?

"Bad luck," one of the other riders said.

"I'd say good luck," another said. "You could have been leaving here in an ambulance tonight."

"Seven seconds on Macabre should be worth ten on any of the other bulls in the chute tonight."

Cannon acknowledged the comments with a nod and a shrug. Nothing else was needed. They all knew the disappointment of losing to a bull.

"Mighty tough way to make a living."

The voice was unfamiliar, gruff, but with a rattle that came with lots of years of living. Cannon turned to see who'd spoken.

Reality sent a shot of acid straight to his gut. As if tonight hadn't already been bad enough.

"What are you doing here?" Cannon asked.

"I came to see my son ride," R.J. said. "No law against that, is there?"

Probably should be. "You've seen me," Cannon said. "Now what?"

"We need to talk," R.J. said.

Cannon wasn't interested in pretending he had any fatherly feelings for a man who hadn't given a damn about him when he could have used his help. And he wouldn't play any part in the old man's search for redemption before he died.

Actually, he'd figured R.J. was already dead by now. Or maybe everything he'd said about the inoperable brain tumor at the bizarre reading of his will had been lies. He wouldn't put anything past R. J. Dalton.

"I know you have no use for me," R.J. continued. "I probably deserve that. We still need to talk. And I have someone you should meet."

"Look, R.J., you had your say at the reading of your will. I wasn't interested then. I'm still not. I don't play games."

"Looks like you were playing a potentially deadly one tonight."

"That's work, not a game. And it's my business."

"So is what I have to tell you."

"Then spit it out."

"Okay. You think I'm a lousy father. I agree. But unless I miss my guess, you're about to get the chance to prove you're a hundred times better at it than I ever was."

"I don't know what you're talking about."

"You will in a minute. Come with me."

Crazy old fool. Cannon couldn't even begin to guess what kind of absurd scheme he was working now. He leaned against the wooden railing that separated the contenders from the rest of the arena as R.J. ambled off without looking back.

Every muscle in his body complained silently, aches and pain seeping in like the bitter cold of a West Texas winter morning. He craved a hot shower, a couple of over-the-counter painkillers with a six-pack to wash them down.

Then he'd plop on the lumpy mattress back at the motel. No place like home, and a lonely motel room was as close to home as he'd been since he'd finished his tour of duty with the marines.

But something had brought R.J. clear out to Abilene to talk to Cannon. Doubtful the old coot would just turn around and drive home without saying whatever he'd come to say. Might as well get it over with.

Cannon followed in the direction R.J. had gone. He spotted him a couple of minutes later, standing near the wooden bleachers. A stunning young woman stood next to him, cuddling a baby in her arms.

Surely R.J. didn't have the testosterone to father another child at his age. And even if he had, why would he think Cannon would give a damn?

The woman turned toward him and attempted a smile that didn't quite work. Her gaze shifted from him back to the sleeping baby.

R.J.'s words about his getting a chance to prove himself as a father echoed through his mind. If he thought Cannon was going to raise this baby for him he was nuts. So was the infant's mother.

A more troublesome angle struck him. Surely, R.J. wasn't insinuating Cannon could have fathered this baby.

He studied the woman. Fiery red hair that cascaded around her shoulders. Deep green eyes. Not a woman a man could easily forget, yet she didn't stir any memories for him.

"I'm Hadley Dalton," she said as he approached. "Your half brother Adam's wife. And this is Kimmie." She held up the baby for him to get a better look. The infant stretched and rubbed her eyes with her tiny balled fists, but then settled back to sleep.

So this was Adam's child. Cannon exhaled, releasing the dread and the breath he hadn't realized he'd been holding. "Cute baby. You and Adam did well."

"But that's just the thing," R.J. said. "It's not their baby. You're her dad, or at least some woman down in Houston claims you are."

Macabre's hooves couldn't have packed a bigger wallop.

Chapter Four

Cannon took a long swig of the cold beer. It did nothing to ease the shock or to relieve the aches in his joints and muscles. R.J. and Hadley sat across the booth from him in the nearby café where they'd gone to finish their discussion. The infant slept in Hadley's arms.

The confusion he'd felt back at the arena was growing worse instead of better. "I don't even know anyone named Brittany Garner. I definitely didn't have a child with her. She evidently has me confused with someone else."

"She seemed pretty sure about her facts when she dropped Kimmie off with us," R.J. said.

"She could be just trying to get money out of *you*," Cannon said. "If she knows anything at all about me, she knows I'm not worth conning."

"She's a detective," Hadley offered. "Surely she wouldn't be working a con."

"Anyone can have business cards printed," Cannon said. "That doesn't prove she's a cop."

"She's a cop all right," R.J. assured him. "Your half brother Travis is a homicide detective himself in Dallas. He had her checked out. She's legit and apparently good at her job."

She might be a detective, but Cannon wasn't convinced he'd slept with her. "How old is this woman?"

"Looks to be in her late twenties," R.J. said. "'Bout your age. Sky-blue eyes. Tall. Thin. Strawberry-blond hair. Damned good-looking if that helps jog your memory."

It didn't. "Awful young for a detective," Cannon commented, not that it mattered. He was twenty-seven himself and he'd already finished a stint with the marines and made a name for himself on the rodeo circuit.

"How old is Kimmie?" he asked.

"Three months, according to Brit Garner," R.J. said.

Cannon went over the basics in his mind. Kimmie was three months old. This was the first week in December. If Kimmie was his, she would have been conceived about a year ago. That would have meant he had to be in Houston last December.

The big Houston Livestock Show and Rodeo was always in March. He'd participated in that, but didn't recall being in Houston any other time. Of course, he might have passed through on his way to somewhere else. He'd have to check his calendar.

He wasn't into one-night stands, but that didn't mean he'd never given in to temptation. He definitely hadn't been in a relationship then, or any time in recent memory. Have a few good times with a woman and she was ready to pick out furniture and run your life.

A one-nighter with a gorgeous Houston detective that he didn't remember. Extremely unlikely.

"You can get a paternity test," Hadley said. "That's the only way you can know for sure if you're Kimmie's father."

"A paternity test." He sounded like a nervous parrot. But he couldn't even begin to wrap his head around the possibility that the baby sleeping in Hadley's arms could be his.

"I hear they're easy to get these days," R.J. agreed. "If you're short of cash, I can front you the money."

"I'm not the father," Cannon insisted, but his stomach had twisted into a huge, gnarly knot.

Kimmie began to stir. She stretched and yawned and then tried to poke her entire fist into her wide-open mouth. Hadley moved her to her other shoulder, but the baby continued to fuss.

"She's hungry," Hadley said. "Would you like to hold her, Cannon, while I get her bottle from the diaper bag?"

Hold that squirming ball of life? Not a chance. A puppy, he could handle. But this was a real live baby.

"I wouldn't know how," he said.

"I s'pect you better learn," R.J. said. "Not only how to hold her, but also how to feed her and change her and even bathe her—that is, if she turns out to be yours."

R.J. was already a believer. Cannon could tell by that knowing look in his eyes even though his pupils were half-hidden by the bags beneath them and the loose skin that drooped over his lids.

Kimmie started to cry. Cannon's muscles bunched. The prospect of fatherhood struck him with raw fear, the kind of paralyzing fright he'd never felt when climbing atop a bull.

"Maybe you should stay at the Dry Gulch Ranch while you have the paternity testing done," Hadley suggested. "There's plenty of room since R.J. is the only one actually living in the original ranch house now. The rest of us have built our own houses on the Dry Gulch now.

"I'd be close enough to help you with Kimmie if

you're at the ranch, but I can't stay here. Adam and I have two young daughters of our own who need me."

Stay at the Dry Gulch and then owe his worthless biological father for the favor. The prospect was repulsive. But what other options did he have? He couldn't walk out of here tonight with a baby in his arms and no idea how to care for her.

He had six days before his next rodeo, time he needed to get over his sore shoulder. But what if the paternity test proved it was his baby. Then what? Drag Kimmie around in a saddle blanket?

The baby had a mother. Detective or not, she'd have to take over the parenting chores until the kid was old enough to at least tell Cannon why she was crying.

Great attitude. If he wasn't careful he'd rival R.J. for the Worst Father of a Lifetime award.

Cannon finished his beer while Hadley fed the baby. "How many times a day do you have to do that?"

"About every four hours during the day. Kimmie has a healthy appetite. She goes longer between feedings at night."

"She takes a bottle at night, too?"

"She sleeps through most of the night but wakes up around five in the morning for a feeding. The good news is she goes right back to sleep after that, and usually doesn't wake up again until about eight."

No wonder the mystery detective was ready to hand the infant off to him. She was probably sleep deprived. Only what kind of mother would trust a man like him with their child?

Either Detective Brittany Garner had no idea what he was like or she was one totally irresponsible mother.

"I need to go to Houston and talk to Detective Garner," he said. "I hate to ask, Hadley, but if you'd watch

Kimmie just for another day or two, until I can get the paternity test and sort all this out, I'd really appreciate it."

"You want me to take her back to the Dry Gulch Ranch?"

"Just for a few days."

"I can manage that."

"But no more than a few days," R.J. cautioned. "If Kimmie turns out to be your biological daughter, then she's your responsibility. Yours and the mother who dropped her off like a stray kitten."

R.J. was a fine one to give advice on parenting. Cannon was willing to bet he'd never in his life changed a diaper or gotten up at five in the morning to poke a bottle at a crying infant.

If the test came back positive—which he was almost certain it wouldn't—Cannon would at least make a stab at being a dad. There had to be a book that would help.

Sure, parenting by the book. About like a guidebook could teach a man how to stay on a mad, bucking bull for eight seconds.

"Are you driving back to Dallas tonight?" Cannon asked.

"We're flying back," R.J. said. "Tague Lambert, one of our neighbors, flew us down in his private jet. He's waiting at the small airport just west of town."

"So if you'll just take Kimmie with you, I'll drive to the ranch when I finish my business with Brit Garner," Cannon reiterated.

"You can fly back with us," R.J. offered. "Get the testing done in Dallas, might even be able to schedule it for tomorrow. Then you can wait until you have the facts to contact Kimmie's mother. You can use one of the vehicles at the ranch to take care of business."

"I don't go anywhere without my pickup truck," Cannon said, dismissing the offer. The less time he spent around R.J. the better.

The conversation dried up and died while his mind searched for reasons this baby couldn't be his and why some woman was trying to screw him over.

Once Kimmie had her fill and spit the nipple from her tiny, heart-shaped lips, Hadley set the almost empty nursing bottle on the table and shifted the baby in her arms. "Don't you want to at least hold her and say hello before we go?"

Cannon shook his head, though he figured it made him look like a jerk. "I've never held a baby before. I'm afraid I'd do it wrong and hurt her."

"You won't." Hadley stood and walked to his side of the booth. "Stand up and hold out your arms. I'll show you how to cradle her."

He stood, but kept his arms to his sides. "I don't think I should...."

"Nonsense." Hadley handed the baby off to him.

He took her reluctantly, standing stiffly while she fit the baby into his arms.

Kimmie's eyes fluttered, eyes the same general color as his, only lighter. Cannon's breath caught in his throat.

The infant was practically weightless, but not still. She squirmed and started to fuss as if she knew he didn't have a clue what he was doing. At least she was smart.

Cannon touched her chin with a fingertip. Her skin was as soft as silk. She made a gurgling noise and kicked and swung her little arms like a wind-up toy.

Her short, chubby fingers somehow caught and wrapped around the one he'd used to touch her cheek.

An emotion he didn't recognize shot through him and settled in his heart.

He had never been more afraid in his life.

BY THE TIME Cannon returned to his hotel room, the shock had worn off enough that the aches and pains had checked back in. He headed straight for a shower, shedding his clothes as he went. For the first time he noticed the rip in his jeans and the dirt stains blotching his Western shirt.

Stripped naked by the time he reached the bathroom, he glanced in the mirror. The area around his rib cage was already turning an ugly shade of purple.

Macabre was no doubt sleeping comfortably in his stall, probably dreaming of what he'd do to the next sucker crazy enough to climb on his back.

Cannon turned the knobs on the shower until the spray was steamy hot. He stepped in and let the water sluice over his head and run down his aching body.

He closed his eyes, but the relief he'd hoped for didn't come. Instead, an image of Kimmie rocked his mind. Could she possibly be his daughter? He racked his brain trying to remember his schedule for last December.

Nothing stood out. His life was a steady stream of rodeos and towns he barely saw except for the arenas where the action took place. After years on the circuit, they ran together like gravy ladled over a plate of biscuits and sausage.

He remembered the big events. Dallas. Austin. Houston. San Antonio. Phoenix. Las Vegas. Hell, he even made it up to Montana on occasion. It all depended on the points he needed and how big the purse was.

There had been women. Not that many, but a few. Never married ones, at least not knowingly. And he stayed clear of the underage buckle bunnies who hung around the arenas and flirted shamelessly with any cowboy who'd give them the time of day. Plenty did. They could get a man in big trouble.

More to the point, he kept a supply of condoms handy—just in case.

The way he saw it, there was damned little chance that Kimmie was his daughter.

So why had he felt that quake deep in his gut when Kimmie had accidentally latched on to his finger? Couldn't be because he had some kind of secret longing to father a child.

He had his future all planned out. His winnings from the rodeo were his ticket to making it happen. A kid would put the skids on his dreams faster than a bull could clear the chute.

He should call Brittany Garner tonight and tell her she had the wrong man.

No. Better to see her face-to-face. If he had sex with her, he'd surely remember her once he was looking at her. If he'd been sober enough to get it up, then his brain cells should have been functioning at least at a minuscule level.

He soaped his body, gingerly, especially over the bruised flesh. Then he rinsed and stepped out of the shower. He grabbed one of the bleached white towels from the shelf and wrapped it around his waist.

The dull pounding at the base of his skull that had been playing background drums for him ever since the fall intensified. He took the bottle of extrastrength painkillers from his duffel and shook two into his left hand. He swallowed them with a chaser of water he'd cupped in his hand from the faucet.

Rummaging in his shaving duffel, he dug out a toothbrush and squeezed a roll of minty jell along the bristles. The brushing did little to rid his mouth of the coppery taste that had taken hold the second he'd learned he might be a father.

Fatigue stitched with dread settled in hard as he walked to the bed, dropped his towel to the floor and threw back the heavy spread. Tomorrow he'd make the long drive to Houston. Tonight he had to get some rest.

Sleep came almost instantly. Unfortunately, it didn't last. By four in the morning, Cannon was behind the wheel of his pickup truck, pulling out of the hotel parking lot. Brit Garner's business card was deep in his pocket.

Talk was cheap, especially from a detective who admittedly slept around. A paternity test was all it would take to prove that she was wrong.

THE CLERK AT the police precinct stared at Cannon, her gaze focused on the angry raw scrape that colored his right cheek. "Are you here to file an assault complaint?"

"No. I'm here to see Detective Brittany Garner. Is she in?"

"The detective is with someone in her office now. What's your business with her?"

"Personal."

The middle-aged clerk leveled her gaze, her features hardening as if she suddenly found his visit threatening or just downright annoying. "Detective Garner is very busy, but give me your name and I'll see if she has time to see you."

"Cannon Dalton and she'll see me."

The clerk rolled her eyes at him as if he was just another nuisance in her day. "Wait here."

The wait was short. The clerk returned less than a

minute later. "The detective will see you now. I'll walk you to her office."

He followed the clerk down a narrow corridor, taking a left at the end of the hall. She opened a door and motioned him to go in.

R.J.'s description hadn't done the stunning woman behind the desk justice. She did look vaguely familiar, but damned if he could place her. Probably reminded him of some movie star or supermodel. She had the body and the looks for either one.

"I'm glad you finally found time to stop by, Mr. Dalton. We need to talk." Her voice was stern, her manner stiffly authoritative. All cop. Not quite what he'd expected from a woman who was about to say, *Hey, guess what? I had your baby.*

Maybe Kimmie wasn't her daughter, after all. But surely the Houston Police Department didn't have the staff to send homicide detectives out to find deadbeat dads.

Cannon let his gaze travel over her while she slid some loose papers into a brown envelope. Striking eyes, the color of a summer sky. Hair was shiny and straight and fell past her shoulders. Long bangs were tucked behind her left ear.

Finally she sat down and told him to do the same. He settled in the straight-backed metal chair across from her desk. He looked her in the eye. Hers were accusing. They matched her smug expression.

"I'm glad you stopped by. This will be much easier to deal with in person."

"Might have been easier if you'd talked to me before you dumped your kid on R.J.'s doorstep."

"I didn't dump. I *delivered* Kimmie to her grandfather since her father wasn't around to accept responsibility for her welfare."

"Part of your official duties as a detective?"

"As a matter of fact, it was."

"And how did you reach the conclusion that I'm Kimmie's father?"

"Maybe I should refresh your memory."

"You definitely should."

"Marble Falls, Texas. Last December. The Greenleaf Bar. Does that mean anything to you?"

Marble Falls. Last December. A resort-sponsored rodeo. He groaned as the pieces started to fall together.

"The woman in Greenleaf Bar was you?"

"You don't remember?"

"Vaguely."

He struggled to put things in perspective. That had been a hell of a night. He'd stopped at the first bar he'd come to after leaving the rodeo. A blonde had sat down next to him. As best he remembered, he'd given her an earful about the rodeo, life and death as he'd become more and more inebriated.

She must have offered him a ride back to his hotel since his truck had still been at the bar when he'd gone looking for it the next morning. If Brit was telling the truth, the woman must have gone into the motel with him and they'd ended up doing the deed.

If so, he'd been a total jerk. She'd been as drunk as him and driven or she'd willingly taken a huge risk.

Hard to imagine the woman staring at him now ever being that careless or impulsive.

"Is that your normal pattern, Mr. Dalton?" Brit asked "Use a woman to satisfy your physical needs and then ride off to the next rodeo?"

"That's a little like the armadillo calling the squirrel

road kill, isn't it? I'm sure I didn't coerce you into my bed if I was so drunk I can't remember the experience."

"I can assure you that you're nowhere near that irresistible. I have never been in your bed."

"Whew. That's a relief. I'd have probably died of frostbite."

"This isn't a joking matter."

"I'm well aware. But I'm not the enemy here, so you can quit talking to me like I just climbed out from under a slimy rock. If you're not Kimmie's mother, who is?"

"My twin sister, Sylvie Hamm."

Twin sisters. That explained Brit's attitude. Probably considered her sister a victim of the drunken sex urges he didn't remember. It also explained why Brit Garner looked familiar.

"So why is it I'm not having this conversation with Sylvie?"

"She's dead."

The words sank in slowly, changing everything. "I'm sorry," he said honestly. The how and why of all of this seemed less important now. A baby would grow up never knowing her mother. A baby that might be his.

He tried to wrap his mind around the new development. The death had to be recent. Kimmie was just a baby. "How did your sister die?"

"She was murdered."

A new jolt shook his system as the situation grew even more disturbing. He muttered a few careless curse words, not out of disrespect but out of desperation. He didn't see how things could get much worse, but from the look on Brit's face, he had a feeling they were about to.

"I get the feeling I should be calling in a lawyer about now," he said.

"Not if you have nothing to hide. You're not currently a suspect in her murder, Mr. Dalton, if that's what you're thinking."

Currently the operative word. "Have you arrested a suspect?" he asked.

"Not yet."

"Do you have one?"

"No."

"A motive?"

"It's an open investigation. I can't really discuss the details with you."

"Exactly what can you share, Detective?"

Brit stood and walked around to the front of her desk, propping her shapely backside on the edge of it. Hard-edged, probably tough as nails, but hard to get past the fact that she looked more like a starlet playing a cop than an actual detective. There had to be a story there somewhere.

"What specifically would you like to know, Mr. Dalton?"

"First, how about calling me Cannon? If I am Kimmie's father, then we're practically related."

"Okay, what do you want to know, Cannon?"

"For starters, why would you hand over your niece to a man like R. J. Dalton, or to me, for that matter, since you think I'm such a lowlife?"

She hesitated, then exhaled slowly as if she were giving in against her better judgment. "I'd planned to take that up with you after we have the results of the paternity test in hand, but since you're so eager to discuss details, I guess we can talk now."

"Then we finally agree on something."

Brit glanced at her watch. "Do you mind if we talk

over a sandwich? I haven't eaten since breakfast and I need some food and decent coffee."

"Fine by me, as long as I'm not riding to the restaurant in the back of a squad car."

Her full lips tipped into a slight smile. "Not this trip. There's an informal restaurant with quick service just around the corner. We can walk."

"Lead the way."

Actually he had few hunger pangs growling in his stomach, as well. He'd driven straight through, grabbing snacks for munching when he'd stopped for fuel and bathroom breaks.

Snippets of that night in Marble Falls kicked around in his mind as they walked to the café. He hated that his memories of that night were lost in a whiskey fog. Weird considering he wasn't even that much of a drinker. A beer or two every now and then. A six-pack on a bad night.

The night in Marble Falls had been far worse than bad.

Right now he figured he wasn't the only one with questions. And, in spite of Brit's assurances, he figured he was one wrong answer away from becoming a suspect.

That still didn't mean she had her facts right about his being Kimmie's father.

Chapter Five

So this was the rodeo cowboy Sylvie Hamm had found irresistible. Brit had to admit he wasn't the sort of a man who'd go unnoticed in a bar or most anywhere else.

His skin was tanned. His eyes were penetrating—caramel colored with gold flecks that made them almost hypnotizing when his gaze locked with hers. His hair was a sun-streaked brown, unruly, thick locks falling rakishly over his brow.

He needed a shave, but the rough growth of whiskers only added to his blatant masculinity, as did the angry, skinned blotch on his left cheek.

Worn jeans that fit to perfection, white Western shirt, sleeves rolled to the elbows. And a sauntering charisma and Texas drawl that left no doubt he was the real deal.

Put that package of screaming virility in a cozy bar with a steamy country ballad for background. A few drinks. A belly-rubbing dance or two. Then a burning kiss that rocked your soul…

Brit swallowed hard and shook the sensual images from her mind. Her relationship with Cannon Dalton was strictly business. She'd been angry with him since the day she'd learned that he was Kimmie's missing-in-action father.

But he was also the only link to Sylvie. Aggravating him or making him defensive would not help her cause. Sylvie could have said or done something the night they'd been together that would lead Brit to the killer. She also needed enough information to decide if he would be a fit father for Kimmie.

If not, biological rights or not, Brit would do whatever it took to keep him from getting custody of her niece.

That move would be a last resort. Brit knew more about the rodeo than she did about taking care of a baby—and that was absolutely nothing.

"Jodie's Grill and Deli. Is this the place?" Cannon asked as they approached the green awning that shielded the entrance from the elements.

"Yes. It's larger than it looks from the outside and mostly a lunch spot, so it shouldn't be too crowded tonight."

He hurried ahead to get the door. Their shoulders brushed as she stepped past him. A jolt of unexpected heat surged through her. She stepped away quickly.

What was it about this man that was getting to her?

"Would you like a booth or a table?" the hostess asked when they stepped inside.

"How about that back booth?" Cannon suggested, nodding to one that the busboy was wiping down.

"Certainly, sir."

"Okay with you, Brit?" he asked after the fact.

She nodded, surprised he'd called her by the shortened version of her first name. Rick was the only male in Homicide who did. To everyone else she was Garner.

It was as if she and Cannon had just skipped a few steps of the introductory stage. Perhaps part of the cowboy way, like his swagger and virility.

They followed the hostess past a cluster of occupied

tables to the back corner of the dining area. Brit took the seat that let her see the door. It was a cop thing to always be able to watch and assess what was going on in any situation.

Cannon slid onto the padded bench seat opposite hers and opened his menu. "Any recommendations?" he asked as the hostess walked away.

"Salads are excellent," Brit said. "My favorite is the Greek salad with a side of hummus and pita bread."

"You mean for starters?"

"No. They're large portions."

"To you, maybe. Show me the beef."

"In that case I hear their ribs and burgers are great."

"That's more like it."

When the waitress showed up, he ordered the rib platter with two sides and a beer on draft to wash it down.

Brit ordered her usual with coffee.

The waitress returned quickly with their drinks. Cannon took a hefty swig of the beer, wiped his mouth on the white cotton napkin and plunged right into the reason they were there.

"I enjoy a good mystery as much as the next guy, but not when I'm playing a supporting role. So let's get to the nitty-gritty of this. What makes you think I'm Kimmie's father?"

"I don't just think it. I'm reasonably certain. When we searched her apartment after Sylvie's murder, I found a file that contained a legal document that she'd downloaded from the internet. It wasn't notarized, but nonetheless, it was still clearly her intent that her written wishes be upheld."

"And this document mentioned me by name?"

"Yes. It specified that in the case of her death or an

injury that left her mentally or physically incapacitated, Cannon Dalton, the biological father of her daughter Kimmie, should be notified that he had a daughter."

"There must be more than one Cannon Dalton in Texas."

"Not one whose father owns the Dry Gulch Ranch."

"She put that in there, too?"

"Yes, either you told her the night she got pregnant or she did some research to make sure Kimmie ended up in the right hands."

"So you're just relying on a computer document that anyone could have printed out and Sylvie never mentioned my name to you while she was pregnant?"

"The form was filed with other important papers. I have no reason to believe it was false."

"Whose baby did you think she was carrying?" A husband's? A fiancé's? A current lover's?

"It's a very complicated situation, but the truth is I had never met Sylvie. I didn't even know she existed until she was murdered."

Brit stirred a packet of sweetener into her coffee and then took a sip before meeting Cannon's penetrating gaze.

"How is it you didn't know your twin sister?"

This was getting sticky. She'd rather not delve into her personal life with Cannon. On the other hand, he was Kimmie's father. She had to tell him something.

Brit explained as succinctly as possible about being called to the morgue, glossing over how intensely disturbing it had been to see what looked like a waxed copy of herself laid out on the metal slab.

"A simple DNA test proved that we were twins," Brit said, "and that Sylvie was Kimmie's biological mother.

By the time that was verified, I was neck-deep in the murder investigation."

"That's tough. I wish I could be more help," Cannon said, "but this came at me from out of the blue. Right now I'm drawing a blank about that night."

"I think the appropriate next step for you would be to have DNA testing to determine for certain that you are Kimmie's father."

"I agree. Any suggestions as to how to best go about that?"

"We have a lab here in town that handles the overflow from the police department. That would be the quickest bet. I can call now and find out if they can see you in the morning."

"Then let's get this rolling."

She made the call while Cannon finished his beer and worried the salt shaker with his free hand. She could easily understand his being disturbed by the news he was almost certainly a father.

Fortunately, the lab was able to accommodate.

"They'll see you at nine in the morning," she said once she'd broken the phone connection.

"Where is this lab?"

"Not far from here." She took a business card from her pocket and jotted down the street and web addresses of the lab on the back of the card before handing it to him. "You can get a map with directions at the website as well as pretest instructions about what you can and can't eat or drink before coming in."

"I can handle that. When will I get the results?"

"I'll request a rush, but it depends on how backed up they are at the lab. We should hear in about three days."

"That seems like long time for a rush."

"It's a very busy lab, but extremely reliable. You won't

have to stay in Houston. They'll call you when the analysis is complete. Be sure to check the box on the form you sign for them that you want phone notification."

Cannon took another swig of beer, scrunched his napkin and then turned his attention back to Brit. "Once you suspected I was the father, why didn't you bring Kimmie to me instead of to the Dry Gulch Ranch? I don't live there now and never have."

"Your father was easier to locate."

"Wrong answer. You're a hotshot detective. You could have found me had you wanted to. I'm sure you checked out R.J. and me before you dropped off a helpless infant."

Right again. He wasn't as gullible as she'd expected and definitely not awed by her badge.

"I did investigate you, Cannon. You went into the Marines right out of high school. You list your uncle's ranch near Midland as your permanent address, but he said you haven't actually lived there in years. You have never been married and have no arrest record."

"That doesn't answer my question."

"I'm trying to find Sylvie's killer and I didn't have time to chase you down at a rodeo. And I wasn't about to leave my niece at a dirty arena with a bunch of sweaty cowboys and smelly livestock."

"Don't pretty it up on my account."

"I'm sorry. I know this is new, but this has all been rather shocking to me, as well. Once I learned that your father lived on a large ranch surrounded by family, I decided they could handle taking care of Kimmie and getting you in to see me."

"Fair enough, but if you disapprove of me and my lifestyle so vehemently, why drop her off at all? You could have raised her yourself. I didn't know she existed."

"That would have been illegal and unethical once I found that document. Besides, I couldn't in good conscience ignore my sister's written wishes."

Not to mention that she'd tried caring for Kimmie and found it nearly impossible to work night and day on finding Sylvie's killer, work the rest of her cases and take on the extremely demanding job of taking care of an infant.

She couldn't begin to imagine how Cannon would handle it, but he was the father. He'd have to work out something.

"Where is Kimmie now?" Brit asked.

"At the Dry Gulch Ranch, but that's temporary. I don't have any ties with R. J. Dalton and I don't want him in my daughter's life—if I have a daughter. I'm far from convinced that I do, no matter what your sister wrote on some form."

"The DNA testing will settle that."

"It won't settle what I'm supposed to do with her if the test comes out positive. I can't take care of a baby. I don't even know where to start."

"Maybe you should have thought about that before you got my sister pregnant."

"If I'd been sober and thinking, she wouldn't have gotten pregnant. And, contrary to what you infer, it takes two to tango. I don't push myself on women."

"That you remember."

Cannon emptied the glass of beer and set it down with a loud clunk. "I say we table the rest of this conversation until we know the results of the paternity test." He pulled his wallet from his pocket, took out a few bills and tossed them on the table, then stood to leave. "I'll be in touch."

"You haven't eaten yet."

"I'd prefer to eat where the air doesn't crackle with animosity."

She'd said too much. Her boss had warned her that if she gave her this case Brit would have to keep her emotions out of it. But she'd lost a sister she'd never gotten to meet, a sister who had left a precious baby behind.

The waitress arrived with the meal. Great timing. The overflowing plate of ribs, fries and coleslaw had an immediate effect on Cannon's demeanor.

"I'm sorry for the last comment," Brit said. "It was out of line. Stay and eat. Please."

Cannon sat back down and ordered another beer. After that, he gave the food his full attention.

Brit waited until he bit the remaining shred of meat from the last rib before getting back down to business. This time she made sure to keep her tone nonaccusing.

"Can we start over?" Brit suggested.

He stared her down. "Will it make a difference?"

"Yes. If I could ask you a few questions, it might help with the investigation. I promise to maintain a civil tone."

"That would be worth seeing."

Brit did her best to put aside the irritation toward Cannon she'd been nursing for almost a week.

"I know you said you don't remember much about the evening you met my sister, Cannon, but if I ask you a few questions, maybe it will trigger a memory."

"Worth a try," he agreed. "I'd like to help you. No one deserves to be murdered, especially not a young mother minding her own business."

"Was Sylvie alone at the bar that night or with a friend?"

"I don't remember seeing her talking to anyone else. That doesn't mean she didn't come in with someone."

"Did she mention a boyfriend, maybe one that she was supposed to meet there or had recently broken up with?"

He shook his head. "Not that I remember."

"Did she seem afraid or talk about being afraid?"

He hesitated, his facial expression grim as if he really was attempting to remember a useful detail.

"I'm sorry. I was dealing with some heavy stuff of my own that night. All I remember about your sister is that she was there, drinking beer and putting up with me. I'm not proud of this, but to be totally honest, I don't even remember her being in the hotel with me."

"Then she wasn't still in the room when you woke up?"

"No. *That* I would have remembered. Did you question the bartender and waitresses who work there to see if they knew her?"

"I questioned everyone," Brit said. "No one remembered either of you. But then it has been a year. Some had moved on to other jobs, some to other parts of the country."

Cannon shifted in his seat, looked around until he caught their waitress's eye and signaled for a check. Obviously he was eager to escape her and her questions.

She wouldn't push further tonight. Cannon was probably too bogged down with worrying over the paternity test results to think about anything else.

Brit was convinced the test results would be positive. Whether or not that was a good thing remained to be seen. But she had to admit that she could see why Sylvie had felt an immediate attraction to the sexy cowboy. He was a virile, rough and tough bull rider with a Texas drawl and a piercing stare that could shake a woman to her soul.

Some women. Not Brit, of course.

BY THE TIME Cannon reached his hotel, he was dead tired and ready to crash. Even so, he doubted sleep would come quick or last long. He'd received bad news on top of bad news over the past twenty-four hours and the hits just kept coming.

The murder of a lover he didn't even remember being in bed with. A gorgeous homicide cop who thought of him as a disgusting rodeo bum.

A baby who'd curled her short, stubby finger around his callused one. His heart twisted inside him at the memory. But it didn't change anything. Definitely didn't mean he could give Kimmie what she needed.

Brit surely realized that. Or maybe not. He'd never been good at figuring out women. Brit was even thornier to figure than most.

She had an intensity about her that most of the young buckle bunnies who hung around the arena in their short shorts, bulging cleavage and ready temptation lacked. But then she was older than most of them and a homicide detective.

The kind of woman who either irritated the hell out of a man or turned him on to the point he couldn't think straight. She had both effects on Cannon.

He had an idea there was a real flesh-and-blood woman behind that tough detective veneer but doubted he'd get a chance to see it. He dropped to the side of the bed and pulled off his boots as he gave that thought more consideration.

Brit in a more intimate setting, dressed in something

skimpy and lacy. He imagined tangling his fingers in her shiny hair and gazing into those sky-blue eyes and seeing them glazed with passion.

Enough, cowboy. He yanked off his shirt, then stood and wiggled out of his jeans. He tossed them over a chair and headed for the bathroom.

He was about to step beneath the spray when his cell phone rang. He raced to grab it from his jeans pocket. The ID screen read R. J. Dalton. He resisted the temptation to ignore the call. Like it or not, R. J. Dalton and the Dry Gulch were in his life for the time being.

"Hello."

"How's it going?" R.J. asked. "Did you find out whether or not you're Kimmie's father?"

Cannon explained that the testing would be done the following morning.

"Did you get a chance to talk to Brittany Garner?"

"I did."

"Is she Kimmie's mother?"

"No. Turns out she's Kimmie's aunt." Cannon figured there was no reason to go into details about Sylvie's murder until he knew for certain whether or not Kimmie was his daughter.

"How are things going with the babysitting chores?" Cannon asked.

"Hadley is loving every minute of it. She's like a kid with a new doll. Went shopping today and bought Kimmie a whole wardrobe, like she needs to be gussied up at that age."

"Tell her not to get too attached yet." Or ever, for that matter. Whatever happened, Cannon had no intention of making the Dry Gulch Ranch or R.J. part of his future.

"Baby's right here, kicking like a Rockette in training," R.J. said. "Want to tell her good-night?"

"No." No way was he coochy-cooing over the phone.

"I'll hold the phone close to her," R.J. said, ignoring his response.

Soft cooing and gurgling sounds reached Cannon's ear. His chest tightened. His stomach grew queasy. The tug on his emotions left his throat so dry he could barely manage a mumbled hello.

"She's smiling," R.J. said. "Must know you're her dad."

"Then she knows more than I do at this point." Cannon said his goodbyes and broke the connection.

Heaven help them all if he was Kimmie's father.

He was toweling off after the shower when he suddenly remembered something Sylvie had said that night they'd been drinking together. He rushed out of the bathroom in the nude, grabbed his jeans and dug Brit's card from the pocket.

He'd punched in all but the last number when he changed his mind. What he remembered wasn't a game changer. It could wait until morning. Give him a good reason to see her again.

And that's when it hit him how much he wanted to see the condescending detective again. Could his life get any more screwed up?

BRIT WAS SLAMMED by the terrible sense of mysterious loss again as she pulled into the garage of her tri-level town house. She'd had a twin sister. They might have shared so many things, a closeness only twins are said to experience. If only they'd met before a killer had claimed Sylvie's life.

Now Brit couldn't help but wonder what other secrets were hiding in her past. Were there other siblings? Had she and Sylvie both been put up for adoption or was it only Brit their biological mother hadn't wanted? Why hadn't her adopted parents ever told her about her twin?

Could she have saved Sylvie from the brutal murder had they met sooner?

Now another question seared into her mind. Why hadn't Sylvie told Cannon that she was pregnant with his child? Now that she'd met Cannon, it was hard to picture him as a man to fear.

Self-confident. Lived on the edge. Might never settle down. A heartache in cowboy clothing. Perhaps not the best of men to hang your heart on, but still he'd deserved to know he was a father.

The mystery continued to plague her thoughts as she killed the engine and climbed out of her silver Acura sedan. Hitting the garage button, the door began its descent as she entered the house though the small laundry-mudroom.

She left her keys on the hook by the back door and stepped into the kitchen. Anxiety hit like a bolt of lightning. She wasn't alone. Her hand went for her gun as a pair of large, meaty hands grabbed her from behind. He yanked her arms behind her back with so much force she cried out in pain.

He shoved her into the wall, his own large body pushing into hers as he plied her weapon from her fingers. A heavy clunk sounded as it hit the tiled kitchen floor. A heartbeat later the sharp blade of a knife pricked the flesh at the base of her neck.

"A lesson you should have learned from your father. Piss off the wrong people and there will be hell to pay."

Waves of adrenaline combatted the anxiety, revving all her police intuitions and training. Even with the knife at her neck, she struggled to turn enough to see the man's face. His hold was too tight and the knife drew a stream of blood that trickled down her neck.

"How do you know my dad?"

"Wrong question." He laughed and then coughed a raspy rattle that seemed to come from deep in his chest. The blade of the knife slid across her jugular and then down her arm, a promise of the hell to come.

If she did nothing, he was going to kill her.

Brit kicked backward, connecting with the attacker's right leg hard enough to throw him off balance.

The knife slid to her shoulder, slicing through the flesh painfully as it slashed across her skin, but still he held her arm behind her back so tightly she couldn't move.

"You bitch. Your payback is waiting in the bedroom, all your fault."

He was going to rape and kill her. She bucked the back of her head against him with all the strength she could muster. She heard it crack against his chin.

Unfazed, her assailant pounded his fist into her back and then spun her around to face him. Dizzy from pain, she struggled to focus. All she could make out was a pair of onyx-black eyes glowing like coals.

He hammered her head against the wall with his fist. She sank to the floor, the room a hazy mass of shifting images.

Somehow she spotted the pistol he'd knocked from her hand. She reached for it and her finger found the trigger.

Before she could aim it, his foot connected with her head. Dizzy and disoriented, she aimed into the foggy blur and pulled the trigger.

A filmy black curtain slowly descended on her world.

Chapter Six

Cannon strolled out of the examining room where he'd been swabbed to the nurse's satisfaction. His craving for a cup of strong coffee intensified now that he was allowed to have caffeine.

His muscles were doing some serious protesting of their own, complaining painfully at every move. They'd taken a beating over the past two days, first at the raw power of an angry bull, followed by sitting for hours yesterday behind the wheel of his less-than-luxurious pickup truck.

But he'd done his part. Filled out a multitude of forms and read every word of the documents. He'd also followed the usual list of dos and don'ts from the pre-swabbing directions on the website. He wanted nothing to invalidate or taint the testing. Too much was riding on the result.

Now all that was left to do was the staff and lab director's job of tracking, verifying and performing the statistical calculations. Then he'd know for certain whether or not he was Kimmie's father.

He still couldn't wrap his mind around the full implications of that, but apprehension felt like sandpaper scratching against his nerves.

He ignored the lab exit signs and followed the

odor of coffee down a narrow hallway. He stopped at what looked like a staff lounge. Two uniformed police officers were talking between chomping down on chocolate-covered doughnuts.

"Garner's lucky to have come out of that with only minor injuries."

"Still can't believe the intruder got the jump on her." Garner, as in Brit Garner? Cannon's interest zeroed in.

"Is she still in the hospital?" he asked nonchalantly, as if he had a right to be privy to the information.

"Memorial Hermann."

"And the guy who attacked her?"

"Still on the loose last I heard."

Cannon's muscles bunched into frayed knots.

The cops moved on to a different topic. Cannon filled a to-go cup with the strong brew and left. Time to make a hospital call on the gorgeous detective.

"ALL I REMEMBER of his face are his eyes," Brit said for what seemed like the tenth time in as many minutes. She tugged the sheet again, trying to keep the uninjured shoulder that kept escaping the baggy hospital gown from showing.

Her partner, Rick, paced the room. He was hounding her with questions she really wanted to answer, but she'd already explained what she could remember of the attack. Pulling the trigger was the last thing she recalled. Even that memory was vague, as if it had happened to someone else. Were it not for the bandages, the pain in her left shoulder and her killer headache, she could easily believe it had been a nightmare.

"Did the attacker say anything?"

"Not much, or if he did I don't remember it."

"Try. What did he say when he grabbed you?"

"Something about my father."

"What about your father?"

She struggled to remember through the brain fog. "That I should have learned from him. That I piss people off. I can't recall his exact words."

"He must have said more than that. Think, Brit. But don't overdo it," he added, no doubt remembering the nurse's warnings not to upset her.

"I am thinking." She massaged her right temple as if that could coax the words from their hiding place inside her mind. "He was going to drag me to the bedroom."

"I'm sure he was. Son of a bitch," Rick murmured under his breath as he stopped at the foot of her bed.

"Did his voice sound familiar?"

"No, but then nothing much was registering at the time except staying alive."

"Do you remember shooting him?"

"Somehow I managed to get my hands on my weapon when I was sliding into unconsciousness. I think I shot it once. The next thing I knew I was lying on the floor and my neighbor Janie and officers Bates and Cormier were standing over me. I don't know how long I'd been out."

"Only a few minutes. Fortunately, your neighbor heard the gunshot and came running."

"Janie's head of our Neighborhood Watch group. She knows everything that goes on in our neighborhood. Talk to her. She may have seen the guy lurking around the house before he broke in."

"Bates asked. She said she didn't see anything unusual, but I'll talk to her again."

"And no one saw the man leaving my house after the attack?" Brit questioned, just trying to get things straight in her muddled mind.

"No, but he left a trail of blood across your kitchen to the back patio door."

She tried to rise onto her elbows. The dizziness returned. Rick appeared to be swaying. Rick never swayed. She closed her eyes and let her head fall back to the pillow.

"My blood or his?"

"His, and lots of it. You didn't miss."

"Nice to know he has something to remember me by this morning, as well. Was the lock broken on the patio door?"

"Yeah."

"So much for my alarm system."

"The wires were all cut," Rick said. "He knew what he was doing. He just wasn't counting on you knowing what you were doing."

Satisfaction eased her tension. "Glad I got at least one shot off. Nice to know I can deliver a bullet when I'm passing out."

"A direct hit, too. As much blood as he lost, he should be in a hospital somewhere in the city, but we haven't been able to locate him."

"And you checked with all the emergency rooms?"

"Yep, but we'll find him. We have fingerprints and DNA," Rick said. "If he's in either of those FBI database systems, we should have no trouble getting a positive ID."

Brit tried to push up on her elbows again and this time she made it. She looked around the room. "Where are my clothes?"

"Taken for evidence."

"I can't leave here in this hospital gown."

"Why not? It's your color."

"Not funny."

"That's what Shelly Mince said at the crime scene. She packed a duffel of necessities for you and brought them to the hospital when we finished up at your house last night. You'll want to stay away from there until the place is cleaned up."

"I've seen plenty of blood. Where's the duffel?"

Rick walked over and opened the small closet to the left of her bed. "It's right here. Not that you're going anywhere anytime soon."

"I'm not going to just lie here and stare at the ceiling while the guy who tried to kill me goes on the run and disappears."

"Thanks for that vote of confidence, partner, but you're not the only competent cop in Houston."

"I know that." It didn't change her mind about what she had to do. "What happened to my pistol?"

"We found it at the scene. It's at the precinct."

"At least the rotten bastard didn't steal it."

"On the bright side, he didn't shoot you with it, either."

"Which also makes no sense. Not that I'm complaining. I just need my weapon."

"You don't need one right now," Rick said. "Captain Bradford ordered round-the-clock protection while you're in the hospital. You have an armed guard at your door now."

"Tell Captain Bradford thanks but she can call off the dogs. Now hand me that duffel so I can get dressed. Then you can drive me to the precinct to get a replacement weapon."

Rick shook his head. "No can do. Doctor's orders."

"I feel fine," she lied.

"That's good to hear."

Brit looked to the door for the source of the last

comment. Dr. Simpson, the white-coated young trauma specialist who had taken care of her in E.R. last night stepped inside.

She smiled and eased her head back to the pillow as a new wave of wooziness hit. "Just the man I need to see. I appreciate the wonderful care, but duty calls. If you'll just sign my release papers, I'll give up my bed to the sick and wounded."

"I'm glad to hear you're feeling so well."

"Then you'll sign the release?"

"No."

"Why not?"

"You have a concussion and you lost a good deal of blood from the shoulder wound. You need bed rest and medical observation for at least another twenty-four hours."

"You tell her, Doc." Rick walked over to the bed. "I've got to run, partner. I'll check with you later, but if you remember anything you haven't already told me, call. I'll be out playing cop."

Rick gave his signature wink and double click of his tongue as he escaped, closing the door behind him.

"How's the pain in the shoulder?" the doctor asked.

"I've had worse." She raised her hand and stretched until her fingers crawled across the thick bandage. "When do I get this off?"

"In a few minutes. I'll check the wound and if it looks good, the nurse will apply a new and smaller dressing. How's the headache?"

"Persistent, but the pounding is more like a kid on drums now instead of a jackhammer."

"That's progress. I'll keep you on the current medication. The pounding should disappear entirely soon. How's the vertigo?"

"Much improved."

"Then sounds like you're well on your way to recovery."

"Exactly. So there's really no point in my staying here. I can rest in any bed as easily as I can rest here."

"Yes, but would you? Besides, you're far too unsteady to be left alone."

"I won't be alone. I have a friend I can stay with and I'll come back to the E.R. immediately if there's a problem."

There was a tap at the door.

"Come in," the doctor said.

He'd probably expected the nurse but it was the guard who stepped inside. "You have a visitor," he said to Brit.

"Who?"

"Cannon Dalton. Do you want me to show him in or turn him away?"

Cannon was the last person she'd expected to see this morning, but there was no reason not to see him except that she no doubt looked like she'd been in a fight with a bulldog. She raked her fingers through her tangled hair and pushed it behind her ears.

"Show him in."

Cannon swaggered in, looking even sexier than he had last night, if that was possible. He was clean-shaven, wearing a pale gold Western shirt that set off his eyes.

He took off his black Stetson and held it in his hands, fingering the brim. A lock of sun-streaked hair fell over his brow.

"Tell me you're not here because there were complications at the lab," she said. "That truly would be the last straw this morning."

"I've been swabbed," he said. "No complications. Doesn't look like you can say the same."

"How did you know I was here?"

"Lab gossip. I figured I'd drop by and see if there's anything I can do to help."

His timing couldn't have been better. Now if he'd just go along with her on this. She smiled appreciatively. "I'm feeling fine," she said, "but Dr. Simpson is concerned about my staying alone."

"If that's an invitation to play nurse, I'm at your service."

She breathed a sigh of relief. "There you have it, Dr. Simpson. I won't be alone."

Cannon smiled, walked over and took her hand as if they were old friends—or more. Heat crept through her veins. She looked away, careful not to let him see that his touch had an effect on her.

"I'll be here for you as long as you need me," Cannon said. "Not sure how good a nurse I am, but I can fetch and carry and I make a mean tortilla soup."

"See, Dr. Simpson," Brit said. "I'll be in great hands."

The doctor didn't look convinced. "You have an armed guard here at the hospital. That indicates to me it wouldn't be safe for you to go back to the scene of the crime or not to have protection."

"I'm a cop," she reminded him. "I made a mistake and let the man get the jump on me once. I won't be careless enough to do that again. Besides, haven't you heard? He's in far worse shape than I am. I have no idea why they ordered the guard."

"She can stay at my place," Cannon offered.

"Thank you, Cannon. That settles that."

The doctor closed the chart. "I can't keep you here against your will, Detective Garner, but I think you'll be making a serious mistake by going against my recommendations for continued hospitalization."

Certainly not her first. "I'll follow the rest of your instructions to the letter."

"Your decision. I'll check out the shoulder wound and then have the nurse go through the care instructions with both of you," the doctor said. "But I'll need to see you in my office in three days, or before if your condition worsens in any way."

"Not a problem," Brit assured him.

She'd get Cannon to drive her home and then he could do as he pleased until he got the paternity test results. After all, she was a detective. She knew to stay clear of the crime scene; but that left the rest of the town house.

Good thing she didn't really need Cannon to nurse her back to health, though. Scary to think of what kind of TLC you could get from a guy used to tangling with bulls and women he picked up in bars.

No reason to worry. She would be getting nothing but a ride from Cannon Dalton.

CANNON WAS CERTAIN he was being used. He wasn't sure why at this point or even if it was bad thing. On the surface, having the seductive detective so eager to accept his help was enticing. Which meant there was more to this than the obvious.

He held open the passenger door of his pickup truck while Brit climbed inside. Since she'd asked him to step into the hallway while her wound was dressed, this was the first real look he had at the knot on the back of her head and the thickness of the bandage just below her left shoulder blade.

Whoever she'd tangled with had meant business. Cannon couldn't help but wonder if her attack was somehow related to Sylvie's murder. Either way, Brit was lucky to be alive.

She was a cop. She should be able to take care of herself. If not, he was sure the officers on the Houston police force would do their best to defend their own.

Yet, the need to protect her swelled like an obsession inside him. He couldn't explain it. Maybe it was just a man's natural instinct to protect a woman in danger. Maybe it was the emotional roller coaster he'd been on since Kimmie had dropped into his life. Most likely it was a combination of the two.

"Take the first left," Brit said as he pulled out into the traffic lane. "Then watch for the signs for I-20 west."

"That's not the way to my hotel."

"Of course not. It's the way to my town house."

"The crime scene."

"Right. The scene where some rotten bastard tried to kill me. I need to check it out for myself."

"What part of bed rest and not stressing out do you *not* understand?"

"What part of I'm fine do you not understand?"

So that was the game. She had no intention of following any of the doctor's orders. Cannon swerved, made a U-turn and hit the accelerator.

Brit turned so that she was facing him. "What are you doing?" she snapped.

"Taking you back to the hospital. I signed on to make sure you weren't left alone, not to taxi you around town."

"You're kidding, right? I mean you didn't really think I was going to hang out with you in your hotel room?"

"Yeah. Guess I'm not as sophisticated as you. I usually take a woman at her word when she asks for help."

"I thought you understood and were playing along with me."

"Doesn't really matter what you thought," he said, still prickling. "I'm driving you back to the hospital. After that you're on your own."

"You're as hardheaded as those bulls you ride, Cannon Dalton."

"Don't even try to detail my faults, Detective. You don't know the half of it."

"Look, I'm sorry, Cannon. Let me explain."

"Why bother? I'm just a stupid rodeo cowboy who doesn't get the intricacies of deceit."

She reached across the seat and rested her hand on his arm. "I don't know you well enough to make judgments, but you don't know me that well, either. So give me a break and try to understand where I'm coming from. I risk my life on an almost daily basis to go after killers. It's what I do. The only difference here is that the would-be killer came after me."

"I admire your dedication." He kept driving toward the hospital. "But you're in no shape to go after a jaywalker right now, much less a would-be killer. In my book, trying it is stupidity, not bravery or even duty."

She let go of his arm. "Okay, you win. I'll go to your hotel and rest. But first, just make a quick stop at my house. I need to pick up my computer and some personal items. You surely can't object to that."

He considered the option, knowing she'd probably break her promise the second she got home. But the truth was he wanted to see the crime scene for himself. Not that he had any intention of jumping into the case.

Besides, if he took her back to the hospital, she'd just call a taxi and leave again. At least this way, he'd be there if she had more complications from the concussion.

"On my conditions," he said.

"Your conditions?" Her voice rose. "I'm the one in control...."

He slowed and pulled to the curb. She sputtered like an engine that had run out of fuel. "Okay, let's hear it," she said. "But be reasonable."

"One quick stop at your house, and then on to my hotel. You will rest and stop acting like the safety of the entire town of Houston rests entirely on your shoulders. And stop talking to me like I'm a hired hand."

She rolled her eyes but then managed a half smile. "Deal."

He turned and headed back toward I-20. He decided this was as good a time as any to level with her about the rest of the reason he'd come to the hospital this morning.

"I didn't just come by to check on you this morning."

"Then why did you come?"

"After I left you last night, I remembered something else Sylvie had said when we were in the bar."

She swiveled to face him and zeroed in like a laser. "What is it?"

"I remember Sylvie saying something about time travel. Coming from the past. Going to the past. I may not have heard it right and only remember it because it sounded so crazy to me at the time. And I think she may have mentioned a sister, though I don't remember what she said about her."

Brit turned back to face straight ahead and grew quiet and pensive.

"Are you feeling okay?" he asked after ten minutes of silence."

"Fine. I'm still thinking about the time travel comment. Are you sure she wasn't just talking about her past?"

"I'm not really sure of anything about that night."

Brit understood confusion and not being able to re-member details. She was living it right now. But at least her problems stemmed from a concussion, not a whis-key bottle. She told him which exit to take and he nod-ded in response.

Her head started pounding again. She didn't dare let Cannon know that. He'd turn right around again on a dime.

CANNON HAD A strong hunch that helping Brit escape the hospital had been a huge mistake. On the other hand, he had nothing else to do but sit around and wait for test results, and hanging out with Brit was definitely not boring.

Twenty minutes of heavy traffic later, they pulled up in front of Brit's town house. It was on a cul-de-sac surrounded by other town houses that looked exactly like hers. The streets were deserted, the residents either inside on this glorious fall day or, more likely, at work.

Lawns were meticulously landscaped, separated by thick holly hedges. There were no porches, but each house had impressive brass overhangs to shelter the wide porticos and striking etched-glass-and-mahogany front doors.

The prominent difference was that Brit's front door was striped with police tape.

"I don't suppose you plan to pay any attention to the warning on the tape," Cannon said.

"I don't have to. I'm a homicide detective, remember?"

"How could I forget? I thought they only used that tape when there had been an actual murder."

"Not necessarily. They can use it anytime they don't

want the public entering or disturbing an area. Which is why you'll have to wait for me outside."

Brit started up the walk and then veered to the stone walkway that ran between the thick shrubs that separated her house from the one next to it. Maybe she had decided not to cross the tape.

Cannon hurried to catch up with her. Before he could, a black sedan pulled up in front of the house.

A woman appearing to be in her midfifties, short brown hair in a stylish bob jumped out and stamped toward them. "Stop right there," she called in a voice that sounded a lot like Cannon's evil high-school principal.

Brit spun around. "Captain Bradford. What are you doing here?"

"Looking for you. Your doctor said you'd left the hospital against his recommendations. I figured I'd find you here."

"I only plan to take a quick look around and pick up a few personal items. I'll be careful not to disturb a thing, though I suspect the CSU has all the evidence they need by now."

"Going inside is not a good idea in your condition. Go back to the hospital. Give yourself some time. Rick has everything under control here."

"I'm not here to take over and I'm feeling fine," Brit insisted, though she'd looked unsteady walking.

Brit nodded toward Cannon. "My friend did the driving and he's going to stay with me the rest of the day. If there's any problem at all, he can drive me back to the E.R. at once."

The captain frowned, obviously still agitated.

Cannon extended his hand. "I'm Cannon Dalton, rent-a-nurse."

"Cannon Dalton? As in Kimmie Dalton's father?"

Bradford turned back to Brit before he could respond to her questions. "Care to explain all of this, Detective Garner?"

"There's nothing to explain. Cannon took the paternity test this morning and then offered to stick around and help out."

"So you've pulled a person of interest in your sister's murder into an attempted murder case involving you?"

"No one mentioned my being a person of interest in a murder case," Cannon protested. His hunch had definitely been right.

"You're only a person of interest because I thought you might have information that could lead to finding Sylvie's killer," Brit insisted.

"Regardless, you are not crossing the police line," Bradford said. "Brit can go inside, but first we need to have a talk."

"About what?" Brit asked.

"About what I'd hoped not to upset you with until you were feeling better. But since you're here, you leave me no choice."

"Rick's already told me that there's lots of blood."

"That's not the big problem."

"So what is?"

"Your attacker had obviously been in your house for some time before you arrived home," Bradford said. "He did some redecorating of your bedroom using your personal belongings and posters he'd brought with him."

"I've seen extremely grisly crime scenes before. I can handle it," Brit insisted. "But I want to enter through the patio door just as my attacker did. It helps when I'm working a case."

Brit stamped off. Bradford turned back to Cannon. "You may as well come, too. I don't know what it can hurt at this point and I may need you to help me carry her out of here and back to the hospital when the impact of this hits her. It made me nauseous when I saw it and I haven't had a concussion."

"It's that bad?"

"No. It's worse."

Chapter Seven

Brit entered the kitchen and groaned. "I don't know if this will ever come clean. I don't see how he walked away after losing this much blood."

"That's what we all said," Bradford agreed. "Have you seen enough for now?"

"Not until I see what the bastard did to my bedroom."

Bradford followed her as she left the kitchen. Cannon stayed a few steps behind. He hurried to catch up when he heard a gasp followed by a shaky curse.

When he saw what Brit was staring at, he rushed over and put an arm around her to steady her. He wasn't sure if it was fury or revulsion that had her trembling. Both were appropriate.

"That's Sylvie in the pictures," she said. "That's Kimmie's mother."

The images were so sickening that even Cannon's stomach lurched and threatened to revolt. "What kind of deranged son of a bitch would do something like this?"

"The maniac who killed Sylvie and tried to kill me."

Brit walked over and tore a life-size poster from the wall and ripped it in half. The poster was made from a black-and-white photo of Sylvie lying in an alleyway with her throat slit.

A black lace pantie, apparently Brit's, had been taped

to the image. She bit her bottom lip so hard that her teeth left a temporary imprint.

The other poster photos were merely different angles of Sylvie's dead body. Other pieces of Brit's lingerie had been shaped into evocative positions and scattered around the room, either near or attached to the posters.

The bedcovers were pulled back. Cannon shuddered to even think what the assailant's plans had been for this bedroom had he not been shot before he could drag Brit in here.

If he could get hold of the pervert right now, Cannon was sure he could kill him with his bare hands. With any luck, he'd staggered outside and was lying face-down in the mud after a slow death.

"My fault," Brit stammered. "He said this was my fault. He must have been talking about Sylvie's murder. He must have planned to kill both of us as some kind of payback killing."

"But payback for what?" Cannon asked. "You didn't even know about Sylvie until she was murdered. How would he?"

"If we knew that, we'd have our man," Bradford said.

"Where's my weapon?" Brit asked. "I don't have it or my cell phone and I'll need them both."

"CSU turned them and your handbag in," Bradford said. "They're at the precinct. I'll have an officer deliver them to you, once I know where you'll be staying until the doctor tells me you're ready to go back to work."

"I'll be with Cannon."

Relief flooded his body. He wasn't sure when the lines had crossed, but in his mind keeping Brit safe had become his priority, and finding the sick bastard who did this had become his responsibility. He wasn't going anywhere until he was sure this man was dead or behind bars.

Now he only had to convince her of that.

IMAGES FROM THE night before stalked Brit's mind as they escaped the horrid scene and left through the front door of the house. Cannon's hand was at the small of her back, instantly ready to pull her close if she lost her balance.

She well could. The nausea and the headache had returned with a vengeance.

She was haunted by flashes of strong hands jerking and twisting her arm behind her back. The pounding fist. The paralyzing pain as her skull banged against the wall. The deafening crack of gunfire.

But what if the bullet had missed. Then he would have dragged her to the bedroom and waited on her to come to before he raped and killed her. That had undoubtedly been his plan all along.

He wanted her to relive Sylvie's death knowing that she would die the same way. He would have made sure Brit knew who was getting back at her and why. That was what made revenge killings worthwhile.

But who with reason to seek revenge against Brit could have known she had a sister, when Brit hadn't even known it?

"I'm sorry you had to see that," Bradford said.

"I needed to see it," Brit said. "I need to understand the nature of the maniacal pervert I'm dealing with and that he knew more about my biological family than I did. That could be key in identifying him."

"The CSU worked half the night collecting blood samples, shoe prints, fingerprints and any other evidence they considered useful," Bradford said. "It shouldn't take long to get an ID."

"Rick assured me they also checked all the local emergency rooms for a gunshot victim," Brit said.

"Every hospital within a hundred-and-fifty-mile radius." Brit turned and looked back at the house. "How far was the CSU able to follow the blood trail?"

"To the small man-made creek that runs in back of the town house complex," Bradford said. "Apparently, even with the severe loss of blood, your assailant was still lucid enough to use the water to hide his tracks."

"But he may not have gotten far. Did they search the neighborhood, the bike path through the green area, the park?"

"There's still a team working on that. We'll find who did it," Bradford assured her. "Rick is lead detective on the case, but I've promised him as much manpower as I can spare."

"Rick is capable," Brit agreed, "but I'm the one most affected by this case. Don't you think I should have the lead detective position?"

"Absolutely not. The doctor ordered bed rest. I expect you to follow those orders. I don't want to see you at the precinct for at least a week."

"A week? You can't expect me to do nothing on this case for a week."

"I expect you to follow orders. You've canceled every vacation you've scheduled for the past two years including the one you were supposed to start the morning Sylvie's body was discovered. You're long past due. Get some rest. Read a book. Watch movies. Take a cruise."

"I get seasick."

"Then don't take a cruise, but you're not coming back to work until I clear you. If you decide to stay in

Houston, I can provide around-the-clock protection," the captain offered.

"I can protect myself."

The captain tilted her head and stared at Brit as if there was no reason to state the obvious.

"I realize I let the man last night get the jump on me, but it won't happen again. I can live with taking the rest of the day off if you insist, but a week is unthinkable."

"My decision stands. You can resume your investigation into your sister's murder when you come back to work, but the attack on you is Rick's case from here on out. End of discussion."

Brit could see there was no use to argue further. Keep pushing and Bradford might suspend her indefinitely instead of calling her forced noninvolvement a vacation.

But just because she was officially off the case didn't mean she couldn't do some investigating on her own— under the radar.

Now if she could just get rid of this annoying headache and clear the cobwebs from her mind, she could...

"Ready to go?" Bradford asked.

"I'm ready."

In fact, she couldn't wait to get started. Her first order of business would be getting rid of Cannon, although he'd already proved himself to be a lot more responsible and levelheaded than she'd ever expected.

Still, hanging out with her would only pull the hunky cowboy with the easy smile and hypnotic eyes into trouble. Not much chance she'd have to persuade him. He was no doubt already sorry he'd ever offered his help.

But first she would take him up on the offer of his hotel room. The confusion, headache and urgency were taking their toll.

Fatigue made mush of her muscles. The fog refused to lift completely from her brain. Her headache was becoming more intense.

What she needed was a safe place to fall.

Who'd have ever expected that to be Cannon Dalton's hotel room?

THE HACKING COUGH started again, the blood in Clive's throat strangling him. Pain racked his body as he turned his head enough that the blood dribbled from between his lips.

It had been hours, maybe days, since the bullet bit into his stomach, tearing out tissue and muscle and leaving his insides exposed like a butchered calf. He'd lost track of time.

The room was pitch-black, the air dank and fetid with the smell of death. His death, unless help arrived soon.

Where was the dammed doctor? He should have been here by now.

There was a rattling deep in Clive's chest. He struggled to cough, but his throat closed tight. His lungs began to burn.

He heard footsteps. The doctor was coming at last.

Chapter Eight

The hotel room was quiet except for the sounds of Brit's rhythmic breathing. She'd changed out of her jeans for a more comfortable pair of workout shorts and then dropped to the bed and drifted into sleep within minutes after they'd arrived at the hotel.

Thankfully, Cannon had splurged for a nicer hotel than usual. He'd figured he'd only be in town a night or two at the most and he was too sore to risk a bed that wouldn't be kind to his strained and bruised muscles.

Cannon took out his small laptop, turned it on and waited for the slow start-up on his aging machine. About the only thing he used it for was checking out rodeo schedules and results.

Until he'd learned he might be a father, his life had been simple and uncomplicated. Chasing the dream from one rodeo to another. Hoping to avoid injury so that he could pick up enough points to be in serious contention for the big bucks and the national title.

So far, no national title, but he couldn't complain. He'd earned over $300,000 in prize money last year along with countless buckles and his new pickup truck. Most of the more expensive buckles he'd won were tucked away in a safe-deposit box in Austin. The cash was invested or residing in his savings account in the same bank.

Another good year and he might just start looking for the ranch he planned to settle on when he had enough money saved to stock it.

When that day came, he'd figured he might even find a woman to share the dream. Start a family. Settle down. In the meantime, he was careful to have no surprise packages like Kimmie to shatter the big picture.

One night that he could barely remember may have destroyed it beyond repair. He couldn't drag a baby from rodeo to rodeo. And he wasn't about to dump Kimmie at the Dry Gulch Ranch the way he'd been dumped at his uncle's ranch.

Never wanted. Never liked.

Cannon typed Sylvie Hamm into the search engine and waited to see what it coughed up. He checked out the possibilities. None appeared to match with the Sylvie Hamm who had given birth to Kimmie.

He tried the online social connections and didn't find her there, either. Not a major shock to him. He wasn't on any of the other popular websites for touching base with people he didn't care about, anyway.

He clicked on the newspaper article that had apparently appeared in the *Houston Chronicle* the day after Sylvie's death. It covered only spotty details about her murder, nothing as graphic as the enlarged photos taped to Brit's walls. Photos taken by the killer himself, most likely shot with the intention of showing them to Brit before he killed her.

The article did state that her body had been discovered in a back alley. He recognized the name of the cross streets. He and Brit had passed them last night on the way to Jodie's Grill. The estimated time of death indicated she'd been killed in broad daylight. Her hand-bag and all of her identifications were missing.

So Sylvie had been murdered in the vicinity of Brit's office. He wondered if she lived or worked in the area herself. Or was it possible that she been on her way to see Brit?

Could she have come that close to connecting with her twin sister after all these years only to be killed be-fore they actually met?

Cannon turned to stare at Brit and a crazy kick of awareness rocked his soul. There was no explaining the way the lady detective got to him. He'd always run from complications before. No one came with more complica-tions than Brit and they were multiplying by the minute.

Last night's assailant wasn't just using scare tactics. He'd murdered Sylvie as payback to Brit. There was no reason to doubt that as soon as he was physically able he'd be back to finish off Brit.

The smartest thing Brit could do right now was ac-cept her boss's offer of 24/7 protection—or else get out of Houston and find a safe place to get some R & R. Come to think of it, getting out of Houston was an ex-cellent idea.

She had a week off. She could go anywhere.

Unfortunately, he had a rodeo looming in a few days if his muscles healed enough to give him a fighting chance with the bull.

There was a tap at the door to the hotel room. Can-non jumped to his feet and hurried over before the noise woke Brit. He looked out the peephole. Captain Carla Bradford was standing there with two handbags slung across her shoulder.

Cannon opened the door, checked to make sure his

key was in his pocket and then stepped into the hall-way, closing the door behind him.

"Brit's sleeping," he explained. "I hate to wake her unless this is an emergency."

"No, I just stopped by to give her this." She handed him a black, leather handbag. "Her pistol is inside the zipped pocket. Be careful with it."

"I can handle a gun," Cannon assured her. Fact was, he was licensed to carry and had a pistol in his truck. "I thought Brit said you were sending an officer by with that."

"I was coming this way."

He doubted that was the full story. The captain was too far up the totem pole to be running errands in Houston traffic.

"Is there anything new in the investigation?" he asked.

"Nothing of consequence."

"You mean nothing you can tell me?"

"Nothing personal, Mr. Dalton. This is an active investigation and you are not an officer of the law."

"I'm an outsider. Got it. I'll let Brit know you made a personal delivery of her possessions."

"How is she?"

"She fell asleep right after we got to the hotel and hasn't woken since."

"Good. She needs to rest, although I'm surprised it's in your hotel room, considering the two of you only met for the first time last night. That was when you met, isn't it?"

"It is. I'm loyal and trustworthy, Captain Bradford. And as lovable as a teddy bear—unless someone gives me reason to get tough. Brit is safe with me."

"It's not you I'm worried about, Mr. Dalton. It's a

man who's on a death mission with her as the target. But since I'm here, I'd like to see for myself that she's actually still with you and not out chasing her killer on her own."

"I thought you might." Cannon took the hotel key from his pocket and pushed it into the lock. At the click he opened the door enough for the captain to peek inside.

Brit had rolled over but was still sleeping, her shiny hair haloing the white pillow. The sheet curled around her, hitting just below her T-shirt clad breasts.

"Satisfied?" he whispered.

She nodded as he closed the door. "I don't know how you got her to rest, but if you have any ideas about being a hero and saving her, forget it. You have no idea what you're up against."

"I'm just the chauffeur. I have no intention of playing cop."

"Then we agree on something. Remind Brit I expect her to keep me posted if she leaves town—which I still think is the best decision at this time. Her would-be killer lost too much blood to go chasing her around the country in the next few days."

"I'll give her the message."

By the time Cannon reentered the room, Brit was curled into the fetal position on the far side of the king-size bed, leaving most of the mattress free.

Cannon took off his boots and stretched out on the bed beside her, fully clothed, on top of the covers. His mind wrestled with the situation.

Brit had given in to a nap, but he knew this wouldn't last. As soon as she felt steady on her feet she'd jump right back into the investigation—with or without Bradford's permission. Worse to do it under the radar. That left her without other officers to watch her back.

He agreed that the best decision would be for her to leave the Houston area. Somehow he didn't see that happening—not unless the investigation led her somewhere else.

Nor did he see her spending another day hanging out with him. Or ever seeing him again if she found out he wasn't the biological father of her niece.

Cannon didn't realize he'd fallen asleep until he woke with a burning deep inside his gut. Brit had obviously tossed in her sleep and ended up cuddled against him. One of her arms stretched across his chest. Her bare left leg pushed between his thighs. Her disheveled hair brushed his chin.

Raw, visceral need bucked around inside him. His body grew rock-hard, his erection pushing hard against the zipper of his jeans. The craving to pull her into his arms and find her lips with his raged inside him.

For a second he couldn't breathe. Couldn't swallow. Couldn't produce a rational thought.

Finally he managed a few deep breaths and the good sense to ease himself from beneath her arm and off the bed.

But the damage had been done. There was no denying his infatuation for her now, no pretending that the attraction wasn't growing out of control.

Any way you cut it, Cannon was in for trouble.

BRIT OPENED HER eyes and stretched, confused for a minute about where she was or why. Slowly the details fitted themselves together. The attack. The concussion. The nightmarish posters. Cannon.

She glanced around the room. He was bent over a

computer, his focus glued to whatever he was reading. He was shirtless, shoeless, his hair slightly rumpled. The awareness he ignited hit again, sending her senses reeling.

Had someone told her twenty-four hours ago she'd experience these sensual jolts, much less trust Cannon enough to move into his hotel room, she'd have thought them nuts.

The only explanation was the timing. She couldn't remember having ever felt this vulnerable. It wasn't that she'd learned anything new from the sickening photos, but they'd been upsetting all the same. So was finding out that she might be the reason Sylvie had been murdered.

Still, Brit could have made it on her own. Having Cannon around had made it a lot easier. Even now, she didn't trust herself to drive, and she wasn't about to sit around and twiddle her thumbs for a week, no matter what Carla Bradford had ordered.

She sat up in bed. There was no reoccurrence of the vertigo that had plagued her this morning. The headache was almost gone, as well. Only the dull, thudding pain in her shoulder remained, triggered by her every move. She stretched and slid out from under the covers.

Cannon turned in his chair. His lips split into a slightly crooked smile that deepened the dimple in his chin. "The sleeping beauty awakes."

"Working on it." She was pretty sure the word *beauty* had been applied loosely. Impulsively, she raked her fingers through her hair, tucking the wild mussed locks behind her ears. Then she straightened the T-shirt that had bunched around her waist.

"How do you feel?" Cannon asked.

"Better," she said, thankful it was the truth. "At least

physically. Emotionally, I'm vacillating between fury that I let the lunatic escape last night and frustration that Bradford's ordered me out of the loop."

"From the amount of blood that covered your kitchen floor, I'm not sure the guy is still alive."

"Apparently he was alive enough to get out of the neighborhood."

"He could have had an accomplice nearby driving the getaway car."

"The possibility of having two lunatics out there looking to kill me doesn't make me feel the least bit better."

She glanced at the bedside clock. Ten minutes after five o'clock. Obviously not correct. "What time is it?"

"Ten after five."

"No way. I couldn't have slept that long."

"Yep, you were out of it."

"Why didn't you wake me?"

"Now why would I do that when the doctor said you needed rest and your boss said you were on vacation?"

She slung her feet over the side of the bed. "I wasted a day."

"Worse, you missed lunch," Cannon said.

"I need a shower more than food." She'd never felt dirtier in her life. It was as if the filthy perversion in her bedroom had crept into every cell of her body. "And I'll need to change into something besides these workout shorts and T-shirt to go out."

"How about room service?" Cannon asked. "I checked out the dinner menu offerings. They look pretty good, and you won't have to bother with changing."

"Fine by me." Bread and water would be fine by her this evening.

Cannon picked up a menu and tossed it to the side

of the bed next to her. "Everything from bratwurst to filet mignon."

"I'd best stick to something light until I'm sure the nausea isn't just taking a break."

"But you're not dizzy or nauseous now?"

"Not at the moment. Not even a headache."

"It's the nursing," he said. "I'm extremely experienced in dealing with contusions and concussions, usually my own. Fortunately, I haven't had a concussion since I mastered the art of getting bucked off a bit more gracefully."

"Obviously a man of many talents."

"Yep. See how lucky you are to have me around."

"Let's see, since you've arrived in town I've been attacked and nearly killed. I've had deranged pictures of my sister's murder plastered around the walls of my bedroom. And I've been ordered to take an unwanted vacation. You have a strange definition of lucky."

"But without me riding to your rescue, you could be in the hospital tonight, dressed in that baggy, open-backed gown and about to dine on broth and gelatin."

"There is that." She studied the menu offerings. "I think I'll go with the club sandwich and a cup of tomato soup."

"What do you want to drink?"

"I'll stick with water with lemon."

"How about dessert?"

"None for me. In fact, I can halve the sandwich with you if you want. I'll never eat it all."

"Half a sandwich wouldn't get me past the appetizer stage. I'm thinking a bowl of Texas chili for starters. Followed by the rib-eye steak with fries and a hunk of their fresh-baked bread."

"All washed down with a cold beer," she added for him.

"How'd you guess?"

She shook her head in wonder. "How do you keep from getting to be the size of those bulls you ride?"

"I'm a growing boy."

That wasn't far from the truth. "How old are you?"

"Twenty-seven."

Three years younger than she was. He could have passed for his early twenties. In spite of his appetite, he was in great shape. Lean and hard-bodied. She supposed he'd have to be strong and agile to stay on a bucking bull.

Brit looked around the room for her purse but didn't spot it. "Did an officer drop off my handbag and Smith & Wesson?"

"No, but Captain Bradford did. I think she wanted to assure herself that I hadn't taken you captive. I get the feeling she doesn't like me much."

"Welcome to the club. So where's my weapon?"

"In the closet, inside your handbag."

Cannon made the call to room service. Brit retrieved her phone from her handbag. No calls. She'd hoped for news of suspects from Rick. She checked the pistol and made sure it was easily accessible, loaded and with the safety on. She dropped her phone into her pocket.

Once in the bathroom, she spent agonizing minutes staring into the mirror. Dark circles cupped her eyes. Lines from the pillow creased the skin on her cheeks. Her hair was a disheveled mop.

One thing for sure, Cannon Dalton wasn't hanging around because he was enamored of her looks. Not that she wanted him to be.

She turned on the faucet, dipped her hands under the

spray and splashed the cool water onto her face. She brushed her teeth again. The metallic taste lingered, probably from the drugs. She'd taken two pills before she lay down.

Her mind went back to the problems at hand. She tried to arrange the events of the past twenty-four hours into a rational pattern, but it was like trying to work a children's pegboard, where all the holes were round and all the pegs were square.

The only thing she was sure of was that the attack was an act of revenge and the would-be killer hadn't started with her. For all she knew, he might not be planning on ending with her, either.

He might have a history of convictions and be going after everyone who'd ever arrested him and their families, as well.

That didn't seem nearly as far-fetched when she remembered the killer's comment about her father. Not that she suspected he'd killed her father. Very unlikely that he'd have waited three years to kill again.

Unless he'd been incarcerated between then and now.

After his years in the police business and coming up through the ranks to land the position of chief of police, the number of people who held a grudge against her father was legend.

She took a long shower and then slipped into a pair of worn and comfortable jeans and a sweatshirt.

When she rejoined Cannon in the bedroom, he'd pulled two chairs up to a round table. She took one of them. He took the other. "Feel like talking?" he asked.

"I assume you don't mean about the weather."

"Not much we can do about the weather, though the first cold front of the season is headed our way. Should feel like winter by the weekend."

"That covers the weather. If you have questions about the attack, I'm fresh out of answers."

"I have confidence that you'll get on top of the situation once you're back on the job." He leaned back in his chair and crossed his arms over his broad chest. "I ran a computer search on Sylvie Hamm while you were sleeping."

Clearly Cannon's focus was still on the reason he'd come to Houston in the first place. He was here to find out if he had a daughter. Naturally he'd be curious about Kimmie's mother.

Once he got the results of the paternity test, his work would be done in Houston. There would be no reason for him not to bail on Brit and her problems. She needed to keep that straight in her own mind.

"I'm not sure what you learned about Sylvie on the internet, but I told you most of what I know about her last night."

"Then I must have missed a few of the finer points. How is it you didn't realize you had a twin sister before now? Wouldn't your birth certificate indicate that?"

"I was adopted as an infant so I have an adoption decree not a birth certificate."

"You're a cop. Can't you get a copy of the original?"

"Possibly. I'll try in time, but up until now that hadn't been pertinent to the murder investigation. Finding and arresting her killer was far more pressing than figuring out our birth history."

"Does that mean you haven't identified your and Sylvie's biological mother?"

"I know who our mother was, but she died a few years ago from cancer. I haven't identified our biological father as yet, but Sylvie's stepfather is working in Guam and so far I haven't been able to reach him."

"Was Sylvie also put up for adoption at birth?"

"Her birth certificate didn't indicate that. I did find a copy of her birth certificate in a file with other important papers inside her home."

"Then you should have the name of your birth father."

"None was listed. I assume our birth mother wasn't married. That may explain why we were separated at birth. She might have felt she could only afford to raise one child, or health issues may have made her only feel capable of raising one child. She chose Sylvie."

"Are there other family members?"

"Sylvie has one younger half brother, which makes him my half brother, too, though neither of us knew the other existed."

"Have you been in touch with him?"

"By phone. Briefly."

"Where is he now?"

"I'm not sure. He's a Navy Seal, currently on a secret mission. He said he hasn't even talked to Sylvie in over a year. They kind of lost touch after their mother died. He said his mother had never mentioned Sylvie being a twin and had never mentioned giving up any child for adoption."

"Interesting."

"Yes, though that means he's been zero help in the investigation. But he did have a lot of questions about Kimmie. I think it's likely he'll get in touch with you when he finishes his mission."

"*If* it turns out that Kimmie is my daughter."

"Right." Even without the test results, Brit was almost certain that she was.

"I read online the little the *Houston Chronicle* had to say about Sylvie's murder," Cannon said.

"It covered the basics, which was all we had at the time, not that we have much more now," Brit admitted.

"It gave the address where she was dragged into an alley and stabbed to death. Not too far from your office in police headquarters. Did she live or work in that area?"

"Oddly no. She lived in Katy and worked at home as a medical transcriptionist."

"What was she doing in the city that morning?"

"All I know is that she took a bus into town and got off a few blocks from where she was stabbed to death. We have security photos from nearby buildings that show her getting off the bus and crossing the street. We lost her after that."

"So there was a chance she was coming to see you that morning."

It hadn't taken him long to figure that out.

"That is one of the possibilities we were looking into. I'm not at liberty to tell you more," she said. Not that she knew much more. The clues had dried up like a raisin in the sun—until the posters in Brit's bedroom had linked Sylvie's death with Brit.

She really needed to talk to Rick. He should have something to go on by now. So why hadn't he called? Surely he didn't really believe she intended to follow the captain's orders to stay completely out of this.

"Excuse me," she said, "but I have to make a phone call that can't wait."

She picked up her phone and took it to the bathroom. Better not to drag Cannon into this for his own safety. She had to reestablish the boundaries. No matter how easy he was to talk to, they were not a team.

Rick's number was on speed dial. In seconds, his mobile number was ringing.

"I figured you'd be calling soon," he said as a greeting. "Knew it was only a matter of time before you balked at your forced vacation."

"Glad we have that clear. Why didn't you tell me about the blown-up photos of Sylvie's murdered body when we talked this morning?"

"Because I knew you'd jump out of bed and leave the hospital, which I've heard that you did, anyway."

"Now that I know revenge against me and Sylvie's murder are linked, I have a lot better chance of figuring out who killed Sylvie."

"Really? Let's hear what you've come up with."

"Nothing yet," she admitted reluctantly.

"And I don't see how you will until you learn a lot more about Sylvie than you currently know."

"So what do you suggest?"

"Going with what we know. Figure out who has a serious grudge against you and the opportunity to come after you."

"What have you got?"

"Unfortunately, not a lot," Rick said. "I've spent most of the day checking out every criminal who falls within those parameters."

"Any luck?"

"You've helped send a lot of guys to jail since making homicide detective. You have enemies out the kazoo."

"Name me a good cop who doesn't."

"Good point."

"Who tops the list?" Brit asked.

"There are three suspects sharing top spot. Two male. One female."

"Let's hear them."

"Gary Palmer. You remember him, killed his wife and her lover three years ago."

"One of my first cases after making homicide detective. How could I forget?"

Gary Palmer was running for city councilman at the time, though most thought he had little chance of winning. He'd always sworn his innocence, falsely claimed that Brit had tampered with the evidence. The jury had decided with the prosecution. The evidence against him had been too compelling.

"I remember the trial and the sentence," Brit answered. "He got life without parole."

"And last year he got a new sly, sleazy lawyer who's persuaded a judge he should be retried due to our handling of the evidence."

"That case was handled by the book. I made sure of it."

"Nonetheless, he's out on bail while his attorney prepares for a new trial."

"If he's getting new trial, it seems stupid for him to risk another murder charge. Not that I don't want him checked out, but who else do you have?"

"Hagan Daugherty, better known as the butcher."

"Who could forget good old Hagan?"

Carved up his girlfriend's furniture and her face before plunging the butcher knife into her heart. He'd become romantically fixated on Brit during the investigation and sent her creepy love letters from prison. No one had ever freaked her out more.

"He was placed in an out-of-state psychiatric facility for treatment," she said. "Surely he wasn't released early."

"Afraid so, considered mentally capable of returning to the public two months ago."

He was a definite possibility. She wouldn't put anything past him. "Where is Hagan now?"

"No one seems to know. I've got a team tracking him down. I'll let you know as soon as we get anything on him."

"Which leaves suspect three," Brit said.

"Melanie Crouch."

"The Melanie Crouch who paid someone to kill her rich plastic surgeon husband?"

"That's the one."

Melanie was a piece of work. Attractive. Could pull tears from thin air. Had the jury and the judge in the palm of her hands.

"Melanie did her time and was released last month, a little early, for good behavior," Rick said.

"Yeah. She was a sweetheart. Let's see, how many threatening letters did she manage to get mailed to me from her prison cell?"

"I'd say at least a half dozen that first year. They slowed down after that, but that doesn't mean she didn't keep harboring her grudge."

"Where is she now?"

"According to probation records her official residence is an old farmhouse that once belonged to her grandparents and hasn't been lived in for years. Apparently she inherited it."

"Where is this house?"

"It's near the small town of Oak Grove. Which, if I remember correctly, is also where you dropped off your niece, Kimmie, last week."

"It is, but I can't see Melanie living in an old rundown house."

"My guess is she won't be there long," Rick said. "Or else she can't afford to live anywhere else. Having your husband killed disqualifies a wife from collecting on his insurance and estate."

"I'd be willing to bet she has some cash stashed away," Brit said. "She went to too much trouble to plan the *almost* perfect murder to risk losing everything."

"Yes, but she'd planned to have all his money and would have if you hadn't seen through her grieving-widow act. But, then, it wasn't a woman who attacked you last night."

"No, but she has a record of paying someone else to do her dirty work."

"The assassin she hired to take out her late husband is still in prison. Not that she couldn't hire someone new."

"I'd like to question her as a person of interest. It would also give me a chance to check on Kimmie."

"Fine by me," Rick quipped. "All you have to do is clear it with Bradford and the sheriff of the county where she's residing now."

Bradford wouldn't be easy, but surely the captain would come around after she realized Brit was fine. Besides, they were always shorthanded in Homicide. This would keep Rick or one of the other detectives from having to make the drive up to Oak Grove.

"I've got a call in to the sheriff now," Rick said. "Waiting on him to call me back, but there shouldn't be a problem there. His name is Walter Garcia. He's been sheriff there for quite a while."

Brit's mind jumped ahead. She was on vacation. No reason she had to clear this with Bradford before she made the trip to Oak Grove. It would save time when she got the okay.

Brit's father had always said a good cop did what it took to get the job done.

Brit was a very good cop.

Chapter Nine

Cannon had been suckered. No doubt about it. Following along with Brit's bizarre plans like some tail-wagging puppy. As a result he was driving north on I-45, a few miles over the speed limit, heading to the one spot in Texas he dreaded visiting.

He hadn't bought for a second the idea that she'd decided to follow her boss's order and take a short vacation, out of town, away from the investigation and danger. The shift in plans had come too swiftly and suspiciously immediately after her phone conversation with her partner.

She had something up her sleeve, possibly dangerous and definitely connected to the investigation. But then, he had time to kill while he waited on the test results. Might as well play bodyguard-accomplice to the gorgeous detective instead of just sitting around an expensive hotel in the heart of Houston.

He'd never been one for big-city life. Too much traffic, too many people, no wide-open spaces. But still, he could have done without the Dry Gulch Ranch.

A few days bonding with her niece while she took care of whatever it was that she was planning to do in the Dallas area was all well and good for Brit.

Bonding with a helpless infant who already held

some kind of mesmerizing power over him was the last thing Cannon needed. There would be plenty of time for that if he found out she actually was his daughter. Until then, he could do without poopy diapers and bottle feedings and tiny fingers that curled around his.

And he damn sure didn't need R. J. Dalton. Those days were long gone.

Yet here he was, heading to the Dry Gulch Ranch. Sucker.

Cannon stopped for gas at the Conroe exit. He poked his head back into the car after the tank was filled. "You need anything? Coffee? A soft drink."

"A bottle of water would be nice."

"You got it."

He got his own strong black coffee from the self-serve bar in the convenience store and picked up a bottle of water for her.

When he returned to the car, she was studying a map of Texas she'd pulled from the door pocket of his truck.

"I know the way to the Dry Gulch," he said.

"I was just checking the distance." She folded the map and put it away.

Cannon turned the key in the ignition and drove away from the pumps and toward the interstate entrance ramp.

"Don't you think we should call your father and make sure he's okay with our staying there a few days?

The word *father* kicked up a surge of ire. "Let's get a couple of things straight before we go any farther, Brit. Number one, R.J.'s never been father to me and I have no intention of participating in a happy family charade now. Second, I don't intend to stay at the ranch long. As soon as I get the results of the paternity test, no matter how it comes out, I'm gone."

"What about Kimmie?"

Good question. He hadn't fully faced that yet. But he'd figure it out without the help of R. J. Dalton.

"If I'm her father, I'll find a way to take care of her," he stated, trying to sound a lot more confident than he felt. The truth was, he had no idea what he'd do with Kimmie.

"You have a great support system in R.J. and the rest of your family," Brit said. "If you moved onto the Dry Gulch, I'm sure they'd be a big help in taking care of Kimmie."

"Right. You had me investigated, which means you have to know my lifestyle isn't baby-friendly. I'm surprised you decided to contact me at all since you seem to think rodeo cowboys are an irresponsible lot."

"Sylvie left specific instructions that if something happened to her, you should be given custody of Kimmie. I couldn't very well ignore her wishes. And, by law, you are the next of kin."

"So why drop her off at the Dry Gulch instead of with me?"

"Leave her at a rodeo with wild bulls snorting all around her?"

"Have you ever even been to a rodeo?"

"No. Let's keep it that way."

Not if he could help it. Detective Brit Garner needed a new taste of Texas.

"I don't know what your past is with R.J.," Brit said. "But it would be nice for Kimmie to have a grandfather and uncles, aunts and cousins in her life."

"Apparently your research didn't give you the full story," he said. "Kimmie isn't going to grow up with a grandfather no matter where I live. R.J. has an inoperable brain tumor. His days are numbered, though the tumor hasn't progressed as rapidly as he'd indicated when he invited all his sons and one daughter to the reading of his will."

"He's already had the reading of the will?"

"He's an unconventional man, when it suits his purpose."

"Which was?"

"To prove what a good father he'd have been if he'd been sober or healthy or had given a damn about anyone but himself. Pardon my French."

"I work in the police department, Cannon. I'm used to far worse language than that. So what did the will say that you find so offensive?"

Cannon hadn't planned to get into this with Brit. He couldn't see why she'd even care. But if she was going to spend her days at the ranch for whatever purpose, she'd probably hear some version of the will's stipulations, anyway.

"In order to share in the estate, each sibling is required to spend one full year living on the ranch and assisting in its operations."

"What if R.J. hadn't lived for a year?"

"The will won't be fully executed until the second anniversary of his death. As long as you take up residence before his death, you can make the cut to start your year."

"I can see why some of the people affected might find that kind of manipulation of their careers and lifestyles problematic. But you're a rodeo cowboy. Living at the ranch between rodeos should fit you perfectly."

"Having any part of my life dictated by R. J. Dalton is problematic to me. Besides, I have plans to buy my own ranch and run it my way. Having six people running a ranch will be chaos."

"Maybe," Brit said. "Maybe not. It would all depend on the people."

"I have no intention of finding out."

"What's the payoff if you meet the will's requirements?"

"The estate is said to be worth around eight million dollars. That includes land, house, outbuildings and cash and investments."

"I didn't realize there was that much money to be made in ranching," Brit said.

"There seldom is unless your cows are scratching their backs on oil wells. R.J's aren't, though his neighbors the Lamberts are one of the richest families in Texas."

"If the Dry Gulch is worth eight million, it must be reasonably successful."

"Didn't look that way to me when I was there for the reading of the will. The house was run-down. I didn't see a lot of livestock when I took the tour of the ranch that R.J. provided. Have to admit R.J. did have an impressive group of horses, though."

"He must have gotten the money somewhere. Why did your parents split?"

That, Cannon was not discussing with the gorgeous detective. "Mother had her reasons for leaving. Now I'd best make that call to R.J. so the old coot doesn't meet us at the door with a shotgun. Unless you've changed your mind about staying at the ranch."

"Then what? We'd sleep in the truck."

"I have before. I don't recommend it. There's a small motel in Oak Grove. We could stay there and it would still be convenient for visiting with Kimmie—if that's your only business in Oak Grove."

"No, thanks. I'm intrigued more than ever at the prospect of getting to know Kimmie's grandfather."

That figured. He used the hands-free function in his new truck to make the call. The phone rang so many times he was about to hang up when he heard R.J.'s throaty hello.

"This is Cannon."

"Yep. Recognized your voice. You got those test results back already?"

"Not yet."

"I'll be jiggered. What's taking 'em so long? You'd think they were having to make the DNA, not just figure it out."

"I hope to hear tomorrow, or the next day for sure."

"I'd hope so. Guess you're calling to check on Kimmie. She just left to go home with Leif and Joni for the night. No shortage of babysitters around here. They've all taken to her like a hog to persimmons."

"Glad to hear she's being well cared for." As for the Dalton clan taking to her, Cannon wasn't sure that was for the best. He didn't need them putting pressure on him to bring her to the Dry Gulch for visits.

"I know it's late to be calling you about this," Cannon said, "but I was hoping you were in the mood for company."

"You're not company. You're family. Always got a bed for you."

"I'm not coming by myself."

"No problem there, either. You wouldn't by any chance be bringing Kimmie's mama home with you, now would you?"

"No. Do you remember the police detective who dropped Kimmie off at the ranch?"

"That's the woman I'm talking about."

"Turns out she's not Kimmie's mom. She's actually her aunt."

"Hell's bells. Go figure that. Where's the mama?"

"She was murdered last week."

A period of silence followed. Cannon waited for R.J. to get his mind around that bombshell.

"I'm real sorry to hear that," R.J. said. "They arrest somebody for the crime?"

The conversation was drifting in the wrong direction. "Not yet. We can discuss that later. The reason I'm calling is that Detective Garner has a few days off work and she would like to spend it on the ranch, getting to know Kimmie a little better, if that's okay with you."

"Really? The detective wants to come here? She couldn't get away fast enough when she dropped Kimmie off."

"You'll have to ask her about that."

"Kind of surprising that a Houston homicide detective would be vacationing when her sister's killer hasn't been arrested."

The old man might have a brain tumor but he was astute enough to read between the lines. "Brit will explain about that later," Cannon said. R.J. would probably buy the story that she was just following orders after suffering a concussion.

Cannon wasn't. There was more to the sudden decision to drive to Dry Gulch tonight than just bonding with Kimmie, especially after the past twenty-four hours she'd had.

"Are you coming with the detective?" R.J. asked.

"I'm driving her to the ranch. I'll only be staying until I get the test results."

"So you two are driving up here in the morning?"

"Actually we're on our way there now. Should make

it to Oak Grove about ten and to the Dry Gulch shortly after that."

Brit grabbed his arm. "Eleven," she whispered. "Tell him we'll be there around eleven."

The plot thickened. No surprise. Detective Brit definitely had an ulterior motive. "Make that eleven," Cannon said.

"Okeydokey. I'll probably be in bed by then, but there's leftovers and half a pecan pie in the fridge, made with pecans from right here on the Dry Gulch. Help yourself to that or anything else you see that you want."

"We've eaten."

"A cowboy's stomach can always make room for pie. There's a guest room down the hall and several more upstairs."

"Where will we find a key?"

"No one bothers with keys out here. I'll leave the door unlocked. Usually do, anyway. Armadillos and coyotes can't work the doorknobs yet and don't no troublesome strangers wander this far off the road. At least not since we took care of the troublemaking hombre who made Faith and Cornell's life a living hell."

"Who's Faith and Cornell?"

"Faith's your half brother Travis's wife. Cornell is her son. Talk about a young man taking to the cowboy life. Hard to get him off a horse. Bet he's ridden almost every inch of the Dry Gulch."

Cannon finished the conversation quickly, not about to feign interest in a bunch of people he wouldn't be around long enough to get to know.

Brit was so quiet for the next few minutes he thought she might have dozed off. He upped his speed. She opened her eyes, looked at him and frowned.

"I can arrest you for going more than the speed limit, you know."

"If you were a stickler for the rules, you wouldn't be heading to Oak Grove."

"I'm just taking a vacation as my supervisor ordered."

"Is that so? Then I guess we're going to be making out between the hours of ten and eleven."

"Dream on, cowboy."

"So what are we going to be doing with our time or is that so confidential that if you tell me you have to kill me?"

"Not quite, but the less you know about this investigation, the better off you'll be. So I've been thinking, and I have a proposition for you."

"Unless it's in the same ballpark as making out, the answer is probably no."

"Hear me out. I'm feeling much better now and the vertigo seems to have run its course. So I could just drop you off at the ranch and then borrow your truck for a bit."

"Sorry, my truck doesn't go anywhere without me."

"Then don't say I didn't warn you."

"WHAT IN THE Sam Hill is going on now?" R.J. muttered under his breath as he rambled to the front of the house. He'd figured the detective was mad as a wet hen at Cannon when she'd dropped Kimmie off at the ranch. Now here she was driving to the ranch with him to visit her niece.

Sure hadn't taken Cannon long to cool her down. Must have inherited some of R.J.'s charm where women were concerned. Hopefully he was better at holding on to them than R.J. had been.

R.J. pushed open the screen door and stepped onto the wide porch. The night was filled with the songs of tree frogs and crickets and the call of a hoot owl on a low branch of a lonesome pine. The heaven was a show-case of twinkling stars. A cool breeze tossed around his thinning, gray hair.

Winter was tiptoeing in on them, but there hadn't been a frost yet and it would be Christmas in another couple of weeks. R.J. had never expected to live to see another Christmas, but God was smiling down on him sure as shooting. Not that he deserved it.

He'd pretty much wasted what might have been a blessed life. Didn't even remember half of it. Lost real-ity to booze. Lost his money to gambling. Chased too many women that weren't worth catching while losing the women who were.

He'd been to the post and tied the knot four times and never made one of his wives happy enough that they'd stuck it out to the finish line. Not that he blamed them. He had more demons on his back than most dogs had fleas.

Best he could say for himself was that he'd never killed a man, though he'd met a few that he wanted to. Never got a woman pregnant he didn't marry, ex-cept for Kiki. She stayed around long enough to give birth to their daughter, Jade, and then she'd taken off for Hollywood.

Never heard from her again. Hadn't heard from Jade, either, until the reading of the will, and she hadn't both-ered to call or stop by since. He hadn't really expected to hear from her, but, then, he'd all but given up on hear-ing from Cannon again, too.

Never knew when the odds would change. Something about Cannon made R.J. think they'd really hit it off if they could move past the old resentments.

R.J. would be sittin' in high cotton if Cannon did settle down on the Dry Gulch, at least when he wasn't riding the circuit. Might even marry Brit Garner. He could do a damn sight worse. She was pretty as a pasture full of wildflowers. And Kimmie could grow up right here on the Dry Gulch Ranch.

Two detectives in the Dalton family.

His old drinking and gambling buddies would get a horse laugh out of that.

Not that there was any guarantee Cannon would hang around long. Still, sure be good if he did.

R.J. owed it all to his beautiful neighbor Caroline Lambert. She was the one who'd encouraged him to get in touch with his kids before he was six feet under. She thought every cloud had a silver lining. He'd thought her naive. Now damned if she wasn't right.

Here he was dying and yet he couldn't remember a happier time.

He wondered what Caroline would have to say about Cannon and the detective driving up to the Dry Gulch Ranch together. Too late to call her now, but he'd ask her next time she stopped by to check on him. The Bent Pine Ranch wasn't but a few miles away. That was nothing in the country.

R.J. looked up at the sound of rustling grass. A raccoon crawled from beneath the new azalea bushes Hadley had planted to pretty up the front yard. The creature paid no attention to him as it scurried off to hunt for dinner.

R.J. turned and went back into the house. He was tired to the bone, but he doubted sleep would come until Cannon arrived.

Still seemed odd that the detective was taking a vacation while her sister's killer was on the loose. Unless…

Unless she wasn't actually coming for a visit but to pick up Kimmie and take her back to Houston. Cannon might have told a white lie about not having the results to the paternity test. The baby R.J. and the rest of the family were growing so attached to might not be his granddaughter at all.

His heart felt plumb heavy at the thought. Not that he deserved another precious granddaughter after the way he'd neglected his own kids.

He'd been a fool. No one knew that better than him. Too bad it had taken a brain tumor to get his head on straight.

It was a few minutes after ten when Cannon turned onto a narrow back road about five miles from the last sign of civilization.

Brit had spent the past ten minutes finally trying to explain why they were looking for an isolated farmhouse that might or might not be inhabited by ex-con Melanie Crouch.

"So let me have this straight," Cannon said. "You are out of your jurisdiction, working a case you have been ordered to stay out of, spying on a suspect you have no real evidence to back up your suspicion that she's involved."

"You make that sound like a bad thing."

"Where would I get an idea like that?"

"I can't stay totally out of the case, and not just because I was the one attacked. No homicide detective deserving of the badge would just walk away from an officer's responsibility. And I'm talking about my own sister's murder and an attack on my life.

"Besides, Melanie is a person of interest. She has to be checked out. The department is short staffed due to the money crunch. I'm in the area. It makes sense that I question Melanie, with the local sheriff's knowledge, of course."

"The sheriff you haven't contacted."

"Rick is taking care of that."

"So your partner is in on this?"

"He knows me well enough to know I can't loll around drinking margaritas and watching *Law & Order*."

"No, but if you get fired, you'll have a lot of time for sipping drinks and watching TV. Can this get you fired?"

"I won't get fired if it goes well."

The chance that it might not go well was what worried Cannon. But he understood her position. He'd do the same in her place. Only, in spite of her claims, she wasn't fully recovered. She needed a few days' rest that he was certain she wasn't going to get.

Still, her business. She was cop. She could take care of herself. She didn't need his protection. That was her job.

So why did he feel so responsible for her now? The woman was seriously getting under his skin, that's why. If he wasn't careful he was going to fall harder for her than he'd ever been thrown in the arena.

"So tell me about Melanie Crouch. What makes her a person of interest?"

"Hers was one of the murder cases I worked after my promotion to Homicide."

"When was that?"

"Three years ago, a few months after my father was murdered. He had been one of the top homicide detectives in the state before becoming the much respected chief of police. There was an outcry from the mayor on down that his killer be caught and prosecuted immediately."

"They must have thought you were the best person to solve the case."

"Either that or it was to honor my father. At any rate, I was the youngest female in Houston to ever make homicide detective."

"And your father's killer?"

"Is yet to be arrested. But I will catch him one day. I will never give up until I do."

The angst-ridden determination in her voice said it all. She couldn't come to grips with having never solved her father's murder. If she didn't bring her sister's murderer to justice, it was going to haunt her forever.

Her heart and soul rested on the outcome of this case.

She was one hell of a woman.

"I'm assuming that Melanie Crouch has reason to have a grudge against you."

"Not a legitimate reason. I was only doing my job. She didn't see it that way."

"So exactly what makes Melanie a person of interest?"

"She was arrested for conspiring to kill her extremely wealthy husband. She hired an assassin to break into their house when she was out of town and kill him in his sleep."

"So she had the perfect alibi."

"In New York with two of her girlfriends."

"And you made the arrest?"

"Yes, but not for several months. I'm sure she thought she was home free by then."

"What led you to her?"

"I can spot fake grief a mile away. It just took time to get enough evidence on her to make the arrest."

"So why is she out of prison so soon after having him killed?"

"She convinced the jury that he'd put her though months of verbal and emotional abuse. She was good at it, too. One day she had half the jury in tears, describing how he told her how stupid she was and blamed her for losing the baby she'd wanted so badly."

"Whatever happened to divorce?"

"Prenups. If she filed for divorce, she got none of his wealth. If he died, she got everything. Unless, of course, she was convicted of killing him. But the jury and the judge sympathized with her and she got a very light sentence which resulted in an early parole."

"When was she paroled?"

"Three weeks ago."

"And she has a history of hiring someone to do her dirty work so you wouldn't have expected her to try to kill you herself."

"Exactly."

"So how does your sister fit into this?"

"That I can't explain, but we have to start somewhere."

"At ten o'clock at night?"

"We're only scouting tonight. We'll save the real action until tomorrow."

Brit directed the beam from a pocket flashlight onto a pencil-drawn map she held in her left hand. "We should pass the shell of a mostly rotted out church in a couple of miles. The spire is still standing. Take the first left turn after that and we should see the old Crouch farmhouse about thirty yards off the road."

"Where did you get this information?"

"From Melanie's parole officer while you were finishing off your steak. Slow down to a crawl when we pass the church. I want to see if the Crouch place looks lived-in. If it's clearly deserted, we might take a look around."

"Why do I feel like we're on a witch hunt?"

"There are no witches in Texas. Maybe a few vampires but definitely no witches."

"Ha-ha."

They reached the standing spire in under five minutes. The moon was bright enough that Cannon had no trouble seeing it or the tombstones stretched out behind it. They hadn't passed a house in several miles. Apparently Melanie's only neighbors were the bodies in the graveyard that stretched behind the church.

"Did you see that?" Brit asked.

"See what?"

"Someone in a long white dress was walking among the graves."

"A vampire?"

"I'm not kidding, Cannon."

"It was probably the moonlight and shadows playing on the old tombstones."

"It was a person. Turn around in Melanie's driveway and go back."

He pulled into the driveway and stopped. "Even if you did see someone—even if it was Melanie—you can't arrest her for being in a graveyard that's right behind her house."

"I'm not going to arrest her. I just want to know what she's doing out there. For all we know, she's burying evidence like the knife that was used on me last night."

"Used on you by a man."

"So? You said yourself he could have had an accomplice. Melanie could have picked him up and driven him out here. He could be inside her house right now."

"Or dead and she's digging his grave," Cannon said, finally getting into the spirit of the hypotheses Brit was coming up with.

A minute later, Cannon had turned around, backtracked and parked his truck in what was once a gravel driveway to the ramshackle old church.

He reached for the pistol he kept beneath his seat. He didn't expect to need it, but he'd take it just in case Brit's illusion turned out to be a flesh-and-blood harbinger of death.

One thing was for certain. If Melanie Crouch was roaming around a graveyard at night burying evidence of bodies, she would not be glad to see them.

Chapter Ten

The truck's headlights cast an eerie glow over the assorted collection of cracked and faded headstones that stretched behind the decrepit church. Brit didn't believe in ghosts, yet the scene made her skin crawl and gooseflesh popped up on her arms.

What she had seen was no illusion though it had looked ethereal. From a distance, the woman had seemed to be floating through the grass, the moonlight painting her wild, flyaway hair in silvery highlights.

At first sight, Brit had feared that her head trauma was dragging her brain back into the murky fog.

But she was thinking clearly now. Logic followed that the woman roaming the ancient cemetery practically in her backyard was Melanie up to no good. Why else would she be out there at this time of night?

The timing for their arrival couldn't have been better. Brit didn't need a warrant, didn't even need to be on active duty to stop and check out something as suspicious as a woman alone in a deserted cemetery this time of night. If for no other reason, she needed to make sure the stranger wasn't in danger.

Captain Bradford wouldn't buy the story, but she wasn't here.

"Stay in the truck and wait for me," Brit ordered.

"What?" Cannon quipped. "And miss all the fun? Besides, someone has to have your back."

"Then let's go. But I do all the talking if we confront Melanie. And don't pull that gun of yours. That's a direct police order, Cannon Dalton."

"I won't pull it unless the apparition in white pulls a weapon first. That's the best I can promise."

"The woman I saw was no apparition. For the record, I'm as clearheaded as you at the moment."

"That's not saying much. I'm starting to think that driving you away from the hospital this morning is a sign I'm downright crazy."

"Then stay in the truck."

"We've settled that already. Let's go."

She wasn't convinced he believed her, but he didn't hesitate to jump out of his truck and rush around to open her door. Almost as if they were going on a moonlit stroll instead of traipsing through a neglected necropolis looking for a convicted felon who was capable of most anything—like paying someone to kill Brit and Sylvie.

Brit ground her teeth and started walking, more determined than ever to get to the bottom of this. But as the crypts and gravestones grew closer, her nerves grew more ragged, her hands more clammy.

She took out her penlight and shone it on the first tombstone they came to.

James Canton Black, 1894–1935. The only love of Conscience Everett Black. His love was great. His death years too soon. Sin claimed him and took him from me.

"No wonder this place is crumbling and uncared-for," Cannon said. "The bodies planted here have long since returned to dust."

"'Sin claimed him,'" Brit murmured. "I wonder what that means."

"Who knows? There were a lot of superstitions about death in the old days. There still are, I suppose."

Brit kept her eyes peeled for any glimpse of white as they walked among the graves. She didn't see Melanie, but that didn't mean she wasn't nearby, kneeling behind one of the crumbling stone markers, watching and waiting for them to leave so that she could sneak back to her house unnoticed.

They kept walking, listening and searching for any sight or sound that would lead them to Melanie. The wind picked up, blowing wisps of hair into Brit's eyes almost as fast as she could push them away. The temperature seemed to be dropping by the second.

The grass grew higher and thicker as they approached the back of the cemetery, the tombstones almost swallowed up by the overgrowth.

Brit's uneasiness intensified. She felt as if they were treading water, barely staying afloat in the sea of graves. The chill reached deep inside her now.

The scrape of branches at the top of a towering pine raised the hair on the back of her neck. A rustle in the grass stole her breath. A swish of wings above her forced her to swallow an unbidden scream.

She was determined not to let Cannon see how the setting affected her. She could deal with murders and killers on a daily basis without a twinge of dread, but a dark cemetery on the edge of civilization sent icy shivers up her spine.

Brit's foot caught in a vine as she sidestepped a pile of rocks that had probably once marked a grave. Cannon grabbed her arm and pulled her against him to steady her.

An unfamiliar sensation thrummed though her blood. She fought off a crazy desire to cling to him, but instead she pulled away so fast she almost lost her balance again.

"Are you all right?" Cannon asked.

"Just frustrated," she whispered, not willing to admit that his touch had stirred such cravings inside her.

"You don't have to whisper," Cannon said. "You're not going to disturb the inhabitants."

"I might frighten off Melanie."

"If she's nearby, she's hiding, which means she already knows we're here."

"Then let's just keep looking."

His fingers tangled with hers. "Your hand is as cold as ice. You're not letting this place get to you, are you?"

"Of course not," she lied.

"Maybe we should go. My guess is that if it was Melanie you saw, she escaped into the woods that border the cemetery when we drove up. She's likely at home and snuggled into bed by now."

"You're probably right, but I'm not quite ready to give up, not with so many hiding places in every direction. Besides, I keep thinking I'll discover something here to tie her to my attack."

"You mean something like this?"

Brit turned to see what he'd referred to in such an optimistic tone. Even without out her penlight, she could see well enough to realize that they were standing next to a freshly dug grave. Two gold mums rested on top of the mound of earth.

Brit picked up the flowers. "This explains why Melanie was here. She must have left these on the freshly dug grave, a grave she either dug or had dug within the past few hours."

"A very small grave," Cannon noted. "It would be

impossible to fit an adult in that hole unless he was butchered into small pieces first."

The blossoms slipped through Brit's fingers and fell to the ground at the sickening image. A wave of vertigo hit again, leaving her dizzy and feeling faint. The last thing she needed now was to pass out.

But she couldn't leave yet. "We have to dig up that grave and see if it holds evidence, like the knife my attacker had planned to kill me with last night."

"Don't you think we should turn that job over to the local sheriff?"

"If we do, chances are that Melanie will move it the second we drive away."

"Then we should call the sheriff now," Cannon said. "Depending on how deep that grave is, it could take hours to unearth whatever's buried there without any proper tools. I think you need to get to bed."

He wrapped an arm around her waist protectively. This time she didn't pull away. For the first time in recent memory she felt as much woman as cop. Hopefully it was just the concussion causing that and not her growing infatuation with Cannon.

She stepped away from the suspicious-looking grave. Something slipped beneath her foot. She stopped to see what she'd stepped on. "It's a shoe," she said, stooping to pull a woman's white leather flip-flop from the grass.

She held it up for scrutiny in the beam of her penlight. "It looks almost new. Melanie must have slipped out of it in her hurry to get away from us."

"That looks like its mate," Cannon said, pointing to a bare, rocky spot a few feet ahead of them. He hurried over to pick it up.

"She's a braver woman I am, if she took off through that wooded area beyond us barefoot and in the dark."

Anxiety hit again as Brit heard a soft footfall behind her followed by the sharp click of a gun being cocked to fire. Before Brit could reach for her weapon, the barrel of what felt like a pistol was pressed into the back of her head.

"Hands in the air, palms open or I shoot. Ladies first."

CANNON DID AS ordered and then spun around. The woman giving the orders and holding the pistol to Brit's head was indeed dressed in a gauzy white nightgown that reached her ankles. Her face was vampire pale. Her hair was long and blond, mussed by the wind.

But it was her eyes that let him know she was capable of pulling the trigger. They had a savage look about them, as if she were ready to punch and devour her prey. This was apparently not the way she had looked at the jury.

"Turn around slowly, Detective," she ordered. "Any quick move by you or your friend will get you killed."

Brit turned around. "You're making a mistake, Melanie. The only thing killing me will do is send you right back to prison."

"Wrong. It would also give me immense satisfaction."

"All I did was my job," Brit said. "You hired a man to kill your husband. If I hadn't arrested you, another police officer would have."

"No other officer was going to arrest me. You were the only one who just wouldn't let it go. You were never married. You have no idea what it's like to be married to a two-timing, arrogant bastard like Richard Carl Crouch."

"You're right. I've never been married at all. And

everyone agrees that he was as arrogant as you claimed. But that's in the past now. You've done your time. You're free to go on with your life now unless you do something as stupid as pulling that trigger."

"What are you doing out here?" Melanie asked, her voice low, her tone spiteful. "You have no right to spy on me."

"We're looking for a friend's ranch," Cannon said, answering for her with the first explanation that came to mind.

"In a cemetery?"

"We saw you roaming the graveyard," Brit said. "We didn't know it was you. We were afraid someone was in trouble."

"You lie. You knew exactly where you were. You came out looking to cause trouble for me. It's not going to work. I've done nothing wrong, but I swear I'll kill you before I let you send me back to that prison."

"Why bother? Just leave it to the man you hired to kill me, or is he dead? Did you pay him all of that money for nothing?"

"I didn't pay anyone a dime to get you. You're not worth it."

"If you don't want to go back to prison, put the gun down, Melanie. It's the only way. Kill me and you'll never see freedom again."

"I won't go back to that prison. I won't." Melanie's voice was rising. She might lose control at any moment and pull that trigger. Cannon lowered his right hand, watching for any chance to catch Melanie off guard long enough for him to go for his own pistol.

"You won't have to go back," Cannon said. "You've paid your time. You have your life back. Don't screw it up. Just hand me the gun and the detective and I will walk away."

"You would, but not the detective. She's already itching to arrest me. Why else would she be out here in the dark of night, roaming around looking for any trace of evidence she can use against me?"

"That's not true," Brit said. "What kind of evidence would I find in a deserted graveyard?"

"I can understand your fears," Cannon said. "I'd probably feel the same in your shoes, but pull that trigger and you lose. This time there will be no early parole. You'll spend the rest of your life in prison. Revenge can't be worth that to you."

"I may go to prison but Detective Garner will go straight to hell."

A pinecone dropped from the branches of the towering pine just behind Melanie, startling her. She spun around. In that split second, Cannon pulled his gun and stepped in front of Brit.

"Drop your gun, Melanie."

She stared at him, her eyes leveled at him like a laser.

Brit stepped from behind him, weapon in hand now and pointed at Melanie. "No way can you kill us both before we kill you. Is a split second of revenge worth your life?"

A motor sounded in the background and suddenly the area was bathed in flashing blue lights. From the periphery of his vision Cannon saw that a police car had pulled onto the property and was bouncing across the rocky ground toward them.

Melanie hurled the gun into the maze of tombstones and took off like a bolt of lightning, her bare feet flying across the rocks and grass and heading for the wooded area between her house and the graveyard.

The gun hit a stone marker and ricocheted back toward them, fortunately not going off.

Instinctively, Cannon raced after Melanie. He caught up with her just as she reached the edge of the clearing. He grabbed her arm and pulled her to a halt. Seconds later, Brit and two armed officers of the law were at his side.

"Get your hands off me," Melanie said, throwing in a few four-letter expletives to make her point.

"Watch your mouth," the older lawman ordered. "One more tirade out of you and I'll throw you into jail for disturbing the peace if nothing else. And you can unhand her," he said to Cannon. "If she tries to run again, I'll handle the situation."

Cannon let go of her arm. She backed away from him but didn't run.

"Now would someone tell me what the devil is going on here?"

Brit flashed her ID. "I'm Detective Brittany Garner with the Houston Police Department."

"Who are you?" he asked, pointing a finger a Cannon.

"Cannon Dalton."

"Cannon Dalton." He scratched his whiskered chin. "Name sounds right familiar. You look a little familiar, too. I'm guessing you're the bull-riding son of R. J. Dalton."

"I am." There was obviously no way of keeping that a secret in this part of Texas.

"The woman he was chasing is Melanie Crouch, recently released from prison."

"I know Melanie," he assured Brit. "I'm Walter Garcia, sheriff of this county. My deputy here is Bobby Blaxton."

"I don't know what brought you out here tonight, but your timing couldn't have been better," Brit said.

"I had business in the area, and you're a long way from home, Detective. Mind telling me why you're chasing one of my citizens through a graveyard this time of night?"

Brit explained the situation as succinctly as possible, stressing that they had no intention of doing anything other than to check out the Crouch place before talking to the sheriff the following morning.

"Detective Garner pinned one crime on me. Now she's looking to do the same thing again," Melanie argued, her voice calm and measured.

"If all you were doing was checking out the house, exactly why were you here in the cemetery?" the sheriff asked Brit.

"We glimpsed a woman running through the deserted cemetery," Brit said. "I had no way of knowing if it was Melanie, but I felt it important to ascertain that no one was in danger."

"Is that a fact? Looked like you were chasing her when I showed up."

"Only after she sneaked out from behind one of the tombstones and pulled a gun on us," Cannon explained. He reached down and picked up the gun with two fingers, careful not to smudge the fingerprints.

"I'll take that," the sheriff said.

Cannon handed it off gingerly.

"A gun, huh?" the sheriff said. "Sounds like you got some explaining to do, too, Miss Melanie. How come you have a weapon on you when the specifications of your parole specifically prohibit it?"

"It's for my own protection. A single woman living alone this far out in the country has to have protection."

The sheriff hiked up his trousers and then nudged his Stetson a little lower on his forehead. "If you're so worried about your safety, what are you doing out in this abandoned cemetery this time of night?"

"I buried a kitten out here earlier today. I was visiting the grave. Brought her some flowers I picked up in Oak Grove today."

"You haven't been out of prison but a few weeks. You telling me you got yourself a cat that already up and died on you?"

"I didn't get a cat. Some jerk threw a sack full of kittens out of a truck and left them in the woods to die. I took them in. One didn't make it."

"Can't see any way we're going to get to the bottom of this tonight," the sheriff drawled. "Besides, it'll be pushing midnight by the time I get home and to bed as it is. Cannon, are you and the detective here staying at the Dry Gulch?"

"For now," he admitted.

"Then I'll be out to the ranch in the morning to have a chat with you both. I been wanting to get there to check on R.J., anyway. Might as well kill two birds with one stone."

"In the meantime, what's to keep Melanie from going on the run as soon as we leave?" Brit asked.

"A jail cell. I'm hauling her in for breaking parole by having possession of a firearm."

Melanie uttered a few more curses. "You don't have any proof that's my gun."

"My suspicions and the detective's word is all I need for you to enjoy a stay in the clinker for the next twenty-four hours."

"I can live with that," Brit said.

Garcia fitted the handcuffs around Melanie's wrists.

"You and Dalton go home and get some sleep. I'll be there before noon tomorrow."

Cannon was pleased to take the sheriff's advice. Rest was exactly what Brit needed. He was beginning to fade, himself, now that Melanie was in cuffs.

Within minutes they were on their way to the Dry Gulch Ranch and R.J. The dread swelled again. He was certain the reunion was a mistake. By the time he drove up to the rambling old house, he was sure of it.

Chapter Eleven

Brit rolled down her window as they approached the house. The temperature had dropped a few degrees and a chill crept deep inside her as she studied her new surroundings.

Clouds had rolled in over the past half hour, obscuring the stars and the moon, outlining the house in shades of grisly gray. Intimidating shadows from towering trees stalked the gables and chimneys. The porch swing swayed and creaked in the wind as if occupied by a hostile aberration that resented their intrusion.

Perhaps arriving at this time of night had not been the best of ideas, especially with Cannon already dreading spending the night under his father's roof.

She rolled up her window and opened her door as Cannon shifted into Park and killed the engine. Fatigue washed over her again as her feet hit the driveway. A good night's sleep without incident and they might both feel differently. Her sizzling attraction to Cannon might cool. He might decide he'd had enough of playing nurse and driver to her.

With their two duffel bags swinging from his shoulder, Cannon extended a supportive hand to the curve of her back as she climbed the steps to the wide front porch. He was clearly good at playing the protective role. He might find a way to get away from her quickly when she returned to the tough, in-your-face, risk-taking cop she was normally.

But for now his effect on her was showing no signs of weakening. Spending the night under the same roof might make the unwelcome desires more potent.

Cannon turned the doorknob. The door squeaked open. The dim light of a lamp welcomed them inside. One look around and Brit's foreboding concerning the house vanished.

Hot coals glistened in the giant stone fireplace. Crocheted throws rested on the leather couch and comfortable chairs. A bouquet of fall flowers in a white pottery vase adorned a pine side table, its fragrance blending with the smell of spices.

A pair of wire reading glasses rested on the pages of an opened magazine. A nearby shelf was filled with books of all sizes, except for the top shelf which held framed snapshots. Many were in black and white, the subjects dressed in attire from throughout the former century.

A stunning watercolor of a majestic cinnamon-colored steed ridden by a man in a black cowboy hat, a Western shirt and a pair of shiny black cowboy boots hung above the fireplace.

"It's exactly as I've always imagined these old ranch houses to look," she whispered.

"Old and outdated?" Cannon questioned, not bothering to hide the fact that he didn't like being here.

That was especially strange since she felt as if she were coming home even though she'd never lived outside the city of Houston. "The house has a strong sense of continuity between the past and the present," she said.

Cannon shrugged his shoulders. "Not my past."

"I wouldn't bet on that." She walked over and picked up one of the framed black-and-white photos of an older man. "You have a definite resemblance to this man. He could be your grandfather or at least an ancestor."

"Still would be a stranger to me. Let's check out the guest room—unless you're hungry. R.J. said to help ourselves to leftovers, including pecan pie made with Dry Gulch pecans."

"Hard to turn down temptation like that."

"I would have thought you capable of resisting any kind of temptation, Detective."

A blush burned her cheeks. His teasing too closely edged the truth. But she wouldn't be intimidated by his flirtatious comment. "I can," she agreed, "but I don't always want to."

"Nice to know."

She returned the picture to the shelf and started down the hallway, stopping at the first open door. Again, she was enchanted by the inviting aura of the room. The furnishings were softened by the glow of lamplight. A colorful quilt was pulled down on the king-size bed, revealing a nest of tempting white sheets just waiting to be crawled between.

"It has an adjoining bath," Cannon said, pointing to a door that had been left ajar. "R.J. assured me he'd leave fresh towels out for you."

"I hate that I've put him out."

"If you did, you'd have never guessed by his reaction. He sounded like he was excited to have company."

"I'm sure that you're the one he's excited to see."

"No doubt. One more offspring on which to assuage his guilt."

They left the bedroom and followed the dimly lit hallway to the back of the house. The kitchen was on the left. Cannon reached inside the door, flipped the switch and flooded the space with light.

The focal point was a large marred and well-worn oak table. Brit could easily imagine the large Dalton family gathered around the table, eating, laughing and talking.

Exactly the kind of place she'd imagined her friends had experienced when they'd gone to their grandparents for Thanksgiving and Christmas. Her family had been only her mother and father up until her mother had died when Brit was twelve.

After that it had been just her and her dad. He'd always made a special attempt to spend holidays with her, but that didn't always work out. When it didn't, she'd be invited to the McIntosh's. Aidan McIntosh had been her dad's partner and best friend. Louise McIntosh had been like a second mother to her until the terrible night of Aidan's arrest.

This was not the time to revisit that night in her mind.

Cannon opened the refrigerator and started lifting plastic tops to peek inside the containers. "Looks like some kind of potato casserole, cold fried chicken, field peas and a few slices of hothouse tomatoes. If that doesn't do it for you, there're eggs and I'd wager I can find some bacon or sausage to go with them."

She reached past him and retrieved the pie. "I have mine," she teased. "It's every man for himself."

"And after I've faced the fierce arm of the law for you."

"I suppose I could share a bite or two."

"How about a glass of milk to wash it down?"

"Now you're talking, cowboy."

In minutes, they were at the table, relishing the best

pecan pie she'd ever tasted. Even Cannon seemed to be relaxing in the cozy warmth of the kitchen.

"How did you ever get into something as suicidal as bull riding?" she asked.

"Nothing suicidal about it. I work damn hard to stay alive."

"Exactly. So why not become a doctor or attorney or even a regular rancher like R.J.?"

"The thought never entered my mind. I moved to my uncle's ranch out in West Texas when I was thirteen. Rodeo was the most exciting thing going around there, and we had no shortage of bulls."

"Wasn't your mother terrified you'd get hurt?"

"She was killed in a boating accident. That's why I ended up on my uncle's ranch."

So they had both lost their mother at an early age. That might be the only thing they had in common.

Brit let the subject drop and turned the talk to the totally impersonal subject of the latest political scandal. The minutes flew by as they talked, joked and enjoyed the pie.

"You'd best get some sleep," Cannon said once they'd finished their midnight snack and rinsed their dishes. "Tomorrow promises to be another action-packed day, starting with your meeting with Sheriff Garcia."

"I am beat," she said truthfully. "But still feeling one hundred percent better than I did this morning."

"Not because you followed the doctor's orders."

"How can you say that? I slept all afternoon and during the drive here from Houston. Except for my brief foray into the land of the dead and deranged I was a perfect patient."

"I wouldn't say perfect. And you definitely ignored your boss's demands."

"You would have to bring that up. I'll deal with her when the time comes—if it comes. She won't argue with success." And after experiencing Melanie's emotional state firsthand, Brit was convinced she was their most credible suspect to date, though she still couldn't figure out how Melanie would have known that Sylvie was Brit's sister.

They left the kitchen and went back down the hallway, stopping at the open door that led to the guest room.

Brit looked up at Cannon. "Where will you sleep?"

He met her gaze. His eyes were questioning, as if he were pondering whether that might be an invitation to share her bed. The tension sparked to the point of explosion.

Brit trembled as the possibility of falling asleep in his strong arms filled her senses. She took a deep breath and tamped down the unbidden desire.

"I'm told there are several guest rooms upstairs to choose from," Cannon said. "But I'll be close by. If you need anything, anything at all, just call and I can be here in seconds."

"I'll be fine," she said. "The room is so cozy and I'm so tired, I may fall asleep with my clothes on."

He lingered, then took a step closer, leaning in so that his lips were mere inches from hers. Her heart skipped crazily. Her head felt light. Her stomach fluttered.

She knew she should back away, but her body ignored her brain. She lifted her mouth to his and then dissolved into a deliciously sweet eruption of passion as his lips found hers.

His lips were soft at first, then more demanding. The thrill of their mingling breaths rocked though her like fire. The inhibitions that had become part of her being melted away and she kissed him back, letting the thrill of him wash though her.

The unexpected hunger for him was primal, untamed. Her arms slid around his neck, pulling him closer as her body arched toward his.

When he had the good sense to pull away, her body went weak.

"Don't think the doctor would approve of this." His voice was a husky whisper.

"Probably not," she agreed, though it wasn't her physical health she was worried about but her inability to control her emotions where Cannon was concerned. It wasn't the time or the place. Likely not even the right man, no matter how right it felt right now.

"Good night, Detective."

"Good night, cowboy."

She stood in the door for what seemed an eternity, drowning in the ecstasy.

One thing about Cannon Dalton. When he kissed, a woman knew she'd been kissed.

CANNON SLEPT RESTLESSLY, waking when the thunderstorm went through and several times since, agonizing over the situation he'd fallen into.

Kimmie.

The murder of Kimmie's mother.

The attempt on Brit's life.

The kiss that never should have happened. The kiss that had sent him on a fast track to heaven. The kiss he ached to repeat.

He finally gave up on sleep when the first light of dawn crept through his open second-floor window. He slipped from beneath the covers, surprised to find an icy chill to the air.

He padded to the window in his bare feet, naked, the way he always woke. He hadn't owned a pair of pajamas since he'd left his uncle's ranch at eighteen. He'd always showered before hitting the sack and liked letting everything hang free while he slept.

He stared into the purplish haze of dawn and spotted the first frost of the season, a thin layer of ice that clung to the blades of grass like sugar frosting.

The house was quiet, but the odor of fresh-brewing coffee tantalized his senses. Might as well go down and get his encounter with R.J. over with. Hopefully, he could avoid a barrage of questions about how he planned to take care of Kimmie if the test turned out positive.

And he definitely didn't want to discuss his reasons for not buying into the controlling stipulations of R.J.'s will and becoming one of the Dry Gulch Ranch entourage of followers. But he wouldn't lie to R.J. or pretend to have any interest in moving out here to watch him die.

Cannon slipped into his jeans, shirt, socks and boots and made his way to the kitchen. The light on the automatic coffeepot was green, but there was no sign of life.

Cannon checked the pot. It was programmed to start perking at six o'clock. It was six-ten now, so R.J. would probably come to the kitchen for his morning jolt of caffeine soon.

Cannon took a mug from the cabinet and filled it with the pungent brew. Still restless, he took his coffee outside. The household might be sleeping but the rest of creation was waking up.

Horses neighed. Birds sang and darted among the branches of oaks, sycamores and pines. A bullfrog croaked. A wasp buzzed by his head. Wide-open spaces stretched out over the pasture and to the wooded area beyond.

A man could get used to this life right quick, he thought as he started down a well-worn trail that led away from the back of the house. Waking up at the Dry Gulch intensified his anticipation for the day he had enough money to buy his own ranch and start raising rodeo stock.

And not just any rodeo stock. He aimed to provide the best animals in the business. His bulls and broncs would be the ones the cowboys prayed they'd get to ride, the ones who could guarantee a rider top points if he could stay on his full eight seconds.

Cannon had his future planned to the nth degree.

At least he had until this week. So much for a man's plans when life decided to kick him around. First Kimmie. Now this crazy reaction to Brit. The detective was doing a hell of a job on him. If he wasn't careful, he'd start believing the two of them could make a go of it even though they weren't even heading in the same direction.

He shouldn't have kissed her. She shouldn't have let him. But she hadn't just let him, she'd kissed him back. Now she was taking over his mind. If this was love, fate was playing a rotten trick on him.

Brit was so dedicated to her job that, according to Captain Bradford, she never even took a vacation. That meant living in Houston. He was a bull rider who was always on the road. And when he did settle down, he planned to do it on a ranch.

Their lifestyle differences weren't the worst of it. He might be the father of her twin sister's baby. A baby conceived during a one-night stand with a woman he barely remembered and had never had any real feelings for.

Brit's bitterness over that had been obvious in their first meeting. So had her contempt for his career choice. That bitterness might be shoved to the back burner now but it would resurface when the urgency of the moment faded.

It was preposterous to even dream they could make it as a couple.

But damn, that kiss had carried a wallop. He could still feel it right down to his toes. How in the hell could he ever trust himself around her now?

He turned and walked back toward the old ranch house and the mouthwatering odor of frying bacon. When he reached the back porch, he heard a babble of voices he didn't recognize. Talking. Laughing.

All suddenly interrupted by the wail of a baby. A baby who might be his own flesh and blood. If she was, life was about to come falling down on top of him like trees in a West Texas tornado. If the lab didn't call with results soon, he was going to pop like a cheap balloon.

He said a few curses under his breath, opened the door and stepped inside to face the posse of Daltons who'd obviously arrived while he was taking his walk.

BRIT WOKE TO the clattering vibration of her phone on the bedside table. She reached for it, then hesitated, her mind so lost in the dregs of a deep sleep she didn't know where she was.

Rectangles of sunlight sneaked around and through the slits of opaque blinds. A strange bed. A strange room. Frosty air flowing through an open window.

The Dry Gulch Ranch.

With Cannon Dalton.

How could that have slipped her mind even for a second? Her lips tingled at the memory of his kiss. The momentary confusion lifted as the thrill of it rushed through her veins.

She slid her finger across the phone to take the call. "Hello."

"Did I wake you?"

"Yeah, but that's okay. What time is it?"

"Almost eight. Are you okay?"

"Of course. I'm fine."

"You don't sound too great and you're usually in the office and on your second espresso by now."

"I was kept up half the night by a thunderstorm that has apparently moved on. And I was ordered to stay out of the office, remember?"

"You were also ordered off the case, but you're not complying with that."

"Not until the lunatic who killed Sylvie and tried to kill me is behind bars. Did you locate Hagan?"

"No. Best source of information indicates he's in Mexico."

"What about Palmer?"

"He's agreed to come in and answer a few questions this morning at nine—with his new sleazy lawyer, of course. After that, I've decided I should head north to a chat with Melanie Crouch."

"That would be a waste of time since I'm already here."

"Don't tell me you drove up there last night in the condition you were in?"

"No. Cannon drove me."

"Cannon Dalton?"

"He's the only Cannon I know."

"Correction, partner. You don't actually know him.

You just met him. All you know about him is that he knocked up your sister who was later murdered."

"He had nothing to do with her murder."

"You can't be sure of that."

"Of course I can. I have a sixth sense about guilt. You know that. Anyway, Bradford said I should get out of town and take a few days off. I decided to spend that time with Kimmie."

"So you and Cannon are at his father's ranch. Easy to see how he moved in on your sister so fast. The guy doesn't waste any time."

"He is just being helpful." Easier for Brit to see how her sister fell for him so fast. A good reminder for her to slow down in the romance department. Now to convince her libido of that.

"It's fine by me if you talk to Melanie," Rick said. "But there will be hell to pay if you blatantly ignore Bradford's order. It could even cost you your job."

"I'll talk to her. When she realizes I'm fine, she'll come around. Is she in the office now?"

"Yep."

"What kind of mood is she in?"

"The chief of police was in her office a few minutes ago and they both were frowning."

"Then I'll call and preface my offer to question Melanie Crouch with a reminder of how short staffed and overworked Homicide is."

"What about the headaches from the concussion?"

"Totally gone."

"And the disorientation?"

"Also gone." Thankfully, that was true, at least for now.

"Good. What I called to tell you should make you feel even better."

"Hit me."

"We have an ID on your attacker."

She sat up in bed, her interest intensifying. "Who?"

"A guy named Clive Austin."

"Doesn't sound familiar."

"He goes by Stats. Have no idea why."

"Still doesn't mean anything. Did I arrest him?"

"No, nor did your father. But Stats does have a rap sheet that would stretch around Reliant Center. Mostly in Austin and Dallas."

"What kind of crimes?"

"Started off with shoplifting when he was a preteen. Graduated early to hot checks, burglary and then moved on to armed robbery."

"But he isn't in jail?"

"Not at the present time. His last arrest was in Tyler, Texas, for some elaborate scam to bilk money out of aging widows. He got out of prison on a technicality nine months ago. Word has it he moved back to Dallas and has the mob on his tail for a huge unpaid tab with his bookie."

"No record of murder for hire?"

"No, but there's always a first time for career criminals like him, especially if he needed money."

"Which he obviously does."

"You got it. Now we just need to find out who hired him."

"All the more reason I should be the one to talk to Melanie while you check out other suspects. I can be in her face before you get out of Dallas morning traffic."

"Bradford will insist you keep this by the book and go through the local sheriff."

"I already have. More reason for me to handle this."

She explained the graveyard encounter and how it

had ended with the sheriff's snapping a bracelet on Melanie and carting her off to jail.

"So now Cannon's not only your chauffeur and nurse, but also he's involved in the investigation?"

Rick's tone left no question as to how he felt about that development.

"It wasn't planned, Rick. We were only going to drive by Melanie's house when we spotted her in the cemetery."

"Bradford will be royally pissed if she hears about this."

"There's no reason for her to hear it, at least not yet. With luck, not ever. Now if we've covered everything, I need to get some coffee and call Bradford."

"Call me back as soon as you talk to her so I can plan my day."

"Right."

Once the connection was broken, Brit threw her legs over the side of the bed. The quick movement delivered a sharp pain through her right shoulder and down her arm.

The soreness from the attack seemed more painful today than yesterday or else she was just paying more attention to it now that the headache was gone.

The only consolation was that if she felt this sore, Clive Austin must be in worse shape. He'd lost a lot of blood and apparently hadn't shown up at a hospital. If he had, Rick would have mentioned it.

Paid to kill her. But by whom? Melanie? More important, how did either of them know she and Sylvie were sisters? Would the killing stop now that she'd wounded her attacker or would that only further enrage the person who'd hired Clive?

Brit heard footsteps and voices coming from down

the hall. Probably R.J. and Cannon getting reacquainted but possibly the sheriff who might have decided to pop in earlier than he'd indicated.

Luckily she'd showered last night, so all she had to do was slip into some clothes, brush her hair and join them.

If it wasn't the sheriff, she'd say good morning, get her coffee and then come back to her room and give the captain a call. Better to deal with her after caffeine.

After that, she'd seek out Kimmie. She must be somewhere on the ranch and Brit couldn't wait to see her adorable niece.

But it was Cannon and last night's burning kiss that haunted her mind as she dressed in a pair of black pants and a pale blue sweater.

Boundaries, she reminded herself as she brushed a stain of blush to her cheeks and smoothed her lips with pink gloss. Not only to preserve her professionalism but also to protect her heart.

Determined to keep that in mind, she followed the voices to the kitchen. Her breath caught in her throat when her gaze rested on Cannon.

He was dressed in jeans, a Western shirt and his boots. A heart-stopping hunk of masculinity holding a smiling, gurgling Kimmie in his arms.

Brit's willpower to keep her infatuation in check melted faster than a chip of ice in a sauna.

Shaken by the intensity of her reaction to seeing him with Kimmie, she stepped away from the door before anyone noticed her. Perhaps it was best to call Bradford first. That should cool off the heat Cannon had generated.

She tiptoed back to her room and made the call.

Unfortunately, Sheriff Garcia had called Bradford first. The captain was ready to have her head, and Cannon was the source of her rage.

Chapter Twelve

"Don't be nervous," Faith encouraged. "You'll get the hang of this in no time."

The assurance did nothing to ease Cannon's fears. He was afraid he was holding Kimmie too tight. Or not tight enough. Or not supporting her head in just the right way. Or that she was going to start wailing.

As if on cue, Kimmie started to fret.

"Either I'm doing something wrong or she doesn't like me."

"Try holding her on your shoulder and patting her gently on the back. She may need to burp."

"Burping. Now that's an art I can probably teach her. How do I get her to my shoulder?"

Faith smiled as she helped him readjust his positioning of the wiggly infant.

To Cannon's amazement, Kimmie burped, a good loud one. "Now we're getting somewhere. But you know, we're jumping the gun here with all this parenting practice. I still don't have the lab results."

"I don't need DNA to know this is your daughter, Cannon. She has your eyes and coloring. And she has the Dalton mouth—a crooked twist to her lips when she smiles."

"C'mon. All babies look like this."

"Absolutely not. Look at any of your pictures when you and your half brothers were babies. Hard to tell one of you from the other."

Cannon wasn't interested in Dalton family photos and he didn't see the likeness to him. But he had to admit, Kimmie was growing on him. She'd obviously already captured Faith's heart.

Faith was Travis's wife, one of the many members of the Dalton clan who'd stopped by for a cup of coffee and to say hello this morning after Leif and Joni had arrived with Kimmie and before rushing off to their own lives.

Apparently news had spread quickly that Cannon and Brit were spending the night at the ranch, though he'd gotten the feeling that stopping by the big house for coffee and/or breakfast was routine for most of them.

Faith was the only visitor still here, apparently Kimmie's caretaker for the morning. Perhaps R.J.'s, too. They all seemed to keep close tabs on the father who had never been around for any of them.

At least that was the distinct impression Cannon had gotten at the reading of the will where R.J. had surprised them with the manipulative stipulations and the fact that he wasn't dead. Not a one of his half siblings had been singing the old man's praises that day.

Adam hadn't even stayed around for beer, barbecue and a tour of the ranch. Yet he was the first one to move onto the ranch with his wife and two twin daughters. He was managing all of the daily operations of the ranch now.

Kimmie's good mood was short-lived. She puckered her lips and started to whimper. "I think she knows she's in shaky hands," Cannon said.

"She'll get used to you," R.J. said. "You might as well get used to her, too. If that test comes back positive, as

Faith and Kimmie's detective aunt Brit seem convinced that it will, you'll be her only parent."

As if Cannon needed that reminder, especially by R.J., a man who hadn't cared about fatherly responsibilities until he found out he was dying.

Cannon picked up one of Kimmie's toys and rattled it for her. She quit fussing and her eyes opened wide. Finally, something she liked. She waved her tiny fists, cooing as if she were trying to tell him something.

He wasn't ready to try his hand at baby talk, certainly not in front of Faith and R.J., but he couldn't deny a tug at his heart. Kind of like when he'd first moved to his uncle's ranch and watched a new spindly-legged colt come into the world. Only this time the pleasure was mixed with anxiety.

Kimmie was going to need a real father, one who could change her diapers and bathe and dress her. One who knew what to do when she cried. One who knew about formula and baby food and immunizations.

Cannon wasn't that man.

He shifted and spied Brit standing in the doorway. It hit him again how stunning she was without even trying. No heavy makeup. No fancy clothes. Just a natural beauty.

The thrill of last night's kiss shot through his senses. He did his best to tamp down his arousal before it became embarrassing.

Their gazes met. It wasn't desire he saw there, but the cop toughness she'd greeted him with two nights ago when he'd shown up at her precinct. He wondered if there had been some new development in the case overnight, but he couldn't broach the subject in front of Faith and Dalton.

"Good morning," Brit said as she joined them in the

kitchen and walked over to plant a kiss among the wispy curls on the top of Kimmie's head. "And good morning to you, little angel."

Cannon handed the baby to her without hesitation. To his surprise, Brit was almost as awkward with Kimmie as he was. Nonetheless, she cuddled the infant in the curve of her arm and Kimmie seemed content—at least for the time being.

"I didn't mean to sleep so late," Brit apologized.

"Don't you worry about that," R.J. said. "The storm probably kept you up half the night. It did me, not that I don't always wake up a half-dozen times every night."

"I usually have that same problem, but I slept soundly once the storm passed." She walked over and offered her free hand to R.J. "I'm Detective Brit Garner. We met briefly when I dropped Kimmie off the other day."

"Yep. Glad you're sticking around a little longer this time."

"I apologize for my abruptness, but at the time I was afraid you'd refuse to accept responsibility for Kimmie, and I was neck-deep in a very important murder case."

"Kimmie's mother?"

"Yes, I suppose Cannon explained that situation to you."

"Not in any detail. He mentioned it last night when you were driving up. That's all."

"There's not much more to tell just yet," Brit said. "The investigation is ongoing."

The woman who'd been giving Cannon tips on handling Kimmie stepped closer to Brit. "I'm Faith, Travis Dalton's wife."

"Nice to meet you," Brit said. "Thanks so much for helping care for Kimmie."

"I should be thanking you. It's so much fun to have a baby in the house. But Hadley has done more care-taking than I have. The rest of us have to threaten rebellion to get Kimmie away from her."

"I'm sure Kimmie is thriving on all the attention."

"I'm sorry about your sister," Faith said. "So sad for Kimmie to lose her mother before she ever got to know her. I'm sure it must be difficult for you to deal with the grief and the investigation at the same time."

"I think it would be more difficult if I didn't have the investigation to focus on."

"You did the right thing bringing Kimmie here," R.J. said. "Having my youngest granddaughter around is better than any medicine my doctor prescribes."

"I'm glad to hear that, and I really appreciate you letting me visit her."

"Stay as long as you like. Always room for one or a dozen more at the Dry Gulch. Long as I got a biscuit, you got half."

"Now that's hospitality."

Faith walked over and set a mug of hot coffee on the table near Brit.

"Thanks. You must have been reading my mind."

"No, but I know how worthless I am until I have that first cup of coffee in the morning. How about some breakfast? We had blueberry pancakes and sausage if you'd like that."

"Please don't go to that much trouble."

"It's no trouble at all. I can warm the leftover sausage patties and the pancake batter is already mixed. All I have to do is spoon some on the griddle."

"If you turn down the blueberry pancakes, you'll be missing a real treat," Cannon warned. "In fact, I'll do the cooking while you reconnect with Kimmie."

"Now that's an offer I can't refuse."

Watching her with Kimmie, Cannon wondered why Brit hadn't married and had children of her own. It definitely couldn't be that she hadn't had plenty of men to choose from.

Might just be that she'd chosen a career over family. From the little he'd seen her job didn't seem to leave a lot of time for marriage or babies. Or even for recuperating from an attack.

Or had she simply not met Mr. Right yet?

Scared of where his own thoughts were heading, Cannon forced himself to concentrate on cooking pancakes. He stirred the batter while the griddle was heating. At least Brit had agreed to eat. That must mean the nausea hadn't come back.

Just thinking about the attack sent the anxiety bucking around inside him again. Her life was still in danger.

She was the cop. She had her own gun. She was the protector and would balk at any suggestion she needed protecting. The only reason she was hanging out with him was that she'd needed a driver until she was back to one hundred percent fighting form.

From the looks of things, that was probably now.

He wasn't sure when he'd started thinking otherwise, but he was sure what he was feeling right now. No matter when the lab work came back or what the result, he wasn't going anywhere until he was sure Brit was safe.

R.J. SETTLED IN a kitchen chair. He hadn't done much talking this morning, but he'd done a whole lot of watching and listening. He hadn't quite figured out what Brit and Cannon were doing here together, but he knew there was something cooking between them.

Anyone with half a brain could see that in the way

they looked at each other. R.J. was mighty curious how that came about considering Cannon was the father of her dead sister's baby. Had sure sounded as though he wasn't in her good graces when she'd dropped Kimmie off at the ranch.

Couldn't predict love. It had a way of sneaking up on you without your seeing it coming. Had happened to Leif and Travis and it was working great for them. If Cannon and Brit pulled it off, it would sure be a blessing for little Kimmie.

God's plan, his neighbor Caroline would say.

But R.J. was betting they hadn't driven out here pushing midnight last night just to spend some time with Kimmie this morning, not with the detective still trying to find her sister's killer. R.J. had better sense than to go meddling into that, too. Besides, life had a way of sifting out the weevils if you gave it time.

He leaned back in the kitchen chair. "Never met a female homicide detective before. What made you decide to take on a grisly job like that?"

"My father was a homicide detective before he became the chief of police. He was my idol. I always wanted to grow up and be just like him."

"Must be a good man?"

"He *was.* He was murdered three years ago. I made detective a few months later. I think the promotion was as much out of respect for him as for me, but I love the job. Not the murders, but bringing the guilty to justice."

"Did you find your dad's killer?"

"Not yet, but I will."

"My money's on you," R.J. said. "You ever do any horseback riding?"

"Not lately."

"Might want to try it sometime. I always think clearest on the back of a horse, especially since that tumor started playing havoc with my thinking skills. Life just looks more manageable from the saddle."

"That's an interesting theory. I'd love to test it when I have more time."

"You're always welcome to ride one of my animals. I got some real beauties in the horse barn. You should at least take a walk out to see them while you're here."

"I'd love to do that."

"Catch me at a good time and I'll go with you."

Cannon brought over a plate of pancakes and sausages and set them in front of Brit.

Faith put the syrup and silverware on the table and refilled Brit's coffee mug. "Let me take Kimmie for you while you eat."

"I think you'd better. Wouldn't want to drip syrup on her."

Before she had the first bite down, the doorbell rang.

"I'll get that," R.J. said. "Probably just a neighbor stopping by to say howdy. You keep right on eating."

R.J. took his time shuffling down the hallway. Whoever it was he planned to get rid of them fast. He was hoping for some one-on-one time with Cannon this morning.

He opened the door, surprised to see Sheriff Garcia standing there.

"What brings you out this time of the morning? Got trouble out this way?"

"I just left Ben Campbell's spread. Connie Barrick's son got drunk again last night, ran off the road and rammed through Ben's fence. Car's still sitting there. Back wheels are buried in the muddy ditch. Found Jack Barrick sleeping it off under a tree."

"Ben have any livestock wander off?"

"Nope. Fortunately, all his cattle were grazing in other pastures."

"Well, you're here, might as well come in and have a cup of coffee," R.J. offered reluctantly.

"Coffee will have to wait. I'm here to see Detective Garner."

"What about?"

"Police business. Didn't she tell you I was coming?"

"No, but then we hadn't a chance to do much talking yet. She's just now having breakfast."

"Well, go get her. We got business to discuss—in private."

"Why don't you come on back to the kitchen with me and have a cup of coffee while she finishes her pancakes?"

"I'll have coffee after we talk."

"I'm sure whatever you have to say can wait five more minutes."

"I say we let her decide that. Just tell her that another body connected to her investigation just hit the morgue."

Chapter Thirteen

"What does he mean another body in the morgue?"

"I have no idea, Cannon. I'm just telling you what Sheriff Garcia said. He talked like it would mean something to Brit."

Cannon picked up his pace to keep up with Brit, then grabbed her arm and tugged her to a stop. He looked around quickly, making sure that neither Faith nor R.J. had followed them down the narrow hallway.

"I think you should reconsider talking to Melanie. Let someone else handle this case. Take the day off and spend it with Kimmie."

"I'm fine, Cannon. I'm a cop. I don't run from murders. I find the killers and lock them up."

"When you're healthy. You're not yet."

"I'll handle this, Cannon. I don't tell you how to ride a bull. You can't tell me how to do my job. I'll listen to what the sheriff has to say and then I'll call Rick back and see why he didn't tell me this."

"Call Rick *back?*"

"He called this morning. They have an ID on my attacker. If there had been another murder attributed to him, I'm sure he would have told me."

"Who's the assailant?"

"A man named Clive Austen."

"How is he connected to you?"

"He's not, or at least not that I know of. I've never even heard of him, but apparently he has an impressive rap sheet in the Dallas area. Anything for money except work for it."

"So if Melanie is behind this, she might have just followed her usual modus operandi even though it didn't work for her before."

"That's a definite possibility."

"Do they have an address on this Austin guy?"

"I don't know. Look, Cannon, Rick's not the only one I talked to this morning. I also called Captain Bradford."

"And she didn't mention another victim, either?"

"No, but she had plenty to say about you. I've been ordered not to discuss this case with you and definitely not to get you involved the way I did last night at the graveyard."

"How did she find out about that?"

"Sheriff Garcia called her this morning. Apparently they've worked together before and he wanted to clear up a few questions about my wanting to interrogate Melanie. Bradford was furious—even more about your being with me than the fact that I'd ignored her orders not to get involved."

Cannon shrugged. "I walked with you through a graveyard."

"And encountered a suspect in an active investigation. End result, I am not to interrogate Melanie Crouch today or any other day."

Cannon mumbled a curse under his breath, but he let go of Brit's arm. He hadn't seen that coming but probably should have. Now he'd screwed things up for her. Of course, if he'd let her go into the graveyard without backup, she might be dead. Someone should point that out to Captain Bradford.

"I'd like to be with you when you talk to the sheriff."

"Not going to happen, Cannon. Bradford will yank my rank if I go against her orders on this. Just back off."

Instead, he followed her onto the porch. The sheriff was leaning against a support post. Travis Dalton was climbing the steps. Cannon recognized him from the reading of the will.

"Good morning, Sheriff," Travis said. "What's up?"

Garcia nodded toward Brit and Cannon. "I've got business with Detective Garner. I guess you two have met."

"Not yet," Travis said. "I worked a homicide scene until sunup this morning. Just came home to clean up and get a short nap before I head back into Dallas."

Cannon, Travis and Brit took care of introductions.

"If I can be of any help, let me know," Travis offered.

"I appreciate that," the sheriff said. "I'm just cooperating with the HPD myself. Now if you two will excuse us, Brit and I need to talk."

"You can have the porch," Travis said. "Cannon and I can go inside. I need some coffee, anyway."

Cannon hated being shut out of the discussion with the sheriff, but Brit wasn't going to cut him any slack on this. At least he could run a few of his concerns by Travis.

Captain Bradford couldn't do a damn thing about that.

"DID YOU TELL R.J. that there was another death related to the crime in which Melanie Crouch is a suspect?"

"Yep."

"Who's the victim?"

"Clive Austin."

"You must be mistaken. They've ID'd Clive as the man who attacked me, but he's not dead."

"He is now."

"Where did you get your information?"

"From Carla Bradford."

If Garcia was right, it meant that both Rick and the captain had withheld that information from her. Associating with Cannon was costing her the confidence of her boss and her partner. She had to break away from him entirely.

Garcia walked from the post to one of the rockers. Brit continued to stand.

"Did Captain Bradford say where they found Clive's body?"

"No. Don't hold me to any direct quotes, but the gist of it was that the situation had changed. I asked her what happened. She said Clive Austin had been found murdered."

"That's all she said?"

"It was all she said on that subject. She seemed in a hurry to get off the phone so I didn't question her further. Carla Bradford's a professional. She'll let me know what I need to know when I need to know it."

Apparently that same professional courtesy no longer extended to Brit. She would call Rick the second Garcia left and demand some answers.

"Want to tell me why you didn't give me the straight scoop last night?" Garcia asked.

"I told you exactly what we were doing in that graveyard."

"You didn't mention that you were recovering from an attack and weren't even supposed to be working the case."

"I was feeling much better. And I don't consider checking on a woman running through a cemetery at night an investigation."

"Not exactly the way it seemed to me when I arrived."

"Melanie pulled a gun on me. I reacted the way any police officer would."

He reached down and nonchalantly knocked a black spider off the arm of the rocker. "I'd have felt the same," he admitted. "Reckon Bradford finally came to the same conclusion."

"What makes you think that?"

"That's the real reason she called back a few minutes ago. She wants you to talk to Melanie before she gets lawyered up. Not that I expect her, too. Far as I know, she's dang near broke."

"She wants me to interrogate Melanie?"

"Yep. We'll have to read Melanie her rights since this could lead to her arrest as a suspect in a murder case and not just a parole violator."

"When can I see her?"

"As soon as I get back to Oak Grove. In fact, you can ride into town with me. I'll have one of my deputies give you a lift back to the ranch when you're finished."

"I can be ready in five minutes or less."

"Hold your horses. We're not in that big a hurry. Melanie's not going anywhere. I got some business out this way I need to take care of before we go back into Oak Grove. I'll be back to pick you up in under an hour."

"Perfect." That would give her time to talk to Rick and get the full scoop on where they'd found Clive's body.

Garcia stood and hiked up his khaki trousers. "Bradford did make one stipulation, though. She doesn't want Cannon anywhere near the suspect."

"He won't be."

"Okeydokey. In the meantime, you be careful," Garcia said. "You've had two people try to kill you in two days. As we say around here, you're wallowing in danger."

"I'm a cop. It goes with the job."

BRIT PUNCHED IN Rick's speed dial number on her cell phone.

Rick answered the phone. "Damn, partner. You picked a hell of a time to go running off with a bull rider. You're missing all the excitement."

"Where are you?"

"In a crummy apartment on the southeast side of Houston working a crime scene. What else would I be doing on a beautiful, crisp, perfect-for-fishing morning?"

"Is it true that Clive Austin's body was found?"

"Yeah. I'm here with the body now. Death does not become him."

Killed by her bullet. In self-defense, but that didn't keep a sickening sensation from weighing on her heart like tons of steel. It wasn't the first time she'd shot someone, but it was the first time she'd taken another life.

She'd always known this day would come, but that made it no easier.

"You still there, Brit?" Rick asked.

"Yeah, just trying to get my mind around my first kill."

"Save the angst. Your record is still intact for now. Clive didn't die from your bullet, though he probably would have, given time, since he didn't have sense enough to go to a hospital."

She took a deep breath and exhaled slowly, renewing her equilibrium. "What killed him?"

"His throat was slit."

"Self-inflicted?"

"Seems doubtful," Rick said, "considering there's no weapon on-site. There is a bloodied car outside registered to him, so apparently he managed to drive himself here after the attack. Judging from the condition of the body, I'd place time of death about twenty-four hours ago."

"Who does the apartment belong to?"

"Clive rented it four days ago using an alias he'd used before. There was no furniture except a dirty futon. No food except an open jar of peanut butter, cracker crumbs and a half-eaten candy bar.

"There was, however, beer in a foam cooler and some weed on the floor next to the futon. The heater was humming and roaches were having a party. Clive was the only attendant not having a good time."

"Convenient robbery of an easy, half-dead victim?"

"Doesn't look that way. His wallet, holding two hundred-dollar bills, was still in his pocket."

Her mind rushed ahead as he described how the body had been found.

"If he was a paid assassin, the woman who hired him must have come back and finished him off to keep him from talking," Brit said, breaking in while he was still talking.

"She or *he*," Rick corrected. "Women are definitely not the only ones who hire killers. Either way, it would mean that Clive's killer has now moved into doing their own dirty work. More reason for you not to take the kind of risk you took last night. There are times even the best of cops need backup. Bull riders don't fill that bill."

"Yet one managed to save my life last night."

"A very lucky break. You could have both been killed."

"But the fact that Melanie pulled a gun on me gives even more credence to my hunch that she's the one behind all of this. Of course, I'll have a better handle on that once I've questioned her—if she talks to me. She knows her way around the system. I look for her to clam up until she gets a lawyer."

"In which case, you need to head back to Houston," Rick said. "I suppose rodeo boy is still at your beck and call."

The comment riled her, but it was just Rick's way. She usually gave as good as she got. This time it was different, but there was no way Rick could know they'd kissed and that it was taking all her willpower to fight the swelling attraction.

"I'll call you after I see Melanie and let you know my plans."

"You got it. Stay safe."

"Yeah, you, too. Get back to work."

He had a crime scene to cover. She had a bull rider to catch up with.

CANNON WAS STANDING with Travis, watching several magnificent horses prance around the corral just behind the horse barn. He'd filled Travis in on the barest of details surrounding the attack on Brit and their run-in with Melanie and Sheriff Garcia last night, careful not to give away any information that might be classified.

"Everybody makes enemies in our line of work,"

Travis said. "And we deal with some real loonies out there so you can't take anything lightly."

"So I'm learning."

One of the horses moved to the edge of the fence. Cannon reached out and ran his fingers through the long mane before giving the animal a good ear scratching.

The sun's warmth beat through his shirt even though the occasional gusts of wind were cold and the temperature was in the high forties.

According to R.J., the weatherman had promised another light freeze tonight. An early winter storm was moving in from the west, bringing snow and hail to parts of the south.

No more than the possibility of a few flakes was forecast for Dallas. If they got that, the ground wouldn't be cold enough for it to stick. Heavy snowstorms in Dallas were rare, but even a light snow or coating of ice caused havoc on the roads.

"I'm glad we have this chance to talk alone," Travis said. "I figure that you have your issues with R.J. We all did before we moved onto the Dry Gulch."

Cannon had been expecting but still dreading this conversation. He'd expected it to be initiated by R.J., but probably better discussing it with Travis.

"I guess issues are one way of putting it. More to the point, I have no interest in moving back to the Dry Gulch Ranch. R.J. was never a father to me. I've never been a son to him."

"Far as I know, R.J. wasn't a father to anybody," Travis said. "Not much of a husband, either. He was an alcoholic, a gambler and womanizer."

"That seems to size it up," Cannon agreed. "Great DNA we've inherited."

"Could have been a lot worse," Travis said. "R.J. had a tendency to marry well. At least he did with my mother. Adam says the same, so we have that going for us."

"So what's your point?" Cannon said. "Are you trying to say I owe R.J. something for providing my mother with sperm?"

"Hardly. Forgiving R.J. has been hard going, even worse for Leif, who hated R.J. more on my account than his. But R.J. has heart and he grows on you. And forgiveness has a way of doing as much or more for the forgiver as for the forgiven."

Travis smiled. "Learned that little gem of truth from my wife, Faith. My philosophy never gets much beyond a man's gotta do what a man's gotta do."

And what Cannon had to do didn't involve the Dry Gulch Ranch. Though he couldn't deny that when he'd gone out walking this morning, the ranch had felt more like home than anywhere he could ever remember being.

"I know you love the rodeo and it's been all you needed until now," Travis continued. "But if it turns out you're a father, your life is about to change big-time. Maybe you should at least consider making the Dry Gulch your headquarters. You could hire a nanny to help with Kimmie, but you'd have family who love her around to make sure she's always in the best of hands."

Cannon hated to admit that Travis made sense—for Kimmie's sake. But Cannon had made up his mind long ago. He'd live life on his terms.

"I'm not much of a team player," Cannon admitted. "And the will specifically stipulates I'd have to live here and work the ranch full-time for at least a year."

"True, but R.J. has already bent the hell out of that

provision. Leif's an attorney. I'm with the DPD. Crazy thing is we're both cowboys at heart, same as Adam is. You'd have to blast us out to get us to live anywhere but on the Dry Gulch Ranch now."

"Glad it works for you."

"Just saying, give it some thought," Travis said. "What have you got to lose?"

"Having a ranch of my own." And the freedom to do with it exactly as he pleased.

Cannon looked away and saw Brit heading toward them. He couldn't read her facial expression from this distance, but she was walking fast, long strides, shoulders back, head held high. He hoped that was a good sign and that the news hadn't been as bad as she'd feared.

He pushed Travis's suggestions from his mind as urgent matters took hold. The ache to take Brit in his arms and absorb some of her worry and fears hit hard as she approached. But one kiss did not a relationship make, no matter how electrifying it had been.

"How did it go?" he asked.

"I'm actually not sure yet, but you'll be glad to know that Captain Bradford changed her mind and said it was okay for me to interrogate Melanie Crouch."

"Back in the saddle again," Cannon said. "That is good news."

"Yes it is, but you're still persona non grata as far as Bradford is concerned."

"That figures. Whose body was found?"

"My attacker was found with his throat split. Apparently someone who knew where he was had come back and finished him off."

"When did they find the body?" Cannon asked.

"Within the past hour. My partner had just arrived

at the crime scene to verify the ID of the victim. The maintenance manager called 911 when he spotted what looked like blood that had spilled out from under the door. The officers who responded to his 911 call recognized Clive from the APB bulletin put out on him shortly before that."

"Would that by any chance be Clive Austin?" Travis asked.

"Yes. Have you ever heard of him?"

"More than just heard of him. I have a warrant out for his arrest. He's the primary suspect in an armed robbery of a convenience store last month that left a teenage customer badly wounded and a young clerk dead. If you've got a minute, Brit, we need to talk, detective to detective."

"Guess that's my signal to get lost," Cannon said.

"That's up to Brit," Travis said. "Your being here doesn't bother me. We're hanging out at a corral with family, not in a court of law. Besides, the way I see it, you're already involved or you wouldn't have been in that cemetery getting your life threatened last night."

"You've got a point," Brit said, "though my immediate supervisor doesn't seem to see it that way."

"Works by the book, huh?"

"Most of the time."

"Your call, then, but I doubt you're going to tell me anything that Cannon doesn't already know."

"Right again," Brit agreed.

Travis hooked his heels behind the lowest slat in the wooden fence and propped his backside on the top slat. "So fill me in on the pertinent details of your case."

Cannon propped himself on the top slat, as well. Brit stood between them, rehashing everything that had happened since the attack on her life two days ago.

"Did Clive Austin have any reason to hold a personal grudge against your sister?" Travis asked.

"Not that I know of. I'm sure that's being looked into."

"What about a grudge against your father?"

"Marcus Garner— Again, not that I know of."

"So you're the daughter of Marcus Garner," Travis said. "I've heard of him though never actually met him. He was well-respected in the business."

"And a great man."

"Seems odd that Clive referenced your being like your father if he'd never had dealings with him."

"Dad did a lot to clean up crime in the inner city. That earned him lots of enemies in the criminal population."

"According to Cannon, Melanie Crouch just got out of jail for paying someone to murder her husband," Travis said.

"Yes, Richard Crouch, a very prominent Houston surgeon before he was killed."

"I remember the case," Travis said. "Dr. Crouch was a sleaze."

"Yes, but few people knew that until the trial brought out all his dirty secrets."

"Was the doctor a friend of your father?" Cannon asked, still trying to make sense of this.

"They'd met. I don't know that they were friends."

"That connection could be worth looking into," Travis said. "Did your dad have a longtime good friend, someone he spent a lot of time with? Someone who might know things about him no one else did?"

"Aidan McIntosh. They were in college together and joined the police force about the same time. They were partners for most of the time Dad was in Homicide. He was the best man at my parents' wedding. Their son, Matt, even took me to the senior prom after I broke up with my boyfriend the day before. Of course, we had no idea then that Aidan and Louise's son was already dealing crack cocaine."

"Where is Matt McIntosh now?" Cannon asked.

"In prison for killing two completely innocent people in a drive-by execution. The worst part of all was that Aidan had tried to cover for him before that. But once his son committed murder, he realized he couldn't protect him any longer. He agreed to testify against his son and turn himself in, but only to my father. I think the worst day of Dad's life was when he had to arrest his best friend."

"Is Aidan still in prison?" Travis asked.

"No, he was released four years ago, a year before my father was murdered. He and his wife live in Plano now. He works as a night security manager for one of the shopping malls."

"Might be a good idea to pay him a visit," Travis suggested."

Brit shook her head. "Aidan had nothing to do with the attack on me. I'd stake my life on that."

"But in case Melanie isn't the culprit, Aidan might have insight into who may have paid Clive to do it, especially if the attack on you was connected to your father."

"It's not far to Plano," Cannon said. "We could drive up there this afternoon after you finish questioning Melanie."

"If you do, get back here early," Travis cautioned. "A little ice on the road in Dallas and fender benders pop up at every intersection."

"We won't be coming back to the ranch tonight," Brit

said. "If I'd been thinking clearly, I wouldn't have stayed last night. I will not bring danger onto the Dry Gulch Ranch and I'm afraid my being here is doing just that."

The decision surprised Cannon. She downplayed danger to herself so well that he'd feared she wasn't taking it seriously. He should have known better. Determined enough to do what it took solve the case. Brave enough she'd do whatever it took to bring a killer down—unless the killer got her first.

He had no intention of letting that happen.

"I guess the good news is that if Melanie is the person who paid Clive Austin to kill me and Sylvie, she was most likely taken to jail before she could find someone else to take over for him."

"But we have no proof that Melanie hired him, so your life is still very much in danger," Travis cautioned. "What I can't make sense of is how Melanie would know that Sylvie was your sister when you didn't even know it."

"Maybe she didn't know," Cannon suggested. "At least not when Sylvie was still alive. You and Sylvie looked so much alike that Clive could have killed her believing she was you."

"She was in the vicinity of my office when she was killed," Brit said. "And near the coffee shop that I frequent every morning."

"If that's the case, Melanie Crouch makes a strong suspect," Travis said.

"It gives me a new angle to look at," Brit said. "I have to go back to the house now. Sheriff Garcia should be back to pick me up any minute and I want to say goodbye to Kimmie before I go into Oak Grove with him."

"You know you don't have to stay away tonight,"

Travis said. "The Daltons stick together. And we easily have enough men and wranglers to protect you."

"I can protect myself, but I refuse to put others at risk."

"Then take this." Travis reached into his pocket and pulled out a key ring. He slipped one small silver key from the ring and handed it to Cannon. "This is to my condo in Dallas. I keep it for the nights I can't make it home at all. Gives me a place to grab a shower and a nap."

Travis took a card and pen from his pocket, scribbled down an address and handed that to Cannon, as well. "Call if you need anything, and, Brit, keep me posted. I want to hear how that chat with Melanie Crouch comes out."

They said their goodbyes. Travis lingered at the corral. Cannon took Brit's hand as they walked back to the ranch house together. His need for her was as much about making sure she stayed alive as it was about the physical side of things.

Still, how in the world would he spend the night alone with her in Travis's town house without sleeping with her?

The answer was simple. He couldn't without going nuts.

Chapter Fourteen

Fury raged inside her, all but crippling her ability to think clearly. Everything had been planned down to the most insignificant detail. There was no reason for anything to go wrong.

And yet it had.

Clive Austin was dead. Brit Garner was alive.

But not for long.

That wouldn't give her back the joy and anticipation she'd enjoyed once, but it would make life bearable. Perhaps she'd even be able to sleep again without the terrifying nightmares.

At one time all her life had stretched out in front of her like a field of wildflowers ready to burst into bloom. She had been young and pretty and excited about life.

And then life had crashed down on her, wave after wave of fear and insufferable heartache.

The only thing she had to hold on to was revenge. It burned inside her, gave her a reason to live.

That's why Brit had to die.

Clive Austin had screwed up the perfect plan, but that was only a detour. The perfect ending was coming.

The plans were in motion even now. And this time

nothing could stop them—not Cannon Dalton, not the Houston Police Department and not Detective Brit Garner.

She might spend the rest of her life in prison, but what did it matter? Her life was devastated beyond salvation. Everything that mattered to her was lost.

Someone had to pay for destruction like that.

Chapter Fifteen

Brit felt Melanie's fury the second she stepped into the small interrogation room. The anger hung thick in the air and seemed to drip from the glaring ceiling light above the table that separated them like a tangible entity.

But the woman sitting across the table from Brit was not the ghostly, barefoot nymph who'd haunted the cemetery last night. Today her hair was neatly brushed and she looked totally in control.

Garcia had decided to watch the meeting from behind the one-way glass—nearby in case Melanie became violent, yet out of sight as Brit had requested.

Brit had her own way of questioning, a blend of what she'd learned from her father and her own experience. Some detectives pushed and shoved and browbeat a suspect down until they cracked under pressure.

Brit couldn't have pulled that off if she'd wanted to. She fit more into the good-cop mold. She let her suspects talk freely, pretended to identify with their plight.

Feeling they were winning, the guilty tended to hammer their own points home, defend even the most indefensible behaviors, justify until they ended up providing the very information that would lead to conviction.

But Melanie already hated Brit so she'd be coming into this ready for a fight.

Melanie looked straight at Brit, her eyes shooting daggers. "So nice of you to come by and chat this morning, Detective."

"I am just here to talk, Melanie. I'm sorry we got off to such a bad start last night, but sarcasm isn't going to help."

"Sorry. I must have forgotten my manners. Prison does that to a lady. So let's get down to business. Exactly what crime are you trying to pin on me this time?"

"You mean other than you pulling a gun on me last night and threatening to kill me?"

"You were stalking me in the dark, behind my own house. I feared for my life."

"I wasn't stalking you. I simply checked to see if a woman roaming around a cemetery at night was in trouble."

"You were there because you know I should keep my word and come after you. You turned that jury against me with all your talk of my options. Well, let me set the record straight, Detective. When you live with a man as rich and powerful as Richard Crouch, there are no options."

"You mean no options that wouldn't leave you broke."

"You have no idea what it was like married to a man like Richard. Cross him in any way and you pay. Verbal abuse. Psychological abuse. Mental abuse. There's no end to the ways he could torment you."

All of which Melanie had detailed to the jury from the stand.

"You're right, Melanie. I can only imagine what he

put you through. Flaunting the fact that he was involved with a much younger woman. Knowing it was only a matter of time before he divorced you. A lot of women would break under that kind of pressure."

"There were always other women."

"He must have promised that would never happen again when he left his second wife for you."

"Lies. Every word out of his mouth was a lie. He twisted things around, put words in my mouth, just the way you do, Detective. He deserved to die." Her voice rose with rage, but the venom in her eyes suggested the fury was directed at Brit and not her murdered husband.

"I didn't convict you, Melanie. All I did was give the evidence to the prosecution. I had nothing to do with the trial."

"You had everything to do with it. Your testimony was the one that swayed the jury. I had them in my hands before that. They believed my desperation, understood that Richard had made me an emotional prisoner. They would have known I needed counseling, not a prison sentence."

"If you really feel that way, I can see why you wanted me dead."

"I wanted you dead all right. More than anything in the world I wanted to see you dead. I lay awake night after night thinking of how I'd kill you when I was free."

"I'm sorry you felt that way. I was only doing my job. I can't believe you wanted me dead so badly that you're willing to go back to prison."

"I don't. And that's the only reason you're still alive, Brit Garner. I would rather die than live behind bars. So stay away from me. I paid my debt to this hypocritical society and I'm moving on, leaving you and Texas and every memory of Richard far behind."

"Is that what you told Clive Austin before you killed him?"

Melanie's muscles visibly tensed, the veins in her neck and forehead cording and turning a vivid blue. "I don't know what you're talking about. I don't know a Clive Austin."

"I think you do, Melanie, and it would go much better for you if you tell the truth. Were you in Houston this week?"

Melanie jumped from her chair and repeatedly beat her fist against the table. "I know what you're doing, Detective. I want a lawyer. I'm not saying another word until I get one."

Garcia stepped back into the room. "That's enough, Melanie. You can hire a lawyer, but the only charge against you right now is for breaking your probation by carrying a firearm. If you have anything else to confess, you'd be wise to do it now and hope for leniency."

"Go to hell, both of you. And when you get there, Brit, say hello to Richard for me."

CANNON STOPPED IN front of the old cemetery where they'd encountered Melanie last night. It looked more deteriorated than spooky in the bright light of day.

Not that he'd been scared of ghosts since the Halloween he was five and one had jumped out at him from behind a tree. Even then, he'd kicked the older kid in the shins before he'd run away.

Actually, he'd never been afraid of much in his life, though he had a healthy respect for what a bull could do to a body given half a chance.

But he'd had a crash course in fear the past few days. One truth he'd learned firsthand was that it didn't always come from the outside. Some of it spewed up straight from the gut.

Like the fear of becoming a father when you had no idea how to begin and no time to prepare. The anxiety wasn't just about him but also for Kimmie.

Talk about getting a raw deal from the get-go. The infant's mother had been murdered. Her father might turn out to the worst choice of dad ever. Well, the second-worst candidate. Surely R.J. would top the list.

But the most pressing terror centered on Brit. It bucked around inside Cannon with such force that he hated having her out of his sight for a second. Even now, when he knew she was with Sheriff Garcia, he worried.

All it took was one second of opportunity to slit someone's throat, the way someone had killed Clive. The way someone had attempted to kill Brit.

The fact that she was a trained police officer and insisted she could protect herself did little to lessen his apprehension. He'd been going crazy uselessly sitting around the Dry Gulch. That's why he'd driven out to the cemetery. He figured the police had already acted on information from Brit and checked out the freshly dug mound of dirt, but he might as well make sure.

This time instead of walking around the church, he walked through it, sidestepping broken hunks of concrete and a chunk of the decaying outer walls. The roof was completely gone. The lonely spire was all that was left to beckon visitors to a deserted graveyard.

He stooped to pick up a small broken piece of pottery. He had no idea what it had been, but the remaining shape would work for scooping up loose dirt.

Not as good as a shovel, but it would do. He slipped it into his pocket and made his way to the overgrown graveyard.

It took him ten minutes to find the freshly dug plot in the maze of cracked and crumbling headstones and aged monuments. He kicked most of the dirt away with the heel of his boot then stooped over and scooped until he reached what he thought was a small box.

When his fingers felt the edges, he realized it wasn't a box but a large book. He freed it from the mound and brushed off the remaining dirt with his hand. He was holding a photograph album.

Odd that Melanie Crouch would come to a deserted graveyard at night to bury pictures—unless they were more of the sickening photos Clive Austin had taken of Sylvie after he'd stabbed and killed her.

Cannon opened the book and skimmed the pages. It was a wedding album.

He recognized the bride at once, though Melanie was years younger. By anyone's standards, she'd been beautiful. Young. Shapely.

The bridal gown looked like one of those extravagant concoctions that you saw on the covers of gossip magazines. But the necklace was the real showstopper. A man cold buy a small plane for what that must have cost.

The marriage between Melanie and Richard Crouch had had obviously started off with a bang. It had ended with his murder by the bride looking at him in the picture like he was Greek god that had sprung to life in Armani clothing.

"Police. Put your hands over your head. Try anything funny and you can have your own grave."

Cannon did as ordered. The album fell to the ground,

bounced off the pottery chunk and landed facedown. He spun around and looked into the barrel of a .45.

"Stand still and keep your hands above your head."

The man giving the order had a deputy sheriff patch sewed onto the arm of his khaki shirt. He stooped down and picked up the album.

"This is a wedding album," the deputy said, as if this were some kind of joke. "You're robbing graves for someone else's wedding pictures. What kind of freak are you?"

"I didn't rob a grave. I just unearthed the album from that mound of dirt."

"Are you the one who buried it there?"

"No. I'm Cannon Dalton. I was here with Detective Brittany Garner from the Houston Police Department last night and we spotted the fresh-dug mound."

"And you came back to dig it up?"

"Right. I thought it might contain evidence in a murder case. This is a complicated story."

"I'll bet."

"You can call Sheriff Garcia now. He'll verify what I'm saying."

"You got some ID on you?"

"If you'll let me get my wallet without shooting me."

"Let's see it." He finally retuned his automatic to his holster.

Cannon showed him his Texas driver's license. The deputy took only a second to check it out.

"You must be R.J.'s son—the bull rider."

Cannon nodded.

"I saw you ride once at the Dallas Rodeo. You won first place and you stayed on a bone-buster of a bull to do it."

"Thanks." So now they were old friends. Cannon

looked around. "How did you get out here, anyway? I don't see a vehicle."

The deputy spit a stream of brown tobacco into the grass. "My horse is tethered over at the old Stanton spread. I live down the road so decided to ride over when the sheriff asked me to keep an eye on the house today.

"I saw you poking through the church and the grave-yard and figured you were up to no good. It was quiet, but you still would have heard me if you hadn't been so engrossed in that album."

"Probably so."

"You say you were here with a Houston detective last night."

"That's right."

"That album wouldn't have anything to do with Melanie Crouch, would it? You know she was a Stanton before she married that rich Houston doctor."

"Did you know her when she was Melanie Stanton?"

"Nope. Her parents were both dead and she was long gone before I moved to Oak Grove. My wife and I bought a little land and built us a house out here after she retired from teaching school. Got tired of city life."

"Then you haven't seen Melanie since she got out of prison?"

"I've seen her coming and going. That's it. Just as well. Didn't take her long to get back into trouble."

"Did you hear that from the sheriff?"

"No, but I'm supposed to keep everyone away from the house until he can get a search warrant to go in and look for evidence. That spells trouble to me."

"Guess it does.

"If you're going to call the sheriff, I'd appreciate

your doing it now," Cannon said. "I need to get back to town. In fact, I can take the album to him."

"That's okay. You can go anytime, but I think I'd best hold on to the album and give it to Sheriff Garcia myself."

"Whatever you think best."

Cannon had done what he came for, verified that Melanie had not been out there to bury evidence last night but her wedding pictures. He understood the act considering how the marriage turned out.

But that still left them with no solid evidence against Melanie Crouch. Clive Austin might be dead, but the world was full of lowlifes who'd do anything for a buck—even murder.

Cannon's phone rang. He checked the caller ID. It was Brit.

"All finished here," Brit said. "If you still want to drive to Plano, you can pick me up at the sheriff's office in Oak Grove."

"Works for me. How did the interrogation go?"

"Well enough that I still think Melanie Crouch is a very strong suspect. I'll fill you in when I see you."

"I'm on my way." And he was not letting Brit out of his sight again until he was sure she was safe.

But she'd never really be out of danger. She was a cop. She'd walk right back into danger again. And again. And again.

"YOU'LL NEED THIS," Cannon said. He held Brit's jacket for her as she slipped into it. Then he reached to the backseat and grabbed the sandwiches they'd bought at an Oak Grove coffee shop. Brit could have skipped lunch, but Cannon had insisted on food.

They'd decided to get the sandwiches to go. The

place was entirely too crowded and noisy for private conversation. A small park two blocks from the sheriff's office seemed ideal.

They trekked up a slight incline and chose a picnic table in the shade of a giant oak. The only other people in the park were a young mother and her two children and they were yards away playing on a bright red tubular slide.

"Turkey-and-avocado wrap. This has to be yours," Cannon said as he pulled out her wrapped sandwich and handed it to her. "Real men eat real sandwiches."

Brit took one look at his oversize sub and shuddered. "You won't even be able to get your mouth around that."

"Watch me."

He took a huge bite out of the sandwich, proving her wrong. She lifted their covered cups of hot coffee from the bag and set them on the table next to them.

Cannon delved into the rest of his sandwich like a starving man. She enjoyed watching him eat. Not that there was a lot about Cannon she didn't like. A definite contrast to the way she'd felt about him before they'd met.

That had only been three days ago and yet she felt more attached to him than anyone she knew. It wasn't just the kiss or the way he made her senses strum with awareness. It was the way he'd looked holding Kimmie this morning—nervous, awkward, fatherly. The way he'd come to her rescue at the hospital with no questions asked. The way he'd gone tramping through a dark graveyard with her. The way he'd saved her life.

"I'm all but convinced Melanie is the one who paid Clive to kill me and then killed him when he failed," she said, determined to get her mind off her growing attraction for Cannon.

"So you said when I picked you up. How about some details?"

Brit went over Melanie's response to the questions and then described her reactions when the subject of Clive Austin came up.

"She claimed she'd never heard of him, but her actions and facial expressions said differently. And when I asked her about being in Houston, she demanded a lawyer. It's not the solid evidence we'll need to hold her in jail, but hopefully we'll have that soon. Sheriff Garcia has already requested a warrant to search that old house she's staying in."

"I heard."

"From whom?"

"A very interesting tobacco-chewing deputy who caught me digging up our mysterious mound in the graveyard."

"When were you there?"

"When you called me to come and pick you up."

"You are a constant surprise, Cannon Dalton. You should think about becoming a detective."

"No, I'll take mad bulls over crazy criminals any day."

She listened as he told about finding the buried wedding album.

"Not the evidence I was hoping for," Brit admitted, "but it is very interesting."

Cannon sipped his coffee. "Seems like a lot of trouble to go to when she could have just tossed it in the trash."

"But burying is more symbolic," Brit said. "It gives

closure, a way of putting that part of your life behind you forever."

"I'd say the closure part is not working if Melanie's still out to kill you."

"It does seem a bit odd when you think of it like that, but no one has ever accused Melanie of being rational."

"How much evidence do you need to keep her in jail with no chance of bail?"

"A murder weapon. An explicit connection to Clive. An eye witness. A confession. Any of those would go a long way."

"They don't make this easy, do they?"

"Innocent until proven guilty." Brit dropped the remainder of her sandwich into the empty bag along with both their napkins. "Let's not talk about Melanie or Clive or my attack for the next five minutes. I only want pleasant conversation and a walk down that bike trail that cuts through the trees while I finish my coffee."

"Okay." Cannon stood and tugged her to a standing position. "You pick the topic."

"Let's talk about you."

"Where shall we start?"

Brit dropped their trash into a nearby container as they started toward the trail. "How about when you were a kid?"

"I thought you wanted pleasant."

"Did you have a terrible childhood?"

"Not in the beginning."

"Then let's start there. How old were you when you left the Dry Gulch Ranch?"

"I'm not sure I ever made it to the Dry Gulch, at least not once I was out of my mother's womb."

"Your mother divorced R.J. that quickly."

"That's the way she tells it."

"What happened?"

"She went into labor early. R.J. was off on a drunk and no one could find him. She decided that she didn't want to be married to an alcoholic so she called an attorney from the hospital and started divorce proceedings. At least, that's the way she told it. And if you'd ever met my mother, you'd know she was impulsive enough to do just that."

"That must have been terrible for her. A single parent with a new baby."

"Looking back, I'm sure she didn't let it get her down. My mother was the most upbeat, outgoing, optimistic woman I've ever met. Our house was always full of friends. Men and women. Mom loved music and dancing and had boundless energy. The other kids always liked to hang out at my house to just to be around her."

"Who wouldn't?"

"Did I mention that she was also good-looking— kind of a young Meg Ryan only her hair was red instead of blond. I didn't realize how cute she was at the time, of course. She was just Mom then. Luckily I have pictures of the two of us together going back to the time I was a baby."

"What great memories."

"It was all good—until it ended."

"What happened?"

"She went water-skiing one weekend with a group of friends. Someone in a speedboat slammed into them when she was getting back in the boat. She was crushed in the mangled wreckage. She died in the ambulance on the way to the E.R."

"Oh, Cannon. How sad. You must have missed her terribly."

"I did. I didn't seem to fit in the world without her. I

went home from the funeral with my mother's brother. I don't think he ever liked me. I know I never liked him, but you do what you're told when you're thirteen."

"Someone should have called R.J. and let him know," Brit said.

"My uncle called him and asked him for money for my support. R.J. told him he didn't consider me a son, said he doubted I was even his."

"Surely not."

"I told you this was ugly. Heard enough?"

"Enough that I understand why you have no use for R.J. But something must have changed his mind about you. He seems glad to see you now and he included you in his will."

"Too little. Too late. I'm not interested in his money or his ranch. I had enough of being bossed around by my uncle. I'll have enough money in a few years to buy my own ranch and run it exactly as I please. At least that's the way I had it planned before…"

He didn't finish the sentence, but she knew what he was thinking. Finding out he was a father would wreck those plans. Had Sylvie known that? Was that why she'd decided not to tell him about Kimmie?

Only how well could Sylvie have known Cannon after only one night?

But they had made love even if Cannon didn't remember it. He'd kissed Brit once and pulled away.

"I guess we should get started back to the truck if we want to catch Aidan and his wife before dinner time."

"I think so."

Only he didn't start walking. He trailed a finger up her arm and then tucked his thumb beneath Brit's chin. Her head was spinning as he tilted her head so that she couldn't avoid meeting his gaze and staring into the deep depths of his brown eyes.

Brit felt giddy, suddenly weak. Cannon kissed her forehead, her eyelids—the tip of her nose. Her heart pounded in her chest.

And then his lips met hers and explosions of desire ripped through her body. His fingers tangled in her hair and he pulled her closer. She arched toward him, so lost in the kiss that all she wanted was more of him.

He came up for air, only to trail his lips from her mouth to her earlobe. "I've wanted to do that all day," he whispered. "You are driving me crazy without even trying."

"Crazy can be good."

He slipped his hands beneath the back of her shirt and his fingers danced along her bare skin. She found his lips again and melted into the thrill of him. No one had ever made her feel desirable. No one had ever made every area of her body ache for more of him.

Her phone rang. Her first impulse was to ignore it. But realty pushed through the passion.

"I have to," she said, pulling away.

"Brit, this is Sheriff Garcia. You called it and got it all right."

Chapter Sixteen

Cannon kept his eyes on the interstate, but listened intently, trying to keep up with Brit's analysis of the sheriff's findings. She was ecstatic, talking fast and throwing in so much police lingo he was having difficulty following her.

"How about slowing down and speaking in English?"

"Sorry. Most important development is that Melanie's arrest is imminent."

"I got that part. I'm lost somewhere in the midst of graveyard timing, phone records, new clothes, fuel tank and opportunity."

"Elementary and evidential, babe. Luck and good police work, the two most important weapons in a detective's arsenal."

"Not to mention my Smith & Wesson that came to the party last night."

"That goes without saying. Did I ever thank you for saving my life?"

"Not appropriately," he teased. Or maybe he wasn't teasing. He'd never wanted a woman more—nor been more certain he was heading for heartbreak.

"I could bake you a cake," she teased right back. "Well, actually, I can't cook, but I could buy one from the bakery."

"I'm not that into cake."

"Back to the timing," she quipped, wisely changing the subject before they started something they couldn't stop and risked never making it to Plano.

Brit kicked out of one black pump and pulled her bare foot into the seat with her. She shifted, so that she was facing him. "You played a major part in the timing, without which we wouldn't have hit the evidence jackpot or have a case against Melanie."

"All I did was drive and follow your orders."

"Requests, not orders," Brit reminded him, excitement still singing in her voice. "Fifteen minutes earlier or later and we would have missed seeing Melanie in the cemetery. She wouldn't have pulled a gun on me. There would have been no arrest for breaking the rules of her parole.

"Melanie was carted off to jail so unexpectedly she didn't have time to dispose of evidence. Her handbag and phone were on her bed in plain sight when they searched her house, as were two packed suitcases."

"Did it look as if she were returning from somewhere or leaving?"

"Definitely leaving, most likely permanently. There was nothing left in the drawers of her chest or her dresser. Her luggage was packed with an all-new wardrobe. Most of the clothes still had the tags on them. Most of it beachwear."

"Off to a Caribbean Island or perhaps Mexico," Cannon said, thinking out loud.

"Definitely somewhere warm," Brit agreed. "If we hadn't driven here last night, Melanie and her evidence might have been long gone before she was questioned."

"Not following orders paid off that time," Cannon said.

"Which should put me back in good standing with Captain Bradford."

"Did they find any plane tickets?"

"No, but you can always buy those at the last minute, a common practice of people unlawfully fleeing the country."

"Did she have the requisite fake passport?"

"None was found. But she could have been flying out on a private jet or picking a fake passport up on her way to the airport. I'm sure she wouldn't have any trouble making those arrangements. After almost five years in prison, Melanie surely knows people in low places."

"Will you be able to get a transcript of the phone calls between Brit and Clive?"

"No, but we have the date and times the calls were made, whether they were incoming or outgoing and the lengths of the calls."

"And Clive Austin's name actually came up on the phone records?"

"Yes, but we're talking about the records on the phone itself. It was a prepaid phone, the kind you can buy at any convenience store. She probably planned on destroying it before she fled the area."

"When were the calls made?"

"They talked twice two days before my attack, both calls short and initiated by Clive."

"That doesn't quite add up if Melanie was the one looking to hire him."

"The first contact with him was likely made in person through a trusted third party."

"That makes sense," Cannon said. "I doubt a killer for hire would be advertising. How many other phone contacts were there between the two of them?"

"Only one," Brit said. "She called him the morning

of my attack. The phone call lasted ten minutes, plenty of time to go over last-minute details like the location of the apartment where he was found dead. She may have arranged to deliver the final payment there, if all had gone well."

"Sounds like a lot of supposition."

"That's not unusual in murder cases, unless you have an eye witness. But the supposition is based on facts. What the sheriff uncovered provides solid evidence that Melanie was lying when she said she didn't know Clive and that there was communication between them just prior to Clive's failed attempt on my life and his murder."

"You mentioned discovering a key to a safety deposit box in her handbag when you were speed talking. How does that fit into the evidence framework?"

"There's no direct link at this point, but it does indicate she had something of value. It was always suspected that she had made off with some gold bars and a few very expensive pieces of jewelry that were never accounted for after Richard Crouch's murder. Selling them on the black market would explain where she got the money to hire Clive and pay for her stylish new wardrobe, and leave enough for her to live on once she'd settled in paradise."

"Must have been a chunk of shiny rocks to bring in that kind of dough."

"Her late husband was a very rich man."

"Any idea who fenced the gold and jewelry?"

"No, but they found a receipt for a full tank of gas purchased at an Oak Grove service station four days ago. Her tank is almost empty now. She'd have never used that much gas just driving into Oak Grove and back."

"So we have motive, ability and opportunity," Cannon said. "Gotta hand it to Sheriff Garcia. That was a nice day's work."

"Agreed. He's a far shrewder investigator than I would have guessed from our cemetery meeting."

"So what happens next?" Cannon asked.

"Melanie will be arrested for paying someone to murder Sylvie, Clive and me, even though I survived. Those charges will insure she won't qualify for bail."

Brit reached over and laid a hand on his thigh. The slight touch set off a spiral of arousal. It was downright scary that a simple touch from her could have that strong an effect on him. Not only did it turn him on physically, but also it felt familiar, as if her hand belonged there, and that touched him on a dozen other levels.

"Seriously, I can't thank you enough for the part you played in all of this, Cannon. I'm not sure why you ended up at the hospital the morning after my attack, but I'm sure glad you did."

"I'm not sure why I did, either," he said truthfully. "Guess it was meant to be."

"I like that sentiment."

"Do you still want to go to Plano?"

"I would—if you don't mind. I'd like hear what Aidan McIntosh thinks about the case against Melanie. Most of all, it would give me a chance to ask him if he knows anything about my adoption."

"Good thinking."

Brit's mood lightened dramatically as they drove the last few miles toward Plano. He'd barely been able to resist Brit when she'd been obsessed with finding Sylvie's killer and her attacker. Now she was completely intoxicating.

His phone rang as they exited the freeway in Plano. "R.J.," he said, willing to let the call go unanswered.

"You have to answer it," Brit urged. "It could concern Kimmie."

Reluctantly, Cannon took the call and switched to speaker so Brit could listen in on the conversation.

"I hear you two swooped in and showed Garcia how to solve a murder case in record time," R.J. said.

"Brit and the sheriff did the work. I just hung around and watched."

"That's not how Garcia is telling it. He's ready to hire you on the spot."

"Tell him I appreciate the offer, but I'll stick to bull riding."

"Travis said you two were going to stay in town tonight because Brit didn't want to bring any trouble our way. Never was any need for that but sure as shootin' ain't no reason for that now. Adam and Leif are grilling Dry Gulch steaks tonight. No trouble to add two more."

"Don't count on us for dinner. We're in Plano right now and I'm not sure how long we'll be."

"What in Sam Hill are you doing way up there?"

"Taking care of some personal business." He wasn't about to start explaining his comings and goings to R.J.

"Even if you get here late, would be nice to have you. Tomorrow's Saturday and the whole family will be around. Be a good chance for you and Brit to get to know everyone. If Kimmie's your daughter, Brit will be part of the family, too."

As if that were an honor. "No use to rush things."

"No use to make things harder than they have to be, either, Cannon. Up to you, but Leif's daughter, Effie, and Faith's son, Cornell, have big plans for the morning. They're calling it our first ever annual Christmas

Tree Search. Everyone will be splitting up into teams and going out on horseback to see who can find the most perfect Christmas tree. My neighbor Mattie Mae is coming over for the fun. She'll be here to watch Kimmie."

"I doubt we can make it."

"You do what you think's best, but you'll be missed."

Brit barely waited until the connection was broken to light into him.

"Did you have to be that rude? They're taking care of your daughter."

"*Possibly* my daughter. And I appreciate that, but I'm not going to play the happy-family game when I have no intention of making R.J. part of my life."

"He's your father and he's reaching out to you. Would it hurt you to at least give him a chance? It's not as if he'll be around forever."

"He was never around, not for me. Wouldn't even admit I was his son."

"He's admitting it now. At least talk to him. Tell him how you feel and why. It might be good for both of you to get things out in the open."

"I just can't see the point of it."

"Have it your way, but I want to go back to the Dry Gulch tonight."

Now he'd ticked her off—the last thing he'd wanted to do. "Afraid to stay alone with me at Travis's condo?" he teased, hoping to get her back in a good mood.

"Not afraid in the least," she said. "Didn't you hear R.J.? I'm part of the family, and I don't want to miss the first ever annual Christmas Tree Search."

AIDAN MCINTOSH POURED a double shot of Scotch into a glass while he waited for Brit's arrival.

He figured the talk tonight would concern Sylvie, since he'd only had one short conversation with Brit since her sister's death. Marcus had always hoped that Sylvie and Brit would meet someday when the time was right. Aidan didn't see the time as ever being right.

Brit's father had always been a hero in Brittany's eyes, bigger than life, more an idol to her than any movie or sports star.

Aidan didn't have the heart or the right to soil Marcus's memory.

He took his drink to the family room. His wife joined him there seconds later. "You should have told Brit we were busy."

"We're not busy."

Her hands flew to her narrow hips. Too narrow, to his way of thinking. She was so thin she could have hidden behind a two-by-four.

"Don't go all pious on me, Aidan McIntosh. It's not as if you haven't lied to her before. 'Anything to help out a friend.' Well, look where that got you. Look where it got our son."

Aidan was used to her bitterness and endless nagging about his shortcomings and how he'd failed his family. Through the years he'd learned to shut her out like static on an old radio. Tonight every word from her mouth seared into his conscience.

"You don't owe her anything, Aidan. You definitely wouldn't owe her father as much as a damn if he called from hell."

"Don't start again, Louise. It's not Marcus's fault our son is in prison. Matt made the decisions that ruined his life. He fired the gun that killed innocent people."

"Matt didn't mean to kill the innocent victims. You know that. My Matt is not a killer."

"You've been going over and over this for years, Louise. Please, just give it up."

"How can you give it up, Aidan McIntosh? Marcus Garner ruined your life, and you were his best friend."

"Marcus did the same as I'd have done in his shoes, the same as any honest cop would have done. I broke the law by covering up for Matt's drug dealing. I had to pay the price."

"Still making excuses for Marcus after all these years. Your son and your career were everything to you. Marcus stripped that from you as callously as if you were a stranger he'd passed on the street."

"I took them from myself, Louise."

He'd been too busy enforcing the law to pay attention to what was going on under his own roof. Had he been tuned in to it, he'd have realized that Louise was covering for Matt and his growing drug habit.

The addiction. The dealing. And finally the drive-by shooting that had left a teenager and an innocent child dead and another wounded.

"It's time to tell Brittany the truth about her father, Aidan. She's a big girl now. She can handle it. Marcus doesn't deserve your protection and neither does she."

"Let it go, Louise. We've been over this a hundred times. For God's sake, just let it go."

"No. Not this time. Either you tell her about her so-called adoption or I do."

The doorbell rang.

"I mean it, Aidan. You tell Brittany or I will. Marcus shattered our lives. He stole the one person I loved more than life itself while protecting his own daughter from even a hint of his sins."

"Marcus is dead, Louise. He has been for three years now. Let it go. You can't hurt him. Instead, you're destroying yourself. But if it will help you move past this hatred, I'll tell Brittany everything."

The doorbell rang again. "I'll get it," she said, walking away and smiling as if she'd won some nefarious game. It was the first time he'd seen her smile in years.

BRIT EXCHANGED A warm hug with Aidan. Louise, as always, was more aloof. Louise's affection for Brit had died when her son had been sentenced to life in prison.

At nineteen, Brit hadn't fully understood her pain. After years of seeing the effect of death on so many, she understood it all too well now.

"It's good to see you again, Louise."

"It's been a while. What brings you here tonight?" Louise asked, avoiding any indication that she was glad to see Brit.

"We were in the area and I wanted to drop by and say hello. I hope we didn't pick an inconvenient time."

"Not at all," Aidan said.

"Good. I'd like you to meet a friend of mine." She did the introductions.

Aidan shook Cannon's hand. "Glad to meet any friend of Brit's. Are you with the HPD, too?"

"Afraid not," Cannon said.

"He's a professional bull rider," Brit said. She'd love to add that he was the father of Sylvie's son, but she couldn't very well make that assertion when Cannon wasn't convinced yet.

"Bull riding's tough business," Aidan said. "And the rodeo doesn't sound like city-born-and-bred Brittany's choice of entertainment. How did you two meet?"

"Just good luck on my part," Cannon said.

"Suffice it to say a bull did not bring us together,"

Brit added, trying to decide how to segue away from small talk to the real reason she was here.

Louise reached into her pocket and pulled out her cell phone. "A text," she said. "I'm sorry. A minor emergency has come up that I need to take care of. I really must go, but I'm sure Aidan can entertain you."

Again the timing couldn't have been better, Brit decided, though she doubted there was really an emergency that had pulled Louise away.

"Can I get you a drink?" Aidan asked as soon as Louise had left the room. "I'm having Scotch on the rocks, but I have most anything you'd like. Bourbon? Vodka?"

"A glass of white wine if you have a bottle open," Brit said. "Otherwise water would be fine."

"How about a Riesling?"

"Perfect."

"That was always your mother's favorite wine."

Cannon asked for beer.

"You two take a seat and make yourselves comfortable. I'll get the drinks and join you in a minute."

"I'd say Louise is less than thrilled to see us, or is she always like that?" Cannon whispered once Aidan was out of earshot.

"She's been less than thrilled to see me ever since my father arrested her son for the murders that sent him to prison for life."

"Guess that could put a damper on a friendship. I get the feeling she and Aidan aren't on the best of terms tonight, either. We may have interrupted a family squabble."

"Possibly. We won't stay long."

"Probably a good idea, anyway, if you still want to

drive back to the Dry Gulch tonight. We're already
going to catch Friday-night traffic."

Aidan returned with their drinks. Brit and Cannon
had settled on the nutmeg-colored sofa. Aidan paced.
He was definitely upset about something.

"Have you made any progress in apprehending Sylvie Hamm's killer?" he asked.

Brit couldn't have hoped for a better opening. "We're
making progress. I can't discuss the case yet, but I think
we may have her killer in jail."

"That is good news."

"Yes, I wish I could say the same about Dad's killer,
but I'm still getting nowhere with that. It's incredibly
frustrating."

"I'm sure it is, but you'll get there one day, probably
when you least expect it."

"I hope you're right. Actually, we came here tonight
because I have a few questions that I hope you can answer."

"Shoot."

"I know how close you and my dad were, right from
college on. He must have shared a lot of things with
you."

"Some."

"Did he ever mention that I had a twin sister?"

Aidan drank the last half of his Scotch in one gulp.
"He did. I've kept those secrets for thirty years, but I
guess it's time you know the truth."

Chapter Seventeen

"I know that he was my father in every way that mattered. No one could ever take his place, but I'd like to know more about the adoption. Mainly I'd like to know why Sylvie and I were separated at birth and why I was never told I had a twin."

"Marcus was your biological father, Brit. You need to know that before you can understand the rest of the story."

The statement caught her off guard. Aidan had seemed so serious, but surely he was joking. Only he didn't look like he was joking.

Aidan buried his head in his hands for long seconds before he looked up again and met Brit's steady gaze. "Sylvie's mother and Marcus were lovers. You and Sylvie were born of that love."

Brit swallowed hard, unwilling to believe Aidan's words. "You must be mistaken. My dad loved my mother. He never even looked at another woman. Everyone who knew him said that."

"And they'd be right, except for a woman named Gabriel Hamm. He fell for her the second he met her."

"Are you sure?" Brit tried but couldn't keep the tremble from her voice.

"I'm sure," Aidan said. "I was there the night they met."

"Was it a one-night stand?" Someone her father had hooked up with the way Cannon had hooked up with Sylvie and gotten her pregnant.

She'd had a hard time reconciling the stranger who'd gotten Sylvie pregnant with the man she'd been steadily falling for over the past few days. But at least Cannon had been single. Her father had been married.

"It wasn't a one-night stand," Aidan said. "Marcus and Gabriel met in Austin when we went back for one of our fraternity brothers' wedding."

"Was Mother there, too?"

"No. Joyce was presenting a paper at a psychology conference in St. Louis. She and your father weren't getting along particularly well at the time. She wanted him to leave the police force and find a job where he didn't put his life on the line. He refused. You know your dad. He loved police work. I can't even imagine him sitting at a desk all day."

Nor could Brit—but an affair. Cheating on her mother and then bringing Brit home for her to raise. But he'd left Sylvie behind.

"I'm not making excuses for Marcus, Brit. He wouldn't want me to. He never made excuses for himself. He loved your mother in his own way. He always did right up until the day she died. But he loved Gabriel, too. He was different with her, more carefree. I swear I could always tell when he'd been with her."

"How long did the affair last?"

"Almost two years, until Gabriel became pregnant with you and Sylvie."

"Don't tell me he deserted a woman pregnant with his twin daughters?"

"No. She deserted him, before she even knew there were twins. The guilt got the better of her, I guess. She moved away and told him she never wanted to see him again, that she was going to give the baby up for adoption. Marcus took it hard. As hard as I've ever seen him take anything, and, believe me, we'd been through a lot together."

"But she didn't give Sylvie up—only me."

"That wasn't the original plan. Somehow your dad found out when she gave birth. He showed up at the hospital and once he saw you and Sylvie he begged her to let him adopt both of you. But she had fallen in love with her babies, too, and changed her mind about adoption."

"But I was adopted."

"Your dad could be very persistent when he set his mind to it. And he definitely set his mind on raising you. He'd always wanted a big family. Joyce couldn't have children and wasn't sure she wanted a family. But somehow he talked her into the adoption without letting her know the truth."

"More lies."

"He was human. He had his faults. We all do, Brit. Your dad and I probably had a few more than our share. I'm not sure how the decision was made about which twin he'd adopt, but I do know that he loved you from the first time he held you in his arms. Joyce did, as well. Both of them loving you so much was what turned their marriage around."

"How can a marriage built on lies be great?"

"Because there was more there than lies. I didn't tell you this to turn you against your dad, Brit. I probably shouldn't have told you at all, but I felt terrible when Sylvie was killed. I know that you two might have been close had you been given the chance."

"Did you ever meet Sylvie?"

"Only once, a few months after her mother died. Gabrielle had told her the truth when she realized she wasn't going to make it. Sylvie paid me a visit. She questioned me about Marcus and you. She said she might look you up one day, but she wasn't ready yet. I figure wanting to meet you was what brought her to Houston."

"And to her death."

"She was traveling into someone else's past to find herself," Cannon said. "That's what she told me the night I met her. I don't know why it popped into my head right now, but it did and suddenly it makes sense."

"I wish I'd met her before she was killed," Brit said. "I wish I'd met Gabrielle. So sad to have a twin sister and a biological mother I never knew. Too bad my dad never thought of giving me that."

It was the first time she'd ever thought of him as less than perfect. Turned out he was just a man.

"If you're interested, you have a half brother, as well," Aidan said. "Gabriel and her new husband had a son. Sylvie said he's a navy SEAL and quite a hero."

"I've talked to him," Brit said. "I got his name after Sylvie was killed and gave him a call. He never knew about me," Brit said. "Perhaps I'll try to meet him in person one day."

Right now, she just wanted to go back to the Dry Gulch Ranch and Kimmie.

Like Sylvie, she needed to rescue her present from all the secrets of the past. What better way to start than by loving her adorable, completely innocent niece?

Learning the truth about her dad had opened her eyes to a lot of things. As for Cannon and his irresponsible one-night stands and the paternity test that he hoped would save him from the responsibility of parenthood, he could go back to his bulls.

How could she ever have thought she was falling in love with him?

IT WAS ALMOST ten o'clock by the time Brit and Cannon arrived back at the Dry Gulch. They'd stopped for dinner at a restaurant and then were delayed for another hour due to a wreck on the interstate.

The house was quiet and dark, but they had called earlier to let R.J. know they were retuning tonight. The door would be unlocked and their beds ready and waiting. Brit was more than ready to climb between the crisp white shirts and cuddle beneath the warm quilt.

Unfortunately, her enthusiasm for participating in a search for the perfect Christmas tree had vanished. Her heart felt heavy, her mind bogged down with learning the truth about the man she'd practically worshipped for all the years of her life.

Once inside the house, Cannon walked her to the guest room. He lingered at the door. "I hate seeing you so upset, Brit. Is there anything I can do to help? Offer a shoulder to cry on or use as a punching bag to vent your frustrations?" He trailed his fingers down her arm and tried to take her hand.

She pulled away. "I'll be fine. I just need a little time to absorb everything I learned about my father tonight."

"Why do I get the feeling you are taking your anger toward your father for mistakes he made years ago out on me?"

"I'm not."

"So why do you pull away when I touch you and won't even look at me when we talk? A few hours ago I was the knight on the white horse who'd ridden to your rescue. Now suddenly I'm the enemy."

"You aren't the enemy. You came through for me when I needed you, and I appreciate that. But I'm no longer suffering from a concussion and Melanie Crouch is behind bars. The urgency has passed. You can go back to your life. I can go back to mine."

"You make this sound like a business deal."

"Think of it as a release from a contract you never meant to sign. You don't have to stick around to wait on the results of the paternity test. The only tie you might have to Kimmie is biological, just like you said about your relationship to R.J. Well, you can walk away without even feeling guilty. If any sacrifices are to be made, I'll make them. I'll take care of Kimmie."

"Whoa. You're way off base. I didn't see any of this coming, I'll grant you that. But if Kimmie's my daughter, I'll take full responsibility for her. I don't know how yet, but I'll find a way. I've never shirked on an obligation."

"And Kimmie would be your obligation?"

"I didn't mean that the way it sounded. You're upset. I get that. Let's call it a night."

"First, satisfy my curiosity, Cannon. How many one-night stands have you had? How many women have you slept with that you don't even remember the next day?"

"So that's what this is about?"

"You didn't answer the question."

Anger flared in Cannon's eyes. "I don't intend to start explaining everything in my past life to you. But just for the record, I don't make a habit of getting drunk and picking up women in bars. I'm not saying I've never had a fling that was purely physical, but those times are few and far between."

"Yet you admit that's all you shared with Sylvie."

"I can't explain that night or what was going on in her mind. I'm not perfect. It's a foolproof bet she wasn't, either. Maybe she'd had the kind of day you had today or the kind I'd had that night. Maybe all either of us needed was a place to feel wanted and safe for a few hours."

"What kind of night does it take for you to make love to a woman you feel nothing for?"

"Okay, you want the truth. Here it is. It takes watching your best friend get his brains kicked out by a mad bull. It takes holding him in your arms while he breathes his last breath. It takes telling his wife who's expecting their first baby that he's never coming home again."

His voice dropped to a husky whisper, sadness replacing the anger in his eyes.

"I'm not your father, Brit. But it's awful easy for you to preach forgiveness and understanding when it applies to me and R.J. and then be quick to turn against your father, a man who never once stopped loving you."

Brit was trembling as Cannon turned and walked away.

Tears filled her eyes as she crossed the room and dropped to the bed. Before she'd looked at a double of herself lying on that cold hard slab—before Kimmie and Cannon had dropped into her life—she'd known who she was and exactly what she wanted.

Now all her priorities had been scrambled beyond the point of recognition. Sylvie had been looking for her future in the past. But the past couldn't be changed. It couldn't be relived. It could only be learned from, the good cherished, the bad released.

Brit was about to throw her future away.

She jumped from the bed, rushed to the bathroom,

washed her face and brushed her teeth. She shed her clothes and pulled on her robe.

Heart pounding, she raced down the hallway and up the stairs. She tapped at the first closed door.

Cannon opened it. He looked surprised but wary. "Is something wrong?"

"No. Everything is right—unless you don't want me."

"I'm not looking for a one-night pity stand, Brit."

"Good, because I'm thinking more like a new beginning with the option of indefinite. But I'm warning you, if you make love with me tonight, you are going to remember it for the rest of your life."

He opened his arms and she stepped inside them, sure of only one thing. There was no place she'd rather be than in his bed tonight.

BRIT AWAKENED TO mouthwatering smells wafting up from the kitchen and a gentle ache in her thighs. Deliciously sweet memories of making love to Cannon danced through her senses.

She rolled over to crawl back into his arms. He wasn't there. She did the next best thing and pulled his pillow against her naked breasts. Breasts that would never be the same after being massaged, nibbled and sucked by Cannon until she'd thought her nipples would become permanently erect and puckered.

The musky scent of Cannon and of their lovemaking still clung to the sheets and his pillow. She breathed it in, savoring it the way she had his every touch last night.

His fingers had explored every inch of her. His lips had teased and tasted until he'd driven her mad with wanting him.

When she'd reached the mind-blowing edge of orgasm, he'd trailed his probing tongue and ravishing lips back to her mouth and kissed her senseless.

And then he'd raised his beautiful naked body over hers and entered her with one heart-stopping thrust of his rock-hard erection. Both wild with desire, they'd ridden the wave of passion home.

Totally spent after that, she was certain it would take days of recovery before either of them would be able to make love like that again.

Two hours later, she'd been proven wrong. Now she wondered if she'd ever be able to get enough of his loving.

But it was morning and the Christmas Tree Search was waiting. She threw her legs over the side of the bed, padded across the room to the window and opened the blinds. Tiny white flakes of snow were falling from a slightly overcast sky.

It had to be a good omen.

She dressed quickly in jeans and a pullover sweater that wouldn't be too hot in the house but would provide a nice layer of warmth beneath her jacket. Her stylish leather riding boots didn't fit the cowboy tradition, but they would do just fine. It was going to be a beautiful day.

Excited voices, all seemingly talking at once, reached her ears the moment she opened her door. The wonderful family Cannon refused to be a part of. She hoped that would change—for his sake and Kimmie's.

And for hers. Who wouldn't want to be part of this family?

She couldn't imagine how Cannon's and her jobs and lifestyles would mesh, but she wouldn't let herself worry about that now. Nor would she think of all the secrets Aidan had shared with her last night.

The day was rife with pleasure and anticipation. She'd let nothing spoil it.

CANNON HELPED ADAM arrange the warm quilts in the seat of the small horse-drawn carriage. "This is a beauty. Where did you get it?"

"On the property. It was in an old barn near the northwestern edge of the spread that hadn't been used in years. Leif, Travis, Cornell and I decided to tear down the barn. The carriage was buried under a stack of old pine logs."

"It must have taken a lot of work to restore it."

"It took some time, but well worth it. Lila and Lacy love going for a ride in what they call their Santa Claus carriage. The difference between sleigh and carriage is a still a little fuzzy with them."

"I heard how excited they were at breakfast."

Adam laughed. "I don't doubt that. They never go unnoticed. I missed the first three years of their lives and then almost lost them to a kidnapper. I know what they mean to me."

"They were kidnapped from the ranch?"

"No, from Hadley's mother's house in Dallas. It's a long story. I'll save it for a cold winter night. We'll get plenty of those in January and February. Right now you and the detective best get saddled up or the rest of the group will be hollering at you. The rules say we all leave at once and get back here in two hours."

"What's the prize?"

"The chance to have your tree in the family room at the big house. That's where we all gather for stories

and songs before midnight church services on Christmas Eve and for opening gifts on Christmas morning."

"That sounds like a lot of togetherness."

"It is, but there's plenty of alone time on the Dry
Gulch. Wide-open spaces. Best fishing and hunting in
the county. Great swimming hole in the summer. I realize you have issues with R.J. We all did. We all had
reason to. But you can't hang on to past hurts forever.
The old resentments will eat you alive."

Interesting theory, but Cannon wasn't being eaten
alive and he wasn't buying the theory.

"Guess I better get back to the tack room. I'm sure
Brit is revved for riding."

He walked the few yards to where he had left everyone saddling their mounts for the morning ride.
The horse barn was quiet and empty now. Well, almost empty.

R.J. finished washing his hands in water from a hose
spout and wiped them on the legs of his baggy jeans. "I
was wondering where you got off to."

"I was helping Adam ready the carriage."

"Good. Glad you got to spend some time with him.
He's a good man. Knows more about life in his thirties
than I ever learned."

Cannon didn't doubt that. "Have you seen Brit?"

"She left here a few minutes ago on Miss Dazzler.
That's my special horse. Wouldn't let just anybody ride
her, but I like Brit a lot."

"So do I." More than he'd ever imagined possible.
"What horse do you want me to ride?"

"Raven. He's already saddled and ready to go, and
waiting for you at the corral. That's the starting point for
this competition Effie and Cornell are so excited about."

"I'd best head over there. Don't want to keep the crowd waiting."

"Won't kill 'em to wait another few minutes."

"You got something to say to me, R.J.?"

"Just need to get a couple of things off my chest."

"Let's hear them."

"I know I didn't do right by you. I wasn't there when your mother died, same as I wasn't there for Leif and Travis. But I did try to help out when I could get my hands on some money. There wasn't much of that back then."

"Hard to believe when there is supposedly millions now."

"I didn't lay it out in the will, but I've told the others so I might as well level with you. I didn't earn that money. Sure as hell didn't save it."

"So where did you get it?"

"I bought a one-dollar lottery ticket in Oak Grove. Damn thing hit the jackpot. Well, not one of those gigantic jackpots, but a few million after taxes was bigtime for me. Went from poor rancher to millionaire overnight."

That explained a lot, though it didn't change Cannon's mind about the man.

"I sent what I could to your uncle to help pay your way when you were growing up, Cannon. I know it weren't much, but I paid for your braces like he asked me to. I borrowed and sent him the money for your medical expenses that time you fell out of the tree and broke your leg."

"You must have me mixed up with one of your other sons. I never had braces. I fell out of several trees, but I never broke any bones. You never sent me or my uncle as much as a birthday card."

R.J. shook his head. "I don't have my facts mixed up. If your uncle says differently he's a lying son of a bitch. Sorry to put it so bluntly, but that's the dadgum truth. You believe who you want. I can't do nothing about that. I just want you to know that there's a place for you and Kimmie here and I'd be mighty proud if you decided to move to the Dry Gulch."

No ready response came to mind. "I appreciate you and the rest of the family helping out with Kimmie." It was the only honest answer he could give without laying more guilt on a dying man.

THEY HAD TAKEN the horses to a trot and then a gallop, slowing again when the sting of the icy wind became more painful than the exhilaration.

Brit stuck out her tongue to catch a snowflake. "Just look around you, Cannon. The massive trunk and crooked branches of that ancient oak tree. The clear, rocky bottom of the shallow stream. The carpet of pine straw and crunchy leaves. I never dreamed the Dry Gulch would be this beautiful in the falling snow."

"Then enjoy. It won't last long. It's freezing this morning, but we're supposed to reach a high of thirty-seven this afternoon. It will all melt."

"But it's here now and beautiful. I love the way summer and fall tangle for control deep into the winter in this part of Texas."

"You seem to be loving everything today," he teased.

"Maybe because I had a great night."

"There's more where that came from."

"I'll hold you to that."

They rode side by side along the stream for twenty minutes or more and then detoured into the woods.

"You'd best start staking out the perfect tree," Cannon said. "We'll need to head back soon if we want to meet the deadline and get there before the hot cocoa and sugar cookies are all gone."

Brit scanned the area. "Do you have any idea how to get back?"

"Sure. Just follow the north star."

"It's daylight."

"I knew that sounded too simple to be true."

He was teasing. She should have known he'd been paying attention to the way they'd come while she'd just been enjoying the ride.

Now it was time for her to do her job. She scanned the area as they walked the horses down a winding trail that went right through the woods. A few minutes later they came to a clearing at the top of a hill.

And there it was. Standing alone. A beautiful evergreen. A trunk as straight as a fence post. Lots of branches laden with forest-green needles.

"That's it," Brit said, pointing to the tree. She dismounted and untied the bow from the loop around her belt. Cannon took her reins as she darted off to crown her chosen tree.

Cannon tethered the reins to a low-hanging branch of a sycamore tree and joined her.

"It's perfect," she declared as she secured the bow to the highest branch she could reach.

"Absolutely perfect."

Only Cannon's voice had grown husky and his eyes were on her instead of the tree. He took her in his arms and she melted into his kiss as the snowflakes fell in their silent wonderland.

If a moment could last forever, she'd choose this one.

The moment didn't last nearly long enough.

"Do we have to go back so soon?" she asked when Cannon pulled away.

"It's my phone. It's vibrating, but I can ignore it."

"We shouldn't. It could be important."

"Okay. Your call." He took the phone out of his pocket and looked at the display.

"It's the lab."

Chapter Eighteen

Emotions Cannon couldn't unravel crashed down on him. He hadn't expected them to call on a Saturday. The past few days had been the longhand version of eight seconds on the bull, a tangled mesh of fear and anxiety and passion. He wasn't ready for this.

But he couldn't postpone the truth.

"Hello."

"Is this Cannon J. Dalton?"

"It is."

"We have the results ready from your paternity testing. You can pick them up Monday through Friday during our regular office hours."

"Can't you just tell me over the phone?"

"Wait. Let me see if you specified that on your form."

He'd specified it. The wait seemed endless.

"Congratulations, Mr. Dalton. You're the father of Kimmie Marie Hamm."

The news hit like a bolt of lightning even though he'd thought he was prepared.

"Would you like me to mail the full written report or would you rather come in and pick it up?"

His emotions were spinning so wildly it took a few seconds to digest her question.

"Mail it to the Oak Grove address that I gave you."

He barely heard the rest of her spiel. He turned off his phone and dropped it into his pocket.

"I'm Kimmie's father, just like you said."

She slipped her hands into his. "Are you okay?"

He had to think about that for a moment. "Yeah. I'm okay. I'm not sure about Kimmie. I have no idea how to take care of her."

"Most new fathers don't. You'll learn."

"Are you going to teach me?"

"I'm as much a novice as you are. I realized that the week she stayed with me. But I'll help you all I can. So will your family. They already love her."

"I feel kind of like life as I know it has been ripped out from under me."

"It will definitely change," Brit said. "There will be lots of adjustments, but you'll make a wonderful father."

If he did, no one would be more surprised than him.

But strangely, he wasn't as upset as he'd expected to be. In fact, he had that same warmth creeping into his chest as he'd felt the first night he'd held Kimmie and she'd curled her tiny fingers around his.

"Shall we go back to the house and share the news?" Brit asked.

He managed a shaky smile. "I should have bought cigars."

THE REST OF Saturday and into Sunday morning had passed in a blur and a frenzy of celebration. You'd have thought he'd just won a Nobel Peace Prize instead of finding out that he was a father.

Cannon would be glad when the hoopla settled down. He had endless decisions to make about how to take care of an infant on the rodeo circuit. Maybe he should just kidnap R.J.'s grandmotherly-type neighbor Mattie Mae and take her with him.

It was eleven o'clock on Sunday morning and he and Brit were stuck in slow-moving traffic on the outer limits of Houston. His old doubts were returning at the speed of the jerk on the motorbike who'd just passed them on the shoulder.

"I'm not good with you staying in that town house alone."

"I live there, Cannon."

"Do you remember what it looked like the last time you were in it?"

"I remember vividly. It doesn't look that way now. I just talked to the cleaning service. The police tape is down and the place has been scrubbed so clean I'll think it's been renovated."

"I still don't think you should be alone until…"

"Until what? Every criminal in Houston is arrested and behind bars? That is never going to happen. If it did, I'd be out of a job."

"I could hire you as a nanny."

"I'd become a buckle bunny with a baby on my hip. That would be over-the-top disgusting."

"You could start a new trend."

She reached across the console and brushed her hand up and down his thigh.

"Plying me with sexual favors will not assuage my worry."

"I know you're afraid for me, Cannon. Police work and going after murderers is new for you. But it's what I do. I'm a detective. I handle investigations. It's not like I'm out chasing down killers every night."

"Clive Austin almost killed you."

"Clive Austin is dead and the woman who hired him is in jail and will be for a long, long, time."

She made sense. He knew that, but knowing and feeling were entirely different things.

Brit was convinced that Melanie was the one who'd schemed to kill her and killed Sylvie and Clive Austin in the process. But what if she was wrong? What if all the supposition and circumstantial evidence had led them to the wrong conclusion? Or what if Melanie had managed to hire another killer even before she'd sliced Clive's throat?

And what if he was going overboard with this? It would be as bad as if Brit was making decisions about his life, telling him to give up bull riding and get an office job.

The anxiety swelled again when he pulled onto her street and spotted a black sedan parked in Brit's driveway.

"Looks like you have company."

"Unexpected company," Brit said. "I don't recognize the vehicle."

Cannon parked his truck behind the car, blocking it in. He killed the engine and jumped out of the car to check things out. Brit, of course, was right behind him.

He recognized the driver immediately, despite the fact that her eyes were swollen and red, her mascara smeared and running down one cheek like black tears.

"Louise, what's wrong?" Brit asked.

"Aidan left me," she muttered between near hysterical sobs. "After you left last night, he got drunk and started calling me names. He said it was my fault he'd lost his job. My fault our son was in prison. I couldn't reason with him."

"I'm sure he's sobered up by now," Cannon offered. "He probably doesn't even remember what he said."

"He may be sober, but he hasn't been home since Friday night and he's not answering his phone. For all I know he's dead." The hysterics started again. "You have to help me get him back, Brit. You have to tell him it's not my fault. I can't live without Aidan. He's all I have."

"Let's go inside," Brit said. "I'll make some hot tea. We'll talk and figure out what to do."

Louise nodded, opened the door and practically fell out of the car. Cannon grabbed her arm for support.

"I've got it from here, Cannon," Brit assured him.

"Are you sure?"

"I'm sure. I'll call you later. Drive safely. I'll see you soon."

There was nothing left for him to do but drive away.

BRIT WAS TERRIBLE with handling hysterical women. She and Louise hadn't been close in years. Going to see Aidan Friday night may have been the biggest mistake in her life.

She led Louise through the front door of her town house and into her cozy living room. "Take this chair," Brit urged, tugging her to the most comfortable seat in the room. "Try to calm down. I'll heat some water for tea."

Once the tea bags were steeping in the hot water, Brit walked to the bedroom door and peered inside. All traces of the brutal attack had been scrubbed away just as her cleaning lady had promised. Still, an icy tremble climbed Brit's spine as thoughts of the horrid pictures filled her mind.

When the tea was ready, Brit put it on a tray and started back to the living room. Thankfully, Louise's body-racking sobs had grown silent. Perhaps now she'd listen to reason.

Aidan might have gotten drunk after their emotional talk the other night. Heaven knows, she'd felt like doing that herself, and she never drank to the point of intoxication. But Aidan and Louise had been through hell and back together. Brit couldn't believe he'd leave her now.

He'd be back. In the meantime, hysterics weren't going to help.

"Tea's ready," she said as she rejoined Louise.

"Thank you, bitch. Now sit it down and don't make another move."

Brit stared into Louise's cold, tearless eyes and at the pistol she held with both hands. Panic rose in her throat.

She set the tray on an end table. "Put the gun down, Louise." She struggled to keep her voice low and reassuring. "I don't know what happened between you and Aidan, but it's not my fault. Killing me won't solve anything."

"It may not, but it will make me feel a whole lot better."

The hysterics had been an act. Louise had crossed the line between sanity and madness and somehow her anger had turned to Brit.

"I've never done anything to you, Louise. You must know that. You were almost like a second mother to me when I was growing up. I would have never hurt you."

"You didn't have to. Your father did enough for both of you. Pretending to be Aidan's best friend all those years. Expecting Aidan to keep his dirty little secrets while he destroyed our lives. You are just like him. You've always been just like him. Even at your prom, you lied and told your father my son was on drugs."

"My father never…"

Brit's words died as the truth suddenly hit home. It wasn't Melanie who had hired someone to kill her. It was Louise. The comment from Clive about her father made sense now.

But Melanie had Clive's phone number in her phone. Why? Unless ….

"You and Melanie Crouch were partners, weren't you? You pooled your money and hired Clive Austin to kill me."

"Dragging Melanie into this was all Clive's idea. When I refused to pay him what he wanted, he tried to persuade Melanie to pay him for the same job— double dipping so to speak. She refused. In the end the bumbling thug agreed to kill you for what I'd offered to pay him."

"Only instead of paying him, you slashed his throat."

"He was trash. The world is better off without him. The same way it's better off without your father."

The pieces were all falling into place. The nauseating truth swelled inside Brit's chest until she could barely breathe. "You hired someone to kill my father, didn't you? While Aidan was at the funeral crying with me, you must have been celebrating your success."

"Marcus deserved it. He destroyed my husband and my son. He tore our family apart. I swore to wipe out his family the way he did mine. That's why you have to die, Brit. It's why Sylvie had to die."

"No one else needs to die, Louise. You've taken enough revenge. Think about what you're doing. Stop the killing."

"I will, after you're dead. You're the last one. I've run out of money. That's why I have to kill you myself. Strange how much I'm looking forward to it. Once you're dead, maybe I can sleep at night."

Louise was mad, far past reasoning. Brit had to find a way to stop her. "You won't get away with this, Louise."

"Oh, but I will. Thanks to you, Melanie is already in jail for hiring Clive Austin to kill you. When they find you dead, they'll be convinced she hired someone else to kill you. Case solved."

"Cannon knows you were here when he left, Louise. If you pull that trigger, he'll know it was you who killed me."

"Cannon saw me in tears, weeping over an argument with my husband. An argument I staged and pushed until Aidan walked out on me. He's done it before. He always comes back. He's a good man, not a cheat like your father."

"Hand me the gun, Louise. We were so close once. You don't want to kill me."

"I have to kill you. You must see that. But you're lucky, Brit. It will all be over for you in a matter of seconds. You can't imagine how many nights I've cried myself to sleep, praying that I would never wake up."

No. She couldn't die. Not like this. She had to be there for Kimmie. She had to tell Cannon how much she loved him.

Brit scanned the room, looking for a distraction, a weapon, for anything to give her a fighting chance.

She lurched for the heavy glass lamp and hurled it at Louise just as she pulled the trigger. The bullet hit the lamp. Sharp shards of glass rained down on them. Louise howled and grabbed her right eye. Still, she kept coming at Brit, one eye bloody, the other open, the pistol poised to shoot.

I love you, Cannon and sweet Kimmie, I love you so much. I don't want to lose you. This is not the way this was supposed to end.

Chapter Nineteen

Cannon stopped for gas one block from the entrance to I-45 North. He still couldn't shake the unwanted anxiety or get the case against Melanie Crouch out of his mind. He agreed she was a suspect and should be in jail, but there were far too many assumptions for him to fully buy her guilt.

And too many unanswered questions. Why bury your wedding album for symbolic closure if you were still holding a murderous grudge against the cop who arrested you for killing him? Why waste your money on hiring a killer instead of using it to support you in paradise for the rest of your life?

And then there was the comment tying the attempted murder to Brit's father. From what he'd heard, there were no apparent ties between Clive Austin or Melanie Crouch and Chief of Police Marcus Garner. No reason to suspect Melanie knew Sylvie was Brit's sister.

They should be looking for someone like Louise McIntosh, who hated Brit's father and knew the truth about Sylvie and Brit's relationship.

Someone like Louise.

Truth hit with the force of a hatchet, the blade landing right in the center of Cannon's heart. He jerked the gas hose from his tank, jumped in his truck and took off. Someone yelled at him from the service station. They could damn well stick the hose back in the pump themselves. If his fears were right, every second counted.

He turned the corner on squealing wheels as adrenaline rushed through his veins. Louise's car was still parked in the driveway.

For once he prayed his instincts were all wrong, that Brit and Louise were having tea and talking about the rotten way Aidan had treated his wife. The praying didn't stop the grinding fear in the pit of his stomach.

His tires screeched as he swerved into the driveway and stamped on his brakes. He grabbed his pistol, bounded from the truck and raced to the door, prepared to shoot off the lock if it came to that.

His hand was on the doorknob when he heard the booming crack of gunshot followed by a piercing scream. Choking panic balled like acid in his throat.

He turned the doorknob and pushed through the front door, his weapon poised to shoot. A chair came flying at him; he ducked just as he saw Brit pounce on Louise and knock her to the floor.

Brit shoved a glass paperweight into Louise's face. But Louise kicked and managed to get away just long enough to reach for a gun she must have lost in the scuffle. Before Cannon could stop her, Louise's finger closed around the trigger.

He jumped over an overturned table and wrestled the pistol from her hand a heartbeat after she fired. Blood shot into the air like an eruption.

Louise fell back to the floor, a pool of crimson blood already pooling on her shirt.

Cannon stepped over her and dropped to the floor next to Brit. "Are you all right?"

"All but my pride, but poor Louise. She's bleeding badly, Cannon. You have to help her."

Before he could, four armed cops crashed into the room, weapons pulled. One looked at Brit and then aimed his gun at Cannon's head.

"Police Officer. Guns down," Brit ordered. "Suspect down and injured. Cannon and I are unhurt."

A police officer she recognized stared at her. "Detective Garner?"

"Right," she said. "I was attacked, but not shot. I think the suspect was hit by her own ricocheting bullet."

One cop called for an ambulance. Another checked Louise's pulse and tried to stop her bleeding.

The officer she knew crossed the room to stand over Brit. "You sure you're all right, Detective Garner?"

"I am, Officer Cormier, thanks to my friend Cannon. If he hadn't arrived when he did, I'd be dead."

"How did you guys get here so fast?" Cannon questioned. "I didn't even get a chance to call you."

"The detective's got good neighbors. They called when they said a suspicious car was parked in her driveway. We heard a shot as soon as we drove up."

"Good work."

Cannon gave Brit a hand, tugged her to her feet and pulled her into his arms. "Am I going to have to spend the rest of my life rescuing you?"

"Do you have something better to do, cowboy?"

"Yeah, I do. I'll tell you about it as soon as we're alone. But don't worry, I'll always have your back."

She stretched to her tiptoes and put her lips to his ear. "Why stop with my back? You can have all of me."

That was a promise he planned to hold her to for the rest of their lives.

Epilogue

New Year's Day at the Dry Gulch Ranch

R.J. sat on the front porch swing, watching the action as the Dalton women scurried in and out of the house like ants.

"Are we expecting the Texas Army National Guard at this picnic?" he asked as Hadley passed with a four-layer chocolate cake.

"No, just half the neighbors in Oak Grove. It's a triple celebration. Don't want to leave anyone out."

"Triple. What more is there than New Year's?"

"You'll see."

Leif and Cannon pulled up in Cannon's pickup truck and started unloading yet another picnic table from the bed of the truck.

"Did you guys buy out the local hardware shop?"

"Nope, all borrowed," Leif called.

And they'd all be needed. When folks around Oak Grove came to a picnic, none came empty-handed. They'd end up with enough food to stock the biggest restaurant chain in Texas.

Once the table was unloaded, Cannon climbed the steps to the porch and poured himself a glass of cold lemonade that Joni had brought out from the kitchen not five minutes ago.

"Real nice to have you and Kimmie here for the day," R.J. said.

"Glad to be here," Cannon said.

"How's it going trying to take care of her and keep up with the circuit?"

"It has its challenges, but I'm making it—for now."

"Good to hear. What's the latest on Louise McIntosh?"

"She's still in the hospital being treated for complications with her chest injury. Her physical situation is improving but her mental condition is deteriorating."

"I hear hate and resentment can do that to you if you hold on to it long enough. Seems there are lots of ways to ruin your life. I'm just lucky I got a second chance at happiness, however long that chance turns out to be."

"On that topic, I've got something I'd like to talk to you about."

"I'm nothing but ears."

R.J. listened to Cannon's plans, his heart warming at every word out of Cannon's mouth. If he kept it up, the light jacket Faith had insisted he wear on this incredibly sunny day would start suffocating him.

"I don't see how that would be a problem," R.J. said. "This spread's big enough you can easily carve out a section to breed and raise rodeo stock. Build a place of your own like the others have or move into the big house with me. Lord knows there's room, and I'd appreciate the company."

"I'm just in the thinking stages."

"I understand that, too. Is Brit included in this thinking?"

"She's a major part of it."

"How does she feel about that?"

"I haven't asked her. I'm almost scared to. Her life's in Houston. She seems to like it that way."

"Likes and dislikes change like the seasons. Even Kimmie opened her mouth for pureed bananas this morning."

"You got a point. Now I better get back to work before the guys come looking for me."

R.J. leaned back in the swing and smiled. It would be plum dandy to have Cannon and Kimmie move onto the ranch. But a man needed a woman.

He closed his eyes and pictured a young lady with hair the color of fresh-mowed hay and a smile that had made him melt just to look at.

His first love. Still alive, or so he'd heard a month or two ago. He wondered what she was doing today and if she still liked double-dip ice-cream cones.

A few minutes later he was snoring away and Gwen was dancing barefoot through his dream.

By SUNSET THE last of the guests had packed up their picnic baskets and headed back to their own farms and ranches.

Cannon's plans were all in place.

Kimmie was spending the night with Hadley and Adam, much to the delight of her four-year-old cousins, Lacy and Lila. The champagne was iced and waiting. Adam had just hitched the ranch's two most dependable geldings to the carriage. The quilts were folded and waiting.

And Cannon was so nervous it took three times to zip his jacket.

He went looking for Brit and found her standing on the porch looking up at the heaven full of stars.

"It was a perfect day," she said. "I loved it when Joni

and Leif stood up and announced together that there would be a new Dalton arriving in six months. That bought a few whoops and hollers from the crowd."

"The Dalton clan is definitely growing," Cannon agreed.

"My very favorite moments were when you and the rest of your half brothers all stood and gave your special toasts to R.J."

"I don't think any of us expected he'd break down and cry," Cannon said.

"There were a lot of tears in that crowd. I was one of the ones who wept to see him so touched and to see you be a part of it. You've come a long way in a short time, Cannon. I'm so proud of you."

"I still have a ways to go. How about taking a moonlit ride with me?"

"In your truck?"

"In the carriage?"

"Just the two of us?"

"Did you want someone else?"

"No. Just you."

A few minutes later they arrived at Cannon's favorite place on the whole spread. A hilltop that looked down on a curve in the creek and acres of rolling pastureland.

He slowed the horses to a stop, reached in his pocket and wrapped his fingers around the tiny ring box. He'd mentally prepared himself all day to hear the word *no* from her lips, but now that he was about to pop the question, he couldn't deny how desperately he wanted Brit to say yes.

Holding the reins in one hand, he put his other arm around her shoulder and pulled her close. "I love you,

Brit Garner. I love you so much I can't even think straight anymore."

"I love you, too, Cannon Dalton, so much that I am finally thinking straight. For the first time in my life, I know who I am and what I want."

"What do you want?"

"I want stars over my head and to be surrounded by laughter and love the way we were today. I want to be part of a family like the Daltons who laugh and cry together, who have their own interests and passions but are always there for one another, too. I want to spend lots and lots of time with Kimmie."

"Is that it?"

"No, I want love in my heart, passion in my soul and joy in the morning. I want you, Cannon Dalton. I love you so very, very much."

"Then I guess it's time for this."

He got down on one knee in the carriage and pulled the ring from his pocket. "Will you marry me, Brit Garner? I promise not to wear my boots to bed or make you go to rodeos, and not to come home with a hair on my shoulder that doesn't match my horse's mane. I promise to always give you the best eight seconds of my day."

"You've got yourself a deal, cowboy."

"What about the HPD?"

"They'll just have to learn to get along without me. I gave them my all while I was with them. Now I plan to be far too busy loving you and taking care of Kimmie, at least for now. That's not to say I might not talk Sheriff Garcia into hiring me one day in the future."

"I can live with that."

Cannon pulled her into his arms and when he touched his lips to hers, she knew she was home to stay.

Their pasts had shaped them and the good and the bad would always be part of them. But their love would guide their future. It would be one ecstatically glorious ride.

* * * * *

"I'll do whatever it takes to protect you. That much is true. This case has been hell."

The weariness in his eyes caused her heart to stutter.

"I need to know you're not going to disappear on me again."

"You have my word."

If only she could be certain. "You know I love you."

"Then, believe in me. This is different."

"How? What's different this time?"

"I know what's at stake."

"But you're hiding something now."

She steadied herself for the lie.

"You're right."

If she hadn't been sitting, his admission would've knocked her off balance.

"I can't tell you everything, but as soon as this is over, I will. You have no idea how much I need you. I need to know you have faith in me."

She answered with a kiss and a silent prayer he'd come back alive.

GUT INSTINCT

BY
BARB HAN

MILLS & BOON

Published in Great Britain 2015
by Mills & Boon, an imprint of Harlequin (UK) Limited,
Eton House, 18-24 Paradise Road, Richmond, Surrey, TW9 1SR

© 2015 Barb Han

ISBN: 978-0-263-25294-1

46-0115

Harlequin (UK) Limited's policy is to use papers that are natural, renewable and recyclable products and made from wood grown in sustainable forests. The logging and manufacturing processes conform to the legal environmental regulations of the country of origin.

Printed and bound in Spain
by CPI, Barcelona

Barb Han lives in North Texas with her husband, three beautiful children, a spunky golden retriever/poodle mix and too many books to count. When not writing, she spends much of her time on or around a basketball court. She's passionate about travel. Many of the places she visits end up in her books. She loves interacting with readers and is grateful for their support. You can reach her at www.barbhan.com.

My deepest thanks to my editor, Allison Lyons, for challenging me and making me a better writer. To my agent, Jill Marsal, for her brilliant guidance and unfailing support. To Brandon, Jacob and Tori, for encouraging me to work hard and inspiring me to dream. To my husband, John, for walking this journey side by side with me—I love you. And a special thank-you to readers, and especially my girlfriend's mom, Linda Tumino, for being so very passionate about books.

Chapter One

Luke Campbell bit back a groan. Why did Julie Campbell—correction, Julie *Davis*—have to interrupt a killer in the middle of one of his "projects"?

His ex-wife's landscaping business had brought her to the doorstep of one of the most devious serial murderers in Luke's career. A knot tightened in his gut as he pulled in front of her small redbrick town house in a North Dallas suburb, the one they'd shared, and parked his truck.

An emotion he refused to acknowledge kept him from opening the door and stepping into the frigid night. How many times had he wished he still lived in that house after he'd come home from active duty a wreck? How many times had he prayed he could go back and change the past since then? How many times had he missed the feel of her long silky legs wrapped around him, welcoming him home? *Too many.*

Hell, he wasn't there for a reunion. She was in jeopardy, and his job was to protect society from national-security threats and major criminals. Keeping her safe was the least he could do after the way he'd hurt her.

He stepped into the crisp evening air.

A young detective with a thick build and sun-worn face approached. "Evening, Special Agent Campbell. Not sure if you remember me, but I worked the Martin crime scene earlier."

"Detective Wells. Thank you. I appreciate the call." Luke shook the outstretched hand in front of him.

"I wouldn't normally bother you with something like this. My boss thought you'd be interested."

The young guy reported to Detective Garcia. Garcia's judgment was dead-on. "What do you have?"

He waved another detective over. "This is Detective Reyes."

Luke shook hands with the detective.

"Show him what was taped to Ms. Davis's window earlier," Detective Wells said.

The officer used tongs to hold out a standard-size piece of white paper. The words *I hope you enjoy your dance with the Devil. Be in touch soon, Rob* were handwritten.

"Whoever wrote this has good penmanship." Luke noticed. He took note of the capitalization of the word *Devil*. The tension between his shoulder blades balled and tightened as he reread the name. His killer, Ravishing Rob, never left a clue as to whom he would target next. If this was him, why would he change his M.O.?

One reason came to mind. Anger. Rob was meticulous. Julie had interrupted his ritual killing, which he'd described as more of a turn-on than sex. That might be enough to trigger a variation.

Luke couldn't ignore another possibility. This could be a copycat. Julie's picture had been splashed all over the news and internet.

Then again, Julie had black hair just like all Rob's targets.

He examined the neat print. Cursive would give more clues to Rob's personality. With his high IQ he was smart enough to know that, too, which made the capitalization of *Devil* even more poignant. "Whoever wrote this took his time."

Luke pulled an evidence bag from his glove box and pointed at the note. "I'll send this up for analysis."

The detectives nodded.

"Can you spare one of your uniformed men for the night? I'd like someone to keep watch on the alley behind her house."

"Sure thing," Detective Wells said. "I made some notes after interviewing Ms. Davis. Do you want to take a look?"

"Absolutely." Luke studied the page. He focused on the word *boyfriend*. The knot tightened in his gut. The thought of another man's arms wrapped around Julie ignited his possessive instincts. He still wanted her, needed her. Those selfish emotions had caused him to stay at the town house to be near her when he'd returned from Iraq a broken man. The front-row seat he'd had to her pain—the hell he'd caused—when he pushed her away day after day had forced him to man up and leave before he permanently damaged her. Intelligent and beautiful, she deserved so much more than him. He glanced up at the detectives who were waiting for his response to the report. Not wanting to give away his bone-deep reaction to her, he skimmed the rest and handed it back. "Good information. Send my office a copy of the report when it's filed."

Detective Wells gave a satisfied smile. "I'll keep a man outside tonight. Let me know if you need anything else."

"Will do." Luke turned and walked toward the house. A thought stopped him at the base of the stairs. What if she wasn't alone?

The detective's notes said she'd been dating a dentist on and off. Was he here?

Davis had been her maiden name, which meant she was still single. Even so, she might be *on* with the dentist again. After the day she'd had, he might be there with her in Luke's house. *Old house,* he corrected, ignoring the all-too-real tug of emotion at seeing the place again.

Taking the couple of steps to her porch in quick strides, he clenched his fists.

The thought of Ravishing Rob targeting Julie didn't do good things to Luke's head. He knocked on the door and his chest squeezed as he thought about seeing her again.

The solid hunk of wood swung open, and suddenly, there she was, his ideal combination of beauty and grace, staring at him with a shocked look on her face. He could see those long legs where her bathrobe split, her taut hips where the robe cinched. A hunger roared from deep within him. The reality of why he was there chased it away.

Her amber eyes stood out against pale skin. Even red-rimmed and puffy, their russet-coppery tint was every bit as beautiful as it had been the last time he'd seen her. Her shoulder-length hair was still inky black. His fingers itched to get lost in that curly abyss again. Muscle memory, he decided. Besides, the frown on her face and stress in her eyes said he was the last person she wanted to see.

Under the circumstances, he was her best bet.

She opened her mouth to speak, but her ringtone sounded. "Dammit. Hang on."

Bad sign. She only cursed when she was hanging on by a thread.

"May I?" He motioned for permission to enter.

Her gaze narrowed, but then she nodded and turned her back to him. She spoke directly into the phone. "I'm okay. No. I promise. You don't need to come over right now. I'll see you when you get off work."

Was she talking to her boyfriend? The last word stuck. Tasted bitter as hell, too.

One step inside and he almost lost his footing. A wave

of nostalgia slammed into him. The furniture was in exactly the same spot as when he'd left. The coffee-colored leather sofa against the wall to his right. The flat-screen directly across from it mounted on the wall to his left. He could see all the way to the back door from where he stood. Same black pedestal dining table with avocado-green chairs tucked around it. The place looked completely untouched, except all the pictures of the two of them had been removed. She'd probably enjoyed stomping on the frames.

The town house might've looked the same, but it had a different air. Funny how out of place he felt in what used to be his own home.

He folded his arms, parted his feet in an athletic stance and stood next to the door. He wasn't there for a reunion. This was business. And no matter how much Julie looked as if she'd rather crawl out of her skin than be in the same room with him, he had a job to do.

She closed the call and whirled around on him, still wearing her angry expression. There was something else in her eyes there, too. Hurt? "Why did they send *you*?"

"I've been tracking this guy for the past two years. He's my case." He intentionally withheld the part about Ravishing Rob being the most ruthless killer Luke had come across so far in his FBI career.

Her eyes narrowed to such slits he couldn't figure out if she could see him anymore. Then again, she probably wanted to block him out altogether, and he couldn't blame her. She'd pleaded with him to stay, but he couldn't stand watching her pain when he had no way to heal either one of them.

With all the daggers shooting from her eyes, he couldn't tell if she was using anger to mask other emotions. Hurt? Fear? Regret?

"There's no one else they could've sent?" The hollow sound in her voice practically echoed.

"I'm afraid not."

"So the note's from him? You're sure?"

"I need to get a little more information from you to help me decide." Even though she'd already given her account to police and he'd read the jacket, he needed to hear her words. He needed to know what she thought she saw. Maybe she'd remember something that could help put this monster away or help Luke figure out if it was a copycat. "Tell me what happened when you arrived at the scene of the murder this morning."

She shivered, looked lost and alone. "My client Annie Martin wanted to meet with me to discuss landscaping after her new pool was installed. I brought a rendering with me and planned to give my presentation. It was a big project that would start in the spring, so I broke all the planting down into zones." She glanced up at him curiously as if she realized he didn't know the first thing about plants or landscaping, or care. "Sorry, I'm babbling. I'm sure you didn't come here to talk about the details of my business."

"I did," he said quickly. He covered a crime scene the same way, broke it down on a grid. "I want to hear everything even if you don't think it's important. You never know what might spark a memory. Something you didn't think of before when you talked to the police." His hopes she'd be more comfortable talking to him had diminished the second he saw her. He wanted to ask her how she was doing, but decided not to, even though he found he still really wanted to know, needed to know. He'd left things broken between them, and thoughts of the sadness in her eyes every time she'd looked at him still haunted him. Outside of this case, he had no right to know anything about her. Why was he already reminding himself of the fact?

"As soon as I pulled up to her house, I heard a noise. Like a muffled cry or something. I couldn't make it out for sure. She'd asked me to come around back in case she was with contractors for the pool, so I ran to make sure she was okay. I thought maybe she tripped or was hurt. But there was no one out there. She screamed again and I ran to the front door. Someone bolted from around the side of the house about the same time. He killed her, didn't he?"

He locked gazes with her and wished like anything he could protect her from the truth. He felt pained that she'd had to witness this and his heart went out to her. "Yes. You get a good look at him?"

"No." She hugged her arms to her body. "I didn't see anything. By then I heard an awful sound coming from inside. Sounded like an animal dying." She shivered.

He pulled out a pad and scribbled notes. Not that he needed a piece of paper to remember the details of their conversation. His memory was sharper than a switchblade. He needed something to look at besides her fearful eyes. Old instinct kicked in and he wanted to maim the person who'd made her feel that way, offer comfort she would certainly reject. "What happened next?"

"You want to sit down?" She moved to the couch and sat on the edge. She clasped her hands together and rocked back and forth. "It was bad, Luke."

The sound of his name rolling off her tongue was a bitter reminder of the comfort and connection he hadn't felt in a long time. He took a seat next to her but not too close.

Tears spilled down her cheeks. "I don't want to think about it again, let alone say the words out loud."

"I know how hard this is." Every muscle in his body tightened from wanting to reach out and comfort her. He didn't want to press further, but the information he gained could mean saving her life. "It's important you tell me everything. Do you want a cup of tea or something?" He made a move to stand.

"No. I'm fine." The uncertainty in her words made him freeze.

"Anything else you can give me might save another woman from going through this."

"We both know he's going to come after me next." Her voice shook with terror.

"I'm not certain it's him yet. Besides, I'll catch him first."

The suggestion of depending on him for anything after the way he'd hurt her set her eyes to infernos. "I didn't ask you to come."

"This is my territory. My guy. I know him better than anyone else."

"I didn't even know you were FBI." The exasperation in her voice made him clench his fists involuntarily.

"I didn't think it was appropriate to send you Christmas cards after your lawyer sent me papers." It was a low blow and he regretted saying the words as soon as they passed his lips. After all, he'd been the one to leave and force the divorce issue.

She looked straight through him. "I lost track of you after…"

This wasn't the time to talk about their past. It complicated the situation. He was professional enough to look beyond shared history and concentrate on doing his job. He focused his gaze on the opened laptop on the coffee table. There was a picture of Julie at the crime scene beneath the banner Breaking News. Damn. Another reminder that she'd been placed right there for the killer or any other lunatic to see.

The last time the local newspaper printed a story with the headline The Metroplex Murderer Strikes Again, Rob went off. He'd left a message on Luke's cell complaining about how common that made him seem. Luke still hadn't figured out how the man got his number. The man calling himself Ravishing Rob—someone who captivated and then decapitated—had done his research. Efforts to trace the call were futile. He'd used a burn phone. Rob was thorough. He also knew how to play the media.

Reporters had their uses. In this case, they might've issued Julie a death warrant. "You said earlier you didn't get a good look at him. Any idea as to general information like height? Build? Race?"

She shook her head. "I was so horrified. The whole thing shocked me. One minute I was planning to meet a client, like usual, and then I thought the worst-case scenario was that I'd walked into a robbery in progress. The next thing I know, I'm staring at a person whose throat had been slit. I'll never forget her eyes, pleading." She shivered again and tears streamed down her cheeks.

Luke had to grip the pencil tighter to stop himself from wiping them away. He didn't like seeing her cry. He'd seen those tears enough for a lifetime. If it didn't mean saving her life, he'd stop questioning. "When did you find the note?"

"This evening. I'd just gotten home from spending the day at the police station answering questions."

"What time?" he pressed. She might not have gotten a good look at Rob. Rob didn't know that. The reason he'd given himself the nickname Ravishing Rob churned in Luke's thoughts as he sat next to her. Rob had said he charmed his way into his victims' homes or cars before taking them hostage, torturing them and then beheading them with surgical precision. The bastard would never get the chance with Julie, no matter how much swagger he thought he had.

"I'm not sure. All I wanted to do when I first got home was take a shower and get out of those clothes I'd been wearing. I ate dinner alone, a bowl of soup. I decided to slip out and check the mail…and that's when I saw it."

He already knew she'd showered. The smell of her pineapple-and-coconut shampoo filled his senses when he breathed. That she'd eaten alone soothed a part of him it shouldn't. He scooted back and scribbled approximate times on his notepad. "Did you see any cars?"

She shrugged noncommittally, leaning into him for support. The vulnerability in her amber eyes ripped right through him. Damned if the past didn't come flooding back all at once, reminding him of old times they'd shared and the feelings he missed.

He had to remind himself their history wasn't the reason she was leaning on him now. She was scared.

"I'm not sure. You know how this street is. There's always someone parked out there. I didn't pay attention." She tapped her hand on her knee.

"I need you to think."

"I said I didn't know," she barked in the way she did when her nerves got the best of her.

Everything about her body language said she'd just frozen up on him. Fear could paralyze victims. Once the shock wore off, she'd forget. As it was, he had very little to go on. Anything she could give him might paint a more detailed picture, save her life. The profiler had said Rob probably kept something from each of his victims and liked to hunt. A saw was his favorite weapon, but he used guns when necessary to kill them before cutting their throats. He was also a perfectionist. Rob was most likely educated, a collector, and he had weapons. "Dammit, Julie. This is important."

"Don't you have anything from the scene you can use to figure out who it is? Hair sample? DNA?"

"Doubt it. The house is being combed, but I'm not expecting the crew to find anything. This guy's careful, meticulous. Even though you interrupted him, he had the presence of mind to ensure he didn't leave a witness." He didn't tell her the guy normally cut off the heads of his "projects," as he called them. Or about the half-open carton of orange juice they'd found sitting on the counter. Since Rob wasn't able to bleach his victim this time, maybe he'd left behind a print. Doubtful, but Luke hadn't given up hope completely. "A rookie was first on the scene. That doesn't help. I just came from there. If there was evidence, which I doubt, it's most likely gone." He stabbed his fingers through his hair. "Can you think of anything else? Anything different. Doesn't have to be about what you saw. Could be anything about the visit."

Julie's gaze widened. "I was supposed to meet with her on Thursday. She changed our appointment last minute."

"Did you mention that to the police?"

"No. I didn't think about it until just now."

Bingo. New information. "Did she say why she moved the appointment?"

"No. She sent me a text asking if I could come a day early. Said something came up last minute and she needed to leave town right away."

"How long did you have the original appointment on your calendar?" This guy watched his "projects" carefully. Hacked into their computers. Studied their movements. He knew them as intimately as he could without ever having met them face-to-face. At least in this case, he wasn't monitoring her phone.

"Weeks."

Must've been the change in schedule. Damn, if Julie

had just kept the original appointment she'd be in the clear. This guy didn't like an audience. He was most likely planning a way to finish his interrupted work…on Julie. Then again, any crazy with internet access could be targeting her right now. Luke glanced around. "How safe's the neighborhood?"

"I had an alarm installed after you left…"

He'd noticed the keypad earlier. "I think it's best if you stay with a friend for a while."

"I've already thought about that. I have someone coming over later to stay the night."

"Who?" He told himself the only reason he'd asked was to make sure it was someone who would have her back if the killer decided to strike. Not that Luke planned on being far away.

"A friend."

He said a quick prayer it was a female. The thought of another man sleeping in his bed shot a lightning bolt of anger down his spine. "Does this *friend* have a name?"

"Alice."

Relief he had no right to own washed over him. Alice hated him. But she was a helluva lot better than Herb, the dentist. "What time is she coming over?"

"She works until…" Julie checked her watch. Her hand shook. "Actually, she should be getting off soon. I'll give her a call."

Before he could debate his actions, he covered her hand with his. A current he refused to acknowledge pulsed up his arm. He didn't want to offer to stay in a place that brought back so many painful memories. He couldn't count how many times they'd made love on this very couch before he shipped off. Or how cold the leather was against his skin when he slept there every night after his return.

"I doubt anything will happen tonight. He'll want time to regroup. I'll be right out front as precaution."

"All night?"

"Yes. I have an officer stationed out back, too." Luke was almost certain she wanted to poke his eyes out for ever having to look at him again. She still looked damn sexy. Her robe opened just enough for him to see she wore his old AC/DC T-shirt to bed. And since every muscle in his body screamed to reach out and touch her, he figured he'd better put a brick wall between them for safety's sake.

"With this cold front it'll be twenty degrees after the sun goes down. I can't let you do that. You'll freeze to death."

"I'll keep the heat on in my truck."

"It just seems silly for you to be out there when you could set up right here."

She must be awfully scared to make that offer. "I'm pretty certain I'm the last person you want to see. Let alone have sleeping under the same roof."

She folded her arms. He could've sworn he saw a flash of regret or sadness darken her features. "True."

He made a move to stand. Her hand on his arm stopped him. An electric volt shot through him, warming places it shouldn't.

"I thought if I ever saw you again, it would be for different reasons." Her lip quivered, but she compressed her mouth. Damn, it was still sexy when she was being stubborn.

"Yeah. Me, too. For the record, I don't like this any more than you do." Scratch that. He liked this situation boatloads less than anyone possibly could, even her. He'd be lying if he didn't admit to fantasizing about meeting up with her again once he got his head screwed on straight. This scenario had never once entered his imagination.

"Luke."

"Yeah."

"You look...better. I hope you don't mind me saying so."

He smiled and meant it. For some reason those words mattered to him.

"And you seem different now," she said. A melancholy note laced her tone.

The anger was gone from her voice completely now, but the sadness was far worse. Anger he could handle, fight head-to-head. He understood anger. Her sounding broken was a sucker punch to his solar plexus.

Her world had been turned upside down. She was reaching for comfort. He was still the same man she'd wanted to gut a few minutes ago. "Everyone changes a little, right?"

"Nope. Not everyone."

Was she referring to herself or Herb?

Reminders that he had no right to care didn't hold weight. He stood and walked to the door. "I'll check in with the officer stationed out back before I take my post."

Chapter Two

The last person Julie wanted to see after the hell she'd been through today was her ex-husband. How long had it been? Three years? Four?

Worse yet, the deep timbre in his voice still caused her nerves to fizz and her body to hum. The effect he'd had—correction, *still* had—on her was infuriating and not to mention completely out of place under the circumstances.

His expertly defined muscles on a six-foot-one-inch frame made for an imposing presence. Those golden eyes, light brown curly hair, dimpled chin and cheeks brought back memories of lying in bed long after she woke just so she could watch him sleep. Her body reacted to that.

Besides, *that* was a lifetime ago.

Her cell vibrated. She read the incoming text. Alice was on her way. *Good.*

Julie heated water in the microwave and made a cup of chamomile tea to calm herself and give her something to do besides think about her ex. Hadn't she spent enough time trying to get over him? And she was almost certain she had.

Almost.

She threw on a pair of yoga pants and curled up on the couch with the steaming brew. She was less than thrilled her ex had shown up. Even so, she wasn't stupid. He was FBI. She'd do whatever he said to stay alive.

There was some relief that he looked better than when he'd come back from Iraq. Then he'd been a shell of the once-charismatic, -vibrant and -sexy-as-hell man he'd been.

She still remembered the day she'd learned his tour was finished and he'd be coming home. She'd sat on this very couch, where they'd made love more times than she could count, and cried tears of joy.

Nothing had prepared her for the day Luke walked through that door.

She hugged the pillow into her stomach and took a sip of her hot tea.

The cool, courageous and fearless man she'd once stayed up all night talking to was gone. He looked as if he hadn't eaten or shaved or slept in weeks. His eyes were deep set. He'd been dehydrated, starved or both. He barely spoke when he walked through the door and then folded onto the couch.

His vacant expression had startled her the most.

He'd refused to talk. The only thing she knew for sure was something very bad had happened overseas. Her determination to be there for him solidified even though he gave her zero reasons to hang on. Julie Campbell didn't quit. Her father had sown those seeds years before and the crop was fully grown.

Even though Luke had shut her out completely, she was convinced she'd break through and find the real him again. The days had been long and fruitless. Then there were the nightmares. He'd wake drenched with sweat but refusing to talk about it. The slightest noise sent him to a bad place mentally—a prison, one he wouldn't allow her access to.

She held on to their relationship, to the past, as long as

she could before there was nothing left between them but sadness and distance. Then he left.

Seeing him now, he looked different but stronger.

She sank deeper into the couch.

Living on his own must agree with him.

She heard a noise from out back and fear skittered across her nerves. She told herself to calm down. There was a police officer stationed out there and Luke covered the front. No one could hurt her. She was safe. Luke wouldn't allow anything to happen to her.

Even so, a warning bell sounded inside her. She turned out the light in the living room, slipped next to the curtain and peeked out the window. Luke's truck sat out front. Empty. He should be at his post by now. Where was he?

A knock at the back door caused her to jump.

Adrenaline had her running toward the kitchen, needing to know if Luke was there.

The tapping on the door increased and intensified, causing her heart to lurch into her throat.

She forced her rubbery legs to carry her the rest of the way into the kitchen.

"Julie" broke through the pounding noise. Luke's voice gave her strength to power forward.

She cracked the door.

He forced it all the way open and pushed his way inside. His weapon was drawn as he leaned his shoulder against the door for support. His dark eyes touched hers. "Thank God you're safe."

"What happened, Luke? What's wrong?"

"He's here." He tucked her behind him.

A scuffle sounded from the alley. Luke opened the door and bolted toward it.

Julie fought to keep pace, pushing her legs until her lungs burned.

They stopped at the sight of an officer's body lying twisted on the concrete, his radio the only noise breaking through the chilly air.

"Stay right behind me," Luke instructed as he scanned the alley for a threat, his weapon leading the way. "And watch for any movement around us."

She looked everywhere but at the officer, who she feared was too quiet to still be alive. She said a silent prayer for him.

When Luke had checked behind garbage cans and gaps in fences, he moved to the injured man. He dropped to the ground, bent over the officer and administered CPR as Julie kept a vigilant watch.

Luke leaned back on his heels after several intervals of compressions. He looked at her again and his horrified expression almost took her breath away.

"What else can we do? We can't leave him."

"There's nothing we can do now. I tried to revive him. He's gone." The sadness in his voice was palpable as he called it in. He glanced at the officer's empty holster and looked around. "His gun is missing."

A sob broke through before Julie could suppress it.

"We have to go," he said, then twined their fingers.

She noticed blood on his shirt and arms. She stuck close behind him as they bolted back through her house and toward the front door, his gun drawn.

"Alice is on her way," she said.

"We'll call her from my truck and tell her to turn around. I already notified local police. We can't stay here."

By the time they got to the front door, the silhouette of a man appeared against the front window.

Luke's grip tightened on her fingers, and he leveled his weapon at the man's chest.

Julie didn't realize she was holding her breath until the

squawk of a police radio on the other side of the door broke the silence.

Luke tucked her behind him, placing his body between her and the officer, and opened the door. He pointed to the badge clipped on his belt. "I'm Special Agent Campbell, and I called for backup. Where'd you come from? I didn't hear your sirens."

"I received a call of an officer down and was told to proceed with caution until others arrived at the scene. I was nearby."

"He's in the alley," Luke said.

The officer thanked Luke, hopped off the porch and disappeared.

Several squad cars roared up the narrow street, descending on the once-quiet neighborhood in a swarm.

Relief washed over Julie. She glanced up in time to see Alice running toward them, looking panicked.

Julie let go of Luke's hand and embraced her friend on the stairs.

"What in hell is going on?" Alice demanded.

"He was here." Another sob broke through.

Alice's expression dropped in terror. "You don't mean...? How does he know where you live?"

"I don't know. He left a note on my window earlier and now a police officer is dead."

"What note?"

"I was planning to tell you about it when you got here. We weren't sure it was him before." Julie caught her friend giving Luke the once-over.

"That who I think he is?" Disdain parted her lips as her gaze stayed trained on Luke.

Julie nodded.

"What's he doing here?"

"This is his case. He's been tracking this guy for the

past two years. He's the expert, so he's in charge." Julie hoped her friend didn't pick up on the change in her voice every time she spoke about her ex.

"Well, he isn't doing a very good job." Alice spoke loud enough for him to hear.

Julie took her friend arm in arm and turned to face the street, walking down the couple of steps to the sidewalk. "You can't know how much I appreciate you for coming. I didn't realize how dangerous this was when I called you earlier. I wasn't thinking straight. You have to go."

"Wait a minute. Are you worried about that killer coming after me, too?"

"I don't know what could happen next. This whole experience is surreal and I don't want to take any chances." Julie wished she could wake up from this nightmare. Except a little piece of her felt a sense of peace at seeing Luke again. She told herself it was only because she had to know he was all right. After the way they'd left things, she couldn't let him go completely.

"I'd feel better if you stayed with me for a few days," Alice said.

"It's safer for both of us if I stay with Luke. I'm sure he'll find this guy, and when he does, I can have my life back."

"How can you stand to be around him after what he put you through?" Alice asked, incredulous.

"It's different. This is work and our past is behind us," Julie lied. One glance in his direction released a thousand butterflies in her stomach. She rationalized the only reason that still happened was because her body remembered the passion between them. Their sex had surpassed earth-shattering, world-exploding-into-a-thousand-flecks-of-light hotness. The physical had never been an issue. She'd even lured him into bed one more time before he left, hoping they could build from there. The sex blazed, but after was all wrong.

They never got closure on their emotional connection, she reasoned. At least she hadn't. He, on the other hand, looked to be doing just fine.

Maybe a part of him regretted the quick marriage?

Whatever had happened overseas could've expedited his realization they were two strangers who had jumped too quickly into a lifetime commitment. Young people were known to be impetuous with their decisions, hearts.

Alice stared intently at Julie for a few seconds that seemed to drag into minutes. Then came "Well, if you're sure."

"I am."

"Don't worry about me. I'm a big girl," Alice reassured her.

"Yeah? Well, this guy won't care what you are," Julie said. The truth cut like a serrated knife. She looked to Luke for comfort, reassurance. For now, she wouldn't stress about the fact that one glance at him stopped the invisible band from tightening around her chest. Or that his touch warmed her in places it shouldn't.

"Tell me you're not staying here tonight," Alice said.

"I'm not."

Luke motioned for her to come back toward him. He hadn't stopped watching her since she'd stepped away, looking uncomfortable the second she left.

"Promise to stay safe," she said to Alice.

The short blonde nodded and gave Julie another hug.

"This will all be over soon and we'll have lunch at Mi Cocina again. Like normal people," she said. She pulled back and saw big tears filling her friend's eyes.

"Are you kidding?" Alice asked. "After this ordeal,

we're going out for margaritas. Or maybe I'll skip the mixer and go straight to tequila shots."

Julie glanced up at Luke. He'd finished his conversation with the officers but kept his distance. He looked impatient for her to wrap things up.

"Take care of yourself. I'll be in touch," she said to Alice.

Her friend started down the sidewalk.

Luke was by Julie's side in a heartbeat. He must've noticed her shivering, not from cold but from the shock wearing off, because he put his arm around her shoulders. She fit perfectly, just exactly as she remembered. Body to body, the air thinned and then thrummed. Julie ignored the familiar rush of warmth traveling over her skin and making her legs rubbery.

"Where's your friend parked?" he asked.

Julie scanned the vehicles lining the street. "I don't see her car."

"Call her back."

Last thing Julie wanted was to witness a confrontation. "Why?"

"He's around here somewhere." He skimmed the street. "Alice!"

Her friend stopped and turned.

Luke had already flagged an officer. "Do me a favor?"

"Sure thing," the cop said.

"See to it the blonde gets into her car, locks the doors, and then wait until she pulls away." He motioned toward Alice.

The officer nodded. "Sure thing."

Luke turned to Julie and said, "You okay with staying over at my place tonight until we find a suitable safe house?"

The thought of being alone with Luke at his place for

an entire night sent a very different kind of shiver down her body. She downplayed it as her being cold. Looking him straight in the eyes, she asked, "Do you really think that's best?"

He didn't answer her. He had already started walking her toward the house. "Want to grab an overnight bag?"

She nodded. He escorted her inside, washed the blood off his hands and waited while she threw together a few items to get her through the next couple of days.

"Rob's one step ahead of me, if it's him. I don't want to let you out of my sight until I'm certain you're protected," he said low, in practically a whisper, as he walked her toward his truck.

His reasoning made sense. After the way he'd been looking at her all night, she suspected he also probably felt some sense of guilt about how he'd left things before. Maybe he could catch a killer and ease his conscience at the same time.

Maybe she'd get the closure she so desperately needed.

Too many nights Luke Campbell had shown up in her dreams, charming her. If she spent the night with him, fixed the past, then maybe she'd be able to walk away clean, too. And possibly be ready to start a life with Herb. Or someone new. She doubted Herb would want to see her again after she'd told him she needed time to think.

Luke helped her into the truck and scanned the street again before he climbed into the driver's seat.

She glanced back at her once-quiet neighborhood.

People were on their porches or standing at their front windows watching the circus of lights. Police were urging them to go back inside and lock their doors. Knowing a cold-blooded killer stalked her, and seemed intent on never letting up, made blood run cold in her veins.

"Wanna scoot a little closer? You're shivering again."

"I'm fine. It's just been a long day."

He turned the heater up. "Shock's wearing off. I'm sorry this happened. If we saw each other again, I'd hoped it would be under different circumstances."

If. He'd clearly had no plans to seek her out. Why did that make her heart sink?

Because Luke was her only failure in life.

"Breathe in and out slowly," Luke said.

She did a few times. It helped calm her fried nerves. "Where'd you learn to do that?"

He shrugged, kept his gaze focused out the front window. "I took the military up on its offer to see a shrink. She was big on breathing."

Luke Campbell went to counseling? If he hadn't told her himself, she never would've believed it. "I'm shocked. You seemed so adamant about not involving doctors or having someone poke around in your head."

"I made a lot of mistakes when I came home from duty." A beat passed. "Some I could fix."

The power of that last sentence hit her like a tsunami. Perhaps he'd worked on the things he thought worth saving. Their marriage clearly didn't fall into that category. Anger burned through her. "When did you start therapy?"

"Not long before you... Doesn't matter. Point being, it helped." His tone was sharp, his words cutting.

"Before I what?" She couldn't let it go.

"Never mind." He flipped on the turn signal and then turned on the radio.

It was just like Luke to get all quiet as soon as they started talking about something personal. Hadn't that been the true failure in their marriage? He didn't trust her enough to open up.

Julie glanced in the side mirror. A white sedan turned

a little too quickly at the same time they did. "Has that car been following us?"

Luke's gaze narrowed as he checked the rearview mirror. "I've been keeping an eye on him."

"Good. I thought my paranoia was in high gear after the day I've had."

"Most people wouldn't be able to hold it together as well as you have today. I'm really proud of you." His voice was low and masculine, and it sent unwelcome sensual shivers racing through her.

She rubbed her arms to stave off the goose bumps.

"Hold on tight." He cut a hard right without signaling.

The white sedan didn't follow.

"Looks like I was imagining things. Sorry," Julie said, ignoring the electric current pulsing through her at being this near Luke again. Damn body.

"No need to apologize. He landed on my radar, too. Besides, I want you to suspect everyone and everything around you from here on out. I want you to take every precaution until I can put this whole ordeal behind you and restore your previous life."

What life? She almost said it out loud. She hadn't had much of an existence since he'd walked away.

Luke glanced at the rearview mirror again.

"The white sedan just pulled up behind us."

Chapter Three

Luke maneuvered in and out of traffic as he directed Julie to take his cell and call Detective Garcia. If this was Rob, he'd escalated to killing cops to get what he wanted, so murdering FBI wouldn't bother him.

The clue Rob had left earlier with the capitalized word resurfaced in Luke's thoughts. Nouns were capitalized. A noun could be a street name or a town. Luke thought about the word again—*Devil*. Proper nouns were capitalized, too. Could it be his last name?

Bluetooth picked up the call, and Garcia's voice boomed through the speakers. "What can I do for you?"

"I've picked up a tail. If he's not one of yours, I'm going to shake him."

"You should have a white unmarked sedan behind you to make sure you weren't being followed."

Luke glanced at the rearview mirror and caught the quick flash of headlights. "Appreciate the extra eyes. Let me know if he sees anything, will you?"

"Absolutely. I'll text any information we get. So far, he says everything looks cool. We've been interviewing Ms. Davis's neighbors. No one saw anyone suspicious around her house. Didn't hear anything, either. We'll keep on it. Any information coming in from your guys at the Martin house?"

"No word from the team. The tech guys are working on her computer. Maybe they'll get lucky and we'll get an IP address."

"That would be like Christmas morning."

"Or like seeing the Tooth Fairy," Luke agreed. "You already know about the orange juice, right?"

"He take a drink by any chance?"

"Didn't get that lucky. The container was left out half-open."

"Looks like we might have a diabetic on our hands."

"My thoughts exactly. I sent you a snapshot of the note he left behind at Ms. Davis's place. You get a chance to check it out?"

"He sure seemed to like the word *Devil,* if his capitalizing it is anything to go by. Any possibility it's an honest mistake?"

"He's deliberate. He also thinks he's too smart for us. He's been right so far. I'm hoping his arrogance will be his downfall. Any nearby towns by the name of Devil?"

"Good question. I'll have my officers check. What about a last name? We could play around with the spelling and see what comes up."

"I thought about that, too. We'll have to investigate any and all Devils in the state, plus variations. See if there are any men in their early thirties in the family. Wouldn't hurt to check for street names in Dallas, too."

"Consider it done," Garcia said. "I'll keep you posted."

Luke said goodbye and ended the call. He and Garcia had mentally connected the first time they met. They thought alike and had mutual respect for one another. The detective was a good ally to have.

Luke glanced at Julie. She gripped her elbows. "We'll get a detailed report from the evidence response team soon.

The suspect didn't get to follow his usual routine this time, so maybe he left something behind we can tag him with."

"Let's hope."

Luke needed more than optimism to find Rob.

A miracle would work.

Or just a good old-fashioned mistake on Rob's part.

Luke drove into the garage of his town house and parked. "My place isn't big. There's a decent kitchen, and coffee's always stocked."

She half smiled the way she did when she was nervous.

"Right. I forgot you don't drink coffee. Sorry, I don't have any tea."

"I drink coffee now. I only drink tea at night to help me sleep."

He cocked an eyebrow at her, remembering when he'd tried to get her to taste his and she had to hold her nose to get close. "Since when did you start drinking coffee?"

She shrugged. "I missed the smell."

He didn't know what the hell to do with that, so he took off his bloodstained pullover, discarded it and took her on a tour. He walked her through the downstairs, which had a similar layout as her place—shotgun style. "My sisters helped pick out the furniture. It's pretty basic."

"It's nice."

Why did those two words lift the heavy weight bearing down on his shoulders since the day he'd walked out? He decided to ignore it and move on.

"By the way, I thought FBI agents wore dark suits and starched white shirts."

He glanced down at his camo pants and black V-neck T-shirt. "Only the ones on TV. This is pretty standard-issue when we're combing through a crime scene."

"That where you were when they called you?"

He nodded. "I would've been by your place to talk to you tonight anyway."

Upstairs, he brought her to the guest room and stepped aside to let her lead the way. "This is where you'll sleep. I'm right next door if you need anything."

She swallowed hard, and he tried not to notice.

"I'm sure I'll be fine."

The fact that only a thin wall would separate them forced its way into his thoughts. "There's not much more than a bed in here, as you can see, but my family says it's comfortable."

"How are Meg and Lucy?"

"Fine. Meg just had a baby." It pleased him that she remembered his sisters.

Surprise widened Julie's amber eyes. "She's married?"

Being with Julie made the past few years fade away. He realized a lot had happened since they'd last spoken. "She's all grown up now with a family of her own."

"Did she have a boy or girl?"

"A boy."

"Another fine Campbell man," she noted. The pride in her tone caused Luke's chest to swell.

"He's an Evans, but, yeah, he'll always have Campbell blood running through him." He absently rubbed the scruff on his face. "He already acts like one of us. He's taken over their lives."

"Then she married Riley." A melancholy look overtook her otherwise-exhausted expression. "I wish I could've been there. Your sisters were always kind to me. I can't even imagine your gran's reaction to the news. She must be so proud."

"She's beside herself, all right. You know how she is. We had a big barbecue to celebrate the day he came into the world." He smiled, and a little bit of the tension from the day subsided.

"Mind if I ask his name?" She sat on the edge of the bed, folded her hands in her lap and beamed up at him.

"Henry, but we call him Hitch for the way he hitched a ride in all of our hearts." For a second, time warped. There she sat on his guest bed, wearing the AC/DC T-shirt she'd stolen from him. She'd claimed he'd broken it in for her. Conversation was easy, just like old times. He leaned against the doorjamb. Luke forgot how much he missed talking to his wife. *Ex-wife,* a little voice inside his head corrected.

As much as he wanted to stay on memory lane a little longer, he couldn't afford to get sidetracked for so many more reasons than just this case. "I should check in and see what the team has come up with. I'll be downstairs if you need anything."

Her chest deflated. "Okay."

The image of Julie on his bed in his nightshirt stirred an inappropriate sexual reaction. Luke changed his plan and headed to the shower.

The blasting cool water went straight to his throbbing midsection. He folded his arms above his head and braced himself against the wall, allowing water to cascade down his back. He closed his eyes and concentrated on the case.

A distraction right now was about the worst thing. He needed to keep a clear head and his thoughts off those long silky legs of hers. Of course, his body screamed accomplishing that feat would be easier said than done with her under the same roof.

A serial killer wanted to stop her heart from beating, he reminded himself.

He let the thought sit for a minute, bearing the full weight of the returning rock.

The shower helped him refocus. Luke toweled off and threw on boxer shorts and a T-shirt.

Downstairs, he made a sandwich and then booted up his laptop. Skimming through two hundred–plus emails, he took a bite and chewed.

The first email he opened was from the leader of the evidence response team. Preliminary data didn't give them much to work with, other than the orange juice. They'd combed the place in a grid, as per standard operating procedure. Nothing stood out. Didn't seem to help that he hadn't had time to spread bleach everywhere, and especially on the victim. They'd pulled carpet fibers anyway. They'd taken photographs and diagrammed the scene. If they found anything useful, Luke would be the first to know, the team leader promised.

Luke scanned emails for Garcia's name or anything from tech.

Nothing yet on either count.

His cell phone buzzed. He moved to the table and retrieved it.

There were eight texts. They must've come in while he was in the shower. He scrolled through them and stopped at Garcia.

His message said there were no cities or residents named Devil in the state of Texas. But there were twenty-four people in Texas with the last name Devel.

Luke texted Garcia. Excellent. We can split the list and start from there.

Garcia pinged back immediately. I'll email the names and addresses.

Luke replied. I'll take the bottom half.

He thumbed through the rest of his messages. Most were from his family. There was a new picture of Hitch. A pain hit hard and fast looking at the little boy's round cheeks and toothless smile. For a split second, Luke wondered if his and Julie's baby would look like his nephew.

Shaking off the thought, the ache in his chest, he moved to his laptop.

In the system, he pulled up the email from Garcia and scanned all twelve names. He printed the list. Three were female. He'd pay them a visit anyway in case one had a brother, husband or father sharing the name. He put a question mark by their names.

One Devel was dead. He crossed out that entry. Eight names drew more interesting possibilities. Two weren't far. They lived in Addison and Dallas. The other names came from Austin, San Antonio and Houston. He could drive a circle. It would take only a couple of days max to investigate everyone on his list.

They'd start tomorrow.

Since both of his brothers worked in law enforcement, a U.S. marshal and a Border Patrol agent, Luke sent the list to them, as well, asking for background checks, paying special attention to anyone in the medical field.

The stairs creaked and Julie stepped into the room. "Just wanted a glass of water. Hope that's okay."

"Help yourself." He motioned toward the kitchen. Being around her, especially at night, made him want things he shouldn't. He kept his gaze focused on the monitor, where it belonged.

She poured her drink. "Not sure if I can sleep just yet. Mind if I sit?"

"Not at all," he said, but his brain protested. If she knew how his body went on autopilot sex alert every time she was near, he wondered if she'd run. He also wondered if she still made that sexy little groan when he traced his finger behind the back of her knee.

She took a seat across the dining room table from him. "Find anything interesting?"

He glanced up and his heart squeezed. "Not yet. Garcia sent a list of names. We're going on a road trip tomorrow to investigate a list of people who have a last name spelled *D-e-v-e-l*."

"How'd you get that name?"

"From his note. He capitalized the name Devil. We ran variations and this is the best match."

"Sounds promising."

"Might not be anything." They were playing probabilities. The real reason the letter *d* had been written in uppercase could mean something else entirely. Yeah, a copycat. Or Rob could simply be playing with them, waving that big IQ like a you're-an-idiot flag.

She took a sip of water.

He didn't want to get her hopes up, considering they had little to go on. "We don't know if it'll lead anywhere just yet." He looked into her amber eyes and saw that the color had deepened, the way it did when he brushed his lips across hers. Damn.

What time was it?

He glanced at the clock, needing a reality check.

"It's well after midnight," she said, her voice almost a whisper.

"We need to get on the road early tomorrow. I was hoping we could leave by six."

She gasped. "In the morning?"

He chuckled. She'd never been an early bird. Then again, he wasn't, either, when he'd had the chance to lie in bed with her, hold her, kiss her. He could lose an entire day with her in his arms. Nothing else mattered but the two of them, being together. Hell, they'd missed more than a few meals in favor of staying in bed. The war broke him of needing sleep. Broke him of a lot of other things, too.

Or maybe just broke him.

She drained her glass. "Guess I'll head upstairs."

"You want to take something to read?" he asked, remembering how she'd said it helped after he'd been deployed.

The reference didn't go unnoticed by her, as evidenced by her half smile. "I'll be okay. Thanks, though. I didn't think you remembered any of that stuff."

How could he forget? She was all he had thought about when he was locked into that hole in enemy camp.

His gaze touched hers and electricity fired through him when their eyes met. His growing erection tightened at what else he recalled about her body. "It's no big deal."

Her smiled faded too quickly as she disappeared up the stairs. "Okay."

He silently cursed himself for hurting her.

No. It was important to put some emotional distance between them. He was sliding down that slippery slope of needing her more than air again. And he'd only disappoint her.

This time, he'd be selfless. He wouldn't drag her into his crazy world only to destroy her. No matter what it cost him personally.

An hour slipped by before he looked at the clock again. He'd mapped their route and caught up on a few emails.

Checking on Julie was for work, he told himself as he walked upstairs and stood outside her door.

A muffled scream pumped a shot of adrenaline through him.

He burst into the room. "Julie?"

Chapter Four

Luke shot through the door. "I'm here."

Julie sat bolt upright. Fear seized her lungs as the image of her client's slit throat stamped her thoughts.

Her heart raced, tears streamed, and she immediately did what she knew better than to—reached for Luke.

He was already there at her side, kneeling by the bed.

She folded into his arms, sobbing.

"You're safe. I got you," he soothed. He whispered more comforting words that wrapped around her like a warm blanket.

She pulled back. "I'm sorry. I had a bad dream. I'm fine now."

"You're drenched. Hold on." He hopped up and disappeared around the corner.

Water ran in the hall bathroom.

Returning with a cool wet hand towel, he pressed it to her forehead as he sat on the edge of the bed. "This should help."

A shiver raced through her when his finger grazed her cheek. Her pulse sped up another notch.

"Better?"

She nodded. When did he get so good at comforting others?

Whenever it was, she was grateful he was there. Dealing

with this by herself was unthinkable. Then she reminded
herself that Luke was the one who'd walked out.

And yet, her body remembered his touch—the way his
finger grazed the back of her knee, sending a sexual current rippling through her. Naturally her body would remember, react to him being this close. Didn't mean she
wanted to peel her clothes off and let those strong arms
wrap around her naked body.

Did it?

"I'll be okay." She took the hand towel from him and
used it to cool the back of her neck. "What time is it?"

He retrieved his cell from the next room. "Two-thirty."

There were dark circles under his eyes. He rubbed the
stubble on his chin.

"You haven't slept, have you?"

He shook his head and then stabbed his fingers through
his curly hair. "Guess time got away from me. I mapped
out our route for in the morning."

Even with his bloodshot eyes and stray locks, he was
a beautiful man. He'd laugh at her if she said it out loud,
but he was beautiful. "Can you survive on less than four
hours of sleep?"

He bit back a yawn and smiled, revealing a peek at his
dimples. "Yeah."

What would happen if she tried to rest again? The thought
of closing her eyes didn't do good things to her imagination.
The nightmare had felt so real. And yet, depending on Luke
wasn't a good idea, either.

"You don't have to babysit me. I'll be okay," she said,
more so trying to convince herself.

"You had a nightmare."

"I saw her…right before she… That image…her eyes…
will haunt me the rest of my life."

"Wish I had some magic formula to make it all go away."

"Me, too."

"The old saying is true. Time helps. Gives perspective. Dulls the pain."

"So does a good shot of whiskey." She tried to make a joke. Lighten the mood. As it was, she would jump out of her skin if a bunny hopped out of the corner.

"Tried that, too. Doesn't work. Only makes it worse. Then you lose everything important to you." His voice was husky, low.

Was he talking about her?

"I don't run away from things that go bump in the night, Luke. I know how to stick around."

"That what you think I did? Run?"

She needed to get him out of the room because the pain in his words was a presence between them. He sounded vulnerable and she wanted to comfort him. *Her.* Comfort *him.* What a joke. He was the one who'd disappeared on her. He'd ended their marriage.

"Doesn't matter. It's history. I'll try to get some rest. If not, I'll read or something. Not like you being next to me will make much of a difference. I already know you'll leave when I need you most." She was trying to frustrate him into leaving her alone. Because, honestly, if he offered to curl up with her right then, she'd jump at the chance, which wasn't her brightest idea.

Instead of fighting back, he bent forward, clasped his hands together and rested his elbows on his knees. "I deserved that."

A knife through her heart couldn't have hurt any less than seeing the haunted look on his face. He'd been through hell in Iraq. Came home a wreck. But inside, he was always a good man.

She bit back a curse. "Luke, I'm sorry. I shouldn't have said that."

"It's okay." He didn't look at her. His gaze intensified on a patch of carpet at his feet. "I can't change the past, but I'm here now. I want to help. I don't mind keeping you company. You've been through the wringer today."

"I must look washed-out, too." The thought of him sticking around sounded a hundred warning bells inside her. And yet, it was Luke. *Her* Luke. The man who'd once made her chuck all her rules and live in the moment. Truth be known, it was the only time she'd truly felt alive.

"Not at all. You're beautiful."

Hearing him say those words made her body hum and her thighs warm. Did he see the sexual desire flushing her cheeks? "Can I keep the light on?"

"Of course you can." He repositioned himself on the bed next to her, stretched out his more than six-foot frame and linked his fingers behind his head. "Remember when scary movies used to keep you up half the night?"

"True. I always made you change the channel." She laughed, relieved at the break from her internal struggle.

"Because you didn't want the bad stuff to be the last thing on your mind before you went to sleep."

He remembered? Her heart squeezed. She had to remind herself not to get too enthusiastic. He might recall a few details from their past, but they wouldn't be together right now if a serial killer hadn't set his sights on her.

The bottom line? Luke had left and hadn't looked back.

"We could go downstairs and turn on the TV for a while." He took her hand in his. His was big and strong.

Thoughts of the two of them, up late, entwined on the couch eating pizza, popcorn and anything else that was in the kitchen after spending half the night making love assaulted her. Not a good time for that memory. Especially not with him this close—so close all she had to do was move a little bit to the right in order to touch him. "You need some sleep."

He repositioned on his side, facing her. "What I need can't be found with my eyes closed. They've been shut too long already."

Logical thought screamed for her to bolt, to get a grip on her out-of-control emotions—damn dangerous emotions that were on a runaway train aimed for a head-on collision. Because, for a second, it felt as though nothing had changed between them.

Time machines didn't exist.

There was only here and now.

"I wish it were that easy, Luke."

His hand came up to her chin and lifted her face until her eyes met his. "I'm not asking forgiveness. I'd be an idiot not to realize I'm too late. I would like a shot at friendship. Is there any chance you'd consider it?"

Her heart raced when he was this close, flooding her with doubts.

They'd jumped into a relationship with both feet first last time around. Hot, sexy feet. But feet first had turned into a nosedive toward unimaginable pain. She needed his protection and professional skill, so there was no way to get out of spending time with him. Could they take it slow and get to know each other? Her heart said no.

"I can try."

His smile shouldn't warm her and make her feel safe.

"Thank you." His low baritone goose bumped her arms. He leaned over and pressed a kiss to her forehead, not immediately pulling back.

Her pulse kicked up, and heat filled the small space between them. She could see his heartbeat at the base of his throat. The rapid rhythm matched hers.

"I want to stick around to help. Will you let me?"

She nodded ever so slightly.

He eased back to his position on his side, still facing her. "You should try to get some sleep."

"You, too," Julie said, her brilliant amber eyes wide. He missed everything about her—her musical laugh, the way her forehead wrinkled and lips pursed when she really concentrated, her compassion.

He'd been an idiot to let her go.

If he could go back and change the past, he would.

"Nah. I'll be all right." Her fear had ripped through him. "I'll stay here with you. If you don't mind."

"I would like that, actually."

He settled on top of the covers beside her as she curled up next to him.

If he were being honest, she was the one he thought about at night. She was the reason he still couldn't sleep over at a girlfriend's house. She was the reason he kept his heart behind a wall. And he had no one to blame but himself.

He'd made the offer of friendship, praying like hell he could handle it.

Julie had been nothing but sweet to him when he'd returned from the war a wreck. And how did he repay her? He'd pushed her away and ruined the best thing that had ever happened to him.

Minutes ticked by after she closed her eyes.

Her breathing slowed. Rhythmic, steady breathing said she'd drifted into sleep.

Being next to her again made his heart ache in the worst possible way. He'd been off balance ever since he'd ended their relationship. He'd convinced himself she'd be better off without him. All he'd done was hurt her. It was the only call he could make at the time. He'd been broken. Sooner or later, she would've seen it, too, and then what? She'd do the same thing his father had done when life got tough— abandon him so fast that four years later his head would still be spinning. There were about a half-dozen people Luke could trust. And most of them shared his last name. Plus, what if he hadn't come back from his mental prison? He would have been dooming her to a miserable life, too.

The decision had seemed like the kindest one he could make under the circumstances. Except that he hadn't considered what it would do to him.

Walking away from her had nearly torn him apart.

Even today, he was only half a man.

Watching her sleep brought back a flood of memories. The few years that had passed since then shriveled. Having her in his home made them disappear. He wasn't sure what was worse. That he'd been a jackass then or that he had her here but couldn't touch her. His fingers flexed and released. She had been better off without him.

He'd barely pulled himself out of the dark hole he'd fallen in when all but one of his brothers in arms had been ambushed, lined up and shot in front of him. Luke had lived. He'd wasted enough of his life cursing over that little twist of fate. Time to move on.

And now Julie was back in his life.

How many times in the past four years had he wanted to drive by their old place again? Hundreds? Thousands?

Hell, he avoided that entire section of Dallas unless he had no choice. Last thing he wanted was to bump into her at a gas station or store. Even though he always looked for her. Every time he had to be in their old neighborhood, he searched the faces of strangers. Hoped.

Figured living with the torment of never seeing her was his punishment for walking away. He'd never be good enough for her. Nor would he be able to give her what she deserved no matter how much his heart wanted to believe differently.

She made a little mewling sound in her sleep and burrowed into his side. Muscle memory had him hauling her against him, bringing her closer. She rolled onto her side and tangled her leg in his.

With her body pressed to him, rational thinking flew south. He didn't want to risk waking her by moving her, so he didn't. But with her leg wrapped around his and her full breasts against his body, he couldn't stop himself from growing hard. A few pieces of cloth kept them from touching skin to skin. Being this close to the woman he never stopped loving was worse than hell.

This new punishment was probably deserved, too. He let that thought carry him to sleep.

Luke woke, but didn't move. Julie was still asleep and he couldn't bring himself to rouse her. A deep-seated need to protect her drummed through him. Anger at Rob tore through Luke. His body went on full alert and his hands shook, similar to when he'd faced a stressful situation after the war.

"Luke, what's wrong?" Julie eased into a sitting position. The look on her face was a hard slap to reality.

"I'm okay."

"You most certainly are not." She folded her arms.

The old signs of PTSD hadn't reared their heads in two years. What was going on? Wasn't he over those?

This case, being close to Julie, had to be stirring up old feelings—feelings he didn't talk about with anyone. Even in therapy, he'd glossed over his pain. How did he begin to explain to Julie what had happened without reliving the whole experience in Iraq?

"Luke?" Her voice was unsteady. Worry lines bracketed her mouth. Her eyes pleaded with him to say something.

He eased to a sitting position and leaned back against the headrest, closing his eyes against the bright sun streaming through the window. There had been no need to close the blinds. He rarely had company. "What time is it?"

"Ten o'clock." Her voice was tentative, but she scooted next to him.

They were four hours past schedule. "My body started freaking out."

"Like before?" She wrapped her arms around him and put her head on his chest. "Your heart's beating so fast."

"Yeah." The urge to move lost to his need to hold Julie. His body still shook, but with her near, he could deal with it. With her snuggled against him, his world seemed right in ways he knew better than to trust.

She looked up at him with such compassion he almost decided talking was a bad idea. Except that he found he wanted to open up a little more.

"They got much worse. That's why I slept downstairs. I didn't want you to see my weakness."

"I hate what they did to you, Luke." She held tighter to him.

He encircled her in his arms, chastising himself for his momentary weakness. "What they did to my buddies was worse. At least I survived."

"Did you?" she asked quietly, the power of her words a physical presence in the room.

He guessed not. "I'm alive."

"Not the same thing as really living, is it?" Compassion was still in her eyes, but there was something else there, too. Desire?

Did she still want him?

"True. Which I haven't been doing a lot of without you." An impulse to lean forward and kiss her slammed into him.

Her mouth was inches from his. *Way to wreck a friendship before it got started, Campbell.*

He'd wait.

If and when the right time presented itself, he'd test to see if she still moaned when he captured her earlobe between his teeth. Or if she still shuddered when he ran his lips across the nape of her neck. The thought of all the other places he'd kissed didn't help his painful erection, which couldn't be more inappropriate under the circumstances. With Rob, Luke couldn't afford to let his guard down for a second.

"I'm so sorry, Luke. I wish I'd known." She shifted her position and ran her flat palm up his back.

"Sweetheart, I wouldn't do that if you plan to get out of bed this morning."

"Oh." Her eyes widened, and she smiled a sexy, sleepy smile. "That wouldn't do either one of us any good."

"I don't know. I think I'd rather enjoy it." He smiled.

A pink flush contrasted with her porcelain skin. "Me, too," she admitted. "Which is definitely why we shouldn't."

Probably true. Being with Julie in bed was never the difficult part. His erection throbbed harder. "Can't blame a guy for missing you."

"You missed me?" The surprise in her voice twisted his gut.

"Of course I did," he said into her mass of inky hair before kissing her forehead. "Why wouldn't I?"

"It seemed so easy for you to walk away. Never look back. I just figured you were done."

That was what she thought?

How did he explain that he'd left because he couldn't watch the hurt and disappointment play out in her eyes? That he'd known in his heart he would only make things worse for her?

"It was my fault."

"You said that before." She rolled over and tossed the covers off. "We'd better get going."

What did he say wrong? Everything *was* his fault. She didn't do anything to deserve the way he'd treated her.

How did he explain that he was trying to protect her by leaving? Maybe she didn't understand his reasoning, on some level he could see that now, but he was thinking of her at the time. He'd made the best decision he could.

"I thought you didn't love me" came out in a whisper.

He hauled her over to him. "I left because I loved you too much to make you sit and watch me wallow until I pulled myself together. I wasn't sure I could after what had happened overseas."

She blinked up at him, her amber eyes reaching deep inside him. She was the only one who'd affected him like that. Damn that she looked sexy and vulnerable. Did it mean something that she still wore his old AC/DC T-shirt to bed?

She pushed off him and sat up. "Isn't that what families do? They stick around and help each other through rough patches. They don't walk out when things get tough. They stay together and work through problems."

"I already apologized. I don't know what else to say about it." There was no way to make her understand. Luke had always had to be tough. Especially after his father had ditched the family. His eldest brother, Nick, had carried most of the burden. Luke had pulled his own weight, doing whatever was necessary to protect their tight-knit family. One thing he hadn't done was dump his problems on others.

Campbell boys held their own.

"Walking out on someone who loves you is just cruel."

The sadness and pain in her voice almost doubled him over. She folded her arms and gripped her elbows.

True. But walking away was still better than dragging her to the depths of hell alongside him. He still hadn't completely healed.

Before he could say anything else, she climbed off the bed and grabbed her clothes.

He didn't want to be selfish when it came to Julie. It hurt seeing her like this, but maybe it was best if they kept a little distance between them over the next few days or weeks until they wrapped this case.

Maybe the two of them together wasn't such a good thing. He had options. There were safe houses...

Luke's cell buzzed.

He picked up his phone and checked the text.

There was a picture of him and Julie on her steps from last night. His arm was around her. The photo was captioned Hope you enjoy watching her die.

Rob had been there.

Right now, Luke wouldn't have been able to think clearly if he couldn't see for himself that she was safe. Could he be there for her, protect her, and keep his heart out of it?

No choice.

Ravishing Rob wasn't forgiving. He'd set his sights on Julie.

Luke would do whatever it took to make sure Rob failed. Besides, rushing into another killing wasn't his typical style. Normally, he worked on his "projects" for weeks, sometimes months. Mistakes happened when people got in a hurry.

Could he make a slip?

Luke hoped so. He'd be right there to make the arrest. If he could get five minutes alone with the lowlife, Luke would gladly check his badge and gun at the door. Rob wouldn't be anyone's problem once Luke was finished.

The guy was thorough. And he wouldn't stop until he had Julie's head.

Literally.

Chapter Five

"Were you on a call?" Julie walked into the master bed-room dressed and ready to go wearing a pair of jeans, beige boots and a cream-colored pullover sweater.

Luke stood near the bed. He had his hand in his pocket as he stared out the window. From his profile she could see that all color had drained from his face.

"What's wrong?" She froze.

"Had to update my boss."

"Everything okay?"

"Fine." He'd dressed in jeans and a black T-shirt. His muscles stretched and thinned as he walked toward her. The fabric pulled taut across his thighs as they flexed. He was the perfect mix of athleticism and grace.

"You're sure?" She stepped aside to let him pass.

"'Course," he said, and his voice was stiff. Hurt?

How many times had she begged him to tell her what was going on before? He'd refused. And yet, this time he'd been different. He'd opened up to her a little and allowed her a peek inside. The idea of a friendship had seemed possible. So, what had suddenly changed?

All she wanted was an update on the case. What had his boss said?

Once again, Luke was holding back. Not letting her in. As much as she wanted to believe otherwise, nothing was different. Sure, he'd opened up a little. Her and Luke's relationship, trust, had inched forward. So, why was he reverting to his old ways? She could tell that whatever had gone down with his boss a few minutes ago was important.

What was that saying about teaching old dogs?

Luke's trick was to shut her out when he got emotional.

"Do you have eggs?" she asked, resigned.

He nodded as she followed him downstairs.

"We need to move to a safe house as quickly as possible." He stopped on the staircase and cocked his head sideways.

"Why can't we just stay here?" She wished they could plant themselves somewhere. His place was comfortable, and even though she didn't have anything here that belonged to her, oddly it felt like home. Their old town house had been foreign to her ever since he'd left. And yet, she couldn't bring herself to sell.

"I'm afraid not. It was late last night, so this was our best bet for sleep. I don't want to push it, though."

The wooden floors creaked downstairs.

Luke pulled his gun. His cell vibrated. He fished it out of his pocket and checked the screen.

A furtive glance toward her, followed by a narrowed gaze focused on the bottom of the stairwell, and Julie knew something bad was about to happen.

"What did it say?" she whispered.

His movement slowed and became purposeful as he wedged himself in front of her and downstairs.

She put her hand on his shoulder. "Luke. Don't shut me out again."

He handed her his phone.

The text read Come down and make breakfast for all of us. I'm here. And that bitch you're with is one step closer to getting what she deserves.

Luke took his cell from her, peeling back her white-knuckle grip slowly. He fired off several texts before easing down the stairs, weapon drawn, motioning Julie to stay behind him.

She had every intention of being glue.

A knock at the front door made her jump.

Shuffling noises were heard as Luke hopped the last couple of stairs and rounded the corner.

Julie followed. The place looked clear, save for the back door being left open.

The doorbell rang several times.

Luke closed and locked the back door after checking the powder room and announcing, "Clear."

He moved to the front door and to a waiting officer, holding his badge in full view as he opened the door.

The officer greeted him and asked permission to come inside.

Luke nodded. They swept the area one more time for safety's sake as more squad cars arrived out front.

"Anything out of place, sir?"

"No. He managed to disarm my alarm, though, and leave out the back door before I could catch him."

"I'll write a report," the officer said. He spoke into his radio then turned his attention to Luke.

"You didn't see anything outside?"

"No, sir. I heard a noise around the side of the house, called it in and vacated my post to investigate. Everything looked fine."

"The noise must've spooked him." He thanked the officer and let him out, locking the door behind him.

"How'd he get inside?" She repressed the fear nipping at her.

"A skilled burglar can bypass even the best alarm systems. There will be more police protection around this place than we need for the next few hours, but it'll be safe for now."

Julie followed Luke as he moved toward the kitchen, reminding herself to breathe through her stress.

His broad back and strong shoulders were eye level as he walked in front of her. Did he know how difficult it was not to reach out to touch him? Get lost in him? Let him be her strength?

But she'd touched that stove once.

Had the burn marks to prove it.

Wasn't the definition of insanity repeating the same mistake over and over again but expecting a different result?

Besides, seeing the man who'd lit wildfires inside her brought back all sorts of raging memories. And the very real disappointment that he'd been her only failure. Luke had been her biggest regret. And that was playing tricks on her emotions. She'd been ready to move on before. Hadn't she?

Luke stopped and she bumped into his back. God help her, but it was like walking into a brick wall with a much better view. "Sorry about that. Wasn't paying attention. Step aside. I'm sure I can whip something up. What have you got in here other than eggs?"

She moved beside him and glanced around the kitchen.

"Sit." He pointed to a bar stool on the other side of the bar.

"What? You? Cook?"

"Try not to look so surprised."

The corners of his mouth turned up in a sexy little grin. His eyes told a different story. An emotion she couldn't quite put her finger on flickered behind his brown gaze. Worry? Fear?

"Okay. Fine. Let me see what you can do, big man."
She perched on the seat.

Not five minutes later, she had a steaming cup of coffee in her hand. "Thank you, Mr. Campbell."

When she smiled after taking a sip, he shot her an I-told-you-so look.

She rolled her eyes. "Of course you can brew a pot. It's good. But I'm still waiting to be impressed with your culinary skills."

After experiencing his handiwork with an iron skillet, a handful of eggs and chopped veggies, she was too full to eat her words.

She put her hands up in the universal sign of surrender. "Okay. You got me. Where'd you learn to cook like that?"

"My sisters taught me. What can I say, I missed your cooking." He pulled a seat across the island from her and sat down with his own plate. "You really like it?"

"Not bad, Campbell." She leaned back in her seat and folded her arms after swallowing the last bite. Not wanting to get too comfortable in his home, she added, "Where are we heading today?"

"The first two stops are Addison and Dallas. We find something there, and we save ourselves a driving tour of Texas. Just give me a minute to finish eating and throw together an overnight bag. And you should bring your stuff, too. If we hit a dead end around here, we'll head to Austin next."

"Live-music capital of the world." Was he thinking the same thing she was? Their first weekend trip together had been to watch the bats under the Congress Avenue Bridge at sunset.

He nodded, picking up his plate.

"The least I can do is clean the dishes." She moved around the island to where he stood.

Luke didn't immediately move. Nor did she.

The air charged around them, electrified with sexual chemistry. She couldn't deny missing Luke. Or thinking about him. She'd dreamed about him more than she cared to admit in the past few years.

She cleared her dry throat.

He hesitated, then half smiled and walked away.

Was he thinking about all the times they'd abandoned breakfast dishes and made love on the kitchen counter? The island?

She could almost feel his strong hands around her hips, helping her move with him as he thrust deeper and deeper home.

Julie shook off the memory and turned on the faucet, trying not to think about the changes in Luke as she loaded the dishwasher.

He logged on to his laptop. His solemn expression had returned. "The crime scene was clear except for a print in the yard. The team's running analysis on the type of shoe to see if we can find anything there."

"Doesn't sound like they have much to work with."

"Unfortunately, no. I'd hoped for more this time around." He stood and motioned toward the garage door. "The print is unusual. Might give us something else to go on."

Julie followed him and buckled in. "How many people has he…?"

"Six so far."

"All women?" she asked, but figured she already knew the answer.

"Yes."

"And what he did to her…to my client… Does he do that to all his victims?"

"Pretty much." Luke backed out of the garage, watching every movement around them. "Usually worse."

He cut their heads off? A rock sat in Julie's stomach.

She sat quietly for the rest of the twenty-minute drive. As usual, I-635 was a parking lot, gearing up for the lunch rush.

He exited onto the Dallas North Tollway, then took Beltline to Addison Road. "The first name on the list lives on Quorum Drive."

"I remember when these apartments were being built. Thought this area was for young professionals."

"Our guy is smart. Profile says he's probably educated and most likely in his early thirties."

A chill gripped her spine. "Sounds like the kind of person I could walk down the street next to and never realize he's a monster."

"That's what makes guys like him so hard to track. We catch killers with a low IQ quickly."

"So, he could be young, attractive and rich?"

"Yes."

"Then why? Why would someone who has it all need to do…that…to women? Is he crazy?"

"No. Believe it or not, he's not crazy. To people like you and me he seems that way. His actions are calculated, justified in his twisted mind. This guy enjoys researching 'projects,' as he calls them. Once he identifies his mark, he studies her. Learns her daily patterns. We have at least two cases where we know he hacked into their computers."

"Doesn't that leave a cybertrail?"

"He's not stupid. Every IP we follow leads us to a dead end. So far, he's been a step ahead. But he's arrogant."

"With me, in my case, it's different. Isn't it? I wasn't on his radar before."

"No."

She sucked in a burst of air. "Then why me?"

"You fit his M.O. He targets women between the ages

of twenty-five to twenty-seven with black hair. Plus, you may have seen him and you're connected to me." Luke's hand covered hers. "He'll make a mistake and we'll be right there to catch him. He doesn't normally work like this, and that's a good thing. He's moving too fast. I'm not going to let him get to you. That's why you're here with me. I'm keeping you right by my side, where I can watch you at all times."

"I'm glad it's you and not some stranger." She smiled weakly. "No way would someone else care this much."

Guilt or whatever it was that made Luke want to give her life back didn't matter. Her safety in exchange for him being able to walk away with a clean conscience didn't seem like a bad trade.

But could she really trust him? He wasn't the first person who'd been emotionally unavailable. Hadn't her father primed her for men like Luke? Except that she'd believed he was different, had broken all her rules for him, and then he'd shut her out just like her father always had.

Freud would've had a field day.

A little piece of her protested, saying that Luke had been different. The part of her that wanted to believe in him no matter what logical evidence was presented against it. But then, emotions weren't ruled by reason.

Luke pulled into an off-street parking spot and cut the ignition. He double-checked the address on his phone. "Stick behind me."

She did.

Being with Luke brought a dangerous sense of comfort.

LUKE HELD THE door open and waited for Julie to climb out of the cab. She deserved to know what she was up against, so he'd shared case information. Her reaction left him wondering if that had been such a good idea. The part about Luke fearing for her life he'd keep close to his chest.

Luke's hands fisted.

The deranged jerk wouldn't get to her. Not as long as Luke was alive. Period.

Intel said the person in this building wasn't likely the one Luke was searching for. Chad Devel was twenty-six years old. He worked as a sous chef in a nearby trendy restaurant and had had three loud-music complaints at this address in the past six months. He'd been pulled over twice and hauled in for suspicion of driving while intoxicated. He'd pleaded out once. The other DWI case was pending.

Not exactly the kind of guy concerned with flying under the radar.

"Which building?" Julie asked. Her voice still sounded sweet to him, like waking up late on a Saturday morning in a cabin in the woods.

A quick glance at his phone and he pointed to the one on the right. "We're looking for apartment number one hundred fifty."

He'd spotted it as he'd said it. "There. Ground floor."

"Looks pricey."

"Would take someone with a good job to afford a place like this."

"Maybe even with a college degree?" She looked at him intently with those amber eyes. "Do sous chefs normally have degrees?"

"Sometimes." Luke palmed his badge and knocked on the door. Since Chad seemed to enjoy partying at night, he'd most likely still be asleep.

No one answered.

The next knocks sounded off louder, more urgently. "Mr. Devel. Open up."

"Okay, okay" came through the door.

It swung open.

A young guy with curly hair stood at the opened door. He blinked against the bright sun and shielded his eyes with his forearm. His gaze moved from Luke to Julie. "What do you want?"

"Are you Chad Devel?"

The young guy looked as if he'd just stepped out of an Abercrombie & Fitch commercial. He had on boxer shorts and no shirt. He was tall, at least six feet, with a lean runner's build. His sandy-blond hair looked windswept, as if he'd just gotten off a yacht. He rubbed his blue eyes and bit back a yawn.

Luke flashed his badge. "I'm Special Agent Campbell. May we come in?"

Surprise widened the young guy's gaze as he stood there stunned. Typical reaction.

"You didn't answer either of my questions."

"Oh. Right. Yes, I'm Chad. I haven't done anything wrong. My court date isn't until—"

"Where were you the night before last, Mr. Devel?" On first appraisal, this kid looked as though he'd grown up with too much money and free time. Yet, he had a job. Maybe Daddy had cut him off?

"Work."

Easy enough to verify. "And that is where?"

"DeBleu on Beltline close to Midway. Why?"

"May we come inside?" Luke asked again. He'd like the chance to look around. Make certain he didn't need to circle back to this guy later.

"Um, sure." The door swung open wide. "The place is a mess. Had a few friends over last night after work."

Luke stepped inside, motioning Julie to follow. "Can your boss corroborate your story?"

"Yeah. He was there. I worked with Tony and Angie, too. They can tell you where I was. They were here last night. I can give you their phone numbers if you want to check."

Luke pulled out his phone and took the information. The guy didn't fit the profile for Rob, but Luke didn't plan on taking any chances with this case.

Besides, something about Chad had Luke's radar up.

Chad's heartbeat at the base of his throat beat too rapidly. Not exactly probable cause for an arrest, but Luke didn't like it. He'd lean on him a little bit. See if he could fish any information out. He handed Chad a piece of paper and a pen. "Write your name."

He complied.

Luke studied the page. The handwriting didn't match Rob's note, which could be on purpose. Most serial killers didn't warn their victims in advance. Rob was no exception. This was all a big game to the bastard. "Where'd you go to college?"

"Here, locally. Dropped out after a couple semesters."

"Your dad work in the medical field?"

"No."

"What did you study?"

Chad's dark eyebrows knitted. "Finance. Why?"

The apartment was small but upscale. Luke could see to the back door from where he stood in the living room. There were hardwood floors, contemporary furnishings. Ansel Adams black-and-white photos hung on the walls. There were no signs of the souvenirs Rob liked to take from his victims, but that didn't mean he would keep them at his house or out in the open. Empty imported-beer bottles lined the glass coffee table. Sofa cushions were strewn around. "Looks like you had a good time."

"We did. Didn't get much sleep." Chad's gaze darted around.

Half of an unrolled cigar lay open on the glass coffee table, a common place to hide weed. Pot was small-time compared to what Luke was used to seeing. Could Chad be on heavy drugs? K2?

Possibly.

Three years on the job had Luke's interest piqued. While he wasn't there to pop the guy for a nickel bag, Luke didn't plan to share.

Chad needed to sweat, and by the looks of him, he was.

Luke moved to the coffee table, picked up the cigar and rolled it under his nose. "Cuban?"

"No, sir. Those are illegal. That one's from Venezuela." Chad shifted his weight to his other foot. A few seconds later, he did it again.

Luke focused on Chad.

"You like to hunt?"

"Not really. My dad forces us to go on a trip once a year." Chad kept chancing a look toward Julie. Luke didn't like the way Chad looked at her. Then again, after Rob's direct threat this morning, Luke was on high alert.

"Your dad live around here?"

"No, sir. California."

There was another point worth considering. Rob knew what Julie looked like. Chad didn't have a clue when he saw her. Luke had been careful to gauge the guy's reaction to her. There would have been some hint of recognition. Pupils dilated. A twitch.

Chad hadn't so much as lifted a thick brow. "You have any medical conditions?"

"No, sir. Why?"

"You don't take medicine?"

"No."

"Mind if I check your cabinets?"

"Go ahead."

Luke motioned for Julie to stay by the door as he moved to the open-concept kitchen and flipped through cabinets and drawers. No medicine bottles or telltale syringes were present. The bathroom was across the living room. The door was open to the main space. He checked the medicine chest before returning.

"Do you have any relatives in the area?"

"My mom lives in Dallas."

"That it?"

"Yeah...um...no. Wait a minute. I have a half brother, if he counts. My parents divorced when I was a kid. My dad moved out of state with his second wife. They had a kid. Got a text from him last month saying he'd moved here."

Chad's age pushed the boundaries of Rob's profile. His half brother would be even younger. "Must be nice to have family in town."

"Not really. We aren't close. He's flaky."

"That's tough when families split. You two didn't grow up together?"

Chad nearly choked. "Not on my mother's life would she stand for that."

"How come?"

"This woman and my dad had been having an affair since before I was born. Rick, my half brother, is four years older than me."

This put him at the exact age of the profile, which meant nothing if the guy was in California the whole time. Julie's eyes widened. She caught on to it, too.

If the brother had just moved here, he wouldn't show up in any databases yet. "Those hunting trips you mentioned."

"Yeah?"

"Your brother into them?"

"He likes them a hell of a lot more than I do. Why?"

"Do you have contact information for Rick? I'd like to speak to him."

"Um, yeah. I think. It would be on my phone. Hold on." Chad moved to the bar separating the living space from the kitchen and started shifting stacks of junk. Mail, papers, books were tossed around.

Couch cushions were next. He checked behind each one. "Oh, wait. I know where it is."

Chad disappeared into the bathroom, returning a moment later holding up a pair of jeans. He fished in the front pocket and produced his cell. Another few seconds of scrolling through text messages and he stopped on a name. He tilted the screen toward Luke. The name read Rick Camden.

"That's your half brother?"

"Yeah." Chad rolled his eyes and tossed his hair back. "His mom didn't want to give them away by naming him after my father. Turns out, the sleazy bitch worked at my dad's office."

"You have an address?"

"No. Sorry. I haven't even seen him."

The women Rob chose were between the ages of twenty-five and twenty-seven. All had black hair. Had Dad's sleeping around caused Chad or his mother to resent women?

Interesting theory. Luke made a mental note to check into Chad's mother's background, too. Female serial killers might be rare, but the few who crossed the line were vicious. Time to find out if the bloodline could use some bleach.

Of course, that didn't explain the male voice who'd phoned Luke before. Although, she might be *that* crafty. "Doesn't sound like the family recovered once their secret came out in the open." Luke could relate to the bitterness he saw in Chad's eyes at his father's abandonment. He also knew that holding on to anger was like drinking poison and expecting it to kill someone else.

Chad shook his head. "We don't exactly get together for holidays."

Luke took note of Rick's information. "This guy grew up in California?"

"Uh-huh."

The way Rob studied his intended victims didn't mesh logistically with someone who lived out of state. But with money like theirs, he could travel back and forth. Even so, Luke would follow up. He'd become the best because he was thorough.

"What about your brother?"

"Half brother," Chad corrected.

"Sorry. He have any medical conditions you know about?"

"Nah. Not to my knowledge. But then, I wouldn't really know."

"You look like your mom or your dad?"

"My mom."

"You have a picture of her?" He needed to see if Chad's mother had black hair.

Chad produced a photo on his cell phone. The image of him and his mother showed their family resemblance.

"What about Rick's mom? She still alive?"

"Yeah. She's pretty, I guess. She's thin. Has black hair."

Interviewing Rick just became a priority.

"We'll be in contact should we have any more questions," Luke said as he made a move toward the door.

"Can you tell me what this is about, at least?"

"Murder." Luke let the word hang in the air.

The guy shook as if he might unravel. Rob was so detached he'd most likely be calm, no matter what. He didn't see what he did to women as bad. In his eyes, killing them was justified.

"Look, I'm not perfect. I like to party. But I would never hurt anyone on purpose."

With his tanned face and Kennedy family–like good looks, Luke figured it wouldn't be hard to find women who wanted to party with Chad.

"Keep it that way," he said as he opened the door for Julie.

One down. Seven to go. Rick was a better fit to the profile. Too bad he hadn't lived in Texas over the past two years.

"I will, sir."

Based on the guy's fearful expression, he wouldn't be so much as jaywalking anytime soon. Chad knew how to throw a party. Was he a killer?

Luke followed Julie back to the truck with the ever-present feeling of eyes on them. He matched her stride and possessively put his hand low on her back.

A visual scan revealed nothing suspect. Chad's door was closed.

So, what was with the creepy feeling?

Chapter Six

Julie wasn't sure what to expect if she saw a killer face-to-face. Would she even know?

"You were tense in there," she said to Luke on the short walk to the truck.

"I don't like his half brother. I can't ignore the link to the Devel name. His age matches the profile. He likes to hunt. His mother has black hair. We'll know more once we talk to him." He paused for a couple of beats. "The only problem is, the killings are happening in the Dallas–Fort Worth Metroplex, and he's supposedly been in California."

She climbed into the cab of the truck and clicked on her seat belt. "Chad said his half brother doesn't have any medical problems. Isn't your guy supposed to be a diabetic?"

"Could be. Then again, he might've just been thirsty." She had picked up on that. Luke's fingers gripped the steering wheel so tightly, they turned white.

He palmed his cell and punched in Rick's number.

"Interesting."

"What is it?"

"The number's bad. It's been disconnected."

"Does that mean he left town? His brother said he wasn't stable."

"Could be. I'll have Nick check into it." He sent a text

to his brother asking for any information he could dig up about Rick Camden. "Or Chad gave us a fake number."

"He seemed like a typical twenty-year-old to me." She shrugged. "If it turns out he's the killer, I wouldn't be any good at your job."

"He could hold a grudge against his stepmother for ruining his family. Some serial killers are charming and popular, and they can start at any age."

"Oh." That last bit of information sat hard on her stomach. "He was good-looking. A woman might never know who she was dealing with until it was too late."

"That's Rob's M.O." Luke started the engine, pulled out of the parking lot and made his way back onto the Tollway.

"So he calls himself Ravishing Rob?"

"Captivates then decapitates."

A wave of nausea slammed into her as Ms. Martin's face flashed through her mind. Julie bent forward to stave off the bile rising in her throat. She'd stopped him from cutting off her client's head, which hardly seemed like a consolation under the circumstances. And now he wanted hers. "What kind of monster does that to people?"

"I'm sorry. That was too much information."

She dragged in a breath. "No. It's good. I need to hear everything. Believe me, there are moments when I just don't want to know. But I have to be prepared, right?"

"Yes, but you can do this in doses. If this is more than you can handle, I can drop you at the station during the day while I investigate. You'll be safe there."

How did she tell him there was nowhere she'd rather be than with him? That she only felt truly safe by his side? "No. I'm fine. I knew this would be hard. I have to toughen up and stay informed. This might be difficult, but it's important, and I can't close myself off to all the bad things in the world. That could get me killed someday. Plus, what if you don't get back tonight? Where would that leave me?"

"Right now, let's think about something else." His gaze stayed focused on the road in front of him as he moved the pickup through traffic.

"I like it when you include me. I mean, you didn't for so long. This is a lot to process, believe me, but I'd rather know."

"And I'd rather protect you from the truth." His tone was solemn. Regret?

Did he mean now or before? Both?

"Can I ask a question?"

He nodded.

"What happened to you in Iraq?"

"War." His gaze intensified on the stretch of road in front of him. His hands gripped the wheel tighter.

"I know you went overseas, but I mean, you didn't talk about it when you came home. The guys you served with were like brothers…"

His nod was almost imperceptible.

Whatever happened must've been pretty bad. After all these years, he still couldn't talk about it. Not even after all they'd been through in the past twenty-four hours. Maybe he would never be able to share. "Whatever it was, I'm sorry."

"I hope you don't think any of what happened between us was your fault."

"It takes two people to wreck a marriage."

"No. It doesn't. It takes two people to make a good marriage. Only one to destroy it."

"If only I'd—"

He pulled the truck off the Tollway and into a hotel parking lot where he parked.

The force of his stare when he turned to face her threw her. "Believe me when I say you did nothing wrong."

Hot tears of frustration pricked the backs of her eyes. "If that were true, we'd still be married and none of this would be happening."

"I repeat, none of what happened to us was your fault." The intensity of his gaze matched the determination in his clenched jaw.

The words were like bullets through her heart. No matter what he said, it wouldn't change the fact she was a failure. Her father had drilled it into her head that Davises didn't give up. Yet, she had. "How can you say that? It takes two people to kill a relationship, Luke. If I'd been a better wife, you would've been able to confide in me. You wouldn't have walked out."

"I take full responsibility."

"They teach you that in counseling? That it was all your fault?"

"No" came out through thinned lips.

"Why, Luke? Why'd you walk out?" Her emotions were taking over, and she knew she shouldn't ask the question. But she had. Well, she'd said it. Couldn't take her words back now. Everything happening around her made her realize just how fragile life really was. One minute, she thought she was starting to figure out her next move and get comfortable in life, and then everything changed just like before.

"Because I was broken, dammit. I came back damaged. They were killed. All of them." He hung his head low.

The truth crushed down on her rib cage, making it hurt to even breathe. Based on his expression, he seemed as devastated as she felt.

"We were ambushed."

Her heart ached for him. She couldn't imagine what that would do to a person. And yet a little piece of her heart filled with hope. He was finally talking about the past. Telling her something important.

"It was my fault."

She put her hand on his arm, ignoring the pulses of electricity she'd come to expect whenever they touched. "Couldn't have been."

He got quiet.

"I wish I could've been there for you, Luke." She couldn't stop the sieve now that it had opened.

"You were perfect. I wasn't. It was my fault. Everything. I hurt you and I couldn't keep going like that. You didn't deserve to be treated like that."

"I was expendable. You must've realized we'd made a mistake. You didn't want me anymore. You left." Tears streamed down her cheeks.

He brought his hand up and brushed them away, only glancing over at her for a second then quickly shifting back to the empty parking spot in front of them. "Do you want to know how much I wanted you back then? How much I still want you?"

She nodded.

His gaze met hers as the space between them disappeared faster than she could blink.

He leaned into her and kissed her, hard, bruising, hungry.

LUKE EXPECTED JULIE to pull back or push him away. Slap him. She didn't.

When her hands came up and her fingers tunneled into his hair, urging him even closer, he battled every instinct he had to lay the seat down and unleash all the primal instincts that had built up in the years since he'd been gone. He was already hard.

He deepened the kiss. She tasted like honey and coffee with just a little bit of spearmint left over from brushing her teeth this morning.

Her lips moved against his, and he swallowed her soft moan. Awareness zinged through his body, wiring his muscles even tighter.

He thrust his tongue in her mouth, and she met his every stroke.

A niggle of conscience ate at his gut.

Her nerves were fried. She'd been through hell. She was reaching out to him for comfort…and he was crossing the line.

Oh, hell. This was one of those rare times he wished he could set aside what was right for what was right *now*.

The hurt expression on her face a few minutes ago would haunt his dreams.

He shivered then pulled back. "I can't do this."

The back of her hand came up to her swollen, pink lips. Her breathing was heavy but she didn't speak. Her gaze trained out the window ahead of her, as though she was trying to make sense of…this.

He hated hurting her again.

What was broken in him that made him assume everyone would turn their backs on him eventually?

His father?

Luke couldn't deny having his old man walk out before Luke was old enough to say the guy's name had damaged him. His family tree left leaves of betrayal scattered around the earth, which only proved to Luke that he couldn't trust his instincts when it came to love.

Then there was his first love, Chloe. The day she'd bolted was still fresh in his mind. The conversation as vivid today as it had been when they'd had it. With no money to go to college, he'd decided to join the military first. Believing what he had with Chloe was real, he'd shared his plans to save money so they could get married someday. But first, he needed to help his family get out of debt.

She didn't respond well to the fact he needed to help out back home, saying she'd expected to come first in his life. That she'd pouted had caught him off guard.

Chloe demanded he change his plans and join her at the state school she'd planned to attend in the fall. Her look of disappointment when he'd balked was still stamped in Luke's mind. An only child to wealthy parents, Chloe was used to getting everything her way.

But Luke had responsibilities. Commitments. His family had been everything to him and there was no way he'd turn his back on them.

When she couldn't convince him otherwise, she broke it off, but not before she let him know just how much he'd hurt her.

Deep down, he'd realized what he'd had with her was puppy love. Yet, it didn't stop him from licking his wounds from her betrayal or closing off another little piece of his heart to the world.

Didn't people always bolt when life got serious?

It wasn't that much longer after that when he'd met Julie, fallen hard and figured out what real love was. He'd been able to trust it while times were good. But when he came home a mess and saw disappointment in her eyes…he'd assumed she'd do what everyone else had. Walk away.

He'd preempted.

Ringtones broke through his heavy thoughts. He pulled out his cell and checked the screen. His brother Nick was calling. Good. "Did you find anything for me on those background checks?"

"Nothing helpful, I'm afraid. Most of the men on the list are too old. None had medical issues. The only person who comes close to fitting is Chad Devel, who doesn't fit your profile."

"Just left his place. Did you find anything on his half brother?"

"Nothing yet."

"His brother said he just moved to the area a month ago from California."

"And he has no idea where he lives?"

"That's what he says. Doesn't seem to be any love lost between them. The family was split by an affair. Get this— Rick's mother has black hair."

"Not exactly a saw with blood on it."

"True. I'll take any lead I can get in this case," he said wearily. "Dig around a little? See what you come up with? And will you check into his mother, too?"

"Will do. I'll be in touch."

Luke ended the call as Julie touched his arm. "What were you thinking about before?"

"Nothing," he lied, glancing around to get his bearings and register his thoughts firmly in the present. He'd hoped for something interesting to come out of the background checks. He repositioned as he scanned the area, careful to watch for anyone who might be trying to surprise them, ignoring the heat radiating up his arm from her touch. Satisfied they were safe, he settled into his seat and rubbed the scruff on his chin. "I came back a mess. You know that already. What you didn't know is that I was a POW."

"I'm so sorry, Luke." Tears brimmed in her eyes.

An overwhelming urge to lean over and capture those pink lips again assaulted him. As much as he wanted to kiss away her tears, hear her say his name over and over again when she hit the heights of sexual desire, he refused to let his hormones rule. "Beatings and starvation were a couple of their favorite forms of torture. But that just scratched the surface. They saved the worst for later."

And now she knew more than his family and the U.S. government put together. Could he tell her the rest even if he wanted to? He doubted it.

Thinking about it shot his anger level to red-hot alert. The psychiatrist had pushed him to open up and discuss his time in enemy camp. He couldn't. Not even with a trained professional. This was different. He felt less exposed with Julie.

"Did all this have anything to do with the award you hid?"

"You found that?" There'd never been any mention of it before. But then, he hadn't exactly been easy to talk to back then.

She nodded. "I didn't open it, though. I promise."

"Didn't feel like I deserved a medal for living."

Her amber eyes filled with remorse and tears and maybe just a little bit of hope.

There was no fantasy she'd take him back. And yet, for whatever crazy reason, a little piece of the armor he'd secured around his heart cracked.

"You're a survivor, Luke. Not many people can say that."

"No one deserves a medal because they kept breathing." Or for not being there for his squad when they needed him. For all intents and purposes, he'd abandoned them. Just like his own father had abandoned him. How could he live with himself? He'd lived the pain firsthand, so to inflict it on others, willingly or not, was more than he could bear.

She paused, her forehead wrinkling in the way it did when she was concentrating. "You came back so thin. And you'd stopped talking to everyone. Me, your family. You changed so much I almost didn't recognize you."

"There was nothing but anger and hurt inside me. I wanted to lash out. Fight something. Except, there you were. You represented everything good in my life. One look and I knew I didn't deserve you—would never be good enough for you."

He expected anger when he glanced at her to see if there was any possibility she could understand where he was coming from. In Luke's life, he'd learned when things got tough, people left. Instead, Julie gave him compassion.

"That's just not true, Luke. You didn't have to go through that alone."

She touched his hand. Electricity and warmth moved through him, spreading from the point of contact.

Julie. *His Julie.*

He'd asked himself a thousand times what he'd done to deserve her. Even for the short time she'd belonged to him. Never could come up with an answer.

"I didn't know how to open up. Not exactly a Campbell trait. We held our family together by taking care of things, not by moving our mouths."

"I remember how worried they were about you. Especially Gran."

"I got through it eventually." Problem was, when he came up on the other side of that dark hole he'd been in, Julie was gone. He'd pushed her away and didn't have the first idea of how to get her back. Didn't figure he could. He assumed most ships that sailed didn't come back to shore. "For what it's worth, I'm sorry."

"I know."

Luke scanned the lot. His gaze stopped at a sedan parked under the hotel canopy.

"Everything okay?"

He shot a glance toward Julie. Her brow was arched, her forehead wrinkled.

"Not sure yet."

The tension radiating from her body filled the air thickly, but she held her head high.

Why did that make him proud? He had no right to feel anything when it came to Julie.

Tell that to his body. To his heart.

He put the gearshift in Drive and eased toward the car. As he neared, the gray sedan snaked between several cars and sped off. Luke tried to navigate in the same traffic but his truck was too big.

"That car?" She pointed to the sedan.

"Yeah. There's something not right. I can feel it. Let's check it out." He put his pickup in Reverse and made a big circle around the check-in lane under the canopy of the grand hotel.

The car was gone.

Luke hooked a right turn out of the parking lot. People in a hurry didn't wait for lights to change green. They always turned right, and this guy had been in a rush.

A phone call to his boss about Rick and his mother would have to wait. Garcia needed an update, too. Luke made a mental note to do it later and moved on while he scanned vehicles.

Julie's quiet demeanor told him all he needed to know about how she was processing the events. When she was truly scared, she got real still. Fear or not, she never backed down. It was one of the many qualities he admired about her.

Two more right turns and he was on the service road to the Tollway. If the guy hit the on-ramp, it'd be all over. He could disappear into the myriad cars snaking down the road.

If Luke had been able to see a license plate, even a partial, he could call Detective Garcia and have the jerk's home address in ten minutes or less.

"There. Over there. Do you see him?" Julie's voice rose in a mix of adrenaline and fear. "Is that him?"

Luke maneuvered closer to the gray sedan. His left hand was planted firmly on the steering wheel, his right gripping his weapon. "Might be. Let's get a closer look."

The car made a quick left before he could get a visual on the driver.

At least half a dozen cars separated them.

Luke swerved in traffic and sped up. An SUV blocked his view.

Horns honked as he pushed in between cars and cut off others. "If you get a good visual, call out the license plate."

"Okay." Julie pulled her cell from her purse and repositioned in her seat, craning her neck to get a better look.

She had to be scared half to death. The sedan stayed in sight just enough to keep Luke on its tail. Although he'd love to get the license plate, it could be a fake. Whoever was driving seemed to know what he was doing, which brought him back to a point he hadn't wanted to consider but had been eating at the back of his mind all day. The killer had uncanny access to information, which he knew how to use. Another troublesome fact: the man sure knew how to hunt someone.

Even though Rick Camden was an interesting lead, Luke had to consider other possibilities, including the unthinkable. Could Rob work in law enforcement? The officer who'd appeared on the scene first at Julie's town house had disappeared a little too quickly. Was it possible that Luke stared Rob in the face and didn't know it? There had been no sirens, no squad car.

Had Rob gotten away with the crime he'd committed in the alley because he wore a uniform? A chill gripped Luke's spine.

A law-enforcement officer going rogue was one of the

worst possible scenarios. A man trained to kill wasn't a good person to have hunting Julie.

Of course, the guy wouldn't have to be currently on the force. He could be disgruntled, disillusioned, or might have been kicked off. Another possibility was that he might've flunked out of the academy and enjoyed playing cop. Of course, the more likely scenario involved someone who worked in the medical field. Even so, Luke didn't want to rule anything out.

The bastard had somehow gotten Luke's home address. He already had his cell number.

What else did Rob know?

Chapter Seven

"He's gone." Luke sighed sharply. The car he'd been following had disappeared.

"I wish I could've gotten at least a partial plate." Julie gripped her seat belt where it crossed her chest and leaned against the headrest. She sat silent for a long moment. Her forehead creased the way it did when she was concentrating, and her lips compressed into a thin line.

He could tell she was having trouble processing what had just happened. She needed a distraction. "We should think about eating lunch."

"How about that barbecue place at Preston and LBJ?" She blinked her eyes open.

How could he forget? It was their favorite. "Sounds good. Let's check it out."

"Luke."

"Yeah."

"Thanks for telling me what you did in the parking lot before. It helps."

"It was true." Their earlier conversation, being able to tell her that everything had been his fault, had lightened what otherwise would've been a horrendous mood on a screwed-up day. And that shocked him.

Wasn't like him to get all talky and share his feelings with anyone. Even more surprising was that he'd felt better afterward. As if the boulder that had been sitting on his chest since he'd left Julie had dislodged. Still there, but less pressure weighing down on him. Not much else was going his way today and he sure didn't like the feeling of always chasing behind Rob. The coldhearted killer was always a step ahead. Bright guy.

But that she'd believed she was a failure because of their broken marriage pierced right through him. None of it had been her fault. For what it was worth, he'd go back and change everything if he could. But life didn't give do-overs. Luke figured all he could do was move forward and not repeat his mistakes.

Within ten minutes, he'd parked in the busy lot. "Doesn't look like they're hurting for business."

"Nope."

He opened Julie's door and then followed her inside. They got in line and stood in silence, contemplating the menu. After all that had happened, he was glad she had an appetite at all.

Julie took in a deep breath. "I haven't been here in a long time. Still smells the same."

The Barbecue Shack brought back a flood of good memories. "Just like Sunday afternoons at Gran's ranch."

"My mouth is already watering." She turned to face him, smiling. "You guys used to smoke a brisket in the slow cooker all day."

"The food was ready when the sun kissed the horizon."

"Remember all those evenings in the barn after supper?" Her cheeks flushed a soft pink.

"Some of the best nights of my life."

"You come here a lot? You know, since we…"

"No. Not since us."

He put his hand on the small of her back, urging her as

the line moved forward. Touching Julie felt as natural as waking up in the morning.

Nothing in his world had been right in a long time.

"Being here, together, seems a lot like old times, doesn't it?" She turned and pushed up on her tiptoes, planting a kiss on his cheek.

Blood roared in his ears and his heartbeat thundered in his chest. "Yeah. It's nice."

"I like being friends, Luke." Her gaze lingered on his.

"Me, too." Before he could find a good reason not to, his arms encircled her waist. With her body flush to his, more than his heart grew warm. "It's been too long."

"Agreed." She smiled up at him.

He pressed his forehead to hers and released a slow breath.

They both stood rooted, for a long moment, breathing each other in.

Then she turned and took another step forward as the line moved. Her hand reached back and found his.

He twined their fingers and hauled her against him. Her sweet round bottom in a perfectly fitted pair of jeans pressed against him. His control faltered.

He breathed in. The scent of her shampoo, coconut and pineapple, filled his senses.

The line moved another couple of steps forward.

Luke didn't want to budge. He wanted to stay rooted to his spot, with Julie, and forget everything else. The past. The craziness. The now.

The couple in front of them moved. He and Julie were up next to order. She leaned into him a little more.

Too soon, the line cleared, and it was their turn. She stepped aside, moving elbow to elbow.

"The usual?" he asked.

She nodded, reaching inside her purse.

He frowned. "Two plates of brisket."

Glancing at her, he added, "And lunch is on me."

The attendant nodded. "Drinks?"

Luke confirmed.

The young guy stuck out two cups.

Julie took them as Luke paid.

Yeah. This felt a lot like old times. They were damn good times, too. He wasn't kidding when he'd said those months with her was the best time of his life. He'd just been too stubborn and too young to realize letting her go would almost kill him.

"What do you want to drink?"

"Surprise me."

Luke piled mashed potatoes and beans on their plates as she manned the drinks stand. They got their usual booth in the corner.

And for a second, life didn't feel as if it was tilted, slowly spinning off its axis.

The moment wouldn't last.

This case would be over as soon as Luke found Rob. And he would find the SOB. Julie would return to her normal life. To Herb. And Luke would settle into his routine again.

Even though letting her go had almost killed him, he'd survived, hadn't he?

Because suddenly, the thought of trying to live without Julie was a sucker punch and he couldn't breathe.

Shake it off.

He slid onto the wooden bench across from her.

Every bit of him wanted to move across the table and snuggle in beside her, but he needed to keep his head clear.

A few bites into his meal, his cell buzzed. He fished it out of his pocket. The name on the screen read Bill Hightower.

What was the local newscaster doing calling Luke?

"Campbell here."

"Sir, this is—"

"I know who this is. Can you advise me of the nature of the call?"

"Something showed up in a studio here at the TV station that I think you'll be interested in seeing."

"Mind giving me a hint?"

"It's a message. A note for you. From a guy who calls himself Ravishing Rob."

"Did you touch it?"

"I'm afraid so. No one knew what we had at first."

The original prints might've been damaged. Luke bit back a curse. "Who discovered it?"

"One of my producers." The normally even-toned newscaster sounded a little rattled.

"Keep it somewhere safe. Don't touch it. I'll be there in ten minutes." Luke motioned for Julie to finish eating as he ended the call.

"Who was that?"

"A TV reporter. Said he has a message from Rob."

"That where we're headed?" She'd already grabbed her purse and was sliding out of the booth.

"I need to take a look at the evidence. I want to know where Rob left it. Check the area. Talk to the staff. Maybe someone saw something. We'll head to Austin afterward if we can't get an address on Camden. Since we're getting a late start, we'll plan to stay over." The thought of spending the night with Julie in a hotel room didn't do good things to Luke's libido.

"Okay."

"Obviously, my place has been compromised."

"Understood."

On their way out, Luke phoned his boss about Rick and

updated him on the gray late-model sedan, too. His next call was to his older brother, Nick, but he didn't pick up.

On the walk to his truck, Julie slipped her hand in his. Friends? Could he limit their relationship? She felt a lot like home.

The drive downtown to the TV station took longer than he'd expected. Traffic was heavy, which doubled his time.

There was no close parking, so Luke parked in a nearby garage and opened the door for Julie. She made no move to hold his hand again. His mind was elsewhere, and she seemed to understand why.

Even though he'd stopped talking, he hoped she understood this was different. He was still available. This was focus, not completely shutting her out.

Their silence was warm and companionable as they walked the street filled with luxury hotels and apartments. This urban area was like so many, one block upscale, the next graffiti-covered walls and empty beer cans lined the streets.

Workers huddled near doors, smoking.

An argument broke out a few feet in front of them between two men in suits. Fists flew and the crowd parted, creating a circle around the action.

Luke shot Julie a look before jogging toward the pair. "Break it up. I'm Special Agent Campbell, and I don't want to have to arrest either of you."

He tapped the badge on his waistband.

The younger man took a step back and touched his lip. Drops of blood trickled down his chin. "He busted my lip. He wasn't supposed to do that."

He made a move toward the other guy. Luke stepped in between them, his palm flat against Young Guy's chest.

"What do you mean he wasn't *supposed* to do that?"

"Some dude paid us three hundred dollars each to pretend like we were fighting."

A diversion? Luke glanced toward where he'd left Julie. She was gone.

A loud scream split the air.

"Julie." Damn that he'd allowed himself a moment of distraction. She might pay for his mistake with her life. The feeling of guilt and shame washed over him as his body trembled. The all-too-familiar feelings rushed him.

Luke pushed through the crowd toward the sound of the scream. Where was Julie?

He bolted through the bodies surrounding him. There was no sign of her.

His brain couldn't wrap around the fact Rob had her. Thinking about what he would do with her sent an icy chill down Luke's spine.

They couldn't have gotten far.

Worst-case scenarios drilled Luke's thoughts as he searched the street, running. Rob could have stuffed her into a waiting car.

The air thinned around Luke.

In that case, the bastard could already be on the highway heading almost anywhere. Luke cursed. If that was true, it could be game over.

Luke rounded the corner and stopped the first person he saw. "Did you see a woman with black hair come this way with a man?"

The person shook their head. "Sorry."

Anger coursed through Luke. This could not be happening. Period. He'd kept Julie next to him for a reason. Helplessness rolled through him in waves. He refused to acknowledge it. Instead, he rushed to the next person, who was on her cell, and asked the same question while flashing his badge.

She nodded and pointed south. "I'm on hold with the police. I saw a man dragging a woman that way. Couldn't get a good look at her. She was struggling."

"Stay on the phone with the police. Tell them everything you just told me," Luke instructed her as he bolted south, maintaining eye contact to ensure the woman understood.

"Okay. I will." Her voice rose from adrenaline.

"Tell them Special Agent Campbell needs backup." Luke broke into a dead run. His tremors returned. He couldn't even consider the possibility of not finding Julie. *Another few minutes, Rob gets her to a secure location, and it's over.*

Luke stopped at the intersection, glancing left then right. Nothing. She couldn't be gone.

This case was bringing back more of the past than his relationship with his ex.

A HAND COVERED Julie's mouth. She tried to bite it. Couldn't. He must've anticipated the move.

She jabbed her elbow back, connecting with his rib cage.

Her attacker swore. He dropped his hand to force her arms behind her back.

She finally broke free enough to scream again, praying Luke would be able to track her location. Had Rob dragged her too far? Had Luke realized she was gone yet?

Luke was good at his job. He would come, she reassured herself.

The next thing she knew, a bag or some kind of cloth material covered her head, and she was being dragged again. She kicked, wriggled and struggled against the vise-like grip around her hands—hands that had been shoved behind her back.

She managed another scream before she was dropped

and concrete slammed into her. Her head cracked against the unforgiving sidewalk.

He swore again, and then he was gone.

With her hands freed, she pulled off the covering in time to see Luke coming at a full run toward her. She pushed up to a sitting position as he stopped in front of her and dropped to his knees.

The haunted look on his face sent chills up her back.

"You all right?" He scanned the area.

"I'm fine. Go."

He took off in the direction she'd heard footsteps, hesitated, then circled back. "Might be playing into his hands by chasing him. He caught us off guard. I won't let it happen twice."

A small crowd had gathered around her.

Julie stood and shook off the shock. "Someone had to have seen him." She looked around. "Did any of you see what happened to me?"

A Hispanic male wearing a uniform stepped forward. "I was watching the fight. Then I heard a scream and turned to look over here, but by that time all I saw was the back of a man. He was taller than me. About this big." He held his hand up to indicate close to Luke's height.

"Around six feet?"

A few heads nodded in the crowd.

"Yeah. That seems about right. He looked like he might be a runner. Slim but athletic. A few inches shorter than you, maybe." He shrugged. "I couldn't see much more than that."

Luke thanked him, very aware of the fact that the height given matched that of the uniformed officer who'd shown up at Julie's place. "Did anyone else see the guy?"

Shoulders shrugged. A woman confirmed, "I think

that's a pretty good description. His back was turned, so I didn't get a look at his face."

After thanking the group, Luke turned to Julie. "I need to talk to the people who distracted us."

They jogged back to the spot of the earlier altercation. A pair of officers were interviewing the men who'd been involved in the fake fight.

Luke introduced himself, then turned to the older guy in a suit. "Tell me about the person who paid you."

"He was wearing a hoodie and sunglasses, but I could see that he had dark hair."

The young guy nodded in agreement.

"And you didn't think anything was wrong with the picture when he offered you money to fight?" Luke shot a heated look at them.

"Sure I did. At first. I said no," the young guy piped up.

"What changed your mind?"

"He seemed like a nice guy. Said he was playing a prank on his roommate. That it was his birthday. We weren't actually supposed to throw punches." He sneered at the older guy.

"And you believed him?"

"Honestly, I thought I was on one of those TV prank shows at first. Then I thought, what could it hurt?" The young guy shrugged. Looking toward the uniformed officer, he asked, "Am I under arrest?"

The officer shot a glance toward Luke.

"No," Luke said. "But give your information to this officer for his report. If we need to talk to you again, we'll be in touch." He hesitated. "And the next time someone asks you for a favor, I'd suggest you both walk away."

"You bet I will," the young man said.

Luke clamped his hand around Julie's, gripping her tightly. "Let's check in at the TV station."

Another block and they stood in front of American Airlines Stadium. Luke located the glass doors at the entrance to the station and guided them toward the door. Julie's body still shook from adrenaline and fear, and she noticed a tremble in Luke's hand, too.

The big and brave Luke had never seemed quite so vulnerable to her before. Even when he came back from the war, he seemed more angry than anything else. Afraid? No.

He stopped at the door and turned to her. "You okay?"

"Yeah. I'd be lying if I didn't admit to being shaken up, but I'm fine."

"That's my girl." He pressed a kiss to her forehead. "I can drop you off at the police station if you want out. You'd be safe there." His gaze bored deeply into hers. His brown eyes filled with worry and what looked a lot like fear.

"As long as I'm with you, I'll be all right," she reassured him.

"But he got…to…you." His voice broke on the last word.

"And you saved me, Luke."

He took in a sharp breath. "Not good enough. You're sure you want to go through with this? I can take you back to the ranch. There's enough law enforcement crawling in and out of there on a daily basis to ensure your safety. I know Gran would like to see you again."

"Me, too. As soon as all this is cleared, I'd like to go out for a visit. I miss her." The warmth in his gaze nearly knocked her back a step.

This time he planted a kiss on her lips before leading her into the news studio.

The receptionist was a cute and perky brunette. She asked them to wait while she paged the newscaster. An armed guard stood sentinel behind her, nodding toward Luke.

Julie immediately recognized Bill Hightower the second he stepped into the lobby. He was shorter in person than he looked on TV. Blond hair, blue eyes and a million-dollar smile with perfectly straight white teeth. He looked to be in his mid- to late-thirties. He had a crisp, new-car-salesman look about him. Suit on, he was polished and ready for the camera.

His hand jutted out in front of Luke, who accepted the shake without a lot of enthusiasm. For whatever reason, Luke didn't seem to care much for this person.

"I wish you were here under different circumstances." Bill's lips curled down in a frown. His brow furrowed.

Julie had to give it to him—he could sell his words. Maybe a bit too perfectly?

"As do we," Luke said, not appearing affected or impressed by the newscaster's plastic concern.

"It's a pleasure to meet you, Special Agent Campbell. You already know I've been wanting an interview with you for months. I understand you're here for a different reason, but while I have you, I wonder if you'd consider answering a few questions?"

"Call me Luke." He paused. The muscle in his jaw ticked. "You said on the phone that you have something for me."

"Yes. I do," he stalled.

"Then, if you don't mind, I'd like to see it."

The reporter turned his attention toward Julie and put on a charming smile. "And you are?"

"Julie Davis."

Luke stepped in between them, drawing the reporter's blue-eyed gaze. "If we could see the message, we'll get out of your way. I'm sure you're busy and I'd hate to be underfoot."

"No trouble at all."

"Is it here at the front?" Luke pressed.

"No. Follow me." Bill led them down the hall to his office, stopping at the door. He motioned toward a pair of leather chairs as he perched on his desk. "Any chance this is actually from the serial killer you've been following?"

"You know I can't comment on an ongoing investigation." Luke parted his feet in an athletic stance and folded his arms. He'd be intimidating to most men, standing at his full six-foot-one height.

Bill seemed to dismiss the threat. "Then it *is* part of the investigation?"

"I haven't seen the message yet." Luke cracked a smile meant to ease the tension.

"Would you both mind holding on for a minute?"

Luke said he didn't, but his expression told another story. Julie knew him inside and out. She doubted the reporter picked up on Luke's frustration. She could see that he was growing increasingly annoyed.

The reporter disappeared, returning a few moments later with a tentative smile. Was he nervous?

Julie certainly understood the newscaster's trepidation. Rob was a monster. And a desperate one at that. Or was there something else going on?

A shiver raced up her spine thinking about how close she'd just come to being dragged to some random place in that psycho's clutches. Trapped. Icy fingers closed around her heart and squeezed at the memory.

She blew out a breath. Her quick thinking had most likely saved her life. Fighting had worked. No matter what else Rob tried to do, she wouldn't be an easy target. Julie planned to fight.

She already knew what would happen if he got her to another location. He'd been so close moments before. Just thinking about it made her skin sting like a thousand fire-ant bites. She shivered, remembering that the best way to escape a sicko was not to let him take you to a second site. Thank God Luke arrived when he had. She couldn't remember where, but she'd read that an abductor all but assured no possibility of escape if he could get his victim to a different spot where it would be harder to break free.

If she'd had to force the man to snap her neck on the street corner, she would not give him the satisfaction of performing his ritual murder on her.

She was not one of his *projects*.

Bill returned, easing onto his desk, and used a nail clipper to pick up a piece of paper and a hair ribbon.

If the items had been there all along, why did Bill disappear down the hall pretending to go get them?

"It's probably too late, but I secured these from Hair and Makeup on the off chance his print is still there."

Wasn't he being helpful?

Luke eyed the reporter suspiciously, took a small paper bag from his back pocket and nodded. "Much appreciated."

He examined the paper. Deep frown lines bracketed his mouth.

Julie moved closer to get a look.

On the handwritten note was printed "I could be anywhere. Even here. The Devil's in the details, but rest assured, the body count is about to rise."

Chapter Eight

Another cold chill trickled down Julie's spine as she glanced around. He could be anywhere. Even there. Watching.

Bill clasped his hands and leaned forward. "The note isn't signed. Is this actually a message from Ravishing Rob?"

"No comment." Luke's tone was cold. His temper was on a short leash.

"So you're not denying it?" the reporter pressed.

"No comment." Luke closed the paper bag. "Where did you find this?

"I didn't."

Luke ate the real estate between them with a couple of quick strides. His hand fisted when he stood over the man who cowered on his desk. "Look. You want to play games with me? Is that your best move right now, Mr. Hightower? You want to spend the night in jail for obstructing an ongoing investigation?"

"No."

A soft knock at the door turned them around. A small woman stood behind them, holding a white piece of paper with a scribble on it.

Bill motioned for her to come in. After handing him the note, she immediately excused herself and disappeared down the hall without making eye contact with Julie or Luke. That couldn't be a good sign.

"One of my producers discovered them taped to a camera lens." Bill sounded distracted. Whatever she'd handed him got his full attention.

"Which one?" Luke took a step back.

"In the studio."

"I thought the newsroom was secure."

"It's supposed to be."

"How'd the note get there?"

"No one saw anyone come in." Bill shrugged. "I have a few questions for you. Unless you plan to get in my face again."

"You didn't answer mine."

"Funny. You didn't respond to my request for an interview last month. Or the one before that. Or the one before that. Can you give us any idea of Rob's profile? People deserve to know. Otherwise, you're allowing a killer to walk around invisible."

"I'd like to speak to the person who found the note."

Bill didn't make a move. "There are no killers here. I have no reason to believe the person who left this note is an employee of the station."

"That's not your call to make." The pieces fit together. Someone had left the note knowing the person who found it would call the agent in charge of the investigation, who happened to have the killer's new target in protective custody.

The newscaster didn't budge.

"You don't want to talk here? We can head to Lew Sterrett Justice Center if you think everyone would be more comfortable having a conversation there." Luke's steel gaze centered on Bill.

"Fine. The guy who found the note is a producer on the

morning show. His name is Lowell Duncan." Bill loosened his tie, then pushed a buzzer on the phone and asked to see Duncan.

Not five minutes later, a sloppily dressed man in his mid-forties stood at the door. Didn't fit the description of the killer Luke had described, but then, he'd also said it could be almost anyone.

One glance toward Luke told her he was sizing this guy up.

"Come in, Lowell," Bill said sharply.

It was clear the two didn't have a warm-and-fuzzy relationship.

"Sir."

Bill gestured toward Luke. "Special Agent Campbell would like a word with you."

Lowell turned. "Yes, sir. I'm guessing this is about the note I found."

"It is. I appreciate your time. You must be busy keeping this place in line." Luke extended his hand to Lowell. The man smiled and took the hand being offered.

Lowell's tense expression softened as he nodded.

"Can you show me where you found the note?"

"Sure." Lowell turned and backtracked down the hall toward the studio.

Julie stayed close to Luke as they walked down the hall. The room where the morning show was taped was smaller than she'd anticipated. Three walls of windows didn't afford a lot of privacy, either.

Lowell stopped at the threshold. "There's a live broadcast going. But I can point to the camera."

He motioned toward the one positioned front and center, aimed toward the newscaster. "It was here when I came on this morning at four o'clock to work *Good Morning Sun*."

Lowell shoved his hands in his pockets and balanced on the balls of his feet.

"Which entrance do you use to get to work?"

"The one in the alley."

"Did you see anyone around this morning on your way in to work? Anyone hanging around back there?"

"No. Nothing out of the ordinary."

"What about inside the studio? Was anything else unusual delivered or did you see anyone who didn't belong?"

"Nothing out of place. I checked everything. It's part of my morning ritual. The fools on my crew like to mess with me. I never know what's going to happen when I unscrew a lid anymore." He held his hands up, palms out.

"But you didn't call it in until much later? What made you hold on to it?"

"I'm sorry about that. Thought it was a trick at first."

Luke nodded his understanding. Julie figured growing up with a couple of brothers, he could relate.

"What made you decide to call it in?"

"No one claimed responsibility by the end of the show." He glanced from Luke to Julie and seemed to realize neither of them knew when that was. "It's over at ten o'clock."

Luke glanced at his watch. "Does someone always come forward by now? When they play a practical joke?"

Lowell half smiled. "Seems to be half the fun for these buffoons. Getting away with it is the first kick. Laughing about it when it's over comes in a close second. None of the guys even knew it was there."

"How many work on the show?"

"Three full-timers. I've got one intern."

"Are they here by any chance?"

"Nah. They left a few hours ago after the wrap."

Luke cocked an eyebrow.

"I have them come in my office and we talk about what

worked, what didn't. See what we can improve for next time." Lowell had a genuine quality to him. Julie figured he'd make a good boss. Heck, a good person. She wasn't so sure about Bill Hightower.

"I'll need to follow up with them," Luke said. "Can I have a list of names?"

"Sure." Lowell rubbed the scrub on his chin. You need me to round them up? I can call them in if you'd like."

"No. Thank you. I'll swing by in the morning."

"I'll put your name on the list. Feel free to watch the show."

"Will do." Luke smiled. His laid-back expression told Julie he believed Lowell. "Do you always come in at four?"

"Usually. Not much traffic to contend with at that hour, so I'm generally right on time. Maybe a little early some days."

"And you're sure there was nothing different about this morning?"

"Nope. No, sir." He paused as if to take a moment to check his thoughts. "I started to rip it up and toss it in the can, but then Mr. Hightower showed up. I told him what had happened, and he asked to see the note."

"He gets here around ten to do the lunch news?"

"Has to. It's in his contract." Lowell froze as if he'd said something wrong. "I'm sure he would anyway."

Luke nodded. "Then what happened?"

"Next thing I know, I'm being asked to talk to you."

"I appreciate your time, Lowell. Is there an easy way to reach you if I have more questions?"

"I'm almost always here at the station. My house is a few blocks away. I can give you my cell. But the receptionist keeps me on a short leash." He chuckled. "The station always knows where to find me."

Bill reappeared as Luke made a move toward the lobby.

Bill's gaze trained on Julie. "Tell me, Agent Campbell, is it ethical for you to work on a case involving your ex-wife?"

The two men locked eyes.

Luke's eyes flashed fire. "Thank you for your time."

Bill must've realized his story was about to walk out the door. He stood in between them and the exit. "I can keep a secret if it's for a good reason."

"You sure you want to do that?" Luke turned to the reporter and took a menacing step forward, poking his finger in Bill's chest. "Threaten me?"

"I—uh—"

"That really your best move?"

"No, sir."

"Good. I'll be back and I expect your full cooperation. Understood?"

Bill nodded slowly.

Luke twined his and Julie's fingers and stalked toward the exit.

The reporter stayed rooted to his spot. Smart move.

"That guy was a jerk. What the heck's going on with him?" she asked when they were out in the fresh air again.

"Maybe he's just a jerk wanting an exclusive." Luke held tight to her hand.

"Where to next? Austin?"

Luke already had his phone out of his pocket. He let go of her hand long enough to make a call. His first was to Detective Garcia to update him on all that had happened. The next was to his boss. He finished the call as they located the truck. "No. That trip's on hold for the time being. We need to drop off the evidence at the lab before we do anything else. They grab a print and there's no road trip necessary. We'll find our guy."

"How about after that?"

"I realized we have one more location in Addison. One

in Dallas. Then we'll think about hitting the road. The team should be able to lift prints quickly if there's anything to work with on that piece of paper. And we know Rob's here."

Luke started the engine and snaked out of the parking garage, glancing in his rearview mirror.

"What is it?"

"Either someone at the station is involved, or Rob planted the note to make sure we went there." The anger in his tone nearly took her breath away.

"So he could get us out in public? It's not like we're hiding. We've been in plain sight all day."

"True, but he didn't know where we were before. And he ambushed us. He might have been trying to flush us out all along by bringing us to the station. He could've been there hiding since this morning." Luke's jaw ticked. "Or it's possible Hightower faked the note."

"Why would he do that?"

"He's been after me for an interview for months. He could've set up the scenario in an attempt to get me to the station. And our guy could've been following us, waiting for a chance to snatch you."

"A reporter wouldn't resort to this, would he? Isn't that a crime?" Was that why Luke had such a bitter response to Bill Hightower? Or had he just had bad experiences with reporters in general? There was something about their interaction that had Julie wondering what else was between the two of them.

And those last words, the ones about her and Luke. Could Hightower cause problems for Luke at work?

"He did an investigative report on the FBI and tried to dig into my past to expose me, questioning whether or not I could do my job. And, yes, it's a crime."

"I don't remember reading anything in the news about you. What a jerk. I'm so sorry someone would do that."

"He didn't succeed. My boss struck a deal with him so he wouldn't run his story. He kept it quiet in exchange for information."

"Your boss must think a lot of you to do that."

"We take care of our own."

"What he did doesn't seem ethical."

"Believe me, reporters have stepped over the line more than once to get a story. And this guy is no exception." Luke's cell buzzed. He glanced at the screen and then locked eyes with Julie.

"Or maybe this whole thing has been a wild-goose chase meant to distract us so Rob could kill again."

Chapter Nine

"Oh. God. No. What happened?" Julie fought the panic closing her windpipe.

"We're heading north. The house of a twenty-seven-year-old woman is being broken into. A neighbor called in a suspicious-person report. The guy's wearing a hoodie and sunglasses." He hit the gas pedal and sped out of the parking structure.

Julie sat perfectly still, watching as Luke punched data into his laptop at every red light on the road heading north. He'd avoided taking the Tollway since there was a wreck reported, instead opting for a straight shot up Preston Road.

Driving to Plano took less than ten minutes.

Another few minutes that ticked by like years, and they pulled in front of a large two-story brick house. The lawns were neatly manicured in the suburb—a safe place with good schools where bad things weren't supposed to happen. Julie realized heinous crimes could occur anywhere. Recent events had taught her if someone fixated on her there wasn't much anyone could do to stop him. Even a skilled FBI agent like Luke could barely keep her safe.

"Keep close to me." The rich timbre in Luke's voice softened his command.

He parked in front of the residence and palmed his weapon, leading with his gun.

Luke approached the house cautiously. The front door was unlocked, so he turned the knob slowly and shot Julie a look. The overwhelming smell of bleach assaulted her as she stepped inside the door behind him.

Step by step, she followed him into the living area. A glance to the right nearly knocked Julie off her feet. She stumbled backward the moment her eyes made contact with the victim.

The woman's body had been neatly arranged on the couch. Some blood was splattered, but there was surprisingly little. Bleach had been poured on her clothing. But the severed head made Julie's stomach twist, nearly doubling her over. Bile burned the back of her throat, and she tasted vomit.

Luke tucked her behind him, cursing. His massive shoulder blocked most of her view.

The only thing holding her together was Luke. She heard him whisper an apology as he continued through the house, checking behind every door, in each room, every closet.

Sirens wailed in the distance, roaring toward them. Luke had notified local police he was inside the house.

Moments later, lights blared from the street. Luke palmed his badge and met the officers in the yard, tightening his grip on Julie's hand.

"The house is clear," he said to the nearest officer. He relayed other information as Julie stood there, stunned.

The officer thanked Luke and headed toward the front door.

Thinking about what was inside sent a wave of nausea rippling through Julie. "What does he do with the…head?"

"He takes special care with cleaning it," he said in a low voice. "Always puts it in a different place after he chops some hair off. Like a twisted game of hide-and-seek. It's his signature."

"He takes a piece of their hair? What does he do with it?" Julie could scarcely contain her horror.

The answer hit her fast and hard. "He's making a human wig, isn't he?"

Luke didn't answer. Didn't have to. Julie could see from his expression she was right. "This was him, then. I could tell she had black hair."

"Looks like it."

"When did he…?"

"Not long ago."

"How do you know?"

"Normally, we can tell by the blood. When the heart stops, it pools inside the body, so in her position, it was at her feet and ankles."

"You saw that?"

He nodded, his gaze intent on her.

"One look at her and I froze," Julie said. "The bleach. You mentioned that before." She wrinkled her nose involuntarily. "Why does he use it?"

"Makes forensic evidence harder to find, for one. Not impossible, but difficult. Even so, I think it goes deeper than that. He sees these women as unclean, which is how he justifies his actions."

"So, he's cleansing them?"

Luke nodded. "And then punishing them."

Julie trained her gaze on the ground, unable to keep the tears from her eyes or hold her composure. Her stomach revolted.

Before she realized what was happening, his hand was low on her back, ushering her toward the truck.

The chilly breeze was a welcome respite on her warm

cheeks. She stepped on the curb just in time for the first heave.

Luke held her hair off her face and whispered words of comfort.

Embarrassment edged in as her heaves became productive. "I'm sorry."

"Don't be."

Looking at him now, he was different but stronger. Could she continue to let him be her strength?

Even after all they'd been through?

When she really thought about it, she had a habit of being with men who shut themselves off emotionally.

Her father had never been there for her. Not even when her mother died. Julie had been a little girl. She remembered the day vividly. It was the first day of kindergarten. She knew her mother had been sick, but no one had prepared her for the fact her mom might die.

Coming home to the news had made her close herself off, too.

Especially when her father hugged her once, then told her they had to get tight and move on.

Most of her childhood memories had faded, but Julie knew exactly the last time she was hugged by both of her parents that first day of school. Julie hadn't understood the tears her mom shed that morning. She thought they had been for the fact she was going to school.

Little did she know her mom would be gone by the time she got home.

Julie hated first days.

From that day forward, she'd get sick in the pit of her stomach at all firsts. And especially when summer ended and school started again.

Her mother had been the soft, emotional one. Her father

had been all about self-discipline and order. Physically, he was always present, but emotionally? Butch Davis didn't do emotions.

Instead of tucking her into bed at night, he had morning inspections. By the second week of school, Julie had learned how to make her own bed and pass muster.

That first night, he took down all the pictures of her mother and neatly packed them away in boxes, storing them in the attic. He never went up there again. Not even when they moved two years later.

The worst part of the whole ordeal was that he never talked about her mother. Ever. It was as if she'd never existed to him. And Julie knew on instinct she wasn't supposed to talk about her mother, either. He'd remarried before the first anniversary of her death.

There were no complaints about her stepmother. She was a nice woman who cleaned when she got nervous. Supper was on time every day. Six o'clock. Very little real conversation was ever had at the dinner table or anywhere else, for that matter.

Was that why Julie was so lost when it came to talking about her own feelings? Why she couldn't for the life of her find the words to help Luke when he was drowning emotionally after Iraq?

Deep down inside, she knew her father had done the best he could. He'd dealt with what life had thrown at him the only way he knew how. She didn't hate him for her childhood. He'd provided all the basic necessities of a roof over her head and food in her stomach. His way of dealing with emotion had been to shut down and ignore it. He'd developed heart disease in his fifties and joined her mother the same year she'd met Luke.

And yet, the Luke she'd met was nothing like her father. Maybe that was the big draw at first?

No one understood her better than Luke. No one made her laugh like Luke. No one caused her body to soar like Luke.

Theirs was a bond so strong, Julie had thought it to be unbreakable. And that was why she'd trashed every one of her rules and married him a month after they'd met. This kind of connection came along once in a lifetime, she'd reasoned. What they had was real and no one could take it away, she'd told herself.

She'd made herself a promise a long time ago that if she should ever get married and have a family of her own, she'd hug them every day. They would know how very much they meant to her every minute. Because life had taught Julie at an early age those she loved could be taken away in an instant.

She had no plans to waste hers by leaving those she loved wondering about her feelings. This was the relationship she'd thought she had with Luke.

And hadn't she?

Then he'd shipped off. She hadn't recognized the man who came home to her.

Determination forced her to stay in the relationship even after he'd quit. She'd thought surely she could bring him back. Their love could move mountains.

"I know this is hard," he soothed, snapping her mind back to the present—a place she was no longer convinced she wanted to be.

Besides, sure Luke was there for her now, but how long before the wire tripped again and he went all emotional desert on her?

She'd been naive the first time she'd fallen for him. Lucky for her, experience was a good teacher.

"Dammit, Luke. I'm fine."

THE FACT SHE swore didn't mean good things. Luke also didn't like her sharp tone, because it signaled she was overwhelmed.

Of course she was. She wasn't the first person who'd had a visceral reaction to her first crime scene. Technically, it was her second, but she'd been in shock during the first, so it wasn't the same. Her mind was fully aware this time. Processing every sight, smell, sound. Taking everything in.

"We don't have to be here," he soothed.

"I don't want to get in the way of your case. You need to investigate. I can handle this."

"My team will be here to process the scene. The sergeant looks like he has everything under control until then. Nothing says we have to stay." He thumbed away a tear rolling down her cheek.

"I'm in the way."

"No. You're right where you need to be."

She looked up at him with those amber eyes—eyes filled with pain—and his heart squeezed. Another chink in his armor obliterated. Spending time together was a mistake. All his good memories came crashing down, suffocating him at the thought of walking away from her again.

If there was another place to stash her, somewhere far away from him, he would do it.

The reality? He was her best hope.

He'd already thought about sending her to Europe or Mexico to hide. Hell, he'd pay for the trip out of his own pocket if it would do any good.

Rob wanted Julie. He would go to the ends of the earth

to find her. He seemed to know where they were at every step. Had he gotten close enough to bug Luke's truck?

The guy had skills.

Too bad he was on the other side of the law. Luke could use someone with Rob's abilities, if not his morals, on his team.

Not happening. The guy was a cold-blooded killer. Another woman was dead because Luke couldn't get a step ahead of Rob.

Shame and guilt ate away at Luke's stomach lining.

"Luke."

"Yeah."

Those eyes pierced through him. "Get me out of here."

She'd seen enough for one day. He wanted to give her one night of peace.

By the time they reached his truck, his team had texted their location. They were a couple of blocks away. They'd be there in less than five minutes.

Luke checked for a device under his truck and then under the hood. He didn't find anything, which didn't mean much. Gadgets were so small these days they were virtually undetectable. He made a mental note and moved on.

He'd most likely cross paths with his team on the way out of the neighborhood because he needed to stay put for a minute and update the file.

Luke keyed in information before starting the truck and pulling away.

The signature on this killing was Rob's. But the timing was off. Why so soon? What did this murder have to do with Julie?

If Rob was trying to flush them out, he had. He'd been dictating their movements all day, Luke realized.

"Are you thirsty?"

"I could use some water," Julie said, staring out the front window. Her color was slowly returning.

Luke pulled into the first convenience store he could find.

"I need a bathroom, if that's okay," Julie said.

He led her to the back of the place and stood guard at the door.

Five minutes later, he knocked. "Everything okay in there?"

"I'm almost done. I'll be out in a minute."

Another couple of uncomfortable minutes and she came out. She'd pulled her hair back in a ponytail and, from the looks of it, had splashed water on her face.

"Better?"

"I had to get that taste out of my mouth. Luckily, I always keep a travel toothbrush and toothpaste in my purse."

Jealousy flashed through him with the speed of a lightning bolt. Why did she keep those items close at hand? Logic told him it was in case she slept over at her boyfriend's.

Luke walked to the drinks case and pulled two bottled waters.

He had no business knowing why she kept those items in her bag. Anything outside of this case was none of his business. So why did a voice in the back of his head say, *She's mine?*

Julie wasn't *his* anymore. No matter how much it felt like old times being near her. And not just any times, but the good times. He had a life apart from her. She had a boyfriend.

He let silence sit between them as he paid for their water. She followed him to the truck, where he opened her door for her.

Luke made a move to close the door but stopped.

A question was eating away at him.

Before he let this—whatever this was—go any further between the two of them, he had to know.

"Is it serious between you two?"

Chapter Ten

"What?" The question caught her off guard. How did Julie tell Luke that his memory was enough to stop her from being able to get close to any other man?

Should she tell him?

What could she possibly accomplish by pouring her soul out to the one man who'd stomped on her heart? Not to mention the fact that if a serial killer hadn't brought Luke to her doorstep, they wouldn't be speaking right now. If he'd come on his own terms, she could trust his feelings. But this? No.

"We've known each other for a while."

"Oh."

She steeled herself against the pain in his voice. Her heart begged her to tell him the truth. Herb was barely in the picture right now. No man before or since Luke had broken through her walls. He was her kryptonite.

Was that such a good thing?

He'd walked out once without looking back. What would stop him from doing it again?

Neither one seemed to feel like talking on the road. Julie didn't. Not after what she'd seen. Then there were her mixed-up feelings for Luke to contend with. Being with him was the first time she'd felt home in years—ever. And yet, her mind couldn't wrap around making the same mistake twice. What was that old saying? *Fool me once, shame on you. Fool me twice, shame on me.* Sure it was a cliché, but it worked for her.

She closed her eyes and leaned her head against the headrest. Images assaulted her. She rubbed her eyes and then opened them.

Luke pulled into a parking garage, found a spot and then cut the engine. "What is it, Julie?"

"This. My life. It's so screwed up that I can't begin to sort through it." She wasn't just talking about Rob, but she didn't want Luke to know. She wasn't ready to discuss their relationship—a relationship that confused her as much as comforted her. "Where are we?"

"Safe house." He hopped out and was at her side before she could reach for the door handle. His lips were curved in a frown. His disposition had shifted to dark and moody.

Was he still bothered by her admission? False or not, she'd done her best to sell it.

The parking garage was active. Well-dressed couples held hands, walking toward either the elevator or the stairs.

"Where are we?"

"There are condos above the shops on this street. This garage will conceal my truck."

"It's busy here. Is it safe to get out?"

"We'll blend in." He placed his hand on the small of her back and electricity shot through her. Unfair that his touch could heat her body so easily.

They moved to the street and into the crowd of forty-somethings as they made their way down the tree-lined road. There were plenty of couples, but single people were abundant, too. Small groups of women looked as if they were out for girls' night. Pairs of men were on the hunt. The place was bustling with restaurants and shops.

"What time is it?" Julie had barely noticed that it had

become dark outside. Her nerves were stretched thin from the day's events. Images from the crime scene would haunt her for the rest of her life. She wondered if she'd ever be able to close her eyes again without seeing those horrible crimes relived in her nightmares.

"Eight-thirty." He led her to an elevator, pushed the button and waited. "I'll pick up something for supper once we're settled."

She hadn't eaten since lunch, which had been interrupted. Seriously doubted she could now. "I'm not hungry."

"I know. But you need to get something in your stomach. There's a deli on the corner. They make a great panini and tomato soup." His words were crisp and held a sharp edge, which was probably a good thing. Was he still thinking about what she'd said? Good. Because one touch and he'd melt her resolve.

"I'll try."

The elevator doors opened, closed. They stopped on the fifth floor.

Julie followed Luke down the hallway, feeling the weight of the day in every step.

"I called ahead and had someone bring clothing. You want to jump into the shower while I get food?"

"No." How did she tell him? Admit her vulnerability? Should she come straight out with it? "I...I'm scared, Luke."

His arm encircled her waist as they walked down the hallway. "You know I'm not going to let anything happen to you, right."

It wasn't a question.

She nodded as his arm tightened around her, sending currents of electricity pulsing through her body.

He stopped in front of the door, leaned over and then

pressed a kiss into her hair. She leaned into him as he worked the key.

The first thing she noticed when she walked across the threshold was how beautiful and plush the apartment was. The feminine decor was tastefully done. This was clearly not a bachelor pad. She wasn't exactly sure why she thought it would be. "Who provides these places?"

"Nice, isn't it?"

"'Gorgeous' is more like it. Surely this doesn't belong to the government." One look at the hand-scraped hardwood floors and high-end appliances in the open-concept kitchen and she could tell this most certainly was not something Uncle Sam would provide. The sky was clear and she could see lights all the way from downtown Dallas.

"It serves a purpose. Make yourself comfortable." He went to the kitchen cabinet and pulled out two glasses, then retrieved a bottled water from the fridge. He seemed to know his way around rather well.

Had she even known him before he'd left for duty? She believed she had, but she'd been wrong about so much in their life together. She'd also been naive enough to think they could get through anything as long as they were together.

Look how that had turned out.

Julie leaned into the sofa, half listening to Luke call in their dinner order. She heard him end the call as the sound of his footsteps drew closer.

"One of the officers downstairs volunteered to pick up our food."

She smiled, trying to erase the horrible images from her mind. "You want to walk downstairs with me to get it?"

"No. I'll wait here."

"Then keep this with you." He placed a small handgun

on the coffee table. "You remember what I taught you about shooting?"

She remembered a lot of things. And that was most likely her biggest problem now. "Yes."

"Okay. The safety's on. There are officers stationed around the building. Don't answer the door for anyone. You can reach me on my cell. I won't be long." He walked right to her, planted a firm kiss on her lips and then locked the door behind him.

Julie hugged a throw pillow to her chest.

Her cell buzzed. She retrieved it from her purse. Luke had sent a text checking on her. She let him know she was fine and then turned on the gas fireplace.

Sleep would come about as easily as snow in a Texas summer, but fatigue was catching up with her, so she leaned back and closed her eyes.

The image of her client and the innocent woman from earlier had stamped her thoughts.

Sobs broke free before she could suppress them. Tears flooded her eyes.

The doorknob turned. She palmed the gun and held her breath until she saw Luke's face. His presence brought a sense of warmth and calm over her.

He locked the door, set the food on the coffee table and dropped to his knees in front of her. "You're shaking."

She folded into his arms.

Before she could stop herself, her fingers mapped the strong muscles in his back. His hands were on her, then circled around her head, pulling her toward home.

He kissed her with a tenderness that caused a flutter in her stomach.

She wanted to erase the images from her mind, lose herself in the moment and forget about real life where people were hurt and Luke had been with other women.

He deepened the kiss and all rational thought flew out of her mind. One word overtook all others. "More."

JULIE ROSE FROM the sofa onto bent knees. She gripped the hemline of her shirt and pulled it over her head in one motion. All Luke could see was the flesh-colored lacy bra covering her full pert breasts.

"You're even sexier than I remember." He made a move to get up, to reduce the space between them.

Her hands gripped his shoulders before pushing him down. "You, stay right there."

Surrender never felt this much like heaven.

Her jeans hit the floor next and, glory of all glories, Luke's eyes feasted on the matching silk panties. He was already hard, and she seemed prepared to make this end before it began with the way her fingers lingered on the strap of her bra.

"Luke?"

"Yeah."

"I have to ask you a serious question before anything… before *this* can happen."

"You can have whatever you want." He held out his arms. "Take it."

She pushed him down to the floor and straddled him. "All kidding aside."

His body craved to be inside her so badly, he shook. He hoped like hell she was about to ask for more than one night. He'd promised himself a thousand times if he was ever lucky enough to get her back in his bed, he had no intention of letting her out.

"What is it?"

"Do you want me?"

"That's not a serious question."

Her amber eyes bored into him.

"Luke."

"Yeah."

"Do you want me?"

"What kind of question is that? Of course I want you. Do you see what you're doing to me?" He glanced down at his painfully stiff erection.

"I mean, *really* want me." She grabbed his wrists and pulled them above his head.

He looked into her eyes—eyes that possessed kindness, compassion and fire—everything he wanted in a woman. "More than I can ever say. More than you'll ever know. More than I'll ever deserve."

He broke free from her grasp. "I think it's pretty obvious I want this." He picked her up and took her to the bedroom, placing her on top of the duvet. He let his fingertip graze the vee between her breasts. "And this." His finger trailed down her belly to the waistline of her silk panties.

Her stomach quivered and a soft gasp drew from her lips.

He let his eyes take her in for a long moment before trailing his finger across her belly to her hip, making a line up her side. "And this."

"I missed how you fit me physically in every possible way. You have no idea how badly I want to wedge myself in between your thighs and thrust my way home again."

She started to speak but her words caught.

"But you know what?"

Her long dark lashes screened her eyes, but her face was flush with arousal. She shook her head.

"I miss this most of all." He pressed his finger to her forehead. "I miss the way you think. Your wit. How you know exactly what to say to make me laugh when I should be serious."

She restraddled him and then leaned down far enough to press her lips to his.

"I miss those, too."

She slowly pushed up to her knees, her gaze locked onto his the entire time.

Her body was grace and poetry in motion, and Luke couldn't help but stop to appreciate her movements. Yeah, she was sexy as all get-out, but she was so much more. He struggled for the words, the context, but sex with her was like rising to a whole new plane.

No one left him with the same feeling after as Julie had. Everyone else had met a physical need, and that was it.

He'd never known to expect more from a physical act.

She unhitched the silk bra she wore and tossed it to the side in one sweeping motion, releasing her ample breasts and pink nipples.

"You're beautiful." Luke made a move to touch her again, but she shoved him back down.

"Not yet."

"Keep this up and this'll be over before it begins," he half joked. Sex wasn't something he'd indulged in for a long time. The couple of women he'd been with after Julie had left him feeling hollow afterward. He figured he needed more time.

"I happen to know you have incredible stamina, Campbell." Her low, sexy voice rolled over him.

He pressed his palm on her belly. "Confession."

She looked at him.

"It's been a long time."

Her gaze widened.

"Surprised?"

"A guy like you could have pretty much anyone he wanted. I just figured—"

"Wrong. You figured wrong," he parroted, stroking her hip. "I didn't want anyone else."

The thought of someone else touching her could eat away his stomach lining, which was totally unfair. He wouldn't ask if she'd been with another man, with Herb.

She stared at him for a long moment. Her forehead wrinkled in that adorable way when she concentrated. "Confession."

The last thing he could stand hearing about would be her and another man. But he owed it to her to listen. After all, she never would've been with anyone else if he hadn't been such a jerk before. "You can tell me anything."

"I haven't been with anyone. Not since you."

"No one?" he repeated. His heart nearly burst out of his chest, filling with something that felt a lot like love. "Then it's been too long."

He tugged her down and wheeled her around, her breasts flush with his chest. He wasn't sure who managed to get her silk panties off, him or her, but he felt her sweet heat against his erection. Their hands and arms were a tangle, as were their legs as he moved in between the vee of her legs.

She arched her back as he drew figure eights on her sweet heat.

Her hand gripped his swollen erection.

Skin that was softer than silk pressed against him as she guided him inside her moist heat. One thrust and he was in deep. *Home.*

One hand continued working her mound and his other palmed her breast, all while he spread kisses along the nape of her neck. Sucking. Biting.

A low, sexy moan escaped as he rolled her nipple in

between his fingers, moving from one to the other, tugging and pulling as she moved her hips in rhythm with his.

Luke nearly exploded when he sensed her climax was near.

She moaned and rocked and whispered his name until he felt her muscles contracting around his length, and then he felt her burst into a thousand flecks of light.

Her rhythm didn't change as she coaxed him toward the same blissful release.

He thrust deeper and deeper as she flowered to take him in.

He groaned, low and feral, as complete rapture neared, every sense heightened.

Her sweet heat ground on his sex as he gripped her hips with both hands and pushed deeper until he detonated. Explosions rocked through him in the release only Julie could give him. His body tingled and pulsed afterward.

Heaving, he rolled over onto his back.

She turned to face him and settled into the crook of his arm.

He looked deep into her eyes and found everything he'd been missing for the past few years. And yet, now was not the right time for a distraction.

They'd taken the relationship well past friendship and he couldn't remember the last time he'd been this happy, but keeping her safe had to be his priority. "I didn't think I'd get this chance again. To be with you like this." He wanted to tell her he loved her, but he wasn't sure she was ready to hear the words any more than he could promise everything would work out differently this time. He didn't want to scare her away. Everything inside him said she felt the same way. He didn't need to hear the words. Yet. "I'm happy."

She blinked up at him, and he realized he was holding his breath.

The smile she gave him would have kept them warm through a blizzard. "Me, too."

All Luke's internal warning bells sounded. He was in deep with no way out. Hurting her again would kill him. But could he give her everything she deserved?

Chapter Eleven

Julie nuzzled into Luke's side, where she reminded herself not to get too comfortable. Everything could change in an instant. Not that she needed the fact brought to her attention, especially with Rob a step ahead of them. Even a strong, capable man like Luke might not be able to keep the determined killer away.

"What are you thinking?" Luke kissed her forehead.

"About how much I missed this," she lied.

"Your eye twitched. You never were a good liar."

"This is nice. Us talking like this. I missed this."

"Me, too. You have no idea how much." His voice was low and had a gravel-like quality. He moved to face her, hauling her body flush with his and smiling a dry crack of a smile—his trademark. Those sharp brown eyes were all glittery with need. "You know what else would be 'nice'?" He pressed his erection to the inside of her thigh, sending heat to her feminine parts. His breath warmed her neck as he moved to her ear and whispered, "I can't get enough of you."

They made love slowly this time, savoring every inch of each other, as if both knew their time together could end in a flash.

A very real threat stalked her, determined as a pit bull.

And she'd learned the hard way there were no guarantees when it came to her and Luke.

He kissed her again before mumbling something about food. He disappeared down the hall, returning a minute later with plates balanced on his arms.

As they ate, he paused long enough to pepper kisses on her forehead, her nose, her chin. She surprised herself by getting a solid meal inside her.

Afterward, she fell into a deep sleep with her arms and legs entwined with Luke's.

The next morning, Julie blinked her eyes open.

She'd slept a solid eight. The bed was cold in the space Luke had occupied. She glanced around the room. His jeans were gone, but his shirt was crumpled on the floor.

Julie laid her head back on the pillow. The thought of her and Luke back together brought warmth and light into her heart. Would it last?

Clanking noises in the kitchen confirmed his presence in the apartment.

"Luke?"

"Be there in a minute. Don't move." He strolled in a moment later wearing jeans and a serious expression, holding two cups of coffee.

"Everything all right?"

"Yeah. Fine."

But was it? Something was on his mind. He was holding back. If they were going to think about having a relationship, this wouldn't cut it. She needed coffee to clear her head first. Then she had every intention of confronting Luke. She sat up and took the hot brew. *Heaven.*

Luke's cell buzzed before she could properly thank him.

He fished it from his pocket. "What's up?"

He said a few uh-huhs into the receiver before setting the phone down.

"What was that all about?"

"First things first." He leaned forward and pressed a kiss to her lips.

His breath smelled like a mix of peppermint toothpaste and coffee. Her new favorite combination. "What's going on?"

"My boss wants me to check out the news." He pulled a remote control from the bedside table and clicked on the thirty-two-inch flat-screen mounted on the wall.

Julie ignored the obvious reason he'd known it was there. He'd taken others here, maybe even women. A stab of jealousy pierced low in her belly. She refocused as Bill Hightower's face covered the screen. Below him was a ticker tape that read *Serial killer strikes again. Has the FBI been compromised?*

Hightower went on to talk about Luke guarding his ex-wife at the cost of taxpayers.

Luke picked up the phone and held it to his ear. He clenched his back teeth as he listened.

"I'm not leaving the case," he finally said.

He was silent for another long moment as though hearing out an argument.

"I know what he said, but I'm not handing her off to someone else." More beats of silence. "What would you do if this was your wife?"

The sound of the last word as it rolled off Luke's tongue sent tingles through her. She scooted closer to him and rested her cheek on his strong back.

"Take me off the case and you might as well kick me out of the Bureau. By giving away my relationship with Julie, he just made killing her more of a game for Rob."

Had Luke seen this possibility coming?

"I understand. Do what you need to do." He ended the call.

"Everything okay?" she asked as she took another sip of coffee.

"Yeah."

"Sounded like you got in trouble with your boss."

"No. He said what he needed to say."

"Is he taking you off the case?"

"No. It's fine. He trusts me."

"Luke, you're not telling me something." She sat up and faced the opposite wall.

He pulled her closer to him again without managing to spill a drop of her coffee. "That's better."

She couldn't argue being close to Luke was nice.

The look he gave her nearly stopped her heart. His gaze intensified. "Last night changed things between us, right?"

She nodded. "It did for me."

"Good."

Julie needed more time to process exactly how much things had changed, but this was a start. Could she trust it? Her logical mind said no even as her heart begged to disagree. "Maybe we got married too soon back then."

The hurt in his brown eyes nearly knocked her back. "It wasn't too soon for me. Was it for you?"

She didn't immediately answer.

"Do you regret marrying me?" His gaze didn't waver.

"No. It's not that. I was just thinking if we'd met now instead of then, maybe things would be different."

"I regret a whole lot of things. None of them have anything to do with the time I spent with you, Julie. You were the only thing I thought about when they captured me. Thinking about you kept me going no matter how hard they beat me or what else they did."

Pain serrated her heart at thinking about what he'd been forced to endure. No wonder all he wanted to do was close up and forget everything that had happened when he'd finally made it back home. "I'm sorry, Luke. I had no idea."

"How could you when I shut you out?"

"I just wish I could've been more comfort. If I'd known, maybe there was something I could've done to ease the pain."

He kissed her. Hard, then sweet. "I was an idiot. I blamed myself for everything that happened overseas. The shrink said I had signs of PTSD. I thought if you knew how weak I was, you'd leave me."

"Luke, I would never—"

"I know that now. It was in my head then. You didn't walk away. Not even when I pushed you."

Those beautiful brown eyes of his caused her stomach to free-fall. "Then why'd you force me to?"

"Every time you looked at me with pity in your eyes, I felt like less of a man. I came back broken...." Speaking the words looked as though they might kill him. His voice had gone rough. "No one could've convinced me I was worthy of being with you—you were sunshine and happiness and all those things I didn't know how to get back to. If I allowed myself to be happy, it seemed totally unfair to the men I lost."

"But it wasn't your fault. None of what happened to you was. Or them." She kissed him.

"They beat me, starved me, and that was okay. I was trained to handle physical abuse. It was nothing. Men died because of my decision." His voice cracked. "Jared was the baby. I was supposed to bring him home safe. What did I do? Got him killed."

"You wouldn't have done that on purpose."

"It was my fault we were in the situation in the first place. I take that to my grave. We were sent into a red zone. Command couldn't give us much detail about what we were walking into. By their best estimates, we had a little time before the enemy arrived." He paused, taking a deep breath. "We were in formation. Ready. Everything was cool. Then I saw something to my right I couldn't ignore. The area was supposed to be civilian free, but there was this little kid heading straight into the line of fire. I knew it was about to be a bloodbath. I'd killed plenty of men by then. But I couldn't sit back and watch this innocent kid die. I thought I had more time before the enemy arrived. I made the decision to move without proper intel." He turned his face away from her.

"Oh, Luke." Tears welled, but she held them at bay. "Look at me."

Slowly, he did.

"You were trying to save a child." She kissed his eyelids, his forehead. "I'm so sorry."

He was opening up and talking about something real, allowing her to share in his pain—pain that was still raw after all these years.

Maybe they could go back. Correct past mistakes. Maybe she could trust that what was happening between them was real and could last this time.

Or was history the best predictor of the future?

LUKE HAD NEVER spoken about the details of the day he was captured and Jared was killed. Not to his counselor. Not to his family. Not to anyone. "As soon as I grabbed the kid, I ran toward the tree line. All hell broke loose. I got shot before I made it to cover. Jared came running out, firing his weapon wildly. The guys came after him. I'd told them to leave me no matter what happened. They didn't. I should've known better because I would've done the same thing."

"Oh, baby, it wasn't your fault. You didn't have to go through that alone," Julie said.

Her words soothed his aching heart. He'd kept those feelings bottled up for so long, he felt as if he might explode some days. Time healed physical wounds—he had proof on his thigh where the bullet had penetrated him—but emotional scars were a totally different story. Did they ever really heal?

She whispered a few more words that brought a sense of calm over him. For the first time in a long time, he felt the dagger that had been stabbed through his heart had loosened. The constant hollow feeling in his chest was beginning to fill with hope and light. Surprisingly, it didn't feel like a betrayal.

Her breath on his skin as she whispered soothing words brought him back to life.

Julie brought him back to life.

He took her in his arms, pulled her tightly into his chest and released tears of anger and frustration that had been bottled inside him far too long. "Losing my friends made me want to die, but losing Jared…that was the worst. That's why I couldn't talk about him."

"I'm glad you told me, Luke."

He turned away, the familiar feeling of shame washing over him. Luke Campbell didn't cry. Besides, if he looked into her eyes, would he see pity there? He wouldn't be able to stand it if he'd let her down, too.

"Look at me."

Was it confirmation that had him needing to see her? Wiping away the moisture that had gathered under his eyes, he turned and faced her.

Her gaze was steady, reassuring and filled with compassion, not pity. "It's not weakness that makes you feel emotion, Luke Campbell."

"You didn't grow up with brothers," he mumbled, half joking, trying to lighten the mood. Although he'd never cried in front of his brothers, he knew deep down inside that they wouldn't fault him for it. The Campbell family always had each other's backs. Trusting outside of their circle was the difficult part. Luke thought about the soldier he'd helped train who never came home. Luke had nearly died overseas. The torture he'd endured felt like just deserts. But Luke had survived a bullet wound and weeks in enemy camp. He'd lived despite the odds. He finally picked himself up, decided to come home and waited until he could escape. And yet, there wasn't a day that went by he wouldn't exchange his life for any one of the men he'd fought alongside.

Luke had spent a year in counseling before he could round up the courage to visit Jared's parents in Spokane, Washington. He drove his truck from the family ranch. The closer he got, the heavier his arms felt.

"The people who tortured you were savage. Being sad or hurt because you had to watch people you love die doesn't make you weak. Compassion separates good people from bad," she said, cutting into Luke's heavy thoughts. "Think that monster chasing us cares about the lives he wrecks? Ignoring your pain and not facing it makes it grow into a beast."

There was truth in her words and they resonated with Luke. "Guess I never thought of it that way. I thought I had to be the strong one. Hold everything inside."

"Well, you don't. I'm here for you, Luke. You can't always go around protecting me and disappearing. I wanted to be there for you before."

"What about now?" He arched a brow and tried his level best not to reveal how much her answer mattered to him.

"How could I not? My feelings for you haven't changed, but I have."

"Because of me."

"No matter what happens between us, I will always be there for you as a friend."

Hurt darkened his brown eyes, but he blinked it away, kissing her pulse at the base of her neck. He smoothed his palm over her flat belly. "Have I told you how much I like this?"

"Yes."

"Or how beautiful you are first thing in the morning?"

His lips brushed the soft skin of her throat, leading to her pink lips.

"Yes."

"Or how seeing you in my old AC/DC shirt nearly drove me wild the other night?"

"That one I haven't heard."

"It did." He nibbled her earlobe.

"Do you forgive yourself yet?"

"I'm a work in progress." He palmed her breast. Her nipple pebbled in his hand.

Her fingers tunneled into his hair, and she gently pulled a fistful.

He pressed his forehead to hers. "So, where does that leave us exactly?"

"I don't know yet." She paused a beat. "We're a work in progress."

"Sounds fair." He could live with that.

The sounds of his cell vibrating cut into the moment. He glanced at the screen. Jenny from his forensic evidence team was on the line. "I better take this." He kissed her again. On the lips this time. The taste of coffee lingered on her mouth.

"Sorry it's taken so long to get back to you, but we have a match on the shoe print," Jenny said.

"Great. What did you find?"

"This particular shoe isn't cheap. It's handcrafted by—get this—an old man who lives in a small village in Italy. They don't sell a lot because each pair costs over a thousand dollars."

"Not something many men would spend money on." Which didn't exactly rule Rick out, or Chad, for that matter. Luke made a mental note to circle back around to Chad. The phone number he'd given Luke for his stepbrother had turned out to be a dead end.

Was Chad covering for his half brother?

He didn't appear to like Rick. But appearances weren't everything. And blood was blood. Maybe the two were closer than Chad had let on.

More questions that needed answers entered Luke's mind. He needed to interview the young guy's coworkers. See if he could dig up more about the relationship between him and his sibling. "So, what you're saying is whoever owns this shoe has serious funds?"

"Exactly. You didn't find anything missing from the crime scene this time, did you?"

"No. He must not've had time. The trinkets he really likes to take can't be bought. This guy likes hair and scalp."

"We knew that much." Most ritual killers held on to whatever piece of their victim they'd taken in order to relive the event for weeks, months.

"On the shoes, not many people can afford these babies. Fine Italian leather. Good news for us is they leave a specific impression."

"I'd like to see for myself. Maybe I need to dust off my

passport." Disappearing and taking Julie with him had crossed Luke's mind more than once. He needed a minute to sort through all the information he'd gained in the past forty-eight hours.

A chortle came across the line. "You wish. The boss isn't sending you to Italy to check on shoes."

Luke thanked her and ended the call.

He'd especially considered going on the run with Julie until this whole mess blew over and Rob was behind bars. Problem was, Luke was the FBI's best chance at catching Rob. And there were already too many innocent women being butchered in the meantime. Now that this had become personal, the body count was rising. Rob had promised more. In his haste, he would make a mistake. He had to.

Julie had disappeared into the bathroom, returning wearing nothing more than one of his T-shirts and her underwear.

He pulled her onto his lap and kissed the back of her neck.

Luke had a problem. Protocol said he should leave her at the safe house, guarded. Yet, Rob had tricked Luke before and almost got away with abducting her. He couldn't risk that happening twice. Keeping her with him was the only option.

"We have a serious problem to take care of before we leave," he said to her.

She turned enough for him to see her brow furrowed. "What is it, Luke?"

He spun her around to face him and then kissed her. She tasted minty and like dark-roasted coffee. "I can't get enough of you."

Julie broke into a laugh as she lowered her hand to his already straining erection. "Is that so?"

He nodded, groaning as her fingers curled around his shaft and gently squeezed.

"Good. Because I'm not done with you, either."

Chapter Twelve

Luke had reluctantly finished dressing and kissed Julie again before moving into the living room to check his laptop.

He'd received an email from Nick stating that the background check on Chad's mother came up clean. In fact, he and his mother had been on vacation together during one of the murders. Nick was still digging around to find an address for Rick.

Luke glanced up from the screen, and his heart flipped when he saw her. She looked as beautiful as ever. No, more. Her hair was pulled back in a ponytail. A few loose strands framed her face. Her body was amazing. He already knew he'd never get enough of exploring her sensual curves. He logged off before that body of hers got him going again. "Ready?"

She nodded.

He led her to the elevator and then the truck. Backup was all around them, and yet an uneasy feeling still sat in his stomach like bad food.

Of course, every time he walked out the door with Julie he disliked the feeling of being exposed. With one hand on her back and the other ready to grip his weapon, he kept a watchful eye on everyone who passed by.

Rob had succeeded in making Luke paranoid. But the

stakes had never been higher. The thought of what Rob would do to Julie if he got his hands on her… Luke couldn't go there.

A visual scan of the garage yielded nothing.

One of his guys stood in the corner, smoking. He had arm-sleeve tattoos and wore a rock-band T-shirt with ripped jeans. Luke glanced at him for confirmation. The undercover agent popped his chin, giving the all-clear sign.

The restaurant would be easy enough to find using GPS. Upscale places like the DeBleu usually required their waiters to show up at lunch to taste the evening's specials and prepare their stations, so if Luke was lucky the staff would be there.

Traffic was light enough to make it to Addison in twenty minutes. For most of the ride, he filled Julie in on the shoe print left at the crime scene and the news he'd received from his brother. After parking and scanning the lot, Luke double-checked the notes he'd made on his phone.

Inside, a man wearing a long white apron greeted them. "I'm sorry. We're not open for lunch."

"We're not here for food." Luke flashed his badge and introduced himself. "I'd appreciate a moment of your time."

A look of shock crossed the guy's blond features. He introduced himself as Stephen before saying, "Of course."

"I'd like to speak to you about Chad Devel. Is he here by any chance?"

"Afraid not. He's not on the schedule tonight. Why? Did he do something wrong?"

"No." Luke smiled to ease the guy's tension. "I was hoping to ask him a few routine questions while I was here. Did he work on the night of the twenty-second?"

"Let's see. I worked that night. It was a Thursday. Decent night for tips." He glanced right as he recalled the date. "Yeah, he was here."

"Can you verify he was here the entire evening?"

"Yes. We give twenty minutes for dinner break, so he was here all night."

"Doesn't seem like much time to eat."

"I've found if I give longer, they disappear and don't always come back. Twenty minutes is enough time to eat. They put their order in before break, and when it comes up, they hit the back room," he said defensively.

Luke nodded as if he understood, to gain sympathy. "Is Chad a good sous chef?"

"He took a while to train, but once he got the hang of it, he's done all right," Stephen said.

"I hate to ask this question, but is he trustworthy?" Luke figured he'd get more information if he buddied up with Stephen.

"He wouldn't still work here if he wasn't."

"This is a beautiful place," Julie said.

Pride flashed behind Stephen's eyes as he looked at Luke. "You should bring her back for dinner sometime. On me."

"I appreciate it. I'll keep that in mind." Luke paused for effect. "Mind if I speak with a couple of your employees while I'm here?"

"Sure. Which ones?" Being treated with respect seemed to be the trick to getting Stephen to open up.

"Tony and Angie. Are they around by any chance?"

"Unfortunately, only one still works here. Angie quit last night in the middle of her shift."

"Sounds like she left you in the lurch."

"You wouldn't believe. I got it covered, but what a disaster."

"I can only imagine. These kids have no idea what real responsibility is like."

Stephen gave a nod of approval for the solidarity.

"Do you happen to have a good address for Tony?"

"Sure. Give me a minute, and I'll check employee records." The man made a move toward the kitchen but stopped and turned. "Would either of you like a cup of coffee? Tea?"

Luke glanced toward Julie, who smiled and shook her head.

"We're okay. Thanks."

Satisfied, Stephen disappeared toward the sounds of clanking pans.

Quick surveillance of the restaurant showed nothing unusual. Luke hadn't expected to find anything out of the ordinary, but experience had taught him he could never be sure when a case was about to break wide open. And they usually did so in an instant. Gut instinct was honed from years of experience. And his rarely failed.

He moved to block more of Julie with his large frame as they waited for Stephen to return.

The blond manager exploded from the kitchen with a piece of paper in his hands. "I'm sorry."

Luke's body went on full alert—ready for whatever was about to come his way. His hand instinctively went to the handle of his gun resting on his hip.

"It seems word got out you were here interrogating me. Tony ran out the back door." He jogged toward them and stuck out the piece of paper.

The roar of a motorcycle engine sounded from the parking lot. Luke muttered a curse and turned tail after taking the address.

"Thanks for the information," he said out of the side of

his mouth with a dry smile. "And if I were interrogating you, you'd know it."

He winked, motioning Julie to follow.

Camera phone ready, he snapped a pic of the motorcycle as it turned right out of the parking lot. He sent the photo to Detective Garcia.

The guy's address was on the sheet of paper. If it was legit, then Luke would wait for him at his house. Running was never a sign of innocence. This guy was doing something wrong. Luke needed to figure out what.

From the parking lot to Tony's apartment was a three-minute ride. Luke didn't figure the guy would be stupid enough to go home, but that was exactly what he'd done. The motorcycle sat in the parking lot near the address the restaurant manager had provided.

Either this guy was small-time or just stupid. Luke's experience had taught him to reserve judgment until he spoke to someone.

The two-story stucco apartment building had roughly thirty units total.

Tony's was on the second floor.

"I want you so close I can feel your breath," he said to Julie.

She nodded, her wide amber eyes signaling her fear.

"We'll be fine," he reassured her, then ascended the concrete-and-metal stairs at the end of the building.

"You don't think it's him?"

"No. Something's up. But I don't think it's Rob. Believe me, we wouldn't be going in without backup if I thought for a second he'd be here, but this guy's scared, and I need to find out what he's hiding."

She was so close he could hear her blow out a breath behind him. His reassurance seemed to ease her tension a notch below panic. Good. He liked being able to calm her fears.

Besides, what he'd said was absolute gospel. He'd never knowingly face down Rob with her present and without any reinforcements. There was a slight possibility that Rob was working with someone else. If not directly, then someone could be covering his tracks. That someone could be his brother or Chad's friends. The circumstantial evidence against Rick was mounting. A rich dad might do anything to shield his son. Especially if the boy had been abused. But the fact Rick grew up in California worked against them logistically, Luke thought as he rapped on the door. "FBI. Open up."

Silence.

"Open up or I'll break down the door. Either way, we're going to talk. Your choice." Luke didn't have a warrant, so there was no way he would force entry. But the guy behind the door didn't know that. It was a gamble.

The door swung open.

Taking a risk paid off.

A twentysomething guy stood there, wide-eyed. His hand trembled on the knob. "Can I help you?"

"I'm Special Agent Campbell, and I'd like to ask you a few questions."

"Okay." His five-foot-ten frame blocked the opening.

"May we come in?"

"No, sir." The guy's voice shook, too.

"I'm not here to bust you. I need answers. As long as you cooperate, we're good." He intentionally used a calm tone.

"Okay. Did I do something wrong?" The door didn't budge.

"Not that I know of. At least, not yet. Obstructing an ongoing murder investigation is a serious charge."

"Holy crap." He shook his head. "I didn't kill anyone."

"I know you didn't." Luke paused to give the young man a minute to think. "But you might be able to stop a crime."

The guy glanced around. "Can't you ask me right here?"

"There anything inside I need to be worried about?"

"No."

"Are you lying to me?"

"No, sir."

"Then why are you afraid to open the door?"

"I'm not, sir." He glanced around nervously and cracked the door. "Is that good?"

"Better." Luke felt more comfortable being able to see inside. "Do you know Chad Devel?"

"Yes." A mix of relief and apprehension played across his features. "He's a buddy of mine from work."

"You two close?"

"Somewhat. Why? Is he okay?" Concern knitted his dark bushy eyebrows together. He was another one who looked as if he'd stepped off an Abercrombie & Fitch ad. Tall, thin, with thick hair and a sullen look on his face.

"Everything's fine. We're trying to make sure it stays that way."

"Is someone after him?" He scrubbed his hands across the light stubble on his chin.

"Do you know his brother?"

"Rick? Yeah, sure. Haven't seen him in a while, though. He hasn't been coming around to Chad's place."

Interesting. Chad had given them the impression he didn't hang out with his brother.

Guess he'd lied. Luke didn't like liars. "When's the last time you saw him at his brother's?"

"Been a couple of months. Why? Did Rick do something wrong?"

That put him in the Metroplex for a few of the killings. "No. You expecting him to?"

The guy wiped his palms down the front of his pants. "He seems the type. I mean, he hangs around with us but doesn't party. Doesn't say much, either. He's sort of creepy."

"Couldn't he just be straitlaced?"

"That's what I thought at first, too. But then he showed up one night—one look at him and I could tell he was on something."

"Drugs?"

Tony nodded. "Except Chad swore his brother didn't partake, you know."

Luke didn't, but he nodded anyway. "I didn't think Rick lived around here."

"Yeah. He's got a place near Chad."

"Addison Circle?"

Tony nodded. "I've never been to his place, though."

"I didn't realize the two of them were so close."

"Chad's kind of protective of him. Feels sorry for him. Said he had a bad childhood or something."

"Their dad?"

"Nah. His mom. She's some kind of freak, from what Chad says. He doesn't really like his brother. He pities the guy."

Luke didn't see that one coming. Rick fit the profile. His age was on the money. Learning he had an estranged mother made Luke wonder if that had anything to do with the bleach. He cleansed his "projects" then tortured them. This was one angry and twisted guy. Of course, abuse did bad things to a kid's brain. He certainly had the income to be able to afford expensive Italian shoes, or they could've been a present.

He exchanged a look with Julie. She was clearly thinking the same thing.

Except Luke's killer knew the area well. "How long has his brother been living here?"

"On and off for a year, I think."

"Where else does he live?"

"He goes back and forth between here and California now that he got kicked out of medical school."

Luke practically had the wind knocked out of him.

Rob cut his victims with medical precision. Rick had been in medical school? He'd have access to the kind of tools Rob used. "How long did you say he's been here?"

"This time? A year."

"What do you mean by 'this time'?"

"Oh. He came here for high school. His dad shipped him off to an all-male boarding school to get him away from his mother or something. Sent him to Dallas so he'd be close to Chad."

Spending his high-school years here would definitely give him insight into the area. "You have Rick's address?"

"No. Like I said, I've never been to his place. I just know it's close to Chad's."

"You planning on leaving the area anytime soon?"

"No, sir."

"Good. I expect to be able to find you if I have more questions."

"Yes, sir."

"And if you run from me next time, I'll haul your butt to jail. Understood?"

"Yes, sir."

Luke led Julie out the door.

"Chad wasn't exactly honest with us yesterday, was he?" she asked in a whisper.

"Nope."

"We find him and we get our killer, don't we?" Her tone was like a line that had been pulled so taut, it was about to break.

"Looks that way," he said calmly.

"So are we heading to Chad's place?" Her voice hitched on the last word.

"No."

"Why not?" She whirled on him.

"I told you that I wouldn't risk your safety. We can't go back alone." He urged her to keep walking. Truth was, Rob could be watching them right now.

Reality dawned on her as her eyes widened. "Oh. Right. *He* could be there."

Luke followed her down the stairs and to the truck. He opened her door for her and helped her in. "He's near. And I'd venture to guess either he or Chad drives a gray sedan."

She gasped as she buckled her seat belt. "The car that followed us?"

"I didn't believe it was a coincidence then. And I sure don't now." Luke took his seat on the driver's side and scanned the lot. "I need to find a good place for you to hide while I pay our friend another visit."

Her hand on his arm normally brought heat where she touched. This time was different. He could feel her shaking. The idea of being away from her didn't do good things to the acid already churning in his gut. On balance, there was no other choice. Under the circumstances, there was only one option he could consider. Luke fished his cell from his pocket and tapped on his brother-in-law's name in his contacts. "Riley, are you on shift right now?"

"Yes, but I can break for lunch anytime. What's up?"

"I need a favor."

"Anything."

Luke picked a meeting spot halfway between them,

which was fifteen minutes away, and ended the call. He turned to Julie as he started the ignition. "You okay with hanging out with Riley for a while?"

"Of course. It'll be good to see him." Her eyes told him a different story.

"What is it?"

"Nothing." She bit her bottom lip.

Lying?

"You know I'm going to be fine." He glanced in her direction as he pulled out of the parking lot and headed north. They'd agreed on a spot at the border where Plano met Dallas on the Tollway.

She didn't respond.

"I don't take unnecessary risks."

"I know," she said quietly. "This guy is…bad."

"I've dealt with worse," he said, trying his best to sound convincing. Luke meandered onto the Tollway and headed north. He took the Parker Road exit and pulled into the strip shopping center. He hadn't noticed the voice mail registered on his phone. Luke listened to the message from Nick, confirming what he'd just learned—Rick Camden had flunked out of medical school. Nick was working on getting a current address. Luke hit the end button and stuffed the phone in his pocket.

Riley waited in his squad car.

"Give me a minute to get Riley up to speed, okay?" he asked Julie.

She nodded.

He didn't like how quiet she was being, especially since seeing the concern in her eyes.

With his hand on the door handle, he paused. "You know I'm coming back to get you in an hour, right?"

It was then he noticed the tears that had been welling in her eyes. He came around to her side of the truck and pulled her into his arms. She burrowed into his chest, trembling. "Be careful."

"I'll be fine."

He lifted her chin until her gaze met his. He thumbed away her tears. "Look at me. I promise I'll be back in an hour or two. You're not getting rid of me that easy." He winked.

Her nod was tentative.

"I give you my word." He paused for emphasis. "You believe me, right?"

"Yes." Her chin lifted a little higher.

"That's my girl."

He tucked her into the passenger seat of Riley's SUV, the standard issue for patrol in Plano, and asked his brother-in-law to step out for a minute.

Riley did.

"You need a heads-up on this one. This guy's the worst."

"I've been watching the bulletins. Plus, we got information at briefing. We have a lot of eyes looking for him."

"Then you know what he's capable of."

Riley nodded, an ominous look settling over his features.

"Keep her safe." Luke didn't like leaving her, not even with one of the few men he'd trust with his own life. "And be careful. This guy doesn't care about the badge you're wearing. Won't stop him."

"Got it. You, too. Your sister would kill me if anything happened to you on my watch." Riley's attempt at humor succeeded in lightening the somber mood.

Luke couldn't help but crack a smile. "I wouldn't want to be on the wrong side of a postpartum woman like Meg."

"Good thing I love her."

Luke had already started toward his truck.

"Watch your back, man," Riley said.

Luke waved, turned to circle around the vehicle and give Julie another kiss goodbye. "I'll see you after lunch. Save me a taco."

Chapter Thirteen

"It's great to see you again, Riley." Julie tried to distract herself from the fact that Luke was about to face down a ruthless killer. *Possibly* face down, she corrected. After all, the guy might not be home. And, although the evidence was condemning, there was no guarantee they were on the right track. Plus, he was going to see Chad, not Rick.

Her nerves were bundled tight. She feared they'd snap if someone so much as said boo.

"You, too," Riley said.

"Congratulations on two fronts. Getting married and I heard you're a new dad. I bet he's beautiful." Any other time she'd be interested in hearing all the details about the boy's birth and first few weeks in the world, but all she could focus on now was Luke's safety.

"He is. Keeping us on our toes." Riley smiled as he cut across the lot and parked in front of the Tex-Mex restaurant she remembered was his favorite.

"I haven't been here in ages. I miss the food."

"It's almost a sin to live anywhere near here and not visit Eduardo's."

She smiled at his visible display of outrage. "How's Meg?"

"Good. Becoming a mother suits her."

Julie got out of the SUV and met him around the front

of the hood. She couldn't help but check out the people around her warily. Would there ever come a time when she didn't fear someone was watching? Riley stared at her, one hand on the butt of his gun. "Everything okay?"

"Yeah. It's just I always feel like he's close." She shivered.

"You've been through a lot. I can't blame you for being spooked. You want to go somewhere else to eat? Meg's home. I can take you there."

"And make you miss out on Eduardo's enchiladas? Are you crazy?" She tried to shake off the feeling. "Besides, I don't want to get in the way of Meg bonding with her new baby. And I want to hear about Hitch."

Riley followed her inside. As they waited for a table, he leaned toward her and whispered, "Three of my fellow officers are outside."

"I didn't see anyone else." And she'd looked carefully.

"Exactly. They're in plain clothes. Out of sight. But they're there. I called in a few favors after my conversation with Luke."

The hostess greeted them and led them toward their table in between no less than four tables full of uniformed officers from Dallas and Richardson. She guessed it was true what they said about law enforcement sticking together.

She smiled. "More favors?"

He nodded as he took his seat. "Couldn't have Luke worrying about you while he did his job, now, could I?"

Julie let out her breath, realizing for the first time her fingers had been practically clamped together in a death grip. "Thank you."

"He called in for backup. You know that, right?" Riley said, his tone serious.

"I hadn't thought of it, but you're right. Of course he would do that."

"You're safe. He's doing his job. And he's the best. He's survived much worse. A jerk like Rob isn't going to get the best of Luke."

"You're right again." She wished she shared his confidence. Fear of losing Luke rippled through her. If not by Rob's hands, then by some trigger that made Luke shut down again. She didn't want to admit to herself how deeply her feelings ran. She'd sworn no one would have that kind of power over her again. Her feelings for him were resurfacing, but that didn't mean things would magically work out this time.

The waiter came to take their orders. He placed a bowl of chips and salsa on the table.

Riley picked up a chip and dipped it in the salsa. "You okay?"

"I guess. Everything's happening so fast. This guy. He's everywhere but nowhere."

"Everyone's looking for him."

"Between that and being this close to Luke again, I'm confused. Scared."

"He hasn't been the same for the past four years."

"But he picked up his life and moved on. I know he's dated other people."

"After a few years we tried to set him up. Lucy had a friend on the force she thought might help bring him out of his funk."

A jealous twinge fired through her.

"Didn't work. He wouldn't…didn't… She liked him, but they ended up friends. The relationship was purely platonic."

"I'm sure there were others." She didn't lift her gaze to meet his. Instead, she toyed with the chip in her fingers.

"True. Over time. I heard."

"You didn't meet them?"

"No. He never brought them to the ranch."

Her heavy heart filled with light.

Food arrived.

They smiled at the waiter and thanked him.

"Thanks for telling me that." It didn't solve all their problems, but it did ease the sting of how easy it seemed for him to walk away before.

"I just hate to see two people who fit so well together go through what you two have."

"When did you become such a hopeless romantic?"

"Having a baby has weakened me," he joked. He pulled his phone from his shirt pocket and opened a picture then handed it to her.

"Is that him?" Hitch had the Campbell family's dark hair. Brown eyes. Dimpled smile. If her heart could've melted in her chest right then and there, it would've.

Riley practically beamed.

Julie smiled back at him. "One look at that angel's face and I can see why you changed."

She handed the phone to him, took a chip, dipped it in salsa and leaned closer. "Thank you for telling me what you did before. About me and Luke. It helps. But now I'd like to hear more about that beautiful wife and boy of yours."

LUKE HAD CALLED for backup on his way south on the Tollway. Chad wasn't at work. With it being midday, Luke figured there was a good chance the guy was still asleep. He already knew Chad liked to party on his days off.

A squad car was already parked in the lot when Luke arrived. He thanked the SWAT officers and led the way to Chad's place.

Three raps on the door, and he yelled, "FBI. Open up."

Noises came from the other side of the door. Did Chad have company? Rick wouldn't go down easy.

"Might be hot," he told the pair of SWAT officers flanking him.

They stepped aside, following his lead.

He pounded the door with his fist this time. "I hear you in there, Chad. Open up."

A minute later, the door flew open. Chad stood there in his boxer shorts. A young woman, barely clothed, curled up on the couch, hugging a pillow.

"What can I do for you?"

Luke stepped inside and grabbed Chad by the neck, slamming his back against the door. "You lied to me."

Chad shook his head, wincing.

The girl screamed.

"You want to start all over, and tell me the truth this time?"

Chad shook his head. His face turned blood red. "Lawyer."

"Innocent people don't need lawyers, Chad." Luke loosened his grip enough for Chad to speak.

"Dude, I don't know what you're talking about."

"You told me you didn't know where Rick was. Is he here right now?"

Chad shook his head.

"You better not be lying to me. Mind if the officers double-check?"

"Go ahead. I swear he isn't here."

The officers split up, guns leveled.

"Why did you lie to me, Chad?" Luke gripped the guy's neck a little tighter.

"Who told you I lied?"

"I visited your job and asked a few questions. You and

Rick are close, aren't you? What? Didn't you think I'd check up on your story?"

Chad shook his head, gasping for air.

Luke eased up enough for Chad to breathe.

"Stop. You're hurting him," the girl pleaded, hugging the pillow tighter.

"You want a trip downtown?" Luke didn't move his arm from across Chad's chest and neck, but he glanced at her.

"No."

"No, what?"

"No, sir."

"Then stay put and keep quiet." Luke turned his attention back to Chad, keeping the girl in his peripheral view. "Your brother have a medical problem?"

"He's diabetic."

Luke bit back a curse.

"Clear," one of the officers said.

The other repeated the word a few minutes later. They returned to the living room at the same time. One held up a shoe with a gloved hand.

"This the item you're looking for, Special Agent Campbell?"

Luke examined the shoe without touching it, keeping one elbow on Chad's chest. "This is it." He leveled his gaze at Chad.

"What does my shoe have to do with anything?"

"Still playing stupid, Chad?"

"I seriously don't know what you're talking about."

"This your shoe?"

"Yes."

"Then you just bought yourself a trip downtown." Luke turned to the officers. "Gentlemen."

"Hold on a sec. What's going on?" The young man looked genuinely confused.

Luke had to give it to Chad: the guy played stupid to an art form. Either that or he really was in the dark about his half brother's illegal activity.

"This shoe is rare, isn't it, Chad?"

"Yeah. So what?"

"This print was found at the scene of two murders."

The color drained from Chad's face.

"Gruesome murders. Someone's chopping up women with a surgical saw." Luke loosened his grip so Chad wouldn't pass out. Instead, he sank to the floor.

"My dad gave me those shoes for Christmas three years ago."

"Let me guess—he gave your brother the same pair."

"Half brother."

"So I'm reminded."

"And the answer is yes." Sitting on the floor, Chad looked small and devastated. Both hands gripped his head as he leaned his face toward his knees.

"You've been covering for your half brother, haven't you?"

"Yeah, because I feel sorry for the guy."

"Why?"

"His mom is crazy. The only reason Dad left my mom for her was because he didn't want Rick growing up alone. I suspected she did cruel...*things*...to him, but he never talked about it."

"What things?"

Tears spilled onto his cheeks. "I don't know. Torture, I guess. He'd show up with bruises all over his body. Dad would send him here because he couldn't go back to school looking like that. Even as a kid I knew he didn't get them from playing. He wasn't into sports, either. He was pretty brainy. He'd sit in the corner of my room and rock his head back and forth. Sometimes, it'd take days for him to acknowledge me. Whatever Bev did to him was awful. His mom was a twisted bitch."

"That why he soaks his victim's clothes in bleach?"

Chad dry heaved. "I'm sorry. I didn't know. According to my mom, Bev threatened to ruin my dad's reputation and that's why he left us. She manipulated and blackmailed him. I can only imagine what else she did to Rick."

"Or cuts out pieces of their hair and scalps?"

"I would've turned him in myself if I'd…"

Luke bent down to Chad's level. "Where does he live?"

Chad stood, moved in front of the door and pointed to a building across the parking lot. "Right there. Number two hundred and two."

"You listen to me carefully. Your sick bastard of a brother is after someone I love. You run into him, you better tell him this for me. He just made this personal. I'll see him in hell before I let him hurt the people I care about."

Chad nodded slowly.

Luke lowered his voice when he said, "You see him? Tell him he's not the only one who can play games."

He turned toward the officers. "Anything worth running him downtown for here?"

They shook their heads. "If he had anything, he got rid of it before he let us in."

"Mind taking his statement and filing the report?"

"Not at all," one of the officers replied.

"I owe you one." Luke needed to get out of there.

An ominous feeling had settled over him, and all he could think about was getting to Julie.

Chapter Fourteen

Luke updated his report, put out a BOLO—a Be On the Lookout alert—and entered Rick's address into the system with a request for a warrant to search the premises. If all went well, he'd be back at Rick's in an hour, and Julie would be safe. Heck, as long as he was wishing, Rick would be locked up before she finished lunch.

Before Luke left the parking lot, he rounded up the pair of officers and headed toward the apartment across the lot. He rapped on the door several times and listened. No one answered, and the place was dead quiet. Knowing the way this guy operated, he'd watched the events unfold at his half brother's and was long gone.

No answer. No warrant. They'd have to come back.

After thanking the officers, Luke hopped on the Tollway and headed toward Plano.

Seeing a half-dozen officers surround Julie when he arrived at the restaurant lowered his blood pressure to a reasonable level.

Her face lit up when he walked into the room, and his muscles relaxed another notch.

"How'd it go?" She threw her arms open and turned her face to the side slightly.

He'd already seen the tears of relief. He held her until she stopped shaking and kissed the top of her head.

The waiter interrupted, taking Luke's order before disappearing into the kitchen.

Julie took a seat next to him as he turned his attention toward Riley. "I owe you one, man."

"I'll start a tab," he joked, no doubt an attempt to lighten the mood.

Luke smiled his gratitude. "We need a new place to stay. Think you can help out with that?" Staying on the move was their best chance.

"I know of a place. I'd like to keep you inside my city limits. You good with that?"

"Absolutely." Luke figured the best place for them was close to family in case he needed a quick place to stash Julie. Besides, with half of Plano P.D. watching out for them, he'd sleep better at night.

"Find anything useful on your shopping trip?" Riley glanced around, using code on the off chance someone was listening.

Luke nodded. "Wasn't bad. Call you later with the details?"

"Sure. Sounds like you identified what you were looking for."

"It's him. No doubt in my mind."

Officers stood, one by one, and gave a nod toward Riley's table.

Luke shook their hands. After eating and thanking his brother-in-law again, Luke helped Julie into the truck and waved goodbye.

"I'll get back to you with the address we talked about," Riley shouted before he drove off.

Before Luke could put the truck in Drive, he got the text he'd been hoping for. "I have a warrant to search Rick's place. We're heading back to Addison."

Julie's gaze widened. "You found out where he lives?"

"Yeah. And it's right across the parking lot from Chad. I've requested uniformed officers to assist. There'll be plenty of backup. Plus, I already know he's not there."

"How can you be sure?"

"He's too smart, for one. He knows we're onto him. Plus, with the location of his place across from Chad's, he's been watching everything that goes on at his brother's. Chad's most likely telling his brother all about our conversation. The shoe print found at the scene of the murders belongs to a shoe given to Rick for Christmas three years ago, according to his brother."

"Is it safe?"

"I don't know what we'll find at his place, maybe nothing, but I'm one hundred percent certain he won't be there. If I had any doubt, I wouldn't bring you." He glanced at her as he navigated the truck out of the parking lot and headed toward the on-ramp. "You good with this? I can always drop you at the station until we're done."

"No," she said quickly. "I want to go with you. It was agony being in the restaurant without you. Not knowing if something had happened… I'd rather be there."

Luke knew exactly how she felt. Even with officers surrounding her the entire time he was away, he'd had an uneasy feeling. Rick was *that* cunning.

His phone chirped, indicating a text had arrived. Luke retrieved his cell from his pocket and handed it to Julie.

She studied the screen. "It's an address from Riley."

"Looks like we have a place to stay tonight."

"I guess there's no chance we can go back to where we were before?" She sounded resigned to be on the run.

"It's best to stay on the move. That's the only way to keep ahead of Rick. Besides, I don't want to jeopardize my friends any more than I have to." The situation was no doubt wearing her down. She seemed determined to keep fighting and hold her own. Her innate survival instincts would help keep her alive.

Problem was, this case was escalating fast. Too fast.

They arrived back at Rick's apartment before the police. Luke parked the truck and palmed his weapon. He surveyed the parking lot for a gray sedan but found nothing matching the description.

"What did you find out from Chad?"

"It's him. Rick is our guy. In addition to the shoe match, Chad also confirmed his brother is diabetic."

"The orange juice that was left out at my client's house."

"Exactly. Plus, there's a history of mental instability in the family."

"His dad?"

"Mom. The reason Dad left Chad's mom to be with the other woman was because he didn't trust her to be alone with his son. Sounds like she held Rick over his head, too. If news of that got out, it could threaten his professional reputation."

"Sounds bad. What kind of person would hurt their own child?"

"Might explain why Rob chops off his victims' heads. He's trying to make his mother pay."

Color drained from Julie's face. "That's so sad."

"Chad believes there was torture involved, but he didn't talk specifics."

"It's awful what human beings can do to one another."

"Not all kinds of love is good." Luke's had been poison when he'd returned from active duty. Or so he'd thought at the time. Took him a year and visits with a counselor to acknowledge he had the classic signs of post-traumatic stress disorder. The same shame he felt at not being able to save his brothers in arms resurfaced every time he heard Rick killed another innocent victim. Every part of Luke wanted to shut down again with the news. The past two years had been like reliving those early months all over again. Except now that he had Julie in his life again, he had even more to fight for to stay grounded and not let the situation get the best of him.

A dull ache pounded between his temples—a searing headache threatened. He remembered the killer ones he'd had four years ago. They'd almost split his head in two.

Other PTSD signs were returning, too.

Luke shoved them down deep. He had to catch Rick or risk losing everything again.

A pair of squad cars parked in front of Luke's truck. He was informed the SWAT team would be arriving to assist.

"He's clever, so don't expect much," he warned the officers. "We might find a shoe match to crime scenes." He showed them the picture.

A minivan pulled up, the doors opened and a team of SWAT officers spilled out. Luke greeted them and pointed toward Rick's door. "Where can she stay while we check things out?"

"In the squad car with Officer Haines," Officer Melton said.

The SWAT officers took position with the Hammer—the key to the city known for its ability to open all doors.

"One…two…three…" The officer who'd identified himself as the supervisor swung the Hammer, bursting through the lock. The door flew open.

One officer went right. One went left. The third took the middle. The officer with the Hammer held position at the door.

Not three minutes later, the supervisor gave the all clear. Luke strode inside.

The place had a few pieces of modern furniture with a forty-two-inch flat-screen mounted on the wall. Since the space was open concept, Luke could see through to the kitchen with its stainless-steel appliances and granite countertops. In the bedroom, clothes were strewn and cabinets already half-empty. Clearly, Rick had made a hasty exit. Luke bit back a curse. He was so close he could almost feel the guy's presence still in the room. It was pure evil—not that he believed in that.

Besides, even if Rick were the devil incarnate, he'd still spend the rest of his days behind bars just like every other heinous criminal. If found guilty of multiple murders, he might just land an express ticket to death row, where he would be executed.

Luke turned the place over in twenty minutes while SWAT kept a close watch on the door and windows. There wasn't much to see except several cartons of orange juice in the fridge and empty bottles of insulin in the bathroom trash can. Proof he was a diabetic, but not necessarily a murderer. The empty bottles of hair-bonding glue in the trash were far more damning.

Maybe his evidence response team could find hair fibers linking Rick to one of the victims?

Luke updated the SWAT officers and called it in.

With Chad's statement, Rick qualified as a person of interest. It was enough to detain him for questioning. But if Luke had found something more concrete, even a drop of a victim's blood on Rick's clothing, he would feel better. Luke figured the guy would be smart enough to keep his tools somewhere else. But where? Surely not in his car.

The headache that had started in the car raged, causing a burning sensation in the backs of Luke's eyes.

A SWAT officer's body stiffened. "I see a guy who fits the description of the suspect watching us from across the parking lot. He's wearing a cobalt-blue sweatshirt and jeans."

Luke muttered a curse as he tore through the door, giving chase. He heard an officer say he would follow. Luke's full attention zeroed in on Sweatshirt.

The second Luke's foot hit concrete, Sweatshirt bolted. This was the closest Luke had been to the deranged killer. He could feel in his bones that this was Rick. A quick shot of adrenaline pulsed through him, powering his legs forward like rockets.

Rick disappeared in between buildings two hundred yards in front of Luke, but he kept pushing anyway. This might be his only hope of catching the bastard before he hurt someone else.

Anger and frustration coursed through Luke as he reached the buildings. He had to take a guess on the direction Rick went. His odds were fifty-fifty, and they were the best he'd had since this whole journey began two years ago. Luke didn't like it. He could not risk losing the guy this time.

"I'll take right," Luke shouted to the officer following without looking back. Acknowledgment came a second later through labored breaths.

Pushing forward, Luke ran until his sides cramped, his thighs burned and his lungs felt as if they might explode.

Shelving the pain, he ran some more.

He'd lost visual contact with Sweatshirt. The situation was becoming more hopeless by the second. A wave of desperation crashed through him. Then he saw something. A glimpse of cobalt blue sticking out from behind a car.

Luke charged toward it.

The piece of sweatshirt disappeared before Luke could get within twenty yards.

At least he was back on track.

The guy wasn't going to get far, if Luke had anything to say about it. He zigzagged through cars, pushing his body to the limit.

No way was Rick in better physical condition than Luke. If he could get close, he had no doubt he could overpower the guy or outrun him. All the advantage had gone to Rick so far. That was about to change. Luke knew who the bastard was, and so would the rest of the world as soon as Luke called Bill Hightower.

Heck, give him five minutes alone with the piece of human garbage and he'd do more than talk a confession out of him. He'd break him. Another five without the badge, and the man wouldn't walk out alive.

Another turn and Luke was closing in on him. He clenched his fists with the need to get his hands around the guy's neck.

Less than half a city block away, Luke pushed his legs further. Closing in at this speed, he'd be on top of Rick in a matter of minutes.

Before Luke could close the last bit of gap between them, Rick disappeared into a small crowd. There was a barbershop and a travel agency side by side at the place Luke had lost visual contact. After checking through the windows of both, it was clear from the commotion that Sweatshirt had ducked into the first.

A few seconds later, Luke burst through the doors of the barbershop. The few men inside looked startled.

"FBI." He flashed his badge. "There was a man who just ran through here."

Heads nodded confirmation.

"Where'd he go?"

Several men pointed toward what looked like a stockroom.

"Any employees in there I need to know about?" He drew his gun, leveled it.

"No. Everyone's out here," one of the employees said, already heading toward the front door.

"Where does that lead?" Luke asked as he stalked toward the back room.

"The alley."

Luke's hopes the place was sealed were dashed. "Everyone outside until someone with a badge tells you it's clear. Got it?" Luke muttered a curse and hauled himself toward the stockroom.

The door was open. He surveyed the room before entering. Even though it had been staged to look as if Rick had run out the back, he could be anywhere, ready to strike.

Luke took measured steps forward, keenly aware of the fact his guy might be getting away.

Underestimating Rick, believing the obvious, had gotten an officer killed already.

By the time Luke reached the alley, there was no sign of Rick. Didn't stop Luke from verifying what his eyes had already shown him. He doubled back and checked the stockroom one more time as he moved through it again. Luke slammed his fist against the wall and released a string of swearwords.

He pulled his composure together as he walked out front. "Everything's safe. Go inside and lock the doors."

"Thank you." The look of relief on the guy's face was fleeting as he scurried toward the stockroom.

Luke took a minute to get his bearings before making his way to the apartment.

Julie sat in the car of one of the SWAT officers.

"He knows the area well," Luke said to the supervisor, still heaving, trying to fill his lungs with air. Sweat rolled down his neck.

"We sent a couple of guys to back you up. They didn't get anywhere, either. We'll stick around until your team shows up to process the place."

After shaking his hand and thanking him for his help,

Luke walked Julie to the truck. He'd been so close to catching Rick. Anger railed through him. His hands shook. Head pounded.

If anyone else was hurt, how could he ever forgive himself?

A jolt of shame washed through him, and his body trembled.

"Luke? What's wrong?" Concern wrinkled Julie's forehead.

"Headache." He couldn't help but feel responsible for the deaths of the women so far. How the heck did he open up and talk about that? If he'd caught Rick two years ago, more than half a dozen lives would've been saved. Not to mention Julie wouldn't be in this mess.

The tremors started again as his headache dulled.

Fury ate at his gut as he fought the signs of PTSD overwhelming him.

Chapter Fifteen

Luke checked outside the window onto the street. An officer was stationed in front of the house. Everything looked fine. And yet, everything felt off. Why?

"This case," he said under his breath. There was a chill in the air and his warning systems had been tripped. Then again, his internal alarms had been firing rapidly ever since he'd chased Rick.

The small two-story in historic Plano was a good cover, he repeated silently for the hundredth time. One of Riley's friends would be driving past every ten minutes or so, in addition to the marked car on the street.

Luke prayed it would be enough.

He distracted himself by moving to the kitchen and fixing a light dinner of soup and BLTs for him and Julie, placing the meal on the island.

Julie descended the stairs. So beautiful. Her hair was still wet from the shower. Water beaded and rolled down her neck where he'd left a few love bites the night before. If anyone could keep him planted in reality, it was her.

"Feels so good to be clean," she said, taking a seat next to him.

"I can think of a few reasons to be dirty." He leaned toward her, touching elbows. The point of contact still spread heat through his arm. He'd never get tired of her.

A distant sound scarcely registered. Luke stiffened as he glanced toward the street. He raised his head as he scooped her up and instinctively headed for cover.

Tucking her behind the sofa, he set her down gently on the wooden floor. "Stay here until I say different."

Sounds of shouting rose from out front. A scuffle?

Before Luke could get to the window, the crack of a bullet split the air.

Luke immediately jumped into action, pulling his handgun from the waistband of his jeans and placing it in her palm. "Anyone you don't recognize comes through the door, aim and shoot. Ask questions later."

Her eyes were fearful, but she nodded, gripping the handle.

"And call 911. I'm heading out the back. Then I'll slip around the side. Find a safe spot and hide." Luke palmed his own weapon as he moved out the door and motioned for her to lock it behind him.

The porch lamp was on, lighting a small circle around the backyard. He didn't breathe easier until he heard the snick of the lock behind him. Back against the wall, he moved toward the street in the darkness.

The front-porch light was off and the street wasn't well lit. It would take a moment for his eyes to adjust to the pitch black surrounding him.

Luke moved to the black-and-white parked at the curb. No movement inside was not a good sign. He got close enough to see that the officer was slumped over. Luke released a string of curse words under his breath.

A flashback to the war assaulted him. *He watched helplessly as one of his best buddies was shot execution style.*

Luke raged against the memory. This was not Iraq. He was in Plano now, chasing a killer.

Fighting the instinct to run to the injured man, Luke

realized how vulnerable it would make him. How exposed Julie would be if anything happened to him.

Circling back, Luke texted his boss. Confirmation came quickly. More uniforms were on their way.

Rob was cunning. Luke had to give it to him. He was a determined killer.

But what the killer hadn't estimated was Luke's determination to stop him. He'd rather die than allow anything to happen to Julie. The thought of losing her again or, worse yet, having her taken from him detonated explosions of fire in his chest.

Running as fast as his legs would carry him, he reached the back door and knocked softly, not wanting to draw unwanted attention to himself. He pressed his back against the door and leveled his weapon, ready for an attack from the yard.

Anyone tried to cross that grass, Luke would be ready.

His chest squeezed when Julie didn't answer.

"Julie," he whispered, ever watchful of the threat around him. He'd break the door down in a heartbeat.

He knocked again. Still no answer.

Luke spun around and thrust his boot against the sweet spot in the door. It popped open. He wanted to scream her name but knew better.

Easing inside the kitchen, he crouched below the window line and moved through the space. One by one, he opened every door, checking for any sign of her.

The first floor was clear. Luke ascended the stairs, checking doors as he moved stealthily down the hallway toward the bedrooms.

The hall bath was empty, as were two secondary bedrooms.

A clank sounded downstairs.

Every instinct inside him said Rick was in the house.

Luke bit back another urge to call for Julie. He had to find her—now.

And he had to do it quietly.

He eased across the hardwood flooring, stepping around the places where the wood creaked, silently cursing Rick.

Tension pulled his shoulder blades taut. Where was she?

Where would she hide? Luke managed to make it to the walk-in closet in the master bedroom without making a sound.

However, someone was moving up the stairs and not being nearly as quiet. Rick? A cop?

Luke couldn't say for sure. All he could think about was getting to Julie. If she was still here. And that was a big *if*.

His grip on his handgun could crack concrete.

The door to the closet was ajar. The light off. Inside, there were two racks of clothing on either side. The back wall was made of deep shelving.

"Julie," he whispered.

A figure moved to his right.

Before he could get a good look, he had a body pinned against the wall and a hand over their mouth.

As soon as the body was flush with his, he realized Julie was in his arms, safe. He removed his hand.

"Is he here?" she whispered, rocketing into his arms.

"Someone's coming up the stairs. Don't figure we should wait to find out who." He tucked her behind his back and, weapon drawn, exited the closet.

A noise from the hall indicated that option was closed off.

They had two choices. Hide in the master bathroom and ambush the intruder and shoot at the first sign of movement. Or they could climb out the windows and get the hell out of there.

He double-checked that Julie was still armed, motioned

for her to keep her eyes glued to the door and cranked open the pane in the historic house.

There should be just enough room for Julie to slip out. The opening might not be big enough for Luke, but he could cover her until she could get to safety.

Luke touched Julie's arm to get her attention. The ledge was skinny, but she could scale it as long as she didn't look down. This wasn't the time to think about the fact she was afraid of heights.

Her wide eyes stared for a moment before she inhaled a deep breath, tucked the gun in the waistband of her jeans and climbed onto the ledge.

Luke kept his back to the window, facing the door. If Rob walked in, he'd be in for a surprise.

Daring a glance out the window a few minutes—minutes that ticked by like hours—later, he could see that she was safely on the ground, her weapon drawn just as he'd instructed. Pride swelled in his chest.

With Luke being significantly bigger than her, he'd have a much harder time squeezing his big frame through the opening.

As he jimmied his way outside, a noise in the hallway got his heart pumping. Right about that time, he realized he couldn't make forward progress. He tried to reposition so he could shift his weight toward the room and go back but understood pretty quickly he was wedged in too well. In other words, stuck. Adrenaline kicking into high gear, Luke settled into the space half inside the room and half out and leveled his weapon toward the hallway.

"Special Agent Campbell?"

Ice gripped Luke's chest and lowered his core temperature in the split second when he heard the voice. He knew instantly whom it belonged to. Rob.

Was he about to show his face? Finally reveal himself?

That would make Luke's job a helluva lot easier. "You're welcome to come in. I seriously doubt you'll like what you find in here."

A figure lurked just beside the door frame.

Luke took aim but couldn't get off a good round. If he could get a clean shot, he wouldn't hesitate to take it. If not, he wouldn't risk his bullet passing through Sheetrock and into an unintended target.

Rob's eardrum-piercing chuckle split the air.

"You think that's funny? Why not go man-to-man for a change instead of creeping around, preying on innocent women?"

"I doubt you'd understand." Rob's voice was high-pitched, agitated.

Had Luke hit a nerve? Think he cared? Think again.

If the monster showed himself, Luke was ready, which was exactly the reason he knew Rob wouldn't bite. He was an opportunist. Like a vulture, he waited until his prey was too vulnerable to fight back.

The barrel of a shotgun poked into the room.

If Luke repositioned now, could he get a better angle? "You want to kill me in cold blood?"

No answer.

"What? You can't talk all of a sudden? We both know that's not usually your problem, now, is it?" Just a little more to the left. Luke leaned, the window frame blocking his view. "Normally, you're a regular Chatty Cathy. And just as ignorant. Like your mother."

Luke was goading Rob on purpose, trying to see if he could throw him off his game. All Luke needed was one little slip. He was right there. So close Luke could hear the SOB breathe.

If he squeezed the trigger, moved his finger a fraction of an inch, Rob might just drop to the floor. But Luke was responsible for every bullet he discharged and he couldn't risk one going astray. There were too many innocent lives around and his bullet would easily pierce these walls.

"You think you can outsmart me, don't you, Special Agent Campbell?" The voice was somber. Depressed? Did Rob suffer from depression? "You don't understand anything about me or my family."

"No. I don't. Afraid I don't speak ignorant, either."

"I can assure you that your insults won't get you where you'd like to go." Rob's high-pitched chortle belied his words. The controlled anger in his tone said otherwise.

"Let me ask you something, *Rick*. Why not fight me? You know, one-on-one? Instead of always sneaking in the shadows. Hurting people who have done nothing to you." Luke paused, hoping for confirmation.

A choked laugh escaped. "That's where you're wrong. These women are far from innocent. And if I wanted to fight a man, I'd choose a more worthy adversary than you." Rick didn't deny the fact he was Rob.

The floor creaked in the hallway. Rick was on the move, heading the wrong direction.

Luke knew Rick was already gone but needed a visual to confirm. Of course, if he wedged himself back inside the bedroom that would give Rick time to get to Julie on the lawn.

Stuck in the pane, Luke couldn't move another inch, leaving Julie unprotected. Did Rick realize that, too?

"Keep your gun ready and shoot anyone who comes out that front door or around the side of the building, Julie." He hoped she heard him.

Luke patiently worked his way through the window, keeping one eye on the room and his hand secured around the butt of his Glock. He managed to squeeze through the opening and shimmy the rest of the way out the window.

He dropped to the ground, scanned the perimeter and motioned for Julie to follow him around the side of the building.

Her hand visibly shook, but to her credit, she held the gun and her composure intact. *That's my girl.*

On Luke's way to the front of the house, he made a call to his boss to provide an update. Backup was a block away. By the time he reached the streets, he knew in his gut that Rob was gone.

Frustration flooded him. Sirens wailed toward him as he conducted a thorough search of the perimeter just to be sure.

He gave a statement to the uniformed officer who arrived on the scene. The officer who'd been stationed on the street was confirmed dead.

With a heavy chest, Luke walked Julie to his truck.

"We have to move. Find another safe house. Or, better yet, just stay on the road."

Julie fastened her seat belt. "How can he be behind us every step? How can he anticipate our moves?"

"He's cunning."

If Rick knew where Luke lived, he'd also know what he drove. Then he remembered that Rick had been on their tail ever since they'd left the TV station. Everything snapped into place. His head pounded.

"Hold on." Luke popped out of the driver's seat.

"What is it, Luke?"

He examined the bottom of the truck again, running his hand along the boards. Nothing. He popped the hood next and checked every part. The filter. The engine. He ran his hand along the drivetrain and released a string of curse words. "Guy figured out what I was driving. He put a tracker on us."

"So he's been following our movements ever since the TV station?"

"Guess he figured he needed insurance in case you got away. We played right into his hands." Luke removed the device and palmed it. "Now the question is, what do we do with this?"

"Toss it?"

"Not unless I want him to know I found it. No. This is too valuable. And our first real break. He doesn't realize we've made the discovery." Luke tucked the small piece of metal in his front jeans' pocket.

"No, Luke. Turn it in. Get rid of it." Her body visibly shuddered. "Won't your boss know what to do with it? Maybe he can destroy it. Send it to the bottom of the Trinity River."

"Don't worry about it. I know exactly what to do." Luke had a plan. He'd lead the bastard away from her.

Julie didn't know what Luke intended to do with that device, but she had a bad feeling he had no inclination to clue her in. Or was it just a bad feeling in general? Probably a little bit of both. Being close to a murderer moments ago had her skin crawling.

Then again, there wasn't much about this situation that she liked. Worse yet, he'd shut down again, cut her out. The gleam in his eyes said he had an idea. The determined set to his jaw said he didn't intend to share, either.

There was so much about him now that was different than before. She'd never felt closer to him in so many ways. And yet, even though her heart wanted to believe this was different, how could it be? Not if he continued to shut her out at critical times.

A feeling of stupidity washed over her.

Wasn't past behavior the best predictor of future actions? And yet, hadn't she clung to the slim hope this time would be different? That he'd changed?

Was that even possible?

Didn't she read somewhere that behavior was the hardest thing to change? Even if someone wanted to?

There were signs of his PTSD returning, too. The headaches. The sleepless nights. The night sweats.

At least he was talking this time, a little voice reminded her. Not completely shutting her out like before.

Yeah. She guessed that was true.

And yet, he wasn't opening up about what he planned to do with that device.

"Luke, talk to me. Please."

He maneuvered onto the on-ramp of Interstate 75. "Everything will be okay. We're making progress, Julie."

Adrenaline caused his hands to shake on the wheel.

Julie had sat by idly before, but she refused to do it now. If she'd learned one thing, it was that she had to fight for what she loved. "Don't shut me out, Luke. Don't you dare shut me out."

He must've realized the implication of what she said because he immediately exited the highway and parked in a retail lot. "I wouldn't do that to you, Julie."

"You are. I see what's going on, Luke. It's happening again."

"No. It's not. This is different. I need you to trust that I know what I'm doing." He held her gaze as he leaned toward her and captured her face in his hands. "I love you. Nothing is going to change that."

"Look what this is doing to you, Luke."

"I'll do whatever it takes to protect you. That much is

true. This case has been hell." The weariness in his eyes made her ache.

"I need to know you're not going to disappear on me again."

"You have my word."

If only she could be certain. "You know I love you."

"Then believe in me. This is different."

"How? You can't sleep. You're having nightmares again. What's different this time?"

"I know what's at stake. I have you to talk to. And I have been telling you as much as I can."

She couldn't deny he was including her for the most part. "But you're hiding something now."

She steadied herself for the lie.

"You're right."

If she hadn't been sitting, his admission would've knocked her off balance. "Then how is this different? Give me something to hang on to."

"I know what I'm doing now. I can't tell you everything, but as soon as this is over, I will. You have no idea how much I need you."

She held on to his gaze.

"But you can't tell me anything else?"

"Not yet. I need to know you have faith in me."

She answered with a kiss and a silent prayer he'd come back alive.

Chapter Sixteen

Luke figured his best chance to draw Rick out was to use himself as bait. He'd drop Julie off with Detective Garcia and park himself somewhere. But where?

His first choice would be an open place like the Katy Trail. SWAT could easily hide in the nearby trees and cover the perimeter. Or if he used the Nature Preserve in Plano, then snipers could surround the parking lot. When Rick so much as stepped out of his vehicle, he'd be arrested or shot. Problem solved.

But that wasn't the case here. Rick would realize something was off in an instant. Luke would not take Julie to a park randomly in the middle of the day. A restaurant wouldn't work, either. Too public. Rick had already proved he'd kill innocent people if it meant gaining his freedom.

A motel? Nope. Where else? Luke navigated back onto the highway. "I need to investigate a lead."

"I already know the answer to this question, but I'm going to ask anyway. You mean by yourself?"

"Yes."

"And you don't plan to tell me where you're going or who you're investigating?"

"No."

"Is it too dangerous for me to come?"

"Yes." Was he closing himself off to her? He didn't

think so. The only reason he didn't tell her was he didn't want to compromise her.

Hold on.

Was that true?

Or was he falling down that hole again, taking on everything himself? Not allowing her to share in his pain? His hurt?

Keeping his emotions bottled up under the guise he was protecting her?

Luke took a deep breath and kept his focus on the road. "I plan to see if I can draw him out using the tracking device I found on the truck."

He prepared himself for the fallout, expecting her to protest that the mission was too dangerous.

"Where do you plan for all this to happen?"

"Haven't decided that part yet."

He didn't need to look at her to know she was assessing him. She studied him for a long moment.

"What about that ranch in McKinney? It's isolated enough to keep people safe, but other officers could hide in the brush." There was no anger in her voice. Concern and caring were the only notes he detected.

"That was my next thought, too." Luke needed to quit underestimating her. She'd proved she could handle just about anything thrown her way. It was time he acknowledged it. "Grab the phone out of my pocket and dial Detective Garcia's number."

She did.

"Place the call on speaker."

Garcia answered on the second ring.

Luke identified himself. "You're on speaker, Detective. Julie Davis is on the line, as well. I need a favor."

"Name it. This have anything to do with our serial killer?"

"He's my only concern right now. I need more people and a personal guarantee."

"Done."

Luke filled the detective in on the plan to draw out Rick and the location. "One more thing. I want to keep Jul—the victim—out of sight. Here's where the personal guarantee into play. You're the only one I trust to keep her safe until I get back."

"I won't take my eyes off her, man."

"Appreciate it."

"Where should we meet?"

"Knox and Henderson." He'd feel a lot safer if she were in Dallas, far away, when he trapped Rick in McKinney.

"Will do. See you in ten minutes."

Julie ended the call and sat quietly on the ride to the meeting point. They beat Garcia, so Luke parked and waited.

He wished he knew what she was thinking. "Scared?"

"For you."

"Don't be. This is my job. Believe it or not, I'm pretty good at it." He cracked a smile, trying to ease the tension.

"I know. It's just…"

"What?"

"I don't want to lose you again." A few tears fell.

"You won't. Besides, I'm not the one he wants."

"He's already killed two officers who got in his way."

She had a point. He could sugarcoat this all day, but that wasn't exactly being fair to her. "Look. There are dangers to my job. Not just this case. This is what I do, who I am, and I need to know you can handle it."

"I did all right before…" She blew out a breath. "It's you I'm worried about."

He resisted the urge to curse. She was right. She hadn't tried to stop him from doing his job. This was who he was.

He was the one who'd come home and proved he couldn't handle it. She'd been more than willing to stick around and help him through what he was experiencing.

He captured her hand in his and brought her fingers to his lips, kissing the tips of each one. Promises sat heavy. He wanted to be able to tell her everything would be okay, but she deserved proof. "You're right."

This wasn't the time for talk. He needed to show her that he could come back from anything life threw at them and still be himself. How did he tell her there wasn't anything Rick or anyone else could do to him personally that would affect him? The only thing that could hurt him was if Rick got to her.

He unhooked her seat belt and pulled her next to him. "I'm stronger because of you."

Julie looked him straight in the eye. "You come back to me in one piece as soon as this is done."

"You have my word." And he meant it.

He kissed her, hard. Needing to remember the way she tasted, just in case things didn't go as planned.

Detective Garcia pulled alongside them.

"Be safe," Julie said before switching cars.

"Keep a close eye on her for me," he said to Garcia.

"Won't let her out of my sight."

"Thank you." They exchanged a few details about the meet-up location and where Garcia planned to take her. "Call me if anything changes. And if—"

"You just worry about keeping metal out of your own butt," Garcia said. "I'll protect her."

Luke nodded his thanks, put the truck in Drive and navigated out of the lot.

A half hour later, he parked at the McKinney safe house. It sat on an acre of land in northern Collin County. The location was perfect. It'd be impossible for anyone to drive up or get close with a vehicle unnoticed. ATVs and motorcycles were too noisy to use.

Normally, ops took weeks to plan where intel was gathered and scenarios ran through dozens of times before executing. But a small window of opportunity existed here. Luke had no plans to waste any possible advantage he could squeeze out of this.

The house was considered as part of a suburb but the neighbors were far enough away to keep them out of danger. Before Luke arrived, he'd picked up enough supplies to last the night. The place had a male quality to the decor, meaning there wasn't much furniture except what was absolutely necessary. A slipcovered couch and a TV tray for an end table were in the living room. The small dining nook had a table with four chairs. They all matched but looked like relics from the seventies. Especially the wallpaper in the kitchen. Those hues of green and yellow had seen better days.

There was no TV. Today, the place would've been described as open-concept living, dining, kitchen with one bedroom off the living room, but Luke suspected when it was built, the place would've been described as quaint.

If Luke put a kitchen chair in the middle of the open-concept space and opened the door to the bedroom and bathroom, he could see every possible entry point into the place.

He moved to the bedroom and, using the key he'd been given when he used the place last month, unlocked the safe. He pulled an AR-15 and loaded a magazine of silver-tip bullets into the clip. He closed the door, slid the key into his back pocket and pulled a chair into the middle of the room.

Even though he couldn't see any of the SWAT officers, he knew they were there, watching. If something happened to Luke, they still had more than a good chance of capturing Rick. Either way, Julie would be safe.

Of course, Luke's plan involved capturing the bad guy and returning in good health to spend a considerable amount of time with the woman he loved. Preferably naked. If he had anything to say about it, spending the rest of his life with Julie would be a good place to start.

Now all he had to do was sit and wait.

JULIE CLICKED OFF her seat belt and followed Detective Garcia into the small ranch-style house.

"I'd like you to meet my wife, Pilar." The woman he referred to was a couple of inches shorter than Julie and had shoulder-length straight brown hair. Her almond-shaped brown eyes were mirrored in the child's, balanced on her hip. She turned from the stove and smiled. "Welcome to our home."

"Thank you for having me." Julie was corralled to the dinner table along with Garcia.

They were joined by a child who couldn't have been more than five years old.

"This is my son, Juan Jr. Pilar is holding our daughter, Maria."

"You have a beautiful family, Detective."

Pilar set a plate of enchiladas on the table, followed by a bowl of soup. "I hope you like authentic Mexican food."

"Love," Julie said with a smile. What time was it? Luke had to be there by now. Was he okay? Was Rick there, too?

When everyone had a plate, the little one clasped his hands together and pinched his eyes shut. *"Padre—"*

"In English for our guest," Garcia said.

Julie's heart squeezed for how adorable the little boy was as he blushed.

"Sorry, missus."

"No. It's beautiful the way you say it. Go ahead."

"Bless us, oh Lord—" he sighed before continuing "—in these gifts we receive from you. A-men."

"Amen," Julie echoed, ignoring the pain in her chest. For the rest of the meal, she vacillated between wanting Luke's plan to work and wanting it to fail. Either way, she feared for Luke's life.

Even though the food smelled amazing, she couldn't imagine being able to eat. She didn't want to be rude, so she managed to get enough bites down that she wouldn't offend the Garcias' generosity.

Seeing the sweet family gathered around the dinner table made her heart ache to have her own family someday.

There was a time—not so long ago—when she'd thought she and Luke would be holding their own child by now. The image of Hitch's angelic face stamped her thoughts.

Would their baby look anything like its adorable cousin?

Would they ever get the chance to find out?

Instead of dreaming of their future, they were running for their lives from a determined serial killer.

Not running. Not anymore. Luke had placed himself directly in Rick's sights in order to draw him away from her.

She couldn't imagine a future without Luke.

Reality hit hard.

Life could change in a heartbeat. An instant—a changed appointment—was all it had taken to alter her course forever. And yet, it had brought her back to Luke.

Was that destiny?

Would it be his to die at the hands of a monster after surviving so much?

Julie refocused. She had to think positive thoughts for Luke. Nothing could happen to the man she loved. Not again.

She didn't look at the detective when she asked, "Have you heard anything?"

"Not yet." He waited until she met his eyes. "But we will."

With everything inside her, she prayed he was right.

Chapter Seventeen

Four hours and sixteen minutes into the mission, Luke started thinking this had been a bad idea. He'd received a coded text message from Garcia letting him know everything was okay. No matter how much he trusted the detective, his first choice would have been to take Julie to the ranch and have his brothers, Nick and Reed, watch over her.

There simply hadn't been time. Considering they'd pieced this mission together in a matter of an hour, everything had fallen into place well. Even so, not having his own eyes on Julie left him feeling unsettled and tense.

The small ranch mostly used for training exercises made for a perfect location. Four SWAT officers were positioned outside on the grounds in various locations.

Luke sat squarely in the center of the place for so long, his legs were going numb. He stood, dropped to the ground and did twenty push-ups to get the blood flowing again. To his backside was a solid wall. No chance Rick could surprise Luke with this setup.

A dull thump pounded between his ears as a flashback rocked him. This was different, he reminded himself as he rubbed his eyes.

Luke shook off the memory. He was no longer alone. He had Julie.

Movement to his left caught his attention. A shadow crossed the window. House lights were on outside, making it brighter than inside, affording a better view. He had company.

Luke readjusted his earpiece and alerted the SWAT team that they had a guest outside the building. He raised his AR-15 to his shoulder and aimed the scope toward the front door.

His eyes had long adjusted to the darkness. He relied on his other senses, too. A noise came in the direction of the bathroom. If this was Rick, he was not in the house yet.

Luke repositioned his scope, lining his crosshairs with the center of the shower door. Adrenaline pulsed through him in audible waves. Every sense heightened, on fight alert.

He changed position, crouching next to the sofa, and then relayed his new position to SWAT. Rick set foot inside this house and this whole ordeal would be all over.

Another noise came from the other side of the house this time. Luke reached for his thermal binoculars. They confirmed SWAT's presence, but where was Rick?

Luke didn't so much as breathe as he listened for anything that would give him a position on Rick. Find that bastard in the crosshairs of his scope and Luke wouldn't think twice about doing what needed to be done, especially considering how dangerous the man was.

But there was nothing.

Luke cursed under his breath and then relayed the message to SWAT. Everything had been quiet for ten minutes. Instinct said Rick was gone. Could they get to him before he got too far away?

"This party has moved on. I'm going hunting." Luke wasn't about to give up until he knew for certain the search was over.

Ringtones sounded. Luke palmed his cell and checked caller ID. His boss. "What's the word?"

"There's been another murder."

"Him?"

"We believe so. It has his signature written all over it."

"Where?" In the hours he'd waited for Rick, could he have been saving someone's life? Luke took down the address, ended the call and loaded his GPS.

He bit back a curse.

While he'd been waiting for Rick, taking up valuable resources, the SOB had killed someone right down the street. Anger and frustration engulfed him, lighting a fire that had been simmering since Iraq. Another person was dead because of Luke's misjudgment.

The familiar sting of shame pierced him, spreading throughout his body like a flesh-eating bacteria. There was no one to blame but Luke. He'd been shortsighted, acted too quickly, and Rick had capitalized on the mistake.

Luke drove the couple of blocks to the scene. A squad car, lights blazing, was parked in front of the house. A uniformed officer stood on the front lawn of the small ranch house, taking a statement from, most likely, a neighbor.

Luke fished for his gloves in the console and pulled them on.

Eating up the real estate in a few short strides, he flashed his badge and made a beeline for the front door.

The kill had to be fresh because there was no stench coming from the house as he crossed the threshold.

Inside, the scene played out the same way the others had. A black-haired woman, decapitated, sprawled across the couch. Her arms folded, her legs crossed. Luke fisted his hands, angry with himself for allowing the monster to strike again. Did he blame himself? Yeah.

Did he take it personally? Hell yes.

It was his responsibility to catch this creep and get him off the streets. Every time he was allowed to breathe air freely and strike again, Luke failed.

There'd been an attempt to clean up the blood, but splatter marks were everywhere. A substance that looked and smelled a lot like bleach soaked her clothes. Nothing else in the place had been touched.

The house was clean, so there were no dust tracks to indicate if anything had been removed. The place was small but neatly kept.

A few personal pictures of the woman and a child at various stages of the child's life were neatly placed around the room.

The whole scene smacked of Rick.

Guilt ate at Luke's insides. If he'd chosen a different neighborhood, this woman would still be alive. Her child would not suffer the horror she was about to face. Life would go on normally for the two of them.

He'd just cost a child her mother. He swore under his breath. His fingers fisted and released.

Was he beating himself up over this mentally? Yeah. Losing another life to this monster was something Luke would always take personally.

He had to remind himself to calm down. Maintaining his cool could mean the difference between being too hasty and missing something important that might lead to finding the life-stealing jerk who was responsible.

Luke walked the house, checking every window, picture and piece of furniture for clues. He'd check and double-check everything just in case.

The officer who'd been interviewing witnesses stepped inside the house and called for Luke. He met the man in uniform in the hall.

"Did the neighbors see anything?" Luke asked.

"No, sir. I canvassed the surrounding houses after securing the area. No one saw anything out of the ordinary."

"No sudden noises? Screaming?"

He shook his head.

"What's her name?"

"Kimberly Jackson, sir."

"Thank you. Has her next of kin been notified?" Luke opened the notebook app on his phone.

"No, sir. Not yet."

"You have kids?"

"A two-year-old and a newborn."

"Must keep you busy."

"Can't remember what it's like to sleep for more than six hours at a stretch," the officer said, easing his stance.

"Ms. Jackson has a daughter. There doesn't seem to be a father. Can you do me a favor and see to it that her daughter doesn't see her like this? No little girl should have to see her mother in this condition."

"I hear you, sir. Will do. I can't even imagine anything like this happening to my wife."

Luke nodded agreement. "Any idea how the guy got inside?"

"Didn't see any signs of forced entry."

How had Rick charmed his way inside? The likelihood he'd planned this out in advance was slim. This was a crime of opportunity.

"Thanks a lot. For everything," Luke said. Another question ate at him. Why? What good would it do to kill someone here? This was outside his usual kill zone.

The logical answer nearly buckled Luke's knees. Rick already knew where he believed Luke and Julie were, based on the tracking device, and he wanted to create a distraction. Had he hoped to create enough of a diversion to snatch Julie from the scene?

How had he gained entry when nothing indicated the use of force?

Luke scanned the area.

A fresh bouquet of flowers sat in the middle of the kitchen island. A weight lodged itself inside the pit of Luke's stomach as he moved toward the yellow roses.

There was a card. He pulled a small evidence bag from his back jeans' pocket, then opened the note.

It read "She has to pay."

Rick had figured them out. He knew.

The diversion wasn't created to snatch Julie from here. Luke released a string of swearwords. The air sucked out of his lungs in a whoosh at the same time his cell phone sounded, because he already knew Rick wasn't talking about the woman in the next room. He palmed his phone and studied the screen, barely aware he was already in a dead run toward his truck. The text from his boss read...

Garcia's missing.

JULIE FOUGHT THE darkness surrounding her, draining her. A blow to the back of her head had left her nauseated and with a pounding headache, but she forced herself to stay awake and remember what had happened.

Her brain was mush, but a picture began to emerge. The detective had been called into the station. She and Garcia had been walking toward his car when they'd been ambushed. The last thing she remembered was the detective grabbing his chest after a shot had been fired. *Garcia.*

Julie said a silent prayer he would be okay. She couldn't imagine having to look into the eyes of his beautiful children or wife and tell them he was no longer coming through that door or sitting at their dinner table.

Pain so overwhelming and powerful it was like a physical punch assaulted her. Where was Luke?

What had happened to him? Had Rick gotten to him before he'd attacked them?

Another stab of pain tightened her gut at the memory of being thrown in the trunk of a gray Volkswagen Jetta. Looking into Rick's dead black eyes would haunt her for the rest of her life. Which might not be all that much longer if she didn't figure a way out of this car.

Didn't all trunks have an emergency-release lever?

It was hard to move with her hands bound behind her back. Her ankles had been tied together with rope. Could she wiggle enough to break free?

Rick must've been a Boy Scout, because, try as she might, she couldn't gain an inch.

There was only one of him. As much as he seemed superhuman, he was only a man. Men had weaknesses. She would find Rick's and fight him to the death. His intentions were clear. Her throat dried up just thinking about what he'd done to her client, what he would do to her.

Maybe Rick had been in such a hurry, he'd allowed Garcia a chance to live.

Julie bounced around in the trunk. A speed bump? She listened for any sounds that might help her figure out where he was taking her or give her an edge when describing her location later.

No situation was hopeless, she repeated to herself quietly as tears spilled out of her eyes. There had to be a way to escape.

Sirens blared past her. She was still in the city.

How long had they been in the car?

She'd panicked at first. It took her a little while to get her bearings. How much time had she lost in the interim? Ten minutes? Twenty?

Foreboding numbed her limbs. She had to fight it. This couldn't be over yet. Julie worked the restraints on her wrists again. She couldn't get any traction there. She kicked her feet and screamed.

"Be quiet back there." The voice was almost a nervous squeal. Freaked out?

He should be.

Julie had no plans to go down without a fight. What was the worst that could happen? She knew what he had planned and couldn't think of a more hateful way to kill someone.

Trying to reason with this guy wouldn't do any good, either.

Fear barked at her, threatening to consume her. She refused to allow it. If she allowed terror to paralyze her, he'd already won. His victims must've been scared to death in their final moments.

He could do what he wanted with her body, and probably would, but he couldn't touch her mind. She alone had the power to control her thoughts. And she refused to give him the satisfaction of knowing she was afraid.

The car came to a stop before he cut the engine.

This was it.

Julie positioned herself on her back and bent her knees.

The trunk opened and she released a scream, thrusting her feet toward Rick's face.

His head knocked back. He swore, grabbing at his nose and checking for blood. Before he could grab her, she kicked again. Hard. With all the fear and anger she had balled inside her.

He stumbled back while cursing her then disappeared. "Be still. Wouldn't want to have to knock you out before I kill you."

Julie expected to be out in the country, far from the city. But she could hear cars. A highway?

All she could see were stars against the curtain of a black sky. There was a brisk chill in the air.

She curled her legs, ready to strike again.

This time, he surprised her from the side. A quick blow to the head and she struggled to remain conscious. "He won't let you get away with this. You hurt me and he won't stop until he finds you."

She was baiting him, but she hoped he'd tell her what he'd done with Luke. Because if her FBI agent was alive, she doubted she'd be in the back of a trunk, fighting for her life right now.

The thought of anything happening to Luke made it hard to breathe.

Another blow to the head and she wouldn't have to worry about it. She remembered Luke trying to make him angry to force a mistake. Could she do the same?

Her heart hammered against her ribs. The simple act of taking in air hurt.

Let her panic control her, and she'd be dead for sure.

What if Luke lay in a ditch somewhere? What if she could help?

She had to try.

"Come back, jerk, and give me a fair fight."

"I should have taped your mouth shut is what I should've done." His tone was frantic, almost hysterical.

"What's the matter? Don't like being rushed?"

A siren wailed in the distance.

"They're coming for you, Rick."

No reaction.

"How about I call you a simpleminded jerk instead? That is what you are. You think you're clever but you're not." She listened for a long moment.

Nothing.

"You're nothing more than a leech, sucking the blood out of innocent people."

"That's where you're wrong. They're filthy. People are dirty. Mother always said women are nasty creatures who will hurt you the way she hurt me. She was preparing me for my life as an adult. But she has to pay for her sins, too."

She tracked the voice to her left, repositioning her feet in order to deliver a crushing blow as soon as those blue eyes appeared. "Your mom sounds as insane as you."

"Ask your FBI agent how stupid I am. Oh, right, you can't. He's dead."

The blow from those words knocked the wind out of her. Was it true? Her heart screamed no. Rick would say anything to throw her off balance. Exactly what she was doing to him. "Might be. But you won't get away with this. They know who you are. You go home and they've got you. They know your family. There's nowhere left to hide."

A hysterical laugh came from the right.

Julie quickly adjusted her positioning.

"Impossible."

"Is that so? How can you be so sure?"

"I would've seen it on the news."

"Like they'd tell those jerks." Her best bet was to stall for time.

Silence.

"What's the matter? Didn't figure that part out already? They swarmed your house. Found everything. One of the officers called you a deviant."

"You're lying." His tone sounded agitated now. "I'm the most sane person they'll ever meet. Besides, I can tell you're making it up. People wouldn't say that about me. I'm too smart and they know it. Smarter than your FBI boyfriend, that's for sure."

He'd moved closer on the right side.

She repositioned, remembering something Luke had told her about serial killers. "Sorry to tell you, bud, they know who you are. Leave here and you'll spend the rest of your life as a scrawny girlfriend to a man named T-Bone in prison. Guess what? T-Bone won't like the fact you make wigs from your victims' hair. People who kill innocent women rank right up there with pedophiles in prison."

He rose up from the side of the car, anger radiating from his slender frame.

Julie kicked with everything she had inside her.

Rick sidestepped in time to avoid the thrust of her foot. She made a move to reposition, but before she could fire off another blow, her legs were captured. She tried to break free, but even with the extra strength another shot of adrenaline provided, the grip around her ankles was too strong.

A quick smirk followed by an even faster blow to the head stunned Julie as her vision blurred.

Before she could get her bearings, she was on the ground being dragged. Every movement hurt. She raised her head to stop it from being scraped along the pavement, screaming, fighting with everything she had inside her.

"You shouldn't talk to me like that, Mother. All I ever wanted was your approval," Rick mumbled. "You've been bad, too. You have to tell me you love me. You'll do that once I cleanse you. Won't you, Mother?"

What was he talking about? She glanced around. And who was he talking to?

Julie bucked and wiggled, still screaming, but his grasp was too tight. He hauled her in front of a storage unit as if she weighed nothing. He unlocked and opened the door using one hand.

Light streamed inside as Rick shoved her against the wall, forcing her to sit up. All she could see in front of her were boxes. "Please, don't go through with this. Let me go."

Rick moved to the center of the room, his body blocking her view.

He turned around. She got a glimpse of what he held in his hands and her heart pitched. In his grasp, he held a half-made wig of black hair.

Bile burned the back of her throat. She screamed as he forced her to be still, placing the wig on top of her head.

"Be still, Mother. You mustn't get upset with me." He withdrew. A hurt look crossed his features. "Bad things happen when you get angry."

"I'm not her. I'm not your mother. Let me go."

"All I ever wanted was for you to love me, Mother. As usual, you deny me." He rose up, fury rising with him. "Why won't you love me?"

He struck Julie again.

Then everything went black.

Chapter Eighteen

Luke had hit Redial for the tenth time in a row when his cell buzzed. He answered his boss's call immediately.

"We found Detective Garcia a block from his house." His solemn tone sent a fireball of dread rocketing through Luke's stomach.

"Alive?"

"Yes. He took a beating, but he's on his way to Parkland Memorial. The EMT said he's in bad shape, but his numbers are strong."

"And the woman who was with him?" Luke steeled his resolve, fighting against the overwhelming urge to slam his fist into something. Anything.

The beat of silence his boss gave him wasn't a good sign. "I'm sorry, Luke. He got her and disappeared."

A torpedo couldn't have pierced his heart more deeply. "Any witnesses? Any idea where he took her?"

"We have a guy who's talking. He saw a man force a woman into a gray Volkswagen Jetta and head east. We have men combing the area. A chopper's already in the air."

Luke fisted his free hand. "Who else is on the investigation?"

"I have all my men on the case. Rogers, Stevens, Segal. Everyone. Dallas P.D. put some more power behind it.

We're canvassing Garcia's neighborhood, just in case someone saw something but is scared to come forward. I sent out an alert in the system. Plano, Richardson and Garland have teams ready to mobilize on a moment's notice. The BOLO's already out. I got every bit of my people available working toward finding her."

Given enough time, his boss's words would be comforting. The names he'd mentioned would put the pieces together and produce a location. The sand had drained from the hourglass, and Luke had no time to wait.

"You know I appreciate everything you're doing."

"Goes without saying. We're checking property records, the DMV. If this guy or any of his family members own so much as an RV, we'll be on it."

"Thanks for the update. If I get any leads on my end, I'll keep you posted." He needed to end the call. Right now, he wanted—no, needed—to punch something, and he didn't want to risk being pulled from the case for going ballistic.

How could he not?

It was Julie.

His boss knew about the personal connection, and Luke had half expected to be yanked. Figured he hadn't been because he'd been able to put up a good front. He was human. No doubt every agent would feel the same way if one of their loved ones was in a similar situation. The boss would, too. He sure wouldn't sit in an ivory tower and hope for the best. He'd be out beating the pavement with the rest of them.

Luke needed to refocus and recap what he knew about Rick. The guy was sneaky. Luke had to give him that. Bright. The guy liked a good diversion. While they'd been trying to lure him into a trap, Rick had murdered a woman and then got to Garcia. The noises at the ranch couldn't have been him.

Why would he risk killing so close to Luke?

Obviously, to kill again. He seemed to enjoy operating on the edge of being caught. Could that mean he wouldn't take Julie far?

Luke's cell buzzed. Nick's name came up on the screen. "What do you have for me?"

"Reed's also on the line. I put the call on conference. What do you know so far?"

He recounted the day's events.

"Man, I'm sorry. I know how much she means to you," Nick said.

"I'm already digging around in the backgrounds of everyone connected to Rick Camden, financial records," Reed chimed in.

"Your support means the world."

"Reed's contacts through Border Patrol can move mountains," Nick said.

"We'll know something in the next few minutes," Reed said. He paused a beat. "Hold on. I have news. Guess what? His dad rents a storage unit at the crossroads of George Bush and Preston. It's a Dallas address. On the southwest side."

Luke bolted toward his truck. "I know that location. I've driven past it a thousand times. It's just off the street. The place is blocked because of the highway."

"Be careful, bro. We'll send Riley for backup. He shouldn't be too far since you'll be at Plano's back door," Nick said.

Luke tossed the cell on the passenger seat as he turned over the ignition, praying he wouldn't be too late. He couldn't lose Julie again. Not like this.

His only real question was whether or not he'd get there in time to make a difference. Flashbacks of the night he lost his men in Iraq assaulted him as he navigated through the evening traffic in frigid temperatures.

That same helpless, angry feeling enveloped him now as he neared the storage facility.

He gunned the engine and weaved through cars and trucks.

The intersection was busy, but, just as he remembered, the facility was off the road, hidden by the wall that was built to block noise from George Bush Highway onto a nearby neighborhood.

Using hands-free, he called his boss to let him know he'd arrived. He left clear instructions with everyone to creep in. No lights. No sirens.

He ended the call letting his boss know he had no plans to wait for backup.

The gate was closed and this facility did not have on-site personnel. He knew that from past experience dealing with the owners. Security would be loose. An iron fence enclosed the place and there were cameras positioned in the corners. These conditions were perfect for a man like Rick. Man? No. Animal.

A real man wouldn't hurt women.

Luke strapped his AR-15 to his back and scaled the metal fence in one giant hop. A security gate wouldn't keep him from taking down this monster. Without sirens, he had no idea how close backup was, so he wasn't alarmed by the fact he heard none. But it wouldn't be far away.

Either way, he couldn't afford to hang around and wait.

THE PLACE WAS COLD, dark and eerily quiet. Julie worked her hands behind her back, trying to loosen the rope. She hadn't managed any progress so far. After the last time she'd screamed, a piece of tape had been placed over her mouth.

Had someone heard her? Stopped him?

No. If they had, wouldn't she be safe right now instead

of locked in a storage room, wearing a wig the sicko had made from his victims?

Tears slid down her cheeks as fear gripped her. Detective Garcia was most likely dead. She couldn't begin to think about his sweet family when they heard the news. Whatever Rob had done to Garcia, his plans for her would be much more sinister.

Where had he gone? Worse yet, when would he be back?

He'd secured her and disappeared. Painfully aware he could return at any time, she pressed her back against the wall and tried to push up.

She struggled against her bindings. Fear caused her hands to shake, making it that much more difficult to work the knot. Damn that she couldn't break free. If she could surprise him, she might have a chance.

A little piece of her prayed Luke would find her. But what if he was…? No. She couldn't allow herself to think like that. Lose hope and it might as well all be over.

The wind howled, her heart pounding faster with every gust. Could she work the knot? Her fingers fumbled around for the bow in the rope. No use. Her eyes were beginning to adjust to the darkness. Was there anything she could use? She squinted, trying to make out shapes, but couldn't get a clear look.

Could she scoot to the door and wiggle out before he got back? Surely there were security cameras. Wouldn't someone be watching? Only one thing was certain. Sit there. Do nothing. And she was already dead.

The bindings around her ankles made it difficult to scoot across the floor. She rocked her body until she inched forward.

A gust of wind slammed against the metal door. She couldn't suppress a yelp.

There were more noises, which sounded like feet shuffling.

Couldn't be wind this time. Rick was back.

Her heart hammered her ribs as she tensed her body and clenched her fists, preparing for whatever walked under the metal sliding door.

She worked her jaw from side to side, trying to loosen the tape because as soon as that metal grate lifted, she planned to scream.

Was there anything else around she could use? She scanned the enclosure but could see only general shapes and nothing specific.

If she could scoot a little closer to the door, she could bang her head against it and make a loud noise. Anyone around would hear it. Except she was reasonably certain there was no one else around but her and Rick.

Julie managed to inch closer to the door. She held her breath, half expecting it to shoot up any moment and Rick to be standing there, that satisfied and haunting smirk on his face. With his blond hair, blue eyes and runner's build, she could see why he was disarming to women. He looked like a Boy Scout, not a murderer. Ravishing Rob. *Captivates then decapitates.* A chill gripped her, numbing her limbs.

Was that a pair of crutches leaning against the wall? Yet another in one of his many traps to disarm his prey? Blood ran cold in her veins.

How could someone be so cruel?

Movement outside the door gave her the ominous premonition that she was about to be next. Hesitating, waiting for a sign—any sign—that the person on the other side of that door wasn't Rick, she held her breath and listened. If she could manage to get a little closer, six more inches, she could make some noise. Maybe she could draw their attention. The footsteps came closer, paused, then moved on. Couldn't be him. Could it?

She banged her shoulder against the metal door, causing ripples of sound to roll through the room and the door to shake.

"Julie?" came out in a whisper, but the voice was unmistakable. Luke.

With the tape covering her mouth, she couldn't speak, but she didn't let that stop her from trying. She banged against the door again, with more force this time, and shouted—which came out like a muffled scream.

The door slid open enough for her to get a glimpse of him. Her body went limp from relief at seeing his face. Luke was alive. A flood of emotions descended on her like a hundred-foot wall of water.

He pulled the wig off, dropped to his knees and captured her face in his hands, his own emotion visible in the worry lines bracketing his mouth. He pulled the tape off her mouth. "I thought I'd lost—"

"Luke. He said you were gone." Her own emotions made her eyes fill with tears. "How did you find me?"

"My brothers tracked down this storage unit." His kiss was a mix of sweet and needy.

Her sense of relief and joy was short-lived as he immediately pulled back and surveyed the area. Luke's guard was up as he scanned the room. Enough light streamed in to see clearly.

"Where is he?" Luke asked.

"I don't know. He threw me in here and disappeared. I was screaming. Hoped someone heard me and interrupted him."

"He had to know the area was hot. Most likely plans to return later and finish the job. Even if he was caught, he'd still have his final revenge if no one found you." Luke turned to face the opening, his back against the wall as he pulled a knife from his pocket and cut the ropes. His gaze continued to sweep the area as he worked.

As soon as her hands were free, she rubbed them together, trying to bring feeling back.

"Let's get you out of here." Luke shifted his position quickly, and before she realized what he was doing, he'd cut the rope on her ankles, too. His handgun was leveled and ready to fire.

The blood rushed to her feet. She made a move to get up but landed on her backside.

"Give it a minute. Feeling will come back," Luke whispered.

The light streaming in from the door gave Julie a little perspective about what the storage facility was used for. She'd already seen the crutches, but there were other props. A wheelchair was in one corner. There was an open box filled with various ropes and handcuffs. There were tools like saws lying around. Boxes of garbage bags sat on the floor. Uniforms ranging from scrubs to local police blues were strewn around. He had everything he needed right there to get inside someone's house without using force.

Back where she sat, he'd spread several blankets on the floor. He must've been in too big of a hurry to tie her to the pole he'd installed.

Julie rubbed her hands together faster. She didn't want to be caught off guard if he returned. And he would come back. She needed to get the heck out of there.

Luke finished sweeping the area. "I can carry you, but that would leave us vulnerable. Can you walk?"

"I will." Julie pushed herself up and took a tentative step forward. "He's just going to let us walk out of here?"

"He doesn't get to decide." He handed her a weapon and shouldered his AR-15. "On my word, shoot. Got it?"

She nodded.

Squeezing her hand around the butt of the gun brought more feeling back. She followed closely as Luke led the way toward an iron fence to what she hoped would be freedom. Faint sounds of traffic from a freeway could be heard. If only she could move faster. As it was, adrenaline was the only thing keeping her upright.

She didn't recognize anything, but that was because Rick had covered her eyes before. With the parking lot in view, she lowered her weapon.

A blow came from behind, striking Julie on the crown of her head.

Chapter Nineteen

"Luke!" Julie's scream wrapped around his spine like an ice pack.

He pivoted and leveled his weapon at Rick. With the SOB using Julie as a shield, Luke couldn't get a clean shot. She'd dropped her weapon and Rick had kicked it out of reach. The blade of a knife was pressed against her throat. Luke forced himself not to focus on the panicked look in her eyes.

"She doesn't get to live." Rick's agitated pitch was a far cry from his normal controlled tone. His voice practically shook from hysteria. The guy must not have wanted to risk being too far away in case she tried to escape.

"This is between us, Rick. Let her go."

"No. I need her. She's part of this, of me. You wouldn't understand."

Julie's body shuddered.

"She didn't do anything to hurt you. She's not your mother. Just another innocent woman." Luke walked a mental tightrope, balancing between angering and disarming Rick.

"We both know that's not true. She's your wife. I should slice her throat just for that." Rick turned his attention to her. "Don't worry. I'll be quick this time."

Luke needed to get the guy to focus on him. "I understand now. What your mom must've done to you. She made you angry, didn't she?"

Rick's laugh came out as a chortle. "I wouldn't push me if I were you. I can end it all now."

"Then tell me. Why do you hurt people weaker than you? That makes you just like her." He needed to keep Rick's attention away from Julie.

She gripped the arm braced against her chest with both hands. The knife was pressed so hard against her throat, Luke could see an indentation from it. A trickle of blood rolled down the blade. If Luke could somehow signal her to bite or fight, maybe he could get a clean shot. With that knife so close to her throat, even an accidental slip could cut her jugular vein. She'd bleed out before the ambulance arrived.

Luke inched forward, closing the five-foot gap between them a little more. If he could get close enough, maybe he could grab the knife or knock him off balance. Backup should arrive any minute.

Rick took two steps back. "Stay right where you are. Don't come any closer."

"You slit her throat and you've got nothing. I'll shoot you right here and now. And that's a promise."

Rick didn't move.

"What happened? With your mother?"

"She can't cut me out."

"What did she say?"

"That I was out of the family. She kicked me out of the house, just like that. Two years ago. After everything we'd been through. Said she was done with me."

"Why would she do that?"

"I told her I didn't want to play her sexual games anymore. I wanted a real girlfriend like my brother Chad had. And she cut me out of the family."

Luke looked at Julie, needing her to stay focused. He

angled his head back ever so slightly. Did she catch it? Did she understand what he was telling her to do?

She blinked her eyes several times quickly but didn't dare budge.

Good. She understood his message.

In the background, Luke heard several cars pull into the parking lot. The footsteps of what had to be several officers rushing toward them echoed across the empty space between the storage buildings.

"Make them go away. I'll kill us both." Rick was panicking. His gaze darted around and his face muscles pulled taut.

Luke instantly knew what Rick meant. He'd slice her throat and then make a move for an officer, forcing him to shoot. He didn't turn when he shouted, "Stay back!"

The footfalls stopped.

Rick wore the expression of a caged animal. He knew he was surrounded. No matter what else happened, the SOB wouldn't get away this time. There would be comfort in that thought if it didn't involve Julie. Blood trickled down her neck.

Except that none of this was good for Julie. And there was precious little Luke would be able to do to save her.

No way could he allow that to happen. He had to keep the officers back, as well. Maybe he could soften the guy. Make him think Luke was on his side. "There's another ending to this story, Rick. All three of us can walk out of here." He didn't add that one of them would be in handcuffs, but it was true.

"That's not how I see it going down." The lean man's hand shook. More trickles of Julie's blood ran down the blade.

"It doesn't have to be like this. You need help. I can arrange it for you."

Rick backed away a few more steps. If he managed another ten feet, he could slice her throat and disappear around the corner. And he would. Rick knew that Luke wouldn't let Julie die alone. His best chance of escape involved ensuring the woman Luke loved was dying.

"Make the officers go away, or she dies right here."

Luke bit back a curse. "Stay back or he'll do it. I'll meet you guys in the parking lot."

Rick took another step back. One more and it would be too late for Julie.

A distraction was needed. But what?

She must've sensed what was coming because she took a breath and then dropped down, buckling her knees. Her movement must've caught Rick off guard, because he fumbled for her, dropping the knife.

Luke lunged, wedging himself between Rick and Julie. At that moment, Rick punched her, knocking the wind out of her. Her weak ankles were unable to hold her weight, so she went down fast—a crack sounded, skull to pavement.

Luke fended off a potshot from Rick as he glanced down at her. "Julie."

Slumped on her side, she didn't answer.

Rick threw a punch that Luke blocked. He was stronger than the other man, but adrenaline did funny things to baseline strength. Not to mention the fact that Rick had everything to lose if he got caught.

A knife thrust at him. Luke ducked in time to miss the blade. He pivoted left and crouched low, getting a quick visual on Julie.

Her chest moved, so it meant she was breathing. *Hold on, sweetheart.*

Luke looked up in time to see an object the size of a coffee can being hurled at him. He deflected it with his forearm. What the hell was the jar filled with? Lead?

Another object flew toward him. He ducked, losing balance. In the time he gained his footing, Rick was over top of him.

The sound of officers rushing toward them was a welcome relief.

A jab to Luke's ribs took his breath away. The blunt end of a shoe cracked into his stomach.

Luke hauled himself into a squatting position, then burst toward Rick, knocking him back a step.

A kick to Rick's groin had him doubled over and groaning.

The fight inside him was still strong, powered by his freeze, fight or flight response. Rick stepped forward, leading with the knife, jabbing at Luke's ribs. He sidestepped and spun in time to avoid direct impact, even though he felt the blade sear through his flesh. There was enough of a wound for blood to ooze through his shirt.

"Not this time, bastard." Luke ignored the pain in order to keep his full focus on Rick.

Another jab caught Luke under the arm.

More of his blood spilled onto the sidewalk.

This time, Luke would be ready when Rick made his move.

"Oh my God, Luke." Julie must've regained consciousness. At least she would be fine.

Luke didn't dare take his gaze off Rick. Another jab and he might just hit something the doctors couldn't fix.

The telltale step forward came, but before Rick could blink, Luke had spun around and twisted the knife. Rick was knocked off balance. He turned in the direction he fell, landing directly on the blade. The knife stabbed him directly through the chest, piercing his heart as footsteps surrounded them.

Rick made a gurgling sound as blood spilled from the side of his mouth and his eyes fixed.

Luke rushed to Julie's side and pulled her into his arms with the intention of never letting go.

Julie's tear-soaked eyes gazed up at him.

He pulled back and looked her straight in the eyes. "Everything's fine now. He can't hurt you anymore. You don't have to cry."

She buried her hands in his shirt, pulled back and gasped. "No, Luke. It's not okay. You're hurt."

He felt light-headed, cold and a little nauseated.

A stoic-faced medic parted the crowd, his gaze fixed on Luke.

He took note of Julie's pallor. Blood was everywhere. Blood on her hands, her shirt, in her hair.

His blood.

He was fully awake but couldn't make his mouth form words. How did he tell her he was okay? They'd survived. That he was determined to take her home with him where he could take care of her now that this whole ordeal could be put behind them?

He made another move to speak, but darkness was closing in.

The faint sounds of her sweet voice telling him not to die registered.

EMTs blocked his view of her.

Darkness was pulling, tugging.

Fighting against the tide sucking him under and tossing him out to sea took all the energy he could muster.

Luke closed his eyes.

Chapter Twenty

Luke blinked his eyes open. His head felt as if he'd tied one on last night, except that couldn't be true.

He searched the room for Julie. Found her as she slept in the chair next to his bed. His heart squeezed.

A short dark-haired nurse rushed in. "Someone's finally awake."

"Yeah, guess I needed a good night's sleep."

"Or three."

"You're telling me I've been out for three days?" he asked quietly, trying not to wake Julie.

"Uh-huh." The nurse went to work pushing buttons on beeping machines.

The noise must've stirred Julie, because she rubbed her eyes and yawned.

"Hello, beautiful."

She sat bolt upright. "Luke. Oh, thank goodness you're awake. Are you okay?" Riding a bolt of lightning couldn't have brought her to his side quicker. "How do you feel?"

"Better. My head hurts. Nothing a little aspirin won't heal." And yet, seeing Julie there, waiting, energized his tired body. God help him, but she was the light.

"How do you feel?" the nurse asked.

He wanted to ask if she was the one who'd dragged cotton balls through his mouth, but thought better of it.

Her permanent frown gave him a hint that she wasn't the teasing type.

"You can give me a shot, clean me or bandage me, but I'm taking this lady beside me home." Little did they know, he wouldn't stop there. He'd do whatever it took to defend her and make her his.

He made a move to get out of bed but was instantly met with two sets of hands pushing him down.

"That's not a good idea, Luke." Julie's voice left no room for doubt.

"You should listen to her," the nurse agreed. "Before I make sure you can't."

He put his hands up in the universal sign of surrender. "No harm done."

Recent events flooded him. His thoughts snapped to his friend. "What happened to Garcia?"

"He's good. He was treated overnight and released. Told me to call him as soon as you woke up." Julie leaned toward him. "If you listen to the doctor and do everything he says, I promise to climb under the sheets and keep you warm later."

The nurse grumbled about his blood pressure as Julie located her phone and sent a text.

"Sweetheart, I don't plan to be here later." He looked into her eyes and saw home.

"Where do you plan to go?"

"With you. Home." He hesitated, praying to see a flicker of excitement in her gaze.

Instead, she lowered her lashes, screening her amber hues. "Your brothers have been calling every hour. They might have something to say about where you end up. Gran's worried sick. And coming home with me? I don't know if that's such a good idea, Luke. We've been down that road before. Remember? I thought I could fix everything by sticking in there, but what did I really do? Hoped everything would magically turn out okay. I was scared to death to try to make you talk. I didn't know how. I'm just as much to blame for what happened."

"No."

"Don't say it, Luke." Her forehead creased and he could tell she was concentrating hard on her next words. "I didn't give up. That part's true. But I let you mope around and eventually drown in your own sadness. I should've stomped on the floor until you picked yourself up. What did I do? I let you fall apart right in front of my eyes."

He made a move to speak but was met with her palm.

"It's true. I didn't know what to do, so I hoped and waited. When that didn't work, I let you push me into the divorce."

"I didn't give you much choice."

"People always have choices, Luke. I didn't fight for us before. Not like I should've."

"I appreciate what you're saying—"

"Then don't take all the blame. What happened to us was both our faults. We were young. We both made mistakes. I shouldn't have let you get away with closing yourself off to me."

Her words lifted the burden he'd been carrying on his shoulders for the years they'd been apart. "Have I told you how sexy you are when you're making sense?"

He brought his hand up to her chin. "I understand if you think it's too risky or too fast. But if you give me a second chance to do what I should've done when I first got back, you won't regret it."

"And what should you have done before?"

"Take you in my arms and never let go. No matter how dark my life becomes, you're the light. Instead of turning away from it, ashamed, I should've run toward it, both arms open.

"I was young and stupid...ashamed of myself for being weak. But I've learned a man isn't weak because he cares about the people he loves. Especially when they're taken from him too soon. A real man hangs on to the people he loves with everything inside him, until light fills him again and the darkness is gone."

Tears rolled down her cheeks. His gaze moved to the bandage on her neck and he thought about how easily he could've lost her.

He thumbed them away. "No more tears. I don't want to make you cry again."

"That's beautiful. You're beautiful."

He cracked a smile. "No. I'm not. But you are."

"Luke Campbell, you're the most beautiful man I've ever known. That's the person I fell in love with before. Who I am shamelessly and deeply in love with now."

"I love you, too." Relief washed over him. He had every intention of asking her to marry him when the time was right. And when she agreed to be his bride this time, it would be forever. "Will you move in with me when I get out of here?"

"Yes."

"Just so you understand what I'm asking, I don't do temporary."

"Neither do I."

"As long as we're being clear. I have every intention of making this permanent as soon as you're ready."

"I'll do my best not to make you wait too long."

"Take as long as you need, sweetheart. Like I said, I'm staying put for as long as you let me. I love you. I never stopped. You're the only one for me."

"Good. Because I can't imagine getting sick of you anytime soon." She leaned close enough for their foreheads to touch. "I never plan to stop fighting for us, Luke. I love you too much."

"Do you have any idea how badly I want to kiss you right now?"

She pulled back and said, "Then what's stopping you, Campbell?"

"Toothpaste. I haven't brushed my teeth yet and I don't want to send you out of the room screaming from my breath."

The nurse, who had finished fiddling with the machines, turned toward the door. "You two behave in here. He needs rest."

Julie helped Luke brush his teeth. He took a swallow of water as she placed the supplies on the counter. He opened the covers. "Get over here, Mrs. Campbell."

"Is that a request?"

"Command. Why? Did it work?"

"Very effective tactic, Campbell."

She slipped under the covers with him and he pulled her body flush with his. "I'm afraid we can't do anything with the nurse keeping her eye on us."

He pressed her fingers to his lips and kissed each tip before finding her lips. "We can get to the rest later. And believe me, we will. For now, having you right here, holding you, is all I need."

* * * * *

Look for the final book in Barb Han's
THE CAMPBELLS OF CREEK BEND,
on sale in February 2015.

MILLS & BOON®

Want to get more from Mills & Boon?

Here's what's available to you if you join the
exclusive **Mills & Boon eBook Club** today:

- ✦ *Convenience – choose your books each month*
- ✦ *Exclusive – receive your books a month before
  anywhere else*
- ✦ *Flexibility – change your subscription at any time*
- ✦ *Variety – gain access to eBook-only series*
- ✦ *Value – subscriptions from just £1.99 a month*

So visit **www.millsandboon.co.uk/esubs** today
to be a part of this exclusive eBook Club!

MILLS & BOON®

Why shop at millsandboon.co.uk?

Each year, thousands of romance readers find their perfect read at millsandboon.co.uk. That's because we're passionate about bringing you the very best romantic fiction. Here are some of the advantages of shopping at www.millsandboon.co.uk:

* **Get new books first**—you'll be able to buy your favourite books one month before they hit the shops

* **Get exclusive discounts**—you'll also be able to buy our specially created monthly collections, with up to 50% off the RRP

* **Find your favourite authors**—latest news, interviews and new releases for all your favourite authors and series on our website, plus ideas for what to try next

* **Join in**—once you've bought your favourite books, don't forget to register with us to rate, review and join in the discussions

Visit **www.millsandboon.co.uk**
for all this and more today!